THE WITCH'S SECRET

ALSO BY STACIE MURPHY

A Deadly Fortune

The Unquiet Dead

The
WITCH'S
SECRET

A Novel

STACIE MURPHY

PEGASUS CRIME

NEW YORK LONDON

THE WITCH'S SECRET

Pegasus Crime is an imprint of
Pegasus Books, Ltd.
148 West 37th Street, 13th Floor
New York, NY 10018

First Pegasus Books cloth edition August 2024

Interior design by Maria Fernandez

Library of Congress Cataloging-in-Publication Data is available.

ISBN: 978-1-63936-629-3

10 9 8 7 6 5 4 3 2 1

Printed in the United States of America
Distributed by Simon & Schuster
www.pegasusbooks.com

This book is dedicated to the memory of
Thomas Norfleet, who swung a mean putter.
Tom, you are greatly missed and fondly remembered.
Semper optimi citius nos relinquunt

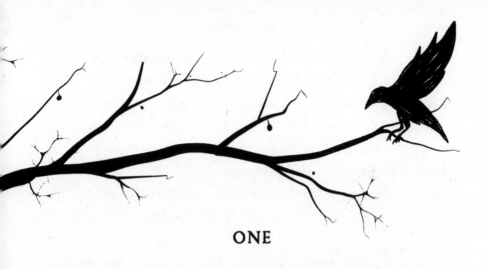

ONE

T he Magisterium, in its eagerness to see me gone, dug deep into its coffers and paid for an express ticket out of Boston. Five days later, by the time I reached St. Joseph, Missouri—as far west as the railroad could take me—their pointless extravagance had become a source of faint and bitter amusement. After a long day's wagon ride from St. Joseph to Atchison, Kansas, I handed over seventy-five dollars, the last of the Magisterium's largesse, in exchange for a stagecoach ticket to Denver City. I boarded, believing I was already as exhausted as it was possible for a body to be.

The ensuing week taught me better. Seven juddering, jouncing days, never stopping for longer than it took to change out the horses. Seven days wearing the same clothes, growing dirtier by the hour thanks to the inescapable dust. Seven days gnawing on meat dried so hard it was like chewing rope and drinking water drawn from streams and huddling beneath the hairy, stinking buffalo-hide blankets the driver handed out against the chill October nights. Seven days sitting with my knees drawn toward my chest so there was room for my luggage beneath my feet. Seven days of catching what sleep I could manage sitting up between my fellow passengers as the coach bucked and swayed along the rutted trail beneath a waxing prairie moon.

I wondered darkly if the Magisterium had weighed the misery of the journey when determining my sentence.

"There's a witch out in the Colorado Territory," Marthe had told me when she emerged from the conclave. "Josiah Merritt. You're going out to him."

I let out a groan. "Another apprenticeship? No one else has had to do so many. I don't see why I should—" I caught a glimpse of Marthe's face, and the protest died on my lips.

"It's not an apprenticeship," my guardian said, looking a decade older than she had a few hours earlier. "You're to be bound."

"Bound?" I repeated, so appalled I could hardly choke out the word. "For how long?"

"Until we decide to unbind you," she said, a hint of steel coming into her voice.

"We? You agreed to this? What about Thomas? And Lisbeth? What's going to happen to them?"

"They aren't your concern anymore," Marthe snapped. "Joya, do you even understand what you've done? Did you think there would be no consequences? You've been warned before. You knew better, but still you—" She cut herself off with a visible effort, then closed her eyes. When she opened them again, they were full of tears. "Child, you don't know how hard I had to fight to get you this much. It's a chance for tempers to cool and memories to fade. It could have been so much worse." She reached for my unwilling hands and clasped them in her own. "This is a gift."

It didn't feel like a gift. My life as I knew it was over, had been over from the moment I decided to go to the Magisterium with what I'd discovered. My freedom was gone. My position was gone. Worst of all, my magic was gone—or it might as well have been. The silver chain the Magistra sealed around my wrist before I left looked like an unassuming little bauble, but a sharp-eyed observer might notice it had no clasp. If I removed it, I would be declared anathema. I'd heard the whispered stories about what happened to such witches. Hanging would be a relative mercy.

I tried to find a way around the binding. Of course I did. It was the first thing I did after the train left Boston. I closed myself in the ladies' lavatory and attempted half a dozen spells. None worked. Each time I tried to draw on my power, the chain grew hot. By the time I gave up and went back to my seat, the skin around my wrist was red and tender, and my chest was tight with a fluttering feeling I managed to identify as suppressed panic. Using my magic had always been like drinking from an endless well. Now it was like trying to slake my thirst by catching raindrops on my tongue.

A dozen times a day I forgot myself and reached for my power. To cast a warmth charm. To sweeten the air in the coach. To help myself sleep. To stop someone's snoring. To urge the horses to run faster. Nothing obvious enough to disturb the other passengers, all of whom were Mundanes. But the sort of thing I had done hundreds—maybe thousands—of times over the years since I'd come into my power. Each time, there was nothing there, and the band around my wrist went hot with warning.

The constant reminders of what I'd lost—of what was being withheld from me, still there, but always out of reach—were a goad and a torment. I'd heard of bound witches going mad, and during the endless days of travel, I wondered if I might become one of them.

When the stage driver bellowed word of our arrival into Eagle's Nest Station, I lifted the canvas flap covering the window and peered out, hoping it at least had an actual privy. I'd passed up the chance to squat behind a bush at our last stop, but there was no way I could last another fifteen miles to the next one.

I was in luck. Eagle's Nest Station consisted of a large barn and a small cabin with a discreet wooden structure behind it. Twenty minutes later, I was waiting to reboard the stage when the sound of approaching riders sent a flutter of concern through the huddle of passengers. The McGills, a Methodist minister and his pigeon-breasted wife, who were horrified that I was traveling alone and had taken it on themselves to guard my virtue, stepped up to flank me on either side. The driver and guard exchanged a tense look, the latter tightening his grip on his rifle. We'd been fortunate on this run, or so I'd heard them say to one another: no bad weather, no broken axles, no sign of Indians along the route.

The driver climbed onto the seat and peered south, shading his eyes against the noontime glare. "Looks like Garvey and Doyle," he said after a moment.

The guard relaxed and glanced at us. "Colorado Rangers," he said. "'S all right."

I edged away from the McGills, trying not to do so too obviously. They were cloying—not to mention years too late with regard to my virtue—but I avoid alienating members of the clergy whenever possible. I don't think the Methodists ever burned any witches, but there's no point in taking chances.

A moment later, three riders cantered into the yard and reined to a stop.

"Afternoon, boys," the man in the lead said, raising a hand to the driver and guard. "I'm damned glad to see you."

"Looks like you caught something this trip," the guard said, his eyes on the man atop the trailing horse.

I followed his gaze and straightened. The rearmost man was slumped in the saddle, his ragged hair hanging over his face. He was coatless, with a blanket draped around him. His hands were manacled, and he had no stirrups or reins. His horse wore a lead rope tied to the saddle horn of the man in front of him.

"Sure enough did," the first rider replied.

"Where are you headed with him?"

"Fort Halleck, but we're not kitted out to take him all the way there ourselves. I was hoping to put him and Garvey on the stage with you and then head back to Denver City."

The stage driver shook his head. "I don't have room for two more. Could maybe squeeze in one extra, but we're not taking custody of him."

The man—Doyle, if the other was Garvey—grimaced. "I've been out two weeks already. He was harder to find than we expected."

The driver shrugged. "Can't help you unless you can talk at least one of them into giving up their seat." He waved in our direction.

All around me, passengers straightened and shuffled their feet. The stage ran every ten hours, so in theory any of us could agree to stay behind and wait for the next one. But I'd been warned that seats were in such demand that you could wait days for an opening. The others must have gotten the same advice, because not a one of them had taken the chance during the week we'd been traveling, even at the stations that offered decent meals or real beds.

Doyle's dour expression as he turned to survey us said he had no expectation of success. "Any of you headed to Denver City?"

A few of us raised our hands. His gaze skipped over me in my fashionable traveling dress and neat kid boots to rest on a pair of rangy-looking brothers whose names I hadn't bothered to learn. "What about you two?"

A wordless conversation passed between the siblings. "We'll ride the rest of the way with you," one of them said with a tobacco-stained grin. "For the cost of our stage tickets."

"I don't have that kind of money and wouldn't pay you that much even if I did," Doyle said, sitting back in his saddle. "At most you're two days out of Denver City."

He spoke as if two more days were nothing much, but the words landed in my gut like a lead weight.

"That's our price," the other brother said.

I had deliberately avoided thinking about how much farther we had to go or calculating exactly how long it would take. The thought of spending another two days trapped in that box with these people was intolerable.

Doyle scowled. "I can't—"

"I have a split skirt in my bag." The words were out of my mouth before I knew I was going to say them.

The rest of the company fell silent, staring at me.

"How long will it take?" I went on. "The ride. Is it faster than the stage?"

Mrs. McGill let out a little yip of dismay and clutched at my arm. "Joya, no. You can't go off alone with him. Why, the very idea."

Doyle ignored her. His expression was guarded. "Faster? Probably not much. But it's more direct. If you're a good rider, we could make the Jensen place tonight and Denver City by late tomorrow."

"What about Josiah Merritt's place?" I asked. "How far is that?"

He looked surprised. "Merritt? That's between the Jensens and Denver City. A day's ride from here."

"So at least a day faster than taking the stage into Denver City and then finding someone to take me to his farm?"

He ran a hand over his unshaven chin before he replied. "I'd say so."

I reached into the coach for my bags. "Then let's go."

⚬—⚬—⚬

Doyle and Garvey took no chances with the prisoner. They left the manacles on as they pulled him off the horse. He let out a pained grunt, and the blanket slipped, revealing a bloodstained bandage wrapped around his shoulder. He shuffled, bent forward like a much older man as they walked him toward the stage, paying no attention to the watching passengers.

At least, paying no attention at first.

As he drew even with me, he stiffened as if startled by something, then lifted his head. His face was flushed with fever, his nose had a scabbed cut over the bridge, and his eyes were ringed with green and yellow patches of healing bruises. They roamed over the passengers, then locked on me with an eerie intensity. He stopped walking and drew a breath, but before he could speak, Garvey jabbed him in the side. It was hardly more than a tap, but the prisoner paled and staggered. His ribs must have been injured in addition to the shoulder wound.

"Keep moving," Garvey said.

I drew back among the clustered passengers as he continued on toward the stage, not liking his scrutiny.

Unfortunately, I wound up back beside the McGills, who took the opportunity to try to change my mind about leaving their company. I ignored their increasingly lurid warnings about how I was imperiling my immortal soul. By the time I'd climbed onto Garvey's horse, they had washed their hands of me, and they pointedly averted their eyes as they climbed back into the coach.

"My best to Bonnie and Sam," the driver called to Doyle as the stage rumbled westward down the trail, Garvey and the luckless prisoner now swaying on its top. Doyle raised a hand in silent response, then clucked to his horse and turned it south, leading the third horse behind him.

I followed. The station dwindled behind us, and sooner than I would have imagined, the two of us were alone on the vast, empty prairie. Very, very alone.

I was used to having my magic to defend myself. But now that wasn't an option, and I eyed the man in front of me in vague, unaccustomed discomfort, abruptly aware that I might have done a foolish thing.

He rode with the ease of a man used to long hours in the saddle. His broad shoulders were rigid with muscle. He wore a heavy leather duster over stained buckskin pants and a shirt so rimed with dust and sweat I couldn't tell its original color. Greasy tendrils of black hair trailed from beneath his hat.

But none of that meant anything about his character. He said he'd been out chasing the fugitive for two weeks. Anyone would be dirty living rough for so long. After a week on the stage, I hardly smelled like rose water myself.

As if he felt me watching him, Doyle twisted in the saddle to look at me.

"Did I hear that woman call you Julia?"

"Joya," I said. "Joya Shaw."

"Joya," he repeated. "I'm Langston Doyle. You're headed to Josiah Merritt's place?"

"He's my uncle," I said, sticking to the story I'd been given before I left.

Doyle frowned. "He's pretty old to have a niece your age. What are you, twenty?"

"Twenty-three. And he's my great-uncle," I added, improvising. "Do you know him well?"

"No," he said. "Met him a time or two, but that's all."

"That's more than I've done," I said. "He's lived in the west since before I was born." I wanted to ask his impression of the man. But it might seem odd. If I were family, surely I'd have heard at least a little about him. I hesitated, but my curiosity got the better of me. "What can you tell me about him?"

"Not much," Doyle said. "He lives about a half day's ride outside Denver City. Keeps to himself. Only comes into town once a month or so. He's got two hired men who live out there with him. Brothers, I think. Mutes, both of them." Now it was his turn to hesitate. "You're traveling alone. Where's the rest of your family?"

As far as I knew, I had no living kin. My parents died when I was six, crushed to death when the shoddy, crumbling tenement we lived in collapsed. I was the building's only survivor.

Magic usually reveals itself during puberty, but it sometimes flares earlier—usually when there's a mortal threat involved. The ceiling above my bed cracking and caving in on me was enough to bring mine on. A mention of my miraculous escape in the *Boston Journal* attracted the Magisterium's attention. They swooped in and took possession of me before my parents were laid in their paupers' graves. I'd been Marthe's ward ever since.

But there was no easy way to explain any of that to Doyle, and I wasn't inclined to try. "I'm from Boston."

He read it as the deflection it was and switched topics with admirable smoothness, turning to face the trail again.

"Long trip for you. Any trouble on the way?"

"No. There were Union soldiers on the train through Missouri," I said, wondering where he fell on the topic of the war.

His voice and posture didn't change. "That's good. It's been ugly there."

"How about here?"

"There have been some incidents. We have a Unionist governor, but there are rebel sympathizers around, especially out in the mining camps. They've formed some militias and tried to do some recruiting, but they haven't gotten far. Especially after earlier this year." He glanced back at me again and must have seen the question on my face.

"A rebel force out of Texas came up the Santa Fe Trail in April, hoping to take the goldfields. The Colorado Infantry and a company of Rangers force-marched four hundred miles from Denver. We caught them at Glorieta Pass. Burned a bunch of their supply wagons and pretty well broke them. There's no more sign of any organized campaign."

There was pride in his voice. When he said "we," he wasn't merely referring to his brother Rangers. He'd been there.

"Good," I said.

He flashed me a surprisingly white, even smile from behind two weeks' worth of ragged beard. Before he could turn back to the trail, I asked the question that had been in the back of my mind since we left.

"Who was that man? The prisoner."

Doyle's face darkened. "His name is Marcus Broaderick."

"What did he do?"

"Kidnapped a woman. From a bro—" He cut himself off, clearly not willing to say the word *brothel* in front of me, then tried cover it with a cough. "Sheriff and his boys went after them. Broaderick got away, although he took a beating doing it." Doyle's face was grim, and my stomach knotted.

"What happened to the woman?"

He hesitated. "Broaderick set the house they were in afire. Left her tied up inside. They didn't get to her in time."

I tried not to imagine it, but I couldn't help myself.

My horror must have shown on my face, because he drew up on the reins. "Are you all right? There's water in my canteen, if you need it."

I straightened. "I've done some nursing. I'm not squeamish. Isn't there a jail in Denver City? Why were you taking him all the way to Fort Halleck?"

Doyle seemed to decide I wasn't going to faint. "Politics," he said in a tone of distaste. "The sheriff is new, and he doesn't much like the Rangers."

I'd spent years watching the members of the Magisterium wage vicious—and often supremely petty—battles over turf and influence, so I nodded my understanding and let the conversation lapse.

We rode for a time in silence while I thought. It didn't seem remarkable that a man like Broaderick might take the opportunity to stare at a woman. I thought of the way his eyes had looked once they fastened on me. I was just as glad he was on his way to Fort Halleck in chains.

I shook off the last of my unease and began paying more attention to our surroundings.

The day was brisk but sunny, the sky overhead an endless blue vastness like nothing I'd ever seen back east. As we plodded along, I breathed in the scent of dry vegetation and distant pines. It was beautiful country, a fact I'd been unable to fully appreciate while crammed into the stage-coach box.

There was no trail to speak of. The grass was thick and brown, beaten down by sun and wind into twisted humps of turf. Our passage set ground squirrels and long-eared jackrabbits to running, and after a while we had a number of enormous birds—golden eagles, Doyle told me when I asked—wheeling on air currents above us. Every so often one would fold its wings and dive, faster than a raindrop could fall, to snatch the prey we'd flushed for them. One took a rabbit so near me that I felt the wind of its downward rush and caught a glimpse of sharp black talons as long as my fingers.

We reached the edge of the Jensens' claim, where Doyle said we would spend the night, just as the sun touched the top of the mountains, and by the time we crested the rise overlooking the homestead itself, the light was fading. It was a tidy-looking place, with a squat, square cabin and a lofted barn.

A pair of shaggy oxen in a split log corral raised their heads and bawled at us as we made our way down the slope. The noise split the still air, and a flock of birds exploded from the hayloft, wheeling away in a clatter of wings and making my horse start. I quieted it and looked around the yard. A pair of quilts hung limp on a line, their bright patchwork muted by the deepening shadows. The kitchen garden, already lying fallow for the winter, was a dark rectangle of earth cut from the pale grass of the yard. There was no smoke coming from the chimney, no lamplight from the windows.

Doyle reined in his own mount, frowning, and cupped his hands around his mouth. "Hello, the house!"

As his voice died away, a cow lowed from inside the barn. The forlorn sound raised the hairs on the back of my neck.

We rode forward, slowly, and my chest went tight as the details of the cabin came into focus.

The front door stood ajar.

"Doyle—"

"I see it." He raised his voice as he swung down from his horse. "Harp? Becca? You there?"

When no response came, he handed me the reins. "Stay here." Doyle strode to the door, pushed it open, and had one foot over the threshold when he froze. There was a half second during which his expression was that of a man who couldn't put together what he was seeing. Then he reeled backward with a muffled curse, his face stricken and his hand fumbling for his gun.

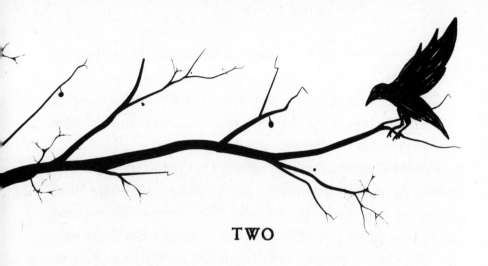

TWO

I reached for my power, then hissed in pain as the silver cuff seared my wrist.

Doyle didn't notice as he spun to face the yard, his weapon drawn. His eyes were sharp, and the big revolver's barrel was steady as he swept the area from one end to the other. After a long moment, he drew in a deep breath and lowered the gun. His shoulders dropped, and he rubbed his free hand across his mouth and chin.

I dismounted and half stumbled toward him, my legs gone wobbly. "What's happened?" I tried to go around him, but before I got close enough to see anything, he reached behind him and yanked the cabin door closed. I jerked to a stop and stared, waiting for him to say something.

When he spoke, his voice was grim, and he didn't look at me. "It's too late to go on tonight. And we can't—" He cut himself off. "We'll have to stay in the barn. Can you water the horses?" He nodded in the direction of the corral. There was a well and trough beside it. "I'll be along in a few minutes."

Without waiting for me to answer, he took a breath, as if steeling himself, then opened the cabin door just wide enough to slide inside, blocking my view with his body and closing it again behind him.

I stared at the door, vaguely offended but too weary to press the matter. As my heart resettled into its normal rhythm, I led the horses to the dry trough and began turning the well crank. The oxen met us, so large up close that I backed away in concern. But they seemed friendly enough, pushing their enormous, shaggy heads into the trough with a degree of eagerness that said they'd been untended for a while.

I drew what felt like endless buckets of water, wondering what Doyle was looking for in the cabin. The Jensens must be dead. And they must not have died peacefully—fever or flux didn't make a seasoned lawman look like that. Or draw his gun.

There were stories of men who'd gone mad and slaughtered their families when the farm failed or the isolation became too much to bear. Maybe Harp Jensen was one of those.

Maybe there'd been an Indian attack, though something about that didn't feel right. The newspapers said most of the Indians had moved to the new reservation the government had given them in the south of the territory. And they would have burned the place, wouldn't they? Or it could have been the rebels. Doyle had said there were militias. But they would have taken the animals, surely, and here the oxen were.

As if to emphasize the point, the cow mooed again from inside the barn.

The barn. My mouth went dry. Doyle hadn't checked it. There could be someone—any number of someones—hiding inside. I dropped the bucket, then fell on my rump as I jumped out of the way of the frigid water while trying not to take my eyes off the barn door.

I was on the verge of shouting for Doyle when I registered that the wooden latch was closed. If there was anyone in there, they were trapped. I let out a breath and pushed myself to my feet, my face hot with embarrassment. At least no one but the oxen had seen me behaving like a ninny.

The cow made another plaintive noise, and I made myself walk toward the door. I flipped up the latch and pushed it open. Harp Jensen had kept the hinges well-oiled, and it swung wide without a sound.

The last bit of lingering daylight was all but gone, and the barn's interior was cave-dark. It smelled of hay and animals. On a shelf inside the door, I made out a battered lard-oil lamp with a box of matches beside it. I lit the wick, my hands still a little shaky. The flame danced as I peered into the shadows.

A pen to my right held a pair of baby goats, who bleated and tumbled over one another, wagging their tails as I approached. I bent to rub their heads, and they latched onto my fingers with their rough little mouths, suckling with frustrated intensity. The cow lowed again, and I turned toward the sound, wiping my wet hand on my skirt.

She pushed her pretty red head over the door of her stall as I approached, and I scratched her between the ears. She mooed at me again and looked at me with pleading brown eyes. "Are you hungry?" I asked. "Is that what's the matter?"

"She needs milking," Doyle said from behind me, and I sucked in a breath and almost dropped the lamp.

"Don't do that," I said sharply as my heart pounded in my ears. "I could've set the whole place on fire."

"Sorry. Didn't mean to scare you." He had the quilts from the clothesline draped over one arm. "I don't suppose you know how? To milk a cow, I mean?"

"No." I knew horses. I'd served an apprenticeship with one of the Magisterium's breeders. But he hadn't kept cows.

"I'll take care of it." He handed me the quilts. "I have a bedroll, but these should do for you, if you don't mind making up a pallet. There's plenty of fresh straw."

I stood with the quilts clutched to my chest as he lifted a tin pail from a hook beside the stall and opened the door. He seated himself on the low stool beside the stall partition, put the bucket beneath the cow's teats, and began sending sharp streams of milk into the pail. A trio of barn cats appeared almost at once, meowing and stropping themselves against his calves.

"Little beggars," Doyle said. "Ought to be out catching your dinner." He reached for a cracked saucer I hadn't noticed before and tipped in some milk. He set it among the cats, and all three crouched onto their haunches and began lapping away.

I waited for him to say something about the scene in the house, but he only went on milking, the steady *hiss hiss* the only sound in the barn.

I ran out of patience. "What happened to the Jensens?"

He didn't raise his head. "They're dead."

I couldn't suppress an exasperated huff. "I gathered that much. How did they die? Is it safe for us to stay here?"

There was a long pause before he replied. "It's safer to stay here than to travel in the dark. We'll be fine." His tone said he expected me to be content with that answer.

One of the cats, an enormous gray beast with tufted ears and an absurdly fluffy tail, stretched and yawned before venturing over to sniff first the hem of my dress and then my outstretched hand. He let me scratch him behind the ears and rewarded me with a purr that sounded like a saw rasping through wood. When he'd had enough, he sauntered away, and I broke apart a bundle of straw and made my mattress for the night.

I waited until Doyle came out of the stall with the full pail to ask my next question. "Shouldn't we bury them?"

He hesitated, then shook his head. "I'll borrow Josiah's hired men and come back tomorrow to do it. But there is another job you could do while I see to the rest of the animals, if you're willing." He held up the pail. "I suspect Becca was bottle-feeding those kids. The bottles and such are probably here somewhere."

He meant it as a distraction—men always think having a small, help-less creature to fuss over will occupy a woman's mind—but I went along with it. He wasn't going to tell me anything anyway. The bottles were easy enough to find, once I knew to look, and the kids clambered over one another in their eagerness to fill their bellies. They fell asleep in my lap when they were done, and I couldn't deny that their warm, heavy presence was pleasant.

Doyle brought a bucket of water with him when he returned. "I thought you might like to wash. I'll step back outside," he added.

A cold bucket bath wasn't nearly enough to wash away the travel grime. I would have given anything for enough magic to heat the water and a clean shift to change into, but it was better than nothing. I called to Doyle when I was finished, and he came back into the barn. His hands and face were cleaner, and his hair was damp. Clearly he'd done his own wash outside.

We ate trail bread and cheese from one of the saddlebags, then bedded down a polite distance from one another, Doyle casually placing himself between me and the barn door.

He doused the lamp, and I began counting. I wondered if he meant to keep watch. But he'd been two weeks on the trail of that fugitive, and by the time I reached five hundred, his breathing was slow and even. I counted five hundred again, then, watching the lump of him beneath his blanket for any sign of waking, I eased from my own bed. I took the lamp and matches with me and padded in my stockinged feet to the barn door. It swung open, and the gray cat slipped out behind me on noiseless paws and disappeared into the night. A moment later there was a rustle of grass, then the squeak of a small animal, abruptly cut off.

The moon was near full, turning the hummocks and hollows of the yard into a watercolor of gray and grayer shadows. The ground was cold beneath my feet as I walked the thirty yards to the cabin, but the goosebumps on my skin were only partly due to the temperature. I both wanted and didn't want to see whatever it was Doyle was trying so hard to hide from me.

There was no lock on the cabin door, or even a proper knob, only a wooden handle. I pushed the door open and stepped inside.

The copper smell of blood and worse hung heavy in the air. Even before I lit the lamp, it was clear I was in the presence of violent death.

The flare of the match was enough to confirm it.

Blood painted the interior of the cabin in great stripes and splashes. There was a dried pool of it an inch from the toe of my stocking. Along with a man's work boot—Harp Jensen's, with his foot still inside—beside it. I got a good view of the sharp stub of his ankle bone poking from the top before I wrenched my gaze elsewhere. It landed on Becca Jensen's head, which lay on the floor by the bedstead, several feet from her torso. Her sightless eyes were pointed in my direction, her mouth open as if she were still screaming.

I was dimly aware that I was panting, making a tiny noise that wanted to be a scream with each exhalation. Everywhere I looked there was some fresh horror. I screwed my eyes closed.

That was the only reason I felt it. The tiny itch against my skin I would have recognized at once—probably as soon as I'd gotten near the cabin—if it hadn't been for the dampening effect of the binding on my wrist.

Magic.

Whoever had done this had been brimful of it. And they'd left a remnant behind.

All magic does that. It leaves traces of itself, like a woman wearing heavy perfume. Those traces can tell you what sorts of spells were worked and even who worked them, if you're skilled enough to read them. There were witches who specialized in doing just that. They'd always made me nervous, since their usual job was to investigate magical malfeasance and testify at tribunals, but now I wished one of them were here. Or all of them. They could handle this abomination, this offense against every pure thing. They could give these poor people justice, and I could walk away and try my hardest to forget I'd ever seen any of it.

I was on the edge of doing precisely that, and justice be damned, when a thought struck me, unwelcome as a slap. As far as I knew, there was only one other witch within five hundred miles. One other person who might be capable of wielding the kind of magic it would take to rip two people apart.

And I was on my way to live with him.

If Josiah Merritt had done this, I needed to know it. I needed to feel the magic that had been used here so I could compare it to his when I met him. If he'd killed these people, I couldn't stay there, no matter what the Magisterium said.

I swallowed hard and opened my eyes enough to locate Harp's boot at my feet, then bent before I could think better of it and put my hand flush against the leather, hoping that would be enough. But magic clings where it has been focused. The magic used in the cabin hadn't been directed against the couple's possessions—it had been aimed at them, at their bodies, their very beings. That was where the residue would be.

I was not going to wrestle Harp's mangled foot from its boot—stars help me, I was *not*. I gulped and cast a desperate look around the scene, trying to find what I needed without absorbing any more of the details. There was a hand—it had to be Becca's—lying on a bench to my right. My stomach lurched, and I damned the Magisterium. This was their fault. I wouldn't even be here if it weren't for them and their blind, stupid dogmatism. I wouldn't be in this cabin with these butchered corpses, knowing I had no choice but to do this if I wanted to be certain I wasn't riding toward a monster.

I ground my teeth and reached out, telling myself it was a wax model of a hand, not real, not part of a murdered woman who had used it to piece quilts and knead bread and feed baby goats.

I put my living hand on Becca Jensen's dead one and felt the magic that had killed her.

It swelled through me, thick enough to taste, foul and malevolent, cloying as rot. I gagged and stumbled outside, only barely making it through the door before my stomach emptied itself beside the threshold. I heaved until it felt as though I would spatter my insides onto the ground, unable to control the spasms until the feeling of that magic began to fade, leaving only an ugly echo. I stood, dizzy, my body still wracked with shudders.

A hand, hard and alive and angry, came down on my shoulder.

I screamed.

I couldn't help it. The lamp fell from my hand and set a tuft of dry grass aflame. Doyle—obviously it was Doyle who had grabbed me—let go, swearing, and stamped out the fire.

"What were you thinking?" he said when it was out, looming over me in the moonlight. "I told you not to go in there."

"I wanted to know," I said, my throat aching and my voice hoarse.

"Why?" There was a mixture of exasperation and bemusement in his voice.

There was no explanation I could give him that he would understand, so I said nothing. I stepped past him and walked back to the barn on numb legs, aware of his aggravated presence at my back the whole way.

"I need you to keep quiet about what you saw in there," he said when I was back on my bed of straw. "It's my job to catch whoever did that, and if wild stories start flying around it will only make it harder."

"I won't say anything," I said, meaning it.

There was no point. He would never catch the culprit. I'd known it as soon as I touched Becca's hand and felt the power clinging to it.

There are a great many kinds of magic in this world. The Africans have their own ways of casting spells, as do the Indians and the Arabs and the Chinese. There's one thing they all have in common, though: they draw on a reservoir of power fed by the natural world. It's all the same power, shaped differently.

What I'd felt on Becca Jensen's hand was something else altogether. Something not of this world. Something wholly, indisputably evil. *Infernal* was the only word I could find that fit. There was no way to prove it, but I was as certain as I could be without having ever felt the like before.

The Jensens had been slain by a demon.

THREE

I lay awake well into the night, trying to remember everything I'd ever heard about demons and their magic. It wasn't much. The Magisterium had ironclad rules against meddling with demons, and I'd never heard of anyone being fool enough to do it.

Most of the reports were centuries old and came from terrified apprentices who had last heard their masters screaming from behind locked doors. The witches involved, once someone ginned up enough nerve to break into their chambers, were always dead. Or, more unsettlingly, simply gone, never to be heard from again.

Demons were beings separate and apart from our world. They could not cross over unless invited, and then only at night—sunrise banished them back to their own realm. Their powers differed, but their goals were always malign. The lore said they could be bargained with and were bound to keep their word, but who knew if that was true?

Perhaps one of the Jensens had summoned a demon and lost control of it. I chewed my lip in the dark, wondering if Mundanes could even do such a thing. If they couldn't have done it, did that implicate Josiah Merritt? And if so, why would he do it?

I slept, finally, but it wasn't restful. An old nightmare came for me. I was trapped beneath the rubble of the tenement where I'd lived with my parents, but my magic did not save me. I was being crushed to death by heavy wooden beams. Dirt and powdered plaster choked me. Fire crackled nearby, heating the air in the pocket where I lay until it felt as though it would sear my lungs with my next breath.

Every facet of the nightmare was familiar, except this time, I was not alone. A malevolent, unseen presence was in the tiny space with me. I knew, with the iron assurance of dreams, it was a demon.

I woke when Doyle pushed open the barn door and the morning sun hit me full in the face. I rolled away from the glare and rubbed at my eyes, my head full of sand. I was still on my pallet when Doyle emerged from the cow's stall with a full bucket. He set it beside me. "Good morning."

"Good morning," I said without looking at him.

"We need to get going soon," he said. "I'd like to get you to your uncle and be back here with enough time to take care of Harp and Becca before dark."

I nodded and sat up, then reached for my boots. I shoved my feet into them and worked the laces with clumsy fingers, then fed the kids while Doyle tended the horses. He talked to them as he worked, the sound of the currycomb against their hides drowning out the actual words but not his low, soothing tone.

I sat beside the goat pen after the kids were finished eating, watching them hop around their enclosure and butt their heads against one another, letting their antics drive the last bits of the dream away as I chewed my own breakfast—another slab of dry bread from the saddlebags.

Doyle approached. "You should take them on to Josiah's with you," he said, nodding at the kids. "And probably the cow, too. I don't know if he keeps one."

"Really?"

He nodded. "Someone has to look after them. I can sort out the rest of the livestock, but I don't have time to be bottle-feeding goats. Once I figure out who Harp and Becca's heirs are, you can either turn them over or buy them."

"All right," I said, rising. I don't know why it cheered me, but it did.

We finished packing and led the horses outside. Doyle tied the kids' legs together and draped them over the pommel of his saddle before mounting. Their plaintive cries trailed off as we rode out, the cow on a long lead rope behind my horse.

I glanced back at the homestead when we reached the top of the rise. The cabin sat in its little valley, bucolic in the morning sunlight. The mountains were vividly bright in the distance, the highest peaks already capped with snow. It looked like so unlikely a location for a demon attack that for a moment I doubted my certainty of the previous night. I'd never felt demon magic before. As far as I knew, I didn't even know anyone who had. How could I be so sure? Couldn't I have misread a mortal killing spell—a particularly nasty one, yes—for something demonic?

But even as I tried to convince myself, my gut cramped with the memory of what I'd felt when I touched Becca Jensen's hand. I wasn't wrong. But I didn't have any idea what to do about it.

The farm fell away behind us, but with our added burden, our progress was slower than the day before. We didn't talk, both of us seemingly lost in our own thoughts.

The eagles found us again, and again they took full advantage. Today they struck me as brutal instead of majestic, with their swift dives and hard, merciless eyes. Dozens of tiny creatures died in our wake, frightened by the false danger of our passage into revealing themselves to the real one circling above. I was half sick with it by the time we stopped to let the animals drink from a creek.

"Who do you think killed them?" I asked, breaking the silence for the first time in hours. Doyle wouldn't be able to solve the murders, but where he thought he ought to be looking might tell me something useful.

The Ranger turned from surveying the opposite bank and lifted an eyebrow.

I tried not to squirm beneath his gaze. "Someone has to pay for that . . . that atrocity," I said.

"I agree." His voice was even. "And I'm going to do my level best to make them. I'm sorry you saw it."

"I'm not," I said.

His expression was dubious, and I willed myself not to flush. It wasn't a lie, even if it wasn't wholly true. Stars knew, part of me—maybe even the greater part—wished I'd never gone into the cabin, never seen the bodies or smelled the blood or recognized what it meant. It would have been simpler that way.

But it wasn't who I was. Giraud, the healer to whom I'd been apprenticed for a time, once said of me that if I'd been in the Garden of Eden the snake would have had an easy job of it—that I would have eaten the apple as soon as it was offered and asked for another.

"I tried to spare you," Doyle said. "Why did you go in?"

"Because you didn't want me to," I said, aware that he might take my answer for nothing more than stubbornness.

It wasn't, but there was no way to make him understand. The world I came from was not the same as his. The capacity for magical power, to say nothing of one's skill in wielding it, had nothing to do with sex. The current head of the council had been elected near unanimously. Some of the members didn't like her, but no one doubted her skill or acumen.

I was accustomed to being treated as an equal—or at least to not being condescended to because I was a woman. The restrictions Mundanes placed on their women, so poorly disguised as chivalry, had never applied to me before, and already I found them burdensome and insulting. I was not a Mundane woman, despite the loss of my magic. Even bound and banished, I was still a witch. I'd had too much taken from me to willingly give away anything else.

I risked a glance up at him, not sure what I expected to see on his face. Dismissal or disgust, probably. Instead, there was sharp interest. A corner of his mouth quirked.

"I've known a few people like that in my time," he said. "Headstrong. Being told not to do something makes them need to do it."

I made a noise that might have been a laugh, if it hadn't been so bitter. "If you only knew. It's part of why I'm out here. I got into some trouble back home, and—"

Doyle's glance at my midsection was a swift, reflexive thing, and the absurdity of it startled a real laugh from me. His eyes flew up to meet mine.

"Not that kind of trouble," I said with a wry look, and I swear he blushed beneath his beard.

"I'm sorry," he said. "I've insulted you."

I was hardly offended, and I would have waved off the apology, but if he felt as though he owed me something, he would be more likely to tell me what I wanted to know. "I'll forgive you if you tell me who you think would have wanted to kill the Jensens."

He hesitated, and that *was* an insult.

"I'm not going to tell anyone what I saw," I snapped. "I already promised I wouldn't."

"I believed you the first time," Doyle said with a conciliatory look. He sighed and capitulated. "Harp Jensen was a Union man. The way I hear it, he got into a bit of a discussion with some rebels last time he was in town. Got a bit heated. I'm going to start by asking some questions about that."

I wanted to ask him how he thought Confederate sympathizers would have made it look as though wild animals had torn the Jensens apart, but before I could decide how to broach the subject, something rustled in the brush behind us. I turned, tensing, and Doyle put a hand on the butt of his gun.

The dense, dry branches of a low bush shuddered, and the gray cat from the Jensens' farm shouldered his way through. He stopped short when he saw us, lashing his tail, then bent to lap from the creek. When he'd finished, he crouched and leapt onto the bundle tied to the packhorse. He stalked across the canvas, then stretched, kneading the coarse fabric with his claws before rolling onto his side and regarding us with an air of entitlement.

Doyle moved as if to shoo him away, but I stopped him with a hand on his forearm.

"If you chase him off, he might end up as eagle food," I said. Truly, I was surprised he hadn't already. He was big, but not nearly big enough to be a match for one of the enormous birds.

The Ranger shook his head and let out a rueful chuckle. "Quite the menagerie you're bringing your uncle. We ought to get going again. We're not more than about two hours out." He remounted and guided his horse out into the creek, pulling the packhorse—with its new passenger—behind him.

There'd been so many stages to the journey, and each had been so difficult in its own way, that I'd had little time or inclination to worry about what lay at its ultimate end. Even as I had traveled toward it, it had felt so far away. But now there was nothing left between me and my final destination. There was nothing left to distract me from the hard fact that I didn't know what was waiting for me.

The Magisterium had sent me out here, so Josiah Merritt didn't have any choice about taking me in, no more than I'd had in coming. At least, that was supposed to be how it worked. In reality . . . Well, I was a long way from home. I knew next to nothing about the man. And that was before I'd had reason to worry he might be the sort who had dealings with demons.

It was early afternoon when Doyle announced that we'd reached Josiah Merritt's land. Ten minutes later, we came around a stand of pines and into sight of the homestead itself. Another step, and a flare of magic sizzled over my skin. I sucked in a startled breath. There was a ward on the property. A good one.

I wasn't the only one who felt it. The horses shuddered as if shaking off flies as it touched them. The cat sat up and sneezed twice, and the kids bleated. The cow, on her long lead rope, let out a low moo as she passed through it a few steps behind the rest of us.

Doyle alone appeared unaffected.

He frowned at the rough log cabin and barn, both chinked with white clay. I could tell from the way his hand rested on his thigh, in quick reaching distance from his gun, that he was wondering if we were about to stumble across another horror such as we'd seen at the Jensen place.

I could have told him we weren't. A ward like the one we'd just encountered was tied to the witch who set it. It was live; therefore, so was Josiah Merritt.

I'd barely completed the thought before the cabin door opened and an old man stepped out. Even from a distance, the scowl on his face was visible. So was the shotgun in his hand. He turned his head slightly in the direction of the barn, keeping his eyes on us, and let out a sharp whistle. A moment later, two dark-haired men emerged. The mute hired men.

Doyle didn't relax as he reined in his horse. "Mr. Merritt," he called. "I don't know if you remember me. I'm Langston Doyle with the Colorado Rangers."

"I remember you, Ranger," the old man said. He wasn't exactly pointing the gun at us, but something about the way he held it said it wouldn't take much. "Who's that you've got with you?"

"I've brought your niece to you," Doyle said.

Merritt's eyes flicked to me.

"It's me, Great-Uncle Josiah," I said before he could say anything. "Joya. I'm Alyse Young's granddaughter."

Only other witches ever recognize the name of the first woman hanged for witchcraft on American soil. Poor Alyse died on the gallows in Connecticut, some forty years before the hysteria in Salem. Claiming kinship with her makes for an effective code phrase.

Josiah Merritt understood it. His face went even more dour, and there was a long pause before he spoke. "Well, you'd best come on, then."

We urged the horses into the yard and reined to a stop.

Josiah gestured, just the flick of a finger, and the hired men came forward in eerie unison. Brothers, Doyle had said. I might have thought they were twins if one hadn't been several inches taller than the other. They moved the same way, had the same dark, shining hair, the same sharp noses and bright, interested gazes. Doyle handed down the goats to the taller man, then leaned over to untie my bags from the packhorse. The cat let out an irritated *mrroaw* at being disturbed, then leapt to the ground and began to wash, elaborately ignoring us all.

"You come from Boston?" Josiah said to me as I dismounted.

"Yes."

"Don't suppose you hauled that cat and them goats all that way?"

"From the Jensens' place," said Doyle, still atop his horse.

I flicked my eyes toward Josiah for any sign of a reaction to the name, but if there was one, I missed it. His face wore the same surly, stonelike expression as before.

"We were there overnight," Doyle went on as he swung down from the saddle. "Need to talk to you about that. And I need to water the horses."

"Peter and Paul will see to it," Josiah said.

I wondered which was which as they led the horses to the trough and began drawing water for them. They cast curious, sideways glances at us as they worked.

I waited for Josiah to invite us into the cabin. Instead, he propped the gun against the wall and lowered himself to a rough bench beside the door, looking up at Doyle expectantly.

"I could use a drink after our ride," Doyle said in a pointed tone. "And I'm sure your niece could as well."

Josiah heaved a sigh. "Paul," he called, and the shorter hired man looked over at us.

There was one question answered, at least.

"Bring the bucket and dipper." Josiah looked back up at Doyle. "Well?"

"The Jensens are dead."

Josiah looked mildly interested. "Both of 'em? What happened?"

"Murder," Doyle said. "They hadn't been dead long when we got there. Had to have been in the last day or so."

I hadn't been thinking in those terms, but he was right. The blood had barely been dry. If we'd gotten there earlier, we might have walked right into the middle of it. I couldn't suppress a shudder, and Josiah glanced at me.

Doyle evidently read it as concern. "I didn't let her see anything," he said quickly.

I almost laughed and bit the inside of my cheek to stop it. There was a lie hidden in a truth if ever I had heard one. He hadn't let me, but I had seen it.

Josiah didn't notice. "Indians?" he asked, frowning. "Haven't heard of any trouble lately."

"I couldn't say," Doyle replied. He gave me a significant glance, clearly intending to remind me that I couldn't, either. "I'd appreciate you keeping an ear out," he went on in a bland tone. "Passing along anything you hear."

"I won't," the old man replied. "Hear anything," he clarified at Doyle's startled look. "Don't get a lot of visitors. Don't go to town that often. Not likely to be able to help."

Doyle accepted the pronouncement with a thinning of his lips. "Well, you should keep a sharp eye out anyway. And keep your gun handy."

"Always do."

The men eyed one another.

"I need to bury the bodies," Doyle said after a pause. "I'd appreciate the use of your hired men. If they go back with me now, we could get it done tomorrow morning. They'd be back here by dark at the latest."

Josiah didn't pause. "No."

"What?" Doyle blinked, clearly taken aback. So was I, for that matter. What kind of man refused such a request?

"Sorry," Josiah said, not sounding in the least regretful. "Can't spare them."

Doyle's face was a study in suppressed irritation. "Well," he said in a sour tone, "I'd best be getting on, then. I've got a long afternoon ahead of me."

Josiah stood and started toward the horses without saying anything further to either of us.

Doyle watched his back as he walked away, then glanced at me and lowered his voice. "You're sure you want to stay here? I can take you on to town if you'd rather."

I tried not to grimace. I would much rather not have stayed, for a long list of reasons. But this was where the Magisterium had sent me, and they wouldn't consider "the old man was rude" a good enough excuse for defying them.

"I'll be fine," I said without looking at him.

He nodded once, then strode forward to take his horse from Peter.

"Appreciate the hospitality," he said to Josiah in a dry tone. He mounted, tipped his hat to me, then set off, the other horses in tow. It was silly, but I felt a pang. I barely knew him, but he was the nearest thing to a friend I had for a thousand miles in any direction.

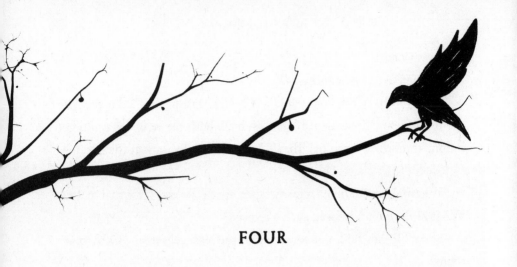

FOUR

J osiah watched him go, his expression guarded.

"I'm—" I began, but the old man shot me a quelling look.

"Wait."

I closed my teeth over a reply and tried not to fidget.

His eyes were intent on the Ranger's back, and he waited until Doyle was around the trees and out of sight before he sighed and turned to me.

There was no hint of welcome in his face. "Who are you, and what do you want?"

"I'm Joya Shaw," I said. "The Magisterium sent me."

"If they sent you, then you should have a letter for me."

"I do." I bent, my heart beating in my ears, and opened my leather valise. The contents had been jumbled around, and for a long moment I couldn't find the letter. The cat approached and stuck his head into the opening. I shooed him away.

"Never much cared for cats," Josiah said.

I glanced up at him. "He took a liking to me at the Jensen place," I said, then went back to rummaging.

"So you thought you'd bring him along?"

"It wasn't my idea," I said, feeling harassed as the cursed animal began batting at one of the bag's flopping handles. "He followed us." With a little spill of relief, I found the letter and straightened.

Josiah put out his hand for it and let out a small *harrumph* as he ran his fingers over the seal. It was charmed, obviously, or I'd have read it on the way. The spell on it would wipe the ink off the paper if anyone but the intended recipient opened it. Once I'd realized how much of my magic was gone, I hadn't dared try to get around it.

Josiah pressed two fingers to the blob of purple wax embossed with the Magisterium's staff-and-stars sigil and closed his eyes, then snapped the seal and unfolded the missive. His scowl deepened as he read.

"Four apprenticeships," he muttered, shaking his head.

My cheeks burned. It usually took a witch only one, perhaps two, placements before they were released from a guardian's oversight. My long period of apprenticeship was a matter of some gossip within the Magisterium. I fought down the urge to speak. Anything I said would sound like protesting too much.

Instead, I took the opportunity to look the old man over while he was occupied, trying not to be too obvious about it. He was nothing but leathery skin stretched over sinew, so thin and brittle he looked as if a good shake might snap him into pieces. He wasn't wearing a hat, and a narrow horseshoe of wispy white hair ringed a head as brown and spotted as a sparrow's egg. Time had plowed deep furrows in his face, and his bushy beard trailed down over his chest, mostly hiding the rawhide thong around his neck. Whatever was on the other end—a charm or amulet of some sort, probably—disappeared beneath the collar of his heavy flannel shirt.

Witches tend to be long-lived, but he looked older than any other I'd ever met. His eyes, however, when he raised them from the letter and focused on me, were sharp and clear.

"Hobbled you, did they?"

Having him put it that way—not bound, not restrained, but *hobbled*, as if I were a horse with a tendency to wander—was a new layer of humiliation. I gave him a stiff nod.

"Let's see it."

I shook the bracelet out of my sleeve and held out my wrist.

Josiah pinched the silver between his thumb and forefinger and closed his eyes, feeling the spell. "Hmm," he said a moment later, letting go and looking at me. "A heavy binding. How much did they leave you?"

I blinked at him. Witches constantly gauge one another's ability, mostly through the size and complexity of the spells we cast, along with how well they work. And we might talk about others' strength or skill, among ourselves and in carefully guarded language. But one witch bluntly asking another, a stranger, no less, how much power they have just isn't done.

"I don't—" I began, drawing myself up to refuse, then managed to stop long enough to consider the consequences of my words. Josiah Merritt had charge of me, by the Magisterium's order. I was on his land, behind his ward, and in his power. The question was beyond rude. But refusing to answer would set us on an even less promising path than we were already on.

And there could be a benefit. If I allowed Josiah Merritt to test what remained of my power, I would have a chance to test his. I could get a sense of his strength. Perhaps, if he'd been the one to summon the demon, it would have left some mark on him.

He was looking at me, waiting for me to finish speaking.

Instead, I pressed my lips together and thrust out my hand.

He took it, and my skin tingled as our magics tasted one another. I frowned, damning the binding yet again. I should have been able to tell to the drop how much power Josiah Merritt had and where his magical affinities lay. Instead, reading him was like trying to feel the engraving on a coin while wearing mittens.

I bit my lip, concentrating. Honestly, it felt as if he had barely any magic at all. But I wasn't sure how far I could trust that impression. The binding was undoubtedly clouding my perceptions. Even so, I would have expected more than—

"They didn't leave you much, did they?" Josiah said, interrupting my thoughts.

My cheeks went hot again at the reminder that however little magic it seemed he had, it was more than I did.

"What did you do?"

"That doesn't say?" I jerked my chin at the letter, my hand still in his.

"No."

"If they didn't see fit to tell you, I'm not sure why I should have to. It doesn't matter." I tried to pull my hand away, but his grip had suddenly become like an iron band, and he gave me a hard look.

"Girl, do not mishear me. I will not have you under my roof without knowing what it is I'm harboring. You'll tell me what you did to earn that piece of jewelry—all of it—or I'll turn you right around and pack you back where you came from. They've all but washed their hands of you by sending you out here. I have an idea they wouldn't be glad to see you back again."

My temper threatened to get away from me, but I managed to keep hold of it. He was right. I didn't know what the Magisterium would do with me if he refused to take me in, but I understood enough to believe Marthe when she said this was the best option. With an enormous effort, I made my voice calm.

"It's a long story," I said. "Can we sit?" I tried again to withdraw my hand. Gently, this time.

He let go and nodded to the bench.

I settled myself on the rough plank seat, trying to decide where to begin. "What do you know about how the war is going?" I asked.

"Denver City has a newspaper," he said. "I see a copy of it now and then. But what's that got to do with anything? That mess is nothing to do with us."

It was true as far as it went. The Magisterium as a body did not involve itself in the affairs of Mundanes. It wasn't uncommon for an individual witch to take an interest in a non-magical dispute and decide to influence events. There had been, for example, at least one American president who didn't know how much of his political fortunes he owed to his wife's discreet spell-casting.

That incident had earned the witch involved a stern talking-to from the council, but since her interference hadn't been obvious to the Mundanes, she'd gotten off with a warning. And low-level practitioners, those not powerful or skilled enough to become Magisterium members, were generally left alone. Hedge witches and wise women could dispense their charms and cures. Stage magicians could add a little something extra to their shows.

But those of us with real power generally knew not to go too far. We did not risk exposing our abilities or becoming tools of a Mundane government. We existed alongside but apart from the non-magical world, and as a rule their political squabbles meant nothing to us. The American Magisterium maintained good relations with the magical authorities in England during the Revolution. The British and French covens had remained in polite contact for centuries, even as their respective countries waged endless wars on one another. But now . . .

I shook my head. "This war is different."

Officially, the Magisterium had always been neutral on the question of slavery itself. Their only firm stance was that no powered individual should be bound to serve a Mundane. They said it lowered us all. For the better part of a century, the Magisterium had been in the habit of seeking out and freeing magically gifted individuals among the enslaved and indentured in the American colonies. We'd had at least a few Negro members for as long as anyone could remember. Some people didn't like it, but the Magisterium had always been clear: just as sex made no difference to one's power, neither did the color of one's skin. The only firm requirements for membership were having adequate magical talent, being able to use it effectively, and being willing to take the oath of allegiance. For decades, there wasn't more than mild grumbling.

As indenture fell out of favor and slavery began dying out in the North, enslaved witches became a purely Southern phenomenon—and a purely Negro one. The tenor of the thing changed. Southern witches who came north, whether for training or to work, became more likely to snub the Negro members. To refuse to sit at table with them or invite them into their private quarters. Most absolutely refused to be apprenticed to Negro masters.

The Magisterium tried to accommodate them, despite protests by the Northerners that giving in to their bigotry rewarded it. One compromise they would not make, however: they would not stop freeing enslaved witches. The traditional method had been facilitating escapes, but some of the Southern witches began to complain. They said it was theft. After Congress passed the Fugitive Slave Act in 1850, there were several ugly incidents—newly escaped witches whose locations were mysteriously leaked to the slave catchers. Freed Negro witches became afraid to leave the Magisterium grounds.

It led to bad blood all around, and the Magisterium ultimately adopted a policy of buying enslaved witches instead, bringing them North and setting them free. That aggravated the Northern witches, who complained of the expense and raised questions about the morality of participating in the slave trade, even if the ultimate result was another free witch.

It was a magical variation on the debates taking place all around the country, and it followed a similar progression. There were polite discussions. Then heated arguments. Factions hardened. Estrangements began. There was a terrible, rising tension to everything. And when the war everyone knew was coming finally started . . .

"Most of the Southern witches left," I told him.

"Only the white ones, I assume," Josiah interjected, and I acknowledged his point with a nod.

Some of those white Magisterium members were from slave-owning families. Some of them weren't but went anyway, feeling that remaining would be disloyal to their home states. And some of them just couldn't tolerate being a Southerner in Boston anymore. The stares when they spoke and the quiet hostility were too much.

"We lost contact with some of the Southern covens almost immediately," I said. "We thought they'd been disrupted by the fighting and would get back in touch when they could, but they didn't. And then we started hearing rumors."

"What kind of rumors?" Josiah asked.

"Strange things happening on the battlefields," I said, looking at him for the first time since I'd started talking. His face was intent. "Bad weather coming out of nowhere. Panic among the Union troops even when they had the advantage. The South is winning too many battles," I said bluntly. "Battles they have no business winning. Battles where they're outnumbered, where they have the worse position and not enough ammunition. At second Manassas earlier this year, the Union troops were outflanked by an entire army they never saw coming."

Josiah's voice was flat, his face expressionless. "You think the Southern witches are helping them."

"We know they are."

"How?"

"Because of me." I swallowed hard and dropped my gaze, determined to tell the rest of the story in the same straightforward way I'd begun. "I told you that most of the Southern witches left. But not all. One of the ones who stayed behind was my . . . friend."

It was no use. I could feel my neck going hot, turning the same ugly, mottled red it always did when I got upset. I shot a glance at Josiah and could tell he was intentionally not looking at me. That made it worse. I went ahead, desperate to have it over with.

"Thomas Brasher Wetherell. The third. Of the Savannah Wetherells."

He'd stayed behind even as most of the others packed their bags because he said he couldn't bear to leave me. We'd been lovers for three months by then, and I was deep in the throes of the sort of rapturous infatuation that feels a great deal like something more.

"One of the other witches who stayed was a woman from Alabama."

Thomas had never shown any special interest in Lisbeth Miller before, but after the war started, I found them talking together in the hallways a few times. They always broke off when I approached. Always appeared to welcome me. Something about their relationship prodded at my insides, made me feel jealous and desperate. I tried asking him about her, casually, and Thomas heard the note in my voice and teased me for it. He said they were talking about their homes. That as much as he adored me, sometimes he needed to hear another Southern voice. Then he took me to bed and did things that left me without the energy to press him further.

It wasn't enough to quiet the worry. I would lie in bed the nights he wasn't with me, doubt gnawing at my insides. I began—not following him, exactly—but finding reasons most days to go wherever he was likely to be, just to see if he was there, and if he was with her. After a few months I couldn't stand it any longer.

"I had to know," I said. "I had to get him to tell me the truth."

Josiah looked at me with hard eyes. "Compulsion?"

"No," I said quickly. Using compulsion spells against other witches was forbidden. Only the council could sanction it, and then only under extraordinary circumstances. "It wasn't a compulsion spell. It was a new spell. One I created."

Josiah scowled in obvious disapproval, and I couldn't stop myself from letting out an irritated huff. None of my teachers had ever liked it, either, when I showed them what I could do.

There were spells for most everything, tried and true and there to use if you could summon and hold enough magic to make them work. But finding a spell to do exactly what you wanted and learning it well enough to cast it could be tedious. I found it much easier to strip bits from spells I already knew and weave them into something new.

But everyone said it was dangerous, and I was forbidden from casting any of the spells I'd created without supervision. I kept doing it anyway, of course, but carefully. By the time I'd decided to build a spell to get the truth from Thomas, I'd had plenty of practice.

"I'm good at it," I said. "I knew it would work."

And it had. I'd begun with a spell meant for loosening stuck objects. You could use it to get a lid off a jar or pull a stubborn stump from a field. I changed it and wove it into the base of a potion meant to create desire. That night, I went to Thomas's rooms with a bottle of his favorite wine in my hands and a phial the size of my smallest finger in my pocket.

I tipped it into his second glass, and when he'd drunk it down, I took his hand and drew him to the bed with a smile. Later, when he was sated and sleepy and unguarded, I whispered the words of the invocation into his neck. A shiver rippled over his skin, and I held my breath as he sighed and settled deeper into the sheets as the spell took hold. I hesitated then, both wanting and not wanting to know.

The need for certainty won out. My mouth dry, I leaned down and put my lips to his ear. I asked my questions.

He answered.

The memory nearly overwhelmed me, and I hauled in a breath so deep I went dizzy, desperate to have it said and over with. "A group of them had decided even before the war started that they meant to help the South win. They had it all planned out. They were afraid the Magisterium would take steps to counter them if they were discovered, so they decided to leave a few people behind." My voice was hoarse.

"Spies," Josiah said.

"Yes. They—" My voice broke. I coughed and tried again. "They drew lots to see who would go and who would stay. Thomas—and Lisbeth—drew the short straws."

He didn't care for me. Had never cared for me. He'd simply needed an excuse to stay behind when the war came. I felt it all again—the fury and humiliation. How long would he have kept up the farce of our relationship if the war had been longer in starting than expected? Which of us had he considered seducing, and what had it been about me that made him choose me? Lost in all the questions I'd been asking myself since the moment I'd uncovered the scheme, I'd almost forgotten Josiah was there until he spoke.

"Council wouldn't like it," Josiah said. "Having cuckoos in the nest."

"No. And it was even worse than that," I said. "They'd sent a few scouts south when we started hearing rumors about magic on the battlefields. None of them have ever made it back. It turned out Thomas and Lisbeth had warned the rebels—given them the names. They're probably dead."

I waited a beat before I went on. "I went to Marthe—my guardian—the next morning and told her what I'd learned. She took it to the council." I raised my hand and shook the bracelet. "They gave me this for my trouble and sent me out here to get rid of me." I couldn't keep the bitterness out of my voice.

"You did the right thing, telling them," Josiah said. Then his voice turned flat as a slap. "And you're lucky they didn't expel you."

I snapped my head up, my mouth falling open. "I didn't do anything wrong. I uncovered a spy ring right in the Magisterium. Who knows how long it would have gone on if I hadn't done what I did?"

"That's self-serving horseshit," he snapped. "And unless you are some spectacular kind of fool, you know it."

I gaped at him.

"You cast a new, untested spell on a fellow witch—one you claim to have cared about, at that—for no better reason than you were jealous. And spare me the spying nonsense," he said, raising a hand to forestall my protest. His face was hard. "You didn't have any idea that's what you were going to find out. You didn't suspect him of anything other than carrying on with that girl. If you had, you could have told someone, let them act on it. You didn't have any high-minded motive behind what you did.

"And it was an illegal spell twice over. You created a new kind of compulsion spell—oh, you don't call it that," he said as I sputtered. "But that's what it was, no matter what you say. You took away his will. You didn't just make him answer your questions. You made him want to. Made him your puppet. It might be worse than compulsion, if you think about it. It was beyond reckless. And you have the nerve to complain that they bound you?" He laughed, but there was no humor in it.

"I almost feel sorry for the council, the miserable wretches. They must have had a time trying to decide what to do with you. You broke the codes half a dozen different ways. But you stumbled over something they needed to know. Hard for them to punish you if they were going to act on what you'd learned. And they didn't have any choice about that. You were lucky," he said again. "You should be on your knees every day thanking your stars that binding you was all they did."

Somehow I was on my feet. "They took my magic away from me," I said in a strangled voice, staring down at him.

The old man scowled back. "They took a loaded gun away from a child. You waved it around with no regard for the damage you could cause, and you proved you couldn't be trusted with that kind of power. I'd be shocked if it's the first time you've gotten into trouble for that sort of thing," he added. "Go ahead. Tell me I'm wrong."

My face went even hotter, and I clenched my teeth together, hating him for having guessed correctly.

He nodded at my silence and stood, stepping to within inches of me. "I thought so. Good thing you're bound. I wouldn't take you in if you weren't, not for all the gold in the hills. Like taking in a mad dog. Just a matter of time before it bites you."

The rage that rose up in me at his words all but blinded me. Every bit of the anger I'd been suppressing since they put the damned bracelet around my wrist and sent me away like a child being put to bed without supper, every bit of the indignity, the fear, the discomfort of the trip—all of it came roaring through me, filling me up until it seemed to spill out of every pore in my body, and all directed at the old man in front of me.

White-hot pain seared my wrist, and I gasped. I'd reached for my power without ever deciding to do it. I staggered away from him, my whole arm throbbing. My fists were clenched. My breath rasped in my throat. It had been years since I'd lost my temper like that. Cold horror filled me as I realized what I might have done if I'd been able.

Josiah waited me out, and when I sneaked a glance at him, his arms were folded, his face impassive.

I dropped my head. "You're going to send me back." It wasn't a question. No one would be willing to let me stay after seeing me lose control like that. Marthe would be ashamed of me. The thought hurt as much as the burn on my wrist, and my throat went thick.

Josiah sighed. "No. Not as long as you agree to abide by some rules."

"What? Why?" I asked, thoroughly shocked. "What rules?"

The corner of his mouth quirked in what might have been dour amusement. "You don't do any magic while you're under my roof that I haven't given you leave to do. No playing with new spells or remaking old ones. Shouldn't be much of an issue, with you bound that tightly," he added, and my face flamed hot again. "And no trying to get around that." He nodded at the bangle.

I stood staring at him for a long moment. "Why would you let me stay after . . . that?"

He sighed. "Why did you come all the way here? Why didn't you snap that thing off your wrist as soon as you were out of Boston? It's charmed, but against your magic, not a hammer and chisel. Why didn't you take it off and take the council's money and run?"

"The Magisterium would kill me," I said.

"From what you've told me, the Magisterium has plenty to occupy their time. A sight too much to send anyone out after a single witch gone rogue. Likely you'd get a good few years before they caught up with you, if they ever managed it."

I didn't speak, and he went on. "That you didn't do that—then, or just now, when I provoked you—tells me there's a limit to your defiance. You aren't willing to make yourself an outlaw. You don't like the council's ruling, but you've decided to abide by it."

"It wasn't much of a choice."

"That's the thing about choices," he said with a shrug. "They're never limitless. And they're most often not what we'd like. You look at the ones available to you and decide which one has a price you're willing to pay. Then you live with it.

"For example, right now, you have several choices. You can stand there until you starve to death. You can start walking in any direction you choose. Or you can agree to my terms, come into the house, and let me give you something for that burn." He strode past me toward the cabin door.

"How do you know I won't change my mind? Make a different choice tomorrow?" I said to his back. "I could decide I'm done abiding by your rules. I could break off the binding and kill you."

Josiah stopped on the threshold and half turned to face me, his expression perfectly, blankly neutral. "You could try."

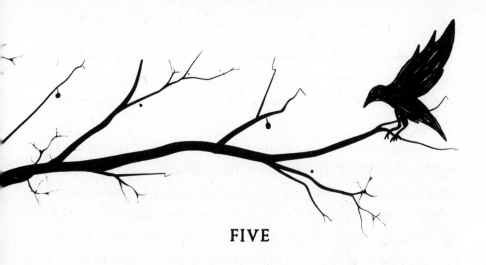

FIVE

He disappeared inside.

I blinked after him, chilled by his response. It made no sense. I had no doubt that without the binding I would be far more powerful than he. He had to know it. So why did he appear to believe he could best me? Was it a bluff? Or a sideways boast that he had power I didn't know about? It wasn't an admission that he consorted with demons, but if I hadn't already been on my guard, I was now.

I took a long moment to gather myself, then followed him into the cabin. The interior was cramped and dark. It stank, predominately of grease and woodsmoke, with an underlying odor I could only describe as "unwashed." It was a single room, rectangular, with a loft on one end. The alcove beneath it held a low wooden bunk, a narrow worktable, and a heavy, iron-banded trunk.

A woodbox sat beside a round-bellied cast-iron stove. Its pipe led through the floor of the loft and presumably out through the roof. On the wall beside the stove was a shelf with cooking implements and a set of tin dinnerware. Canvas sacks—mostly flour and beans and coffee, from what I could see—were piled along the back wall along with other supplies. What was left of the space was dominated by a rough table and a pair of splintery chairs.

It was the most depressing little hovel I'd ever seen. I tried not to let my dismay show as Josiah ducked into the sleeping space and hauled open the lid of the trunk with a grunt of effort. He extracted a ceramic jar and brought it back out to me. The salve inside was badly made, too thick to spread easily, with a gritty texture. I scooped some out with my fingers and patted it on the burn anyway, wondering what his potions must be like if he was this poor an herbalist.

"Thank you," I said, handing it back.

"You're welcome," Josiah replied. "Now, since you came inside, it appears you've accepted my terms, but I'm not going to have you claiming otherwise later. I want to hear you say it."

I lifted my hands in a gesture of surrender. "I accept your terms."

"Which were?"

I ground my teeth. "No magic beneath your roof without your permission. No creating spells or remaking them. And I won't try to remove the binding."

He nodded. "Fair enough. You can have the loft to sleep in—there's a bed up there with a straw tick. I'm too old to be climbing that ladder like a damn monkey." He rubbed absently at his hip, as if pained by the memory of a fall.

I eyed the space. "Where do Peter and Paul sleep?"

"There's a bunkhouse attached to the barn. I'll show you that, along with the cold cellar and the privy."

I followed him outside, grateful to be back out in the fresh air. "I need to feed the kids," I said, stooping to pull their bottles from my bag. "Could one of the men milk the cow for me? Or show me how," I added at his sharp look.

"You'll earn your keep while you're here," he said, leading me past a rooting pig in a pen and a covered chicken run. A rooster crowed a challenge at us from within the wattle enclosure. "I'm not running a hotel."

It turned out, when we reached the barn, that Peter and Paul had already seen to the cow. She was contentedly chewing away in a stall beside a second cow that could have been her twin. On her other side were two more stalls, each of which held a gray-muzzled mule. The nearest bared its teeth at me when I approached.

"Mind your manners," Josiah said, rapping it lightly on the nose. "This is Badger. He's an ornery old cuss. Th' other one's Fox." Fox pricked his ears forward when he heard his name and looked placidly at me over the door of the stall.

Across from the stalls, Peter and Paul had constructed a makeshift pen for the goats. The two hired men sat inside it, looking delightedly at each other as the little animals scrambled over them like living mountains.

They clambered to their feet when they noticed us watching them, ducking their heads as if they expected a reprimand.

Instead, when the old man spoke, it was in the mildest tone I'd heard him use yet. "We've all got work to do. Best be getting back to it. I'll be back in by suppertime," he said to me. "Can you manage to get yourself settled and put something together?"

"Of course," I said, unwilling to admit that I'd cooked as many meals in my life as I'd milked cows. I knew how to make potions. I'd figure it out.

The three men left, and I fed the kids, grateful to have the time alone to order my thoughts. Or try to, at least. They were mostly a muddle. Having gotten through the end of my journey and the much-dreaded initial encounter with Josiah Merritt, the fatigue of the last few weeks caught up with me as I sat on the floor of the barn. I jerked out of a doze, once when the bottle slipped out of my hand and clunked against the floor, and again when one of the kids butted me after he'd sucked it dry.

I scratched their heads a final time, then pushed myself to my feet and trudged back to the house, where I was relieved to find someone had hauled my bags inside. I hadn't eaten anything that day but a hunk of bread, and I was shaky with hunger. There was a pair of corncakes on a tin plate on the back of the stove. The cloth covering them was dirty, but I was too famished to care, and I choked them down with another dipperful of water.

There were banked coals in the stove, and I poked them up and piled in some wood. Once the fire was roaring, I heated a bucket of water to wash, then filled a pot and set several scoops of dried beans to boiling.

They'd been bubbling away for some time, and I was scraping the scorched bits off the salt pork I'd tried to fry when Josiah returned to the cabin. I dished up the meal, but my pride in having produced it died when I discovered that both dried beans and salt pork had to be soaked before cooking.

"Never mind," Josiah said dourly, scraping the hard little rocks back into the pot. He dropped in the charred hunks of meat and covered the whole mess with the lid. "It can soak tonight and we'll have it tomorrow."

We ate fried corn mush with milk for dinner, without talking. I was too exhausted to try to parse the silence, and when my bowl was empty, Josiah told me to go on up to bed. I took the stubby tallow candle he offered and climbed wearily to the loft, which was too low for me to do more than kneel. I'd stoked the fire too high, and the cramped space was sweltering.

I crawled to the single small window and propped the wooden shutter open a few inches to let in some fresh air before turning to regard the bed. The blankets were worn and needed washing in the worst way, and the straw in the tick was limp and sour, but it was a real bed. I stripped down to my shift and fell onto it, my entire body aching with exhaustion.

There would be time enough tomorrow to decide what to do next. I couldn't tell Josiah what I'd seen at the Jensens' farm. Not until I knew he wasn't responsible for it. If he wasn't, there was a good chance he wouldn't even believe me. No one had seen a demon in two hundred ye—

No, that wasn't true. The Jensens had seen one. An image of the inside of the cabin flashed through my mind, and I grimaced in the dark and forced myself to think of something else.

If Josiah was the summoner, telling him about what I'd seen could get me killed. I'd have to tread carefully. I couldn't let him know I knew anything about a demon. I couldn't let him know I suspected him. But if he was consorting with demons, I could write to the Magisterium. Maybe they would recall me to testify. Maybe they would rescind my banishment, or even remove the binding.

But for any of that to happen, I would need proof. There had to be a way to find it.

Before I could follow that line of thought any further, sleep rolled over me like a wave and dragged me under.

⊶

I slept as deeply as I ever had in my life until sometime just before dawn, when the nightmare intruded, again. I gasped awake, sweating, to find the gray cat crouched on my chest, his nose an inch from my own and his green eyes regarding me with unnerving intensity.

With a little huff of relief, I reached up with both hands to scratch him beneath his chin, and he closed his eyes and unleashed another of those thrumming purrs.

Rattling snores from below told me Josiah was still asleep.

"You shouldn't be here," I told the cat in a whisper. "How did you get in?" He opened his eyes as I spoke, and I shifted him from my chest to the tick mattress beside me, relieved to be able to draw a full breath. He settled into the crook of my arm, still purring. We drowsed together until the snores below hitched and became a series of deep, phlegmy coughs.

The cat flattened his ears at the noise, looking displeased, then slithered to the floor. He leapt onto the sill of the open window.

As Josiah muttered and spat below me, I leaned over to watch the cat clamber down the side of the cabin, claws digging deep into the timbers, tail lashing the entire way. A few feet from the ground, he jumped and landed with a thump, then paused to groom himself before sauntering away.

The daylight did my little loft no favors. Everything was coated in a thick layer of dust, and the blankets were even grimier than I'd realized. My clothes were likewise filthy. I wrinkled my nose as I dressed, wishing with all my heart for enough power to cast a cleaning spell. Maybe I could ask Josiah to do it. But the state of the cabin suggested he didn't consider such things to be worth spending magic on. Or that maybe he didn't have the magic to spare for them.

I made my way down the ladder and out to the privy, wrapping my arms around myself in the cold morning air. It was a puzzle. He didn't seem to have much magic—except for all the ways he did. The ward around his property was no trifle. And his casual confidence in his ability to best me if it came to a fight suggested he was more than he seemed.

Finished in the privy, I headed for the barn to feed the kids, thinking about how to find out what I needed to know.

The cat was crouched behind the water trough, peering around the corner at a pair of crows as they pecked at the dirt in front of the barn. I raised my hands, ready to clap and startle them away before he could pounce at them, then held back. Something about the showy way they hopped and fluttered their wings made me think they knew he was there and were enjoying taunting him. Just as he gathered himself to spring, they took to the wing, one after the other, their cawing sounding almost like laughter. He watched them with a disgruntled air as they flew away behind the barn.

He was still staring in that direction when the barn door opened and Peter emerged. The big hired man bent down and scooped him up, giving him a rough pat on the head before returning him to the ground, where he stalked away, affronted.

"Good morning," I said, and Peter looked up at me with a shy smile. "I don't suppose you could teach me to milk the cow?"

His smile broadened, and he nodded and gestured for me to follow him back inside.

It was a comedy of errors, but half an hour later, I'd produced a bucket of milk. Both men watched, apparently fascinated, as I filled the bottles and fed the kids.

I was finishing up when Josiah entered the barn, hardly sparing me a glance. "The rest of that hay ain't going to cut itself, boys," he said from beside the door, and the brothers ducked their heads at me as they left the barn.

"I was hoping to get some laundry done today," I said before Josiah could follow. "Maybe give the cabin a cleaning, too. I don't suppose you have a charm or amulet I could use? Since I can't make one?"

He probably wouldn't up and hand me a demon charm, but anything that would let me examine his own power more closely could be useful.

He shook his head. "Don't generally use magic for such things. But I suppose I can leave one of the boys to help you—laundry is a job of work. Lot of water to haul."

"I'd appreciate that," I said.

"Washboard and tub are there," Josiah said, pointing to a corner of the barn. "Should be a crock of lye soap in the house somewhere." He turned to leave, and I let him get three steps away before I spoke again.

"Is there . . . anything in the house I shouldn't touch?" I tried to sound casual, but even to my own ears, there was an unnatural note in my voice. Stars, I might as well go ahead and announce that I wanted to search through his things.

"Ain't nothing," he said, appearing not to notice anything odd. "No wards or live spells in the house. I've got my lunch, so I won't be back in 'til supper."

"Beans and salt pork," I said, inanely.

He gave me an odd look as he left, and I waited until he was gone to bury my burning face in my hands. I was a terrible spy without my magic. I had to get myself under control.

By the time I hauled the washtub back to the house, Paul was waiting beside the door. On the table inside was another pair of corncakes covered with the same grimy cloth. I made a face. That was one thing that was definitely getting washed today.

I took one of the cakes and offered the other to Paul, who ate it in three quick swallows, hardly seeming to chew.

"I suppose we should get going," I said when he was finished. "We have a long day in front of us."

I had no idea how true a statement it was.

I gathered clothes and bedding and emptied the mattress ticks of their compacted straw while Paul drew and heated buckets of water, stoking the stove until both our faces were red and shiny with sweat. When the washtub was full, I knelt beside it, stirring the contents with the handle end of a broom until the water cooled enough that I could plunge my hands in without risking burns. I rubbed the sodden cloth against the scrub board until my shoulders and arms screamed. The caustic soap stung my hands and made my eyes water.

When I could stand it no longer, Paul took a turn at the wash while I hauled bags and boxes outside and swept the cabin floor, raising such a cloud of dust despite the open door and windows that I thought I might choke. I alternately sweated and shivered, since the air near the stove was too hot and that near the windows too cold.

It was some of the hardest physical work I'd ever done, and I would have given up after an hour if it hadn't been for Paul. Though he could not have been any less miserable than I was, there was not a hint of complaint in his expression or demeanor, and every time I glanced over at him, his stoicism shamed me into pressing on.

At midday, when the first batch of washing was rinsed and wrung, I sent Paul to hang it to dry, then laid my broom aside and ducked into Josiah's sleeping alcove.

The Magisterium's letter lay unfolded on top of his worktable. It was the least important piece of the search, but I picked it up at once. My face flamed as my eyes hurried over the words, written in the spidery script of the Magistra's personal secretary. "Talented, though headstrong and undisciplined" was the nicest thing it said about me, and I forced myself to set it aside instead of reading it a second time. It didn't matter. Josiah had taken me in.

And now I needed to finish searching his things to make sure he wasn't summoning demons.

He had an apothecary box much like the one I'd been forced to leave behind in Boston, though less well-stocked than mine had been. The salve he'd given me for my burn the day before was the most complicated thing it contained. The tray in its bottom held several blank amulets—flat, smooth disks of wood the size of dollar coins. His athame—the ritual dagger he would use for carving spells into them—lay alongside, well-worn and clean of any magic or matter.

His trunk held nothing interesting except for a trio of buffalo robes, a pair of heavy knives in worn scabbards, and a tiny two-shot derringer. Under his bed, he had a money box filled with equal parts coins and nuggets of gold. There were no spell books, no ritual candles, no bottled potions. There was nothing, in short, that indicated Josiah Merritt was anything other than he seemed to be: barely a witch at all.

How, then, to explain that ward? And his unsettling certainty that even if I removed the binding, I wouldn't be able to overpower him?

The search took only a few minutes, and by the time Paul returned, I'd half filled the washtub again. He did most of the work on the second batch of wash, while I concentrated on putting the cabin back in order.

By the time Josiah returned near sunset, the laundry was done, though the last of the clothes were still damp on the line. I'd bathed in the last tub of warm water and was dressed in truly clean clothes for the first time in weeks. The cabin was as tidy as I'd been able to make it, with supplies now stacked neatly along one wall. I waited for Josiah to comment, but he only glanced around the space and grunted before turning to the stove. He lifted the lid on the pot containing the previous night's beans, then glared at me.

"What?" I asked, too tired to hide my annoyance. "They can't have burned."

I'd remembered to add water throughout the day and congratulated myself for my foresight. I hurried over to look. I was correct. The beans had not burned. They and the fatback had, however, boiled down into a pale, grayish mush.

We choked down the mush in glowering silence before I retreated up the ladder to my loft. Worn out and aggravated, I undressed, listening to Josiah muttering as he stumped into his alcove. The mutters stopped as he encountered his own clean and folded clothes, stacked neatly atop the clean blanket that covered a clean bed tick full of fresh straw.

"You're welcome," I called out with vindictive politeness as I dropped onto my own bed.

There was a snort from below before the lamp went out and the cabin was plunged into blackness.

It might have been laughter.

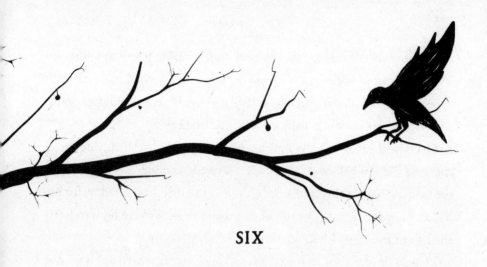

SIX

T he days bled into one another as fall slouched toward winter. The nights grew frigid, and though the cabin was stoutly built, it was cold enough in the mornings that my breath fogged the air. Josiah gave me one of the buffalo robes from his trunk for my bed, but when I asked him to make me a warmth charm, he refused.

"Why?" I asked, baffled. Every witch I knew used warmth charms in the winter.

"You know how they work, don't you? They don't make you warmer. They just make it so you don't feel the cold," he said. "That's dangerous out here with no one to remind you. Your fingers and toes can freeze and you won't know it til they start turning black."

"But you do have someone to remind you," I said. "Peter and Paul are here. And now I am, too. I'll be careful. I only—"

"No," he said, in a tone I'd learned meant the discussion was at an end.

I sighed and resigned myself to shivering.

Each morning, I woke with the cat curled beside me. Sometimes he brought a corpse with him, a mouse or vole, and stared at me with such expectation that all I could do was hide my revulsion and whisper praise as I stroked his back and listened to his satisfied purr.

Once he'd gone—always out the window; Josiah had firmly declared that cats did not belong in the house—I would shudder as I disposed of the evidence of his tiny midnight murders. I named him Shadow for his habit of appearing mostly around dawn and dusk. Where he wandered the rest of the time, I had no idea.

I found the daily toil of life on a farm shocking, city-bred as I was, and without my magic to ease the labor. I swept and scrubbed, fighting the insidious dust that worked its way through cracks and crevices, coating everything in a fine gray-brown film. I milked the cows and scalded the pails and churned cream into butter. I hauled water and wood and hay.

I looked after the kids, though Peter, especially, was prone to beating me to their morning feeding. Both he and Paul enjoyed the little animals, taking every opportunity to pause and watch them gambol, unabashed glee on their faces.

I tried to cook but wound up carrying so many messes out to the chickens that Josiah finally put a stop to it, complaining that I would bankrupt him if I kept running through his supplies at such a rate.

My mortification over the ruined dinners aside, caring for the poultry was a task I enjoyed. The hens were glossy and fat, and I liked listening to their contented clucking as I strewed corn for them and gathered their eggs. That damned nuisance of a rooster was another matter. He strutted and crowed and tried to bully me away from his harem, charging me and pecking at my ankles whenever I entered the run. I took to calling him Percy, after a boy I'd known at the Magisterium school.

Once he'd been christened, I couldn't help but name the rest of them. Penny and Patty and Pernilla were the goldens. Poppy and Pinky were red. And Polly, Prudence, and Pippa were glossy black. Josiah told me I'd regret it when I had to wring the neck of whoever ceased laying next. I ignored him, then was heartsick when something—a stoat or fox—got hold of Pernilla one night when I left the latch open on the coop. I found what was left of her, a mass of feathers and drying gore, beside the privy the next morning. Josiah was sharp with me that day, surly at the loss of a good laying hen and impatient with my woebegone face.

Worse, by far, was the day we killed the pig. It was cold enough, Josiah said, that it was time. The bears were hibernating and would be less likely to steal the meat from the smokehouse while it cured. I begged to stay inside the house until it was over, and Josiah let me, but the pig's sharp squeal still reached me, and the terror in it left me cold to my bones.

Josiah let me miss the slaughtering, but there was no escaping the aftermath. I helped with the bleeding and gutting. I scrubbed bristles from the boiled carcass with a stiff brush. I scraped and trimmed and cut. I skimmed fat and rendered lard and packed salt around sides and haunches. *Just a pig*, I told myself, trying not to remember the inside of the Jensens' cabin, not to see their bodies laid out before me. I stank of sweat and smoke and pork fat by nightfall, and when I fell into bed, my dreams were full of blood.

Josiah seemed unbothered by the whole experience, and I didn't know whether to read any meaning into it or not. There was no overt sign that he dealt with demons or had anything to do with the Jensens' deaths. But there was nothing that obviously cleared him, either.

For my own part, I kept to my word and used no magic. It was the longest stretch I'd ever gone since coming into my powers, and every minute of every day was tinged with a strange, hollow feeling of loss. As bad as it was, though, I was clear-eyed enough to realize it would have been worse if I'd been back in Boston. There, I would have been surrounded every day by people casually doing things I no longer could. I couldn't have borne it, starving while they feasted, being regarded with varying degrees of pity and embarrassment. Here on the farm with Josiah, who lived more or less as a Mundane, I was at least spared that much.

Mostly.

The fire went out overnight three weeks after I arrived, and Josiah set me to relighting it with magic while he watched. A quarter hour of attempts left me with a singed twist of newsprint and a pair of fresh burns on my wrist. I'd managed to make a single big spark. Finally, with the day's work ahead and breakfast still unmade, Josiah grunted, brushed me aside, and lit the stove with a gesture and a word, the whisper of his magic so subtle I felt nothing at all.

I stared at the flames, humiliated beyond measure as Josiah matter-of-factly went about cooking our breakfast. He didn't try to make conversation as we ate, which was no different from any other day, and when he was finished, he packed up a lunch and left me alone to use the last of his burn salve and brood over my failure.

Making fire was one of the most basic uses of magic; one of the first things an apprentice learned to do. Was I even a witch anymore if I couldn't draw enough power to do something so simple? I stared at the binding on my wrist, seized by an almost overwhelming urge to tear it free and drink in power until I burned the magic clean out of myself and died like a horse with the bloat. The pure yearning brought tears to my eyes. I fought them back and went to feed the chickens.

⚬━━⚬

I'd been agitating for a trip into Denver City almost since I arrived. Limited to twenty-one pounds of baggage on the stage, I'd left behind most of my things, and some of them needed to be replaced. I needed to send Marthe a letter. I wanted to see a newspaper and read about how the war was going. And I wanted to hear what people were saying about the Jensens and ask Doyle if he'd learned anything more.

It was coffee that got me my wish. With two of us drinking it, we were running through Josiah's supply. One morning after breakfast, near the end of my fifth week at the farm, he looked at what remained in the cannister and sighed.

"We're going to have to go to town." His expression was glum.

"Is that so bad?" I asked. "I'd think some time away from the farm would be welcome now and again."

"I don't like the crowds," he said, scowling. "And it's better than a half day there in the wagon. Means staying overnight."

"Well," I said, "you don't absolutely need to go. I could do it."

Josiah snorted. "Send you by yourself? Are you cracked in the head, girl?"

I suppressed an urge to scowl. "I traveled all the way here from Boston on my own. I think I can manage a trip to town. I've lived in a big city my whole life. Besides, Peter or Paul could go with me."

"Boston ain't Denver City," he said. "All kinds of things out here you ain't used to. Look at what happened to that homesteader couple."

I might have been imagining the sidewise look he gave me as he said that. "We don't know what happened to the Jensens," I said carefully.

"No, we don't," he said. "And it don't matter. You ain't going by yourself." He sighed as if resigned. "We'll cut stick first thing tomorrow. If it has to be done, best to get it over with." He snatched his hat from the peg beside the door and left.

I was so thrilled I almost danced through the day's work. That night, I wrote my letter to Marthe by the light of the half-inch nub of candle Josiah had allocated to me. I debated whether to tell her about the Jensens and my suspicions about their deaths. But there was nothing she could do. Worrying her would be cruel. I barely resisted the urge to add a pointed line about hoping to see her soon. In the end, I said only that I'd arrived safely and that Josiah was treating me fairly.

The following morning, I was down the ladder, already dressed, a bare instant after Josiah's snores began to turn into the hacking coughs of waking. The sun wasn't up yet when we led the mules from the barn, and the yard was crisp with the first frost of the season. Josiah took Badger, who still snapped every time I came near. The old man let out a pained grunt as he lifted the heavy leather collar over the mule's neck, then stopped to massage his lower back before turning to help me attend to Fox.

"Do you want me to knock on the bunkhouse door and get Peter and Paul to help?" I asked, shivering despite my coat.

"Leave them be," he said without looking at me. "They'll be along directly."

Indeed, only a minute after the sun broke over the horizon, they emerged from the barn and silently took over the job of readying the wagon. Paul turned and trudged back into the barn when it was done, while I clambered into the bed of the wagon and tried to find a comfortable position. Josiah had brought along the buffalo robes, and I twitched one over my lap against the chill. Peter climbed into the wagon seat beside Josiah. The hired man took the reins and slapped them against the mules' hairy backs. With a lurch and a creak of the wheels, we set off.

Some three hours into the trip, the sun had burned off the frost, and I had cast aside the robe. Peter nudged Josiah and pointed south. It was the first time either of them had done more than shift their weight since we'd left the farm, and the movement attracted my attention. I turned to follow the gesture, shading my eyes against the midmorning glare. There was a dust cloud on the southern horizon, small but growing. A minute later, I could make out figures on horseback. A faint whoop reached my ears, and my insides went cold.

Indians.

"Josiah," I said, coming up onto my knees in the wagon bed. "They're coming this way."

"I see them." His tone was guarded.

The distant hoofbeats were barely audible over the pounding of my heart in my ears. I'd read newspaper accounts of what the Indians did to the settlers. Scalpings and other atrocities. Sometimes they kidnapped the women. Fear churned in my gut, and I wished desperately for my magic. There was no way we could outrun them with the wagon, no way to fight them off with nothing but Josiah's shotgun.

They got close enough for me to start picking out individual riders. I began counting, my mouth dry, getting to thirty before Josiah spoke.

"It's High Walking."

The tension had gone from his voice, and I took my eyes off the advancing group long enough to glance at him. He gestured to Peter, who hauled the mules to a stop and set the brake.

The Indians—all men—reined in a wagon's length from us, their small, sturdy-looking horses snorting and stamping. They wore layers of buckskins, heavily fringed and beaded, and their long black hair was tied back with thongs and decorated with feathers. The oldest wore an elaborate headdress of mottled owl feathers, and a heavy necklace of bone and metal covered much of his chest. His face was seamed with age, though he moved with the vigor of a much younger man as he nudged his horse to Josiah's side.

Another man moved alongside him. He was young, wearing a buckskin shirt marked with a distinctive pattern of red and blue beads down the sides. An aide, I supposed, from the careful way he shadowed the older man.

"Greetings, Netse Ôhtseve'hâtse," the elder said. He leaned from his horse, and he and Josiah grasped one another's wrists.

Josiah spoke a string of syllables in response, and I blinked, startled that he knew their language.

They conversed for a few moments before Josiah gestured to me. The Indian gave me an assessing look. His eyes met mine, and I sucked in a quick breath; power fairly radiated from him. He glanced at the bangle on my wrist and pursed his lips, then gave me a small nod before turning back to Josiah.

"It is good that you have taken an apprentice," he said in English. "We are old men now, and there must be someone ready to take our place when we fly to the camp of the dead." He glanced at Peter. "And I see He'heenohkeso still stays with you."

"He does," Josiah said. "And his brother."

High Walking said something to Peter, who chuffed under his breath in response. Apparently, I was the only one there who did not understand their language.

"I will not keep you from your journey," High Walking said. "Be well, Josiah." He called something to his men, and they wheeled away and were gone almost before I could let out a breath.

Peter released the brake and clucked to the mules.

"What was that he called you?" I asked as we began rolling forward once more.

"Netse Ôhtseve'hâtse," Josiah said, the words not coming off his tongue as smoothly as they had from High Walking's. "Means Eagle Flies About."

I let out a laugh. "And Peter?"

"Little Blackbird," he said shortly.

"Blackbird, I could see," I said. "But little doesn't exactly fit. You know them well, clearly. Well enough that they have a name for you."

"I've known High Walking for a long time," he said. "He's their medicine man. A shaman. Done some work together, time or two. His grandson—that young fella behind him—was Nahkôheso. Means Young Bear."

"Why aren't they in the South with the rest of their people? Didn't we give them lands there?"

Josiah gave me a sharp look. "Back in '51," he said, "there was a treaty that said they could have everything around here—it was theirs already, you understand, but the government promised they wouldn't take it away—as long as the tribes didn't bother the wagon trains passing through or burn the forts the army was building. They said there weren't going to be settlements." He made a derisive noise. "That lasted until about half a minute after they found the gold up to the Peak. Miners and settlers started rushing in. The government decided it would make a new treaty—such as it was. Didn't negotiate so much as call some of the chiefs together and tell them how it was going to be. Took most all the land we promised them in '51, gave 'em the smaller reservation down in the southern part of the territory."

"But they accepted the agreement," I said. "They signed the treaty."

"Not all of 'em," Josiah said. "Black Kettle—one of the chiefs—told the government he couldn't sign on behalf of all the bands, but the government didn't care. Most of the bands went, yes. The wagon trains had already been chasing off or killing most of the buffalo, and the gold rush pretty much did the rest. Not more than a few hundred left in the whole territory. But High Walking and his people didn't sign anything, didn't agree to anything. Far as they're concerned, this is still their land." Josiah sighed. "So far the government hasn't made much effort to make 'em go, but I don't know how much longer that will last. The war's taking up most of their energy. Once that's over with . . ." He looked somber.

"Will they fight?" I glanced at Peter, unable to ask the question as plainly as I wanted to in front of him. "With more than guns, I mean? I could tell High Walking is . . . strong."

"That he is," Josiah said. "I've seen him cut loose a time or two. The Cheyenne have rules about such things, same as we do. They mostly don't have to—their warriors are skilled enough they don't need it. But if it's a matter of saving his people? I don't know what he might be willing to do."

As we rode on, I wondered to myself if I already knew.

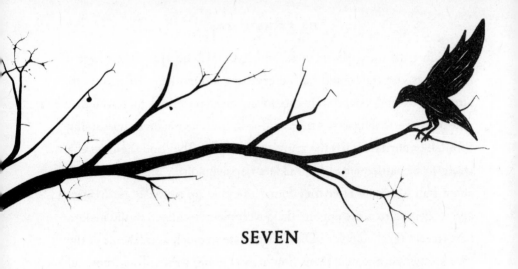

SEVEN

Denver City smelled of pinewood. It had a raw, unfinished look, with wide, rutted dirt streets laid out in a more or less orderly grid and dozens of wooden buildings in various stages of weathering. Wood-plank awnings shaded wood-plank sidewalks, though a few of the nicer-looking storefronts sported striped canvas instead.

Painted signs advertised livery stables, barbers, assayers, apothecaries, dry goods merchants, blacksmiths, and saloons. So many saloons. All appeared to be doing a brisk business, and not merely in liquor. From the upper windows of The Golden Rose, women wearing little more than smiles with their hair flowing free down their backs called out invitations to men on the street with a brazen lack of regard for who might be listening.

"Looking for company, gentlemen?" said a black-haired woman.

"I'll give you two bits for a throw!" a man called back. His companions laughed.

"No two-bit whores here," one of the women said back, lowering the top of her shift to flash a pink-tipped breast at them.

Shouts and whistles filled the air as our wagon lumbered past.

We passed the Broadwell House Hotel, a three-story structure on the corner of the next block. ICE CREAM SOLD HERE YEAR-ROUND, read a sign in the window. My eyebrows went up. For that to be possible, there must be an icehouse somewhere in town. Perhaps Denver City was more civilized than I'd realized. I leaned forward from the bed of the wagon.

"Where do we stay?" I asked. It was too much to hope for the Broadwell House itself, but maybe we'd be somewhere nearby.

In front of me on the wagon seat, Josiah stiffened, then turned, an unmistakable look of chagrin on his face. "There's a bunkhouse at the livery stable. I always stay there. But . . ."

"They don't have women's quarters," I guessed.

"No," he said. "But we'll find you somewhere to stay. Got to be some cheap places around," he added, and I sat back, hoping it would at least be clean.

A quarter of an hour later, Peter pulled the wagon to a stop. Josiah moved stiffly as he climbed down, putting a hand to his hip. I was hardly in better shape after hours in the wagon bed, buffalo robes or no.

A man came out and reached for Badger's bridle, then yanked his hand back as the mule went for his fingers.

"My hired man will tend that one. You can get th' other," Josiah said. His voice was clipped. "I'll need berths for the mules and wagon and a bed in the bunkhouse for the night."

"Not two beds in the bunkhouse?" I tilted my head at Peter.

"He doesn't like staying in town," Josiah said. "He'll camp on the outskirts."

I glanced first at the wagon bed, which held nothing but the robes and my own small bag, then at Peter, wondering how he felt about that arrangement. But, in truth, he looked uncomfortable, drawn in on himself and skittish in a way I'd never seen him. It must be difficult for him among strangers, unable to speak.

I turned back to Josiah, ready to ask where we went from here. But I noticed now that there was a pallor to his face and a sheen of sweat coating his brow despite the cool air. "Are you all right?"

"Old bones," he said, waving the question away like a bothersome fly. "They don't much care for that many hours on the wagon seat. I'll manage. We got work to do." He reached into his pocket for the list he'd made the previous night.

I put my hand out. "Give it to me. I'll take care of it while you go rest. I assume you have a store you prefer?"

Josiah nodded. "Tuttle and Veach, over on Blake Street. I have an account there." He eyed my outstretched hand doubtfully.

I sighed and waggled my fingers. "It's broad daylight. Peter can go with me. It will be fine."

He hesitated, then handed the sheet to me. "They ought to be able to tell you where to stay, too. Nothing too fancy, mind." He rummaged in his pocket and withdrew a small leather purse. He gave it to me, then stepped in close. For a shocked instant I thought he meant to embrace me. Instead, he dipped a hand back into his pocket and withdrew the little derringer I'd seen in his trunk. "You know how to use this?"

I stared at the gun for a moment before I found my voice. "Do you mean for me to buy the supplies or steal them?"

He ignored my joke. "This town ain't safe. Some of the saloons got dead men for breakfast every day—bodies in the street of a morning after fights at night," he explained when he saw the look on my face. He gestured to the gun. "Keep it on you. Don't take it out of your pocket unless you mean to use it. It's no good from more than about a foot away, so don't be waving it around as a threat. But if you plant it in a man's gut and pull the trigger, it will do the job well enough."

I took it, gingerly, and stowed it in the pocket of my dress. Guns had not been part of my education.

"It will be fine," I said again. "Go. Rest."

He didn't argue further, and I wasted no time in leaving, Peter trailing behind me with my bag.

Denver City was no Boston, but it was busy enough to be disorienting after the solitude of the farm. There were only a handful of women in the streets, and most of the men looked rough enough that I was thankful for Peter's silent presence at my back as I made my way to Blake Street and found the store Josiah had mentioned.

Tuttle and Veach was a log building with a two-story false front of milled planks. There was a large front window, its wooden shutters folded back to let in the light. Inside, it was jammed from floor to ceiling with every sort of merchandise. Bolts of cloth and baskets of sewing notions. Barrels of pickles and sweets. Seed packets and gardening tools. Lengths of stovepipe and sheets of tin.

A set of shiny copper cookware hanging from one wall caught Peter's attention, and I left him to admire it as I made my way to the back of the store, where an enormous man stood behind a counter. His face, pink and shining above a striped shirt that resembled nothing so much as a circus tent, lit up when he saw me. "Welcome, miss!" he sang out. "How may I assist you this fine day?"

It was impossible not to smile back at him. "Are you Mr. Tuttle or Mr. Veach?"

He snapped his heels together—or as close to together as he could get them with legs like tree trunks. "A.X. Veach, at your service! And whom do I have the pleasure of addressing?"

"I am Miss Shaw," I said. "My great-uncle, Josiah Merritt, sent me with a list of supplies." I held it up. "He said he has an account with you."

"Indeed, he does!" He put out his hand for the list. His eyes scanned it, then came back up to meet mine. "All the usual. We'll have it all ready to load for him in the morning. So lovely to meet a relation of his. Now, there is nothing on this list a young lady might find interesting. What can I show you while you're here? I have some exquisite lace collars that have just come in from Chicago—machine made, finer than anything you've ever seen."

"I don't have any use for a lace collar right now," I said. "But I'm afraid the boots I brought with me aren't heavy enough for farm work. They're going to be ruined if I keep on the way I have been. I could use a new pair, if you have them."

"Of course I have them," he said, drawing up in near offense. "You'll find no better selection in the whole of the Colorado Territory. Come right this way."

I let him fuss over me and show me his wares, then chose a perfectly adequate pair of boots that cost at least three times what they would have in Boston. The money in the purse Josiah had given me wasn't enough to pay for them, so I asked Mr. Veach to add them to his account.

I spent a long moment looking at the selection of books he had on one of the shelves, going so far as to reach for a new Mary Elizabeth Braddon novel I hadn't read. It would be nice to have something to read in the loft at night. But in the end, I pulled my hand back with a sigh. Boots, I could justify spending Josiah's money on; novels, less so.

I turned back to Mr. Veach. "I wonder if you might be able to direct me to a good boarding house for the night? Someplace clean and safe for a single woman, but not too expensive?"

"You want to go to Bonnie Stover's," he said at once. "Just one block over on Wazee Street. It's a restaurant, not a boarding house, but if you tell her I sent you, she'll rent you a room for the night. Best food in Denver City. I take my dinner there several times a week."

I was sick to death of beans and salt pork and corn mush, so such an endorsement from a man who clearly appreciated his food was good enough for me. I thanked him for the recommendation and turned to leave.

At the front of the store, Peter was still standing before the pots and pans, leaning forward and back again, baring his teeth and waggling his eyebrows, apparently fascinated by his reflection in the polished surfaces. I watched him for a moment, unable to suppress a grin, then got his attention and pointed out at the street. He straightened and followed me.

There was an apothecary shop farther down the block, and I spent more of Josiah's money there. I needed ingredients for more burn salve, and there were several other things he ought to have on hand, even if neither of us ever meant to make a potion. As the proprietor gathered my order, I scanned the labels on the jars behind the counter, impressed with how well-stocked the place was. There were half a dozen vials and several paper packets in my bag by the time we left.

Bonnie Stover's house was a two-story frame building, identical to at least a dozen others we'd passed. But this one had crisp gingham curtains hanging in the windows, and the aroma filling the air outside made my mouth water.

A young girl stood on the sidewalk, making desultory sweeping motions with the broom she held in one hand. The rest of her attention was focused on the book she held in the other. I leaned closer. *The Woman in White.*

"That's a good one," I said.

She started and turned. Her eyes hopped from me to Peter and back again. She couldn't have been more than eleven, with a pointed chin and clear gray eyes. A spray of freckles dotted her nose. Her dark blond hair was plaited, and her bonnet hung down her back, its strings tied at her neck.

"You've read it?"

"Yes," I said. "Last year. I enjoyed it very much."

"I like it, too. I think the—"

"Samantha?" The woman's voice came from above us and inside the house.

Irritation rippled across the girl's face, and she angled her reply toward one of the upper windows. "Down here."

A woman appeared in the window, the slight frown on her face replaced with a look of mild surprise when she saw there were three of us.

"Hello," I called up, shading my eyes from the sun. "Are you Bonnie Stover?"

"I am."

"Mr. Veach at the general store sent me to you. He suggested you might have a room for the night."

"Happy to help," she said. "I'll be right down." She turned her attention back to the girl. "Put down the book and finish sweeping, please. You have other chores to get to. And what have I told you about keeping your bonnet on in the sun?"

She disappeared from the window, and I looked back at Samantha, who scowled as she dragged her bonnet up to shade her face.

"Your mother is right about that, you know," I said. "With skin like yours—"

"She's not my mother," the girl said.

"Oh. Still, she's only—"

Samantha's gaze drifted down the sidewalk behind me, then sharpened. Her face lit up. "Pa! You're back!" She dropped both broom and book and darted past me.

I turned.

The girl had thrown herself into the arms of a man I hadn't heard approaching. He'd bent to hug her, leaving only the crown of his hat visible until he straightened and our eyes met.

It was Doyle.

EIGHT

He looked as surprised to see me as I was to see him.
"Joya? What are you doing here?" He still had one arm around
Samantha. He looked drawn and tired, but he was far cleaner than the
last time I'd seen him, and I was surprised to discover that underneath
the trail grime there had been an attractive man.

Very attractive. He was freshly shaved, revealing a full lower lip and
a jawline so sharp it could split firewood. His dark hair was damp. He
wore the same leather coat as before and carried a pair of worn saddlebags
slung over his shoulder.

"Josiah and I came into town. With Peter," I said, gesturing to the
hired man, who had withdrawn beneath the awning of a neighboring
building. "Supplies." Mostly for a reason to look away from him, I bent
and retrieved the book.

I'd just straightened when the door opened and Bonnie stepped
out. "Miss, if you'd like—" She broke off when she saw Doyle. "Lang,"
she said, pleasure coloring her voice. "I didn't expect you home until
tomorrow."

Give my best to Bonnie and Sam. That was what the stagecoach driver had said to Doyle as we left Eagle's Nest Station that first day. I remembered wondering if they were his wife and son. Now I knew Sam was Samantha, his daughter. And Bonnie was . . . what, exactly? Not Samantha's mother. I glanced at her hand. No ring. And her surname was Stover rather than Doyle. But there was unmistakable familiarity in the way she spoke to both father and child. Perhaps theirs was an informal arrangement. I eyed her. She was slender as a reed and pretty, with enormous hazel eyes and roses in her cheeks. Beside her I felt suddenly round and sallow.

"Just got in," Doyle said. "Stopped at the bathhouse to clean up. Thought that would be easier."

"Are you hungry? Come on in. All of you," she added, widening her glance to include Peter and me. "We'll get you settled."

Doyle looked at me. "You're staying here? Both of you?" He glanced at Peter.

"Just me," I said with a forced smile. "It came highly recommended. I'll send Peter back with a note to let Uncle Josiah know where I am."

Bonnie looked between us. "You already know each other?"

"Joya—Miss Shaw—is the young woman I told you about," Doyle said. "The one I took out to Josiah Merritt's place."

"The one who was with you when you found the—" Bonnie cut herself off with a swift glance at Samantha, who was watching us with a narrowed gaze that seemed too old for her young face.

"Well," Bonnie went on after a moment. "Welcome." She stepped back and ushered us all inside. Doyle didn't lean down to kiss her as he entered, but she did put a familiar hand on his arm as he passed.

Samantha was still clinging to his other side. "Can you stay for a while this time, Pa, or are you leaving again?"

"I'll be here a few days, at least," he said, looking down at her. "I need to go stow these." He twitched the shoulder holding the saddlebags. "And I think you have chores to finish?" He nodded to me, then wove his way through the quartet of long dining tables that took up most of the main room before he disappeared through a door I assumed led to the kitchen.

Samantha sighed and stepped back, turning toward the front door. I handed her the book as she passed me. Her fingers brushed mine, and I experienced my second shock in as many minutes.

Doyle's daughter had the potential for magic within her.

Samantha was too young for it to be more than a seed, coiled and waiting to sprout. But if I could feel it in her with nothing more than that fleeting touch, even through the binding, it meant her potential power was a formidable one.

It was a problem.

Power like that, when it does come, rarely announces itself quietly. More young witches than anyone liked to think about died because they came into their power without warning or anyone to help them. Samantha would need guidance. Someone to tell her what she was experiencing, to teach her how to use it. Back east, there was the Magisterium school. Out here, there was only a crotchety old man who lived half a day's ride away. A crotchety old man . . . and me.

"Miss Shaw?" Bonnie said my name, and the concern in her voice said it wasn't the first time she'd tried to get my attention.

I tore my eyes away from the door and tried to smile. "I'm sorry. I'm afraid I went woolgathering for a moment."

She smiled back. "It's all right. I was saying that I have an extra room upstairs. Lodging is a dollar a night, in advance, and it includes both supper and breakfast."

I found the purse and handed over a dollar coin.

"You don't want to see the room first?"

I shook my head. "I'm sure it's fine. If you have a pencil and some paper, I'll write my uncle a note to let him know where I am."

Peter, still standing by the front door holding my bag, looked hunched and uncomfortable in the unfamiliar space. I wrote a note, hesitating for a moment over whether to include what I'd discovered about Samantha, then decided I could tell Josiah about it the next day. I folded the paper and handed it to Peter. "Take this back to him, please. There's no need for you to stay."

He cocked his head at me as if asking if I were sure.

"I'll be fine," I said. "I know you don't like being in town."

Once he left, Bonnie showed me to my room. Her breathing grew labored as we mounted the stairs, and she stopped halfway up, doubled over by a coughing fit. "Apologies," she said when she'd recovered.

"Not at all," I said, reconsidering the brightness of her eyes and the flush in her face. She had consumption. I wondered how long she'd been sick and how bad it was. Supposedly the drier air in the west was good for consumptives. Maybe that was why she was out here.

I followed her down a hallway until she opened the door to a bright, airy room with a curtained window. A wide bed took up most of the space, with the rest given over to a washstand and basin and a single ladderback chair. A rag rug covered the board floor. It was clean and cheerful, and I was thrilled to think of sleeping there. It made a welcome change from my cramped little loft.

"Oh! Oh my. It's lovely," I said, meaning it.

"I'm glad you like it," she said, with obvious pride. "It's not as fancy as the Broadwell House, maybe, but I like to think it's homier. And the food is better, if I do say so myself. I'll bring you up some water if you'd like to wash."

"I have another errand I need to run first. What time is dinner? I'll be sure to be back in time to wash up."

"Supper service starts at six," she said. "But I'd suggest being back here before then. It'll be getting dark, and the streets aren't safe for a lady after that."

"I'll be back," I said. "Where should I go to post a letter?"

"I'll show you," Doyle's voice came from the hallway.

We both turned.

"I'm headed that way," he said, looking between us. He held a sheaf of papers under one arm.

I glanced at Bonnie, wondering how she felt about him leaving again as soon as he'd arrived. Leaving with me, specifically. But she only smiled.

"How has it been, being out at Josiah's?" Doyle asked as we left the house.

I shrugged. "Fine, more or less. A lot of work. Mostly very dull. And dirtier than I'd anticipated."

"That's farm life, all right." His tone was wry.

I glanced up at him. "The voice of experience?"

"Grew up in a farming family in Iowa."

"How did you wind up as a Ranger in the Colorado Territory?"

"Long story," he said, in a tone that said he wasn't interested in telling it. "Listen, there's something you should know, and with you being out at the farm, I don't suppose you've heard."

"Heard what?"

Doyle stopped on the sidewalk and looked around us. There was no one near. Still, he lowered his voice and stepped so close to me I could feel the warmth of his skin. He smelled like shaving soap and woodsmoke. Something tightened low in my belly.

As soon as he spoke, however, every other consideration fled my mind.

"There was another attack."

I went cold. "What happened?"

"Someone ambushed a Union patrol out of Fort Halleck. Six men. All torn to pieces."

I swallowed hard against the image of six men's bodies strewn over the prairie grass. "When? And where?" My voice was thready, and Doyle gave me a sharp look, as if he feared I would faint. I straightened and met his eyes, trying to tell him I would do no such thing, and he gave me a little nod of acknowledgment.

"Ten days after we were at the Jensens'. About eight miles south of the farm. A Ranger patrol found them."

A pair of men approached, apparently absorbed in their own conversation, but I waited until they had passed to ask my next question. "How do you know exactly which night it happened?"

"The commander's logbook," he said. "He'd written in it that night after they made camp. He recorded where they were."

"Were there any differences?"

Doyle's jaw hardened. "The Jensens never had a chance to fight. The patrol tried. Fired their weapons. Some evidence that the men tried to form up against . . . whatever it was."

"*Whatever* it was?"

He squinted and looked down the street. "Rebels or Indians would have used guns. But there were no bullet wounds in the bodies. The Rangers who found them said it looked more like wild animals had done it."

I began walking again while I tried to think how to respond. "Wild animals didn't kill the Jensens."

"No."

"What are people saying now that there have been two attacks?" I spoke without much consideration, my mind busy with things I couldn't say aloud. I'd been at Josiah's the night of the second attack. Given how hard I'd been working, I'd been sleeping deeply, but I found it implausible in the extreme that he could have summoned a demon without my having any idea of it.

But if he hadn't done it, who had? I was so preoccupied by my own thoughts that it took me a moment to realize Doyle hadn't answered my question. I glanced at him.

The expression on his face was terrible.

"What's wrong?"

"They don't know." The words were almost too quiet to hear.

"What?"

"People don't know the attacks were the same. I only told a few people about the Jensens. Garvey and a couple of others I trust," he said. The words began to pour out of him, as if he'd been holding them back and now the dam had burst. "I didn't want to start a panic. I knew people would blame the Indians, and I didn't want to risk it. Things have been peaceful the last few months. I thought the fewer people who knew, the better. I thought I could find whoever did it and arrest them without getting everyone worked up."

"That was a reasonable choice to make under the circumstances," I began, but he was in no mood to hear it.

"It was the wrong choice," he said, his voice harsh with his effort to stop it breaking. "Maybe if I'd told everyone what happened at the farm, the patrol would have been on their guard. It might have saved them."

"It wouldn't have," I said at once.

"You can't know that," he said. He swallowed hard, and his voice was tight with suppressed emotion when he went on. "I knew some of those men. I should have warned them. It's my fault they're dead."

"It's not," I said.

Doyle didn't reply, but his jaw worked as he stared down the street at nothing in particular. He visibly gathered himself, then blew out a rueful breath.

"I shouldn't be burdening you with this," he said.

"It's all right." I wanted to put a hand on his arm, to offer some comfort, but I held back. He wouldn't welcome it.

He glanced at me. "It's not, but thank you for saying so. I suppose I don't have to tell you—"

"Not to tell anyone? No, you don't."

"Thank you." He paused. "The stage office is there," he said, pointing at a building down the block. Doyle was still carrying the papers, and he peeled one of them off the stack and handed it to me. "There's a notice board inside. Would you mind posting this for me? I need to get the rest handed out to the saloons and shops."

I glanced down at the paper. WANTED, read the heavy black print at the top. $200 REWARD.

Beneath the letters, a vaguely familiar face stared up at me. I frowned, trying to place it. "Isn't this the man from the stage? The one Garvey was taking to Fort Halleck?"

Doyle nodded. "Marcus Broaderick. Garvey got him there and turned him over. He escaped a few days later."

"How?"

"The army didn't say," he replied. "Just sent word down that he was loose again."

"Quite the reward they're offering."

"I'm hoping it will be enough to tempt someone into telling us where he's hiding."

"I'll post it," I said, then hesitated. "About the patrol. It wasn't your fault. You couldn't have—"

"Do you want me to come back for you, or can you find your way to the house without me?" His voice was level, but there was something in his face that warned me against pushing him further. He didn't want to talk about it.

I capitulated. "I'll be fine. I'll see you back there later."

He nodded, then turned and strode away. I watched him go, wishing there was something I could do to relieve the guilt that was obviously gnawing at him. But even if I could tell him the truth, he wouldn't believe it. Would probably be angry with me for making up such a mad story. I grimaced, hoping he would be able to let it go, worried that he wouldn't.

Inside the stage office, there was a line of people waiting.

"I want to send a telegram," said a loud-voiced man at the counter.

"Write it out on this," said the clerk, pushing a slip of paper toward him. "It will go up to Julesburg on the stage and get sent out from there. Reply will take about a week. Next!" he called out.

The notice board was along the back wall, above a table where several people stood, finishing their letters or adding addresses. I found an open space beside a young woman around my own age wearing a dress of blue silk and a stylish hat over a mass of white-blond curls. Her shoulders were tight and hunched as she labored over a sheet of paper. Beside her on the table was a scrap of newsprint.

Dr. R.E. Strycker's Female Renovating Pills.

Removes blockages, stoppages, and suppressions of the natural cycles of females, by whatever cause they be produced. Comprised of simple vegetable extracts and containing nothing harmful or deleterious to even the most delicate constitutions. Warranted to have the desired effect in all cases. Easy to use, with full instructions in every box.

The only necessary precaution is that married ladies who suspect themselves to be in the family way should not take them, as they will surely cause a miscarriage, almost without the knowledge of the patient, so gentle yet active are they.

Do not be fooled by counterfeit formulations. Dr. Strycker's Female Renovating Pills may only be obtained by sending $1 to his office in St. Louis, Missouri. Upon receipt of same, 1 box will be sent discreetly packaged and free of postage.

I stiffened.

Unable to help myself, I looked at the letter she was writing.

Deer Dr Strycker—
Plees send the pills to me at Mrs Roses house in Denver City
I have enclosd 1 doler

I pressed my lips together. There were advertisements for such pills in every paper in the country. Anyone could place one, and desperate women would send money. This poor girl might get a box of pills for her trouble. Maybe they would be harmless—molasses and beeswax, if she was lucky. Maybe they would be full of calomel and make her violently ill without doing a thing for her actual problem. There was about one chance in a thousand they would do what they advertised.

I pinned the poster to the notice board, then took my place in line.

Mrs Roses house. A brothel, obviously. Maybe even the one we'd passed on the way into town. Surprising that they didn't have someone there who could advise her not to waste her money. I was painfully aware of it when she got in line behind me, and I suppressed the urge to turn around and tell her myself. It was none of my business.

It was my turn at the counter.

If she was pregnant, time mattered. It would take at least a week for her letter to reach St. Louis and another week for the pills to arrive. That was assuming they came at all and weren't useless to begin with. Giraud had a recipe for a tea that gave good results, as long as it was taken soon enough. There wasn't even any magic involved. I thought of the rows of jars in the apothecary's shop.

I handed over my letter and paid the postage.

The girl's skirts rustled behind me as she anticipated my stepping away, making room for her at the counter.

Instead, I spun to face her. She blinked at me, startled. Her eyes were as blue as the ocean off the cape, but the rims were pink and puffy. She'd been crying. That decided me.

I stepped closer to her and lowered my voice. "You don't need the pills. There are better ways."

She blushed to the roots of her hair. Her skin was so pale the veins showed blue at her jawline. She must essentially never venture out in the daylight, to have skin like that in this climate. I'd been careful, and still my hands and face were darker than when I'd arrived, and that was with November sun. I didn't like to think what it would be like in the summer.

"The apothecary on Blake Street," I said. "He has everything you need. I can give you a list of what to ask for."

Behind me, the clerk cleared his throat. "Pardon me, but you're holding up the line."

I scowled at him over my shoulder, then turned back to the girl. "Look, let's step outside and talk. If you still want to send your letter after that, I promise I'll leave you be."

She chewed at the inside of her cheek, then nodded. "All right." Her accent was foreign. She turned to leave, and I followed.

Outside, we stood in awkward silence for a moment, each of us waiting for the other to speak.

"I'm Joya," I said finally.

"I am Inge," she said. "You can help me?"

"Maybe. How long has it been since you bled?" I asked bluntly.

She glanced to one side. "I've missed two monthlies."

"Any other symptoms?"

"Yes," she said, her voice clipped. "I am certain."

"All right, then." I reached for the letter and pencil stub still in her hand. I tore the blank bottom half from the paper and wrote the list of ingredients at the top and the recipe on the bottom. I showed it to her. "You can read this?"

Inge scanned the paper and nodded. "It works? You have used it?"

I almost lied, wanting to reassure her. "No," I said after a pause. "I've never needed it." It was true. I'd never been with a Mundane man, and witches weren't fertile together. Giraud's theory was that it was a natural check on our numbers. We had too many other advantages over the Mundanes. Only our relative rarity kept the populations in balance. "But I know lots of women who have," I went on. "It will work. Drink a big cup four times a day until you start bleeding. Then one in the morning and one at night for three more days." I hesitated over the next part, but she was a prostitute. She was unlikely to be offended. "And you shouldn't go with any men until the bleeding has been over for at least a week."

"I understand." She glanced at me. "I have never seen you before. You are new in town?"

"Yes."

"Where do you work? Which house?"

"Oh, no, I'm not—" I cut myself off, not wanting her to think I was offended by the assumption. "I live with my uncle out on his farm," I said instead. "I've worked as a nurse."

"Then you aren't . . ." She trailed off, obviously embarrassed. "You shouldn't let people see you talking to me. They will think we are the same."

"It's all right," I said. "I'm not worried about what anyone thinks." Even as I said it, I was aware that it wasn't entirely true. It must have shown on my face, because Inge put a gentle hand on my arm.

"I thank you for this," she said, holding up the recipe. "Now best for me to go."

I watched until she turned a corner, then began walking back to Bonnie's.

I was perhaps thirty yards from her door when the sound of distant chanting came to me, and I froze on the sidewalk, my mouth going dry, certain for a brief, wild moment that someone was summoning a demon there and then. My head swiveled in every direction as I searched for the source.

A moment later, I found it as a dapperly dressed man turned the corner on the other side of the street, followed by perhaps a dozen boys. They ranged in age from no more than six to at least fourteen, and they were reciting something in a foreign language—Latin, I thought, now that the words weren't as muffled. The man glided along at the head of the pack, carrying, of all things, a buggy whip. He swung the implement as if it were a baton, with such wild abandon that the two foremost boys were forced to duck out of its way with each backswing. They didn't seem to mind, exchanging grins each time the leather whooshed over their heads and never missing a syllable of their recitation.

Ahead of me on the sidewalk, Samantha emerged from the house. She waited for a pause in the chanting, then cupped her hands around her mouth. "Mr. Northcutt! Thank you for the book!"

The man with the whip grinned across the street at her. "You're very welcome," he shouted back, saluting her with the implement. "The *Aeneid*, from line one, in the Latin," he bellowed to the boys, and they began a new chant.

Samantha watched as they made their way down the block, then caught sight of me as I approached. She smiled and held the door open for me, then followed me back inside.

"Aunt Bonnie, Joya is back," Samantha announced.

I straightened a little at that, wondering if there really was a family relationship. It could be merely a courtesy title, used to give Samantha a respectful way to address an elder. I glanced at Bonnie, who looked up from the table she was wiping.

"Miss Shaw, Samantha," she said in a chiding tone. "You know better than that."

Samantha pulled a face, but Bonnie ignored it.

"There are some potatoes in the kitchen that need to be peeled and chopped for supper. Go and get to work on those, please."

Samantha heaved a sigh, then straightened her back and trudged into the kitchen with the dignity of a saint going to martyrdom.

I didn't want to hurt her feelings, so I suppressed the laugh that tried to escape.

"That child," Bonnie said ruefully. "I apologize. I thought I'd have a few more years before the moods and back talk started, but these last few months she's been . . . difficult."

"It's a challenging age, or so I'm told," I said, reassessing my guess about how much time there might be before Samantha's powers began to manifest. I wanted to ask how she and Samantha were related, but if they weren't, it might be awkward, so I kept the question to myself.

"I usually don't lean on her so much," Bonnie went on. "But the girl I had helping me quit to go get married. It's hard to keep help out here—too many single men. I just hope it won't take too long to find someone else." She let out her own sigh, and the weariness in it was evident.

"Could I help?" The words were out before I thought about them.

"Oh, I couldn't ask you to do that—you're a paying guest."

"I don't mind," I said, half surprised to find I meant it. "I have to warn you, I'm entirely useless as a cook, but I can peel and chop."

Bonnie hesitated. "If you're sure, then yes, I'd be glad to have another pair of hands. I'll refund part of your money for the night in exchange."

I followed her into the kitchen and began helping Samantha with the potatoes while Bonnie worked over the stove.

"So," I said to the girl, "you got *The Woman in White* from the man with the buggy whip?"

She nodded. "Mr. Northcutt. He runs the boys' school over on Laramie Street. I like him. He comes here for breakfast most mornings, and he usually brings a book with him. I asked him if he got it from the lending library—I wanted to join, but it costs twenty-five cents a week, so Pa says we can't afford it. He said he had his own collection and said I could borrow whatever I wanted. He said he 'loves to see a young person improving their mind through the written word.'" Her tone was half mimicry, half gentle mockery. She had a good ear—she'd captured the tone and cadence I'd heard on the street.

"What else have you read?"

Samantha and I chattered about books for the next quarter hour. We'd read several of the same ones and agreed about most of them. I was almost disappointed when the pile of potatoes was gone. Bonnie sent Samantha to fetch a canister of flour.

"You're good with her," she said as I joined her beside the stove. "That's the pleasantest she's been in I don't know how long."

"I'm a novelty to her," I said with a shrug. "What's for dinner?"

"Stewed venison with fried potatoes," Bonnie said. "And fresh biscuits with homemade chokecherry syrup. Speaking of which, could you pass me that jar?" She pointed to a jar of dark red liquid on a shelf to my right.

I half lifted it from the shelf, but my grip slipped. The jar fell sideways, and the lid popped off. Sticky red juice splashed everywhere. Some landed on the surface of the stove, where it hissed and began to burn at once, sending sweet-acrid smoke into the air. Some wound up on the floor. Far too much of it landed on me—my sleeve was covered, my bodice spattered.

Bonnie and I regarded the mess in mutual dismay.

"I'm so sorry," I said, mortified.

"Not your fault," she said with a shrug. "Could have just as easily happened to me. We need to put your dress in to soak now, though, or there's no way that stain will come out."

I looked down at myself. I looked like I'd worn the dress to butcher a hog. "I have a clean shift upstairs, but I didn't bring another dress."

"Maybe I have something you can—" She broke off and looked down at her own slight form. There was no way anything of hers would fit my taller, fuller figure. "No, that won't work, clearly. But you're about the same size as my girl who quit. Her baggage is in the storeroom." She pointed to a door on the other side of the kitchen. "She's supposed to send for it but hasn't yet. She probably has something that would work. Why don't you go and look? I'll get started cleaning this up."

I wiped my sticky hands on a rag and did as she said.

The storeroom was full, but in the back corner I found a trunk and carpetbag. I knelt beside the trunk, assuming that was where the dresses would be. There was a keyhole lock on it, but when I tried the latch, it opened easily. Inside, atop a wadded bundle of clothing, there was a messy jumble of papers, a pair of books, and, curiously, a shallow bowl of milky stone.

I frowned, bending closer to look at it. A deep crack ran across the inner surface, ending in a ragged gouge near the bottom where a hunk of the stone had broken free. An inscription spiraled from the outer edge of the bowl toward its center, the final words lost with the missing piece. I could tell it was Latin, but I didn't know the language well enough to translate it. There was an unfamiliar sigil, an interlocking series of circles and triangles, scratched into the bottom. The markings were only visible against the light background thanks to a dark, ink-like substance limning the edges of the scratches.

I picked up one of the papers.

It was a crudely printed broadsheet, folded in half.

FREEMEN! OF TENNESSEE!

THE YANKEE WAR IS NOW BEING WAGED FOR "BEAUTY AND BOOTY." THEY HAVE DRIVEN US FROM THEM, AND NOW THEY SAY OUR TRADE THEY MUST AND WILL HAVE. TO EXCITE THEIR HIRED AND RUFFIAN SOLDIERS, THEY

PROMISE THEM OUR LANDS AND TELL THEM OUR WOMEN ARE
BEAUTIFUL—THAT BEAUTY IS THE REWARD OF THE BRAVE.

TENNESSEANS! YOUR COUNTRY CALLS! SHALL WE WAIT
UNTIL OUR HOMES ARE LAID DESOLATE, UNTIL SWORD AND
RAPE SHALL HAVE VISITED THEM? NEVER! THEN TO
ARMS AND LET US MEET THE ENEMY ON THE BORDERS.
WHO SO VILE, SO CRAVEN, AS NOT TO STRIKE FOR HIS NATIVE
LAND?

I made a face and tossed it aside, then reached for one of the books. It was clearly old, with a cover of worn, dark leather, creased and crumbling around the edges. There were traces of gilt on the raised bits. I turned it over to read the title. *DE VOCATIONE*. Latin again. I opened it. One word leapt out at me, and I didn't have to be fluent to recognize it: *DAEMONIUM*.

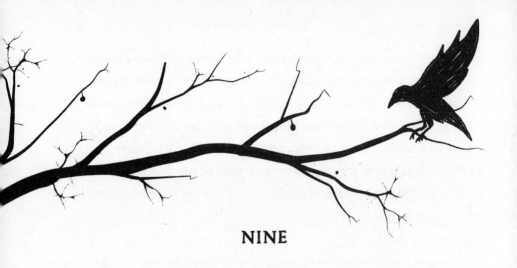

NINE

My breath hissed out, loud in the silent storeroom.

I was still staring at the word when the storeroom door began to swing open behind me. Instinctively, I flipped a fold of cloth over the books and bowl as I turned.

It was Bonnie.

My heart tried to climb up my throat. Did she know what the trunk held? Did she realize I'd seen it?

Her expression told me nothing. "That's Patsy's." She pointed to the carpetbag.

"Oh," I said, trying to keep my voice steady. "I'm sorry. Is the trunk yours? I didn't mean to pry."

She shook her head. "Not mine. It belonged to a man Lang and Garvey arrested."

My heartbeat, already elevated, became a staccato flutter in my chest as pieces began to fall into place. "Marcus Broaderick?" I guessed.

"Yes," Bonnie said, sounding surprised. "How did you—Oh, you were there when they brought him to the stage, weren't you?"

"I was," I said. I closed the trunk and reached for the carpetbag as my mind whirled. The way he'd looked at me. It hadn't been because I was a woman. It was because he'd known what I was. I hadn't felt any magic from him, but that didn't mean much. I'd been far enough away from him that I might well have missed it, bound as I was.

I opened Patsy's carpetbag and pretended to study the contents, but my thoughts were busy elsewhere. Marcus Broaderick was a practitioner. He was the one summoning the demons. He must be.

"Do you see anything that will work?" Bonnie asked.

I grabbed a shirtwaist and skirt without looking at them and held them up to her. "These will be fine."

"Good," she said. "I'll have a bucket ready to soak your things when you come back down." She stepped aside to let me pass, and I was forced to leave the trunk and its contents behind.

Up in my room, I pondered the implications of what I'd seen as I stripped off my soiled clothes.

Marcus Broaderick was summoning demons. He had rebel propaganda in his trunk. The Jensens had been Unionists. A Union patrol had been killed. I already knew from events back east that there were witches helping the rebels. Was Broaderick one of them? Was he part of the same group, or was he acting alone? But he couldn't be completely on his own—he'd been in Doyle and Garvey's custody the night the Jensens had been killed, hadn't he? So there must be others. I'd have to find a way to get a better look at the books in his trunk. And the bowl. I didn't know what it had to do with anything, but if Broaderick was carrying it around with him, it was probably important.

I'd been too distracted to pay attention to the clothes I'd grabbed, but as I finished dressing, I realized I should have considered my choices more carefully. The skirt fit me well enough, but the fabric of the shirtwaist was tissue-thin from washing and tight enough across my bosom that the buttons gaped each time I breathed. I grimaced. It would have to do.

The derringer didn't fit in Patsy's pocket, so I left it in the dresser drawer and hurried back downstairs to give my syrup-stained dress to Bonnie, who took one look at the shirtwaist and handed me one of her bibbed kitchen aprons. I tied it on gratefully and began dishing up food. The meat fell apart at the touch of the serving fork, and the biscuits smelled heavenly. My mouth watered as I carried plates out to the dining area, which was already filling up with men.

The next two hours were a blur. I served plates, poured drinks, and collected coins. I also dodged more than a few wandering hands, pretended to laugh at unfunny—but invariably ribald—jokes, and gracefully declined half a dozen marriage proposals, at least two of which were sincere, though I wondered at Patsy's standards. Doyle came in at some point and raised a questioning brow when he caught my eye. I shrugged and smiled and turned away as a customer called for more biscuits. He was gone when I turned back.

I tried to listen to the conversations happening around me, hoping to hear someone say something useful. Half of the men were miners, so they talked of sluices and claims and other bits of mining lore. The other half mostly talked about the miners, the war, and the chances of getting statehood for the territory. One group of well-heeled men was talking about how to get the planned California railroad to run through Denver City instead of Cheyenne.

It was near the end of the night when I finally heard something interesting. The crowds had thinned out, and there weren't more than a few tables left. Bonnie brought me a plate, and I sat gratefully to eat it. My eyes were closed in pleasure—she was every bit as good a cook as advertised—when a snatch of conversation floated toward me.

"—killed them soldiers like flies—"

My eyes flew open. I didn't catch the next words, and I tried not to be obvious as I scanned the room, trying to figure out who had spoken. It had to have been the pair of men nearest the door to the kitchen. They leaned toward one another over their empty plates, their faces serious. They had the look of miners about them—rangy and worn, with unkempt beards and deeply tanned skin. They were too far away and the room still too noisy for me to hear any more of their conversation. I shoveled the rest of my food into my mouth, then stood with my plate and headed in their direction.

"I'm supposed to bring him another piece of quartz," one was saying as I neared. He broke off as I stopped beside the table.

Quartz. The bowl could be made of quartz.

"Could I take those dishes for you gentlemen?"

They looked down at their plates as if surprised to find them empty, then pushed them toward me without speaking.

"Could I bring you some dessert? Coffee?"

"Nothing," one of them said. Neither spoke, and I stacked their plates atop my own and took them into the kitchen.

Bonnie and Samantha were both there. "Finished already?" Bonnie asked. "Did you get enough?"

"I did, thank you. It was delicious. Do you know the men at the table beside the kitchen door?"

"Why? Did one of them do something?" Bonnie glanced at Samantha.

"No," I said. "I was just wondering who they were."

Bonnie frowned as if trying to recall. "I'm afraid I wasn't paying attention." She picked up a pair of plates. "Let me take these out, and I'll get a look on the way back and tell you."

She bustled out with the plates, and I turned to Samantha, who was scrubbing dishes. "Have you eaten?"

"Earlier," she said. "Venison is my favorite. And I—"

She stopped as Bonnie came back in. "They've gone," Bonnie said.

"Gone?"

"Left the money on the table. What did they look like?"

"They were . . ." I said, then trailed off as I tried to call the men's faces to mind and found I couldn't. I frowned. "They were dressed like miners." I remembered that much. They'd had beards, hadn't they? Or was one of them clean-shaven? I'd just seen them. Why couldn't I picture their faces? Every time I tried, it was like looking at a reflection in a pond once a pebble has been thrown in, all ripples and wobbly outlines.

I'd looked right at them, not more than a minute ago. It must be magic stopping me from recalling them. Some kind of spell or charm.

"Well, there are hundreds of miners. I'm afraid I don't know many of them by sight anyway," Bonnie said. "They come and go so often." She set down the dishes and put a hand on my arm. "I can't tell you how much I appreciate your help tonight."

"It was no trouble. Truly," I said.

"I know you've had a terribly long day, so feel free to go ahead upstairs if you like. We'll finish up down here."

"Thank you," I said, and she smiled at me as she went back to the dining room.

As the door closed behind her, I yanked at the strings on my apron. "Samantha, I've got to go out for a few minutes. I won't be long."

She looked worried. "Pa says it's not safe to be out this late."

"I'll be fine," I said, and was out the back door before she had time to respond.

The backyard was unfenced and backed up to the yard of the building on the next street over, with a privy in between. The alley between the buildings was narrow and dark, and I kept one hand on the splintery wood of the house as I hurried toward the sidewalk, half stumbling on the uneven ground.

They couldn't have gotten far. Surely if I saw them again I'd be able to recognize them. I could find out where they were staying. See how many of them there were. Something.

The wind hit me as soon as I stepped out of the alley, cutting through the thin cotton of the shirtwaist, and goose pimples stubbled my skin. I spared a moment's thought to going back for my coat—the derringer, too, tucked in the drawer where it would do me no good—then decided against it. There was no time. Every second, they were getting farther away. Besides, I wasn't going to confront anyone, only follow them.

If I could find them.

The street wasn't much better lit than the alley. Most of the businesses were closed for the day, their windows dark and shutters drawn. I wasn't sure which direction the men had gone, and I peered both ways down the street, searching for silhouettes. I saw a likely pair and set off after them.

I hadn't gone more than a block before I realized how conspicuous I was. Most of the open establishments were saloons and brothels, and I tried to hurry past the little knots of men gathered outside them, stepping out into the street more than once to avoid having to shoulder through them.

Ahead of me, my two targets disappeared around a corner. I picked up the pace, but by the time I got there they were nowhere to be seen. I scanned the buildings along the street. Several boarding houses, a trio of saloons, and a hotel. I hesitated, then swore under my breath. I'd lost them. To be fair, I wasn't even certain I'd ever had them.

Frustrated, I spun on my heel to go back to Bonnie's and bumped into a different pair of men behind me on the sidewalk.

"Hoo there, little girlie," one said, putting a hand on my arm as I tried to step back. "No need to be in such a rush." He was squat and red-faced, with a straggly, yellowing beard that made his head look as though it sat directly atop his shoulders. He stank of sweat and liquor. He and his companion, a taller, stringy man with a pockmarked face, each held a jar full of cloudy liquid.

"Excuse me," I said firmly. "I have to be going." I looked down at his hand, still on my arm. "Let go of me."

"Now don't be that way," he said. "You bumped into us. Least you could do is stay and be friendly. We just want to talk to you. Been out at camp for better'n a month, haven't we, Johnny? You're the prettiest thing we seen that whole time."

Johnny took a long pull from his jar and angled his body so he was between me and the street. "Me and Seb, we got gold," he said. "Give you some of it for a few minutes of your time."

Moving together, they backed me toward the alleyway, and my heart sped up.

"Ooh, lookit, Johnny. She's hot for it already." Seb's eyes were fastened on my chest. I glanced down. Patsy's too-tight shirtwaist and the cold night air created more of a display than I'd realized.

His hand, which had been on my arm, began to slide toward my breast, and I pulled back and slapped him hard across the face before it could get there. "Get out of my way this instant, or I swear I'll make you regret it."

He grinned, revealing rotten teeth. "Ooh, I like a feisty one. Go ahead and fight if you want to, sugar. Makes it more fun." He jerked his head at Johnny, and the pair of them muscled me into the alley and pushed me up against the wall before I could do more than draw breath to scream. Johnny's hand was over my mouth before I could let it out. There was a rough hand on my breast, another already grasping at the folds of my skirt.

Terror and rage surged through me. I reached for my magic, desperately, and didn't stop, even as the flesh of my wrist began to burn. I couldn't suppress a whimper at the pain, but I didn't let go.

Johnny took it for encouragement. "That's right, darlin', you got a real man tonight—two of 'em, even." He removed his hand and shoved his tongue into my mouth. The taste of him was vile, and I gagged, then bit down on his tongue, hard, and he howled and pulled away, staggering into Seb and sloshing moonshine over the other man's hand and sleeve.

He tossed the empty jar away and spat blood onto the dirt. "Ooo liddle nunt," he said around his mangled tongue.

I tried to dart past them, but Seb snagged my arm and slung me back against the wall so hard the breath went out of me with a little *woof.* He pinned me to the wall with a hand around my throat and leaned in close.

"For that, I'm gonna make it hurt," he said.

The blood pounded in my ears. I couldn't breathe. I clawed at his wrist and kicked at his shins. The fumes from his sleeve seared my nose, and a faint hope flickered within me.

I closed my eyes. I didn't try to fill myself with power. I didn't try to cast a spell. I clamped down on his wet sleeve with both hands and thought of fire. I thought of fire and ignored the pressure in my chest and the pain in my throat and the heat building around my wrist, even as sweat broke out on my forehead and stars began to dance in front of my eyes.

I made a spark.

It wouldn't have lit a stove, but it was enough to set the liquor soaking his sleeve alight. I didn't even know for certain it had worked until blue flames licked over the wool and the pressure on my throat eased as Seb stumbled away from me with a yelp.

I sucked in a wheezing breath, shoved my way free, and ran, glancing over my shoulder as I reached the mouth of the alley.

Seb was doing a herky-jerky dance, waving his arm like a torch, too drunk or stupid to realize it was only fanning the flames. Johnny was batting ineffectually at him. Both men were shouting and cursing. Neither looked like they were thinking of chasing me. Yet.

I wheeled and made it two strides onto the sidewalk before I slammed into something. Someone. A new set of hands gripped my shoulders, and my panicked brain came entirely loose from its moorings. I flailed and kicked, trying to yank away. I stumbled over my own feet and would have landed on the ground if whoever it was hadn't held me up.

"Joya!"

Doyle's voice penetrated the fog of terror. I looked up into his face and went weak with relief.

He glanced past me into the alley, where the fire was now out and the men were regrouping, and his face darkened.

"Did they hurt you?" His voice was low.

"They—" My voice caught in my battered throat, and I tried again. "They grabbed me. I got away." I was aware I was shaking, and that he could feel it.

"I see," he said. "Stay here."

He stepped past me, closing on the other two men with a speed I didn't know he possessed. His arm came up and drove forward like a ram, his fist flattening Seb's nose with a crunch audible from five feet away. The smaller man staggered and went over on his backside with a yowl. Johnny didn't have time to do more than raise his hands in supplication before Doyle was on him. He pummeled them both, thoroughly and in complete silence, leaving them groaning on the ground before he turned back to me. He put a gentle hand on my back and guided me away.

I was too shaken to talk, and Doyle seemed to understand, waiting until the next block to speak.

"Samantha came to my room to get me," he said, shrugging out of his coat and draping it around my shoulders. "Told me you'd left. She was worried about you."

"Apparently she was right to be," I said in a rasping voice that still managed to convey my bitterness. I clutched the coat around me like a cape, keeping my arms and hands inside. It was heavy and warm from his body, but since my shivering was as much from fear and shock as cold, it helped only a little.

He didn't say anything. He didn't have to.

Stupid, I berated myself. Multiple people had warned me Denver City was dangerous at night. I should have listened. I didn't have my magic to shield me anymore. The old, familiar anger at the Magisterium flared up, and it was so much more comfortable than being frightened that I snatched at it like a child grabbing for a sweet. They'd sent me out here without any ability to protect myself, to a place where a woman couldn't walk alone. A place where people were summoning demons—they hadn't known about that, but I was in no mood to be fair. I brooded until we reached Bonnie's, where she and Samantha were waiting for me in the dining room, a lamp on the table between them.

Samantha sprang to her feet when we entered. "Joya! Are you all right?"

"Thanks to your father," I said, trying to smile. "And you, too. I'm sorry for scaring you."

Bonnie stood. "Can I get you anything? Something warm to drink?"

"No," I said. "I'm fine. Don't go to any trouble on my account. But thank you."

"You two go on up to bed," Doyle said to Bonnie and Samantha. "I want to talk to Joya for a minute."

"You'll lock up?" Bonnie asked.

"I will," he said.

When they'd gone, I shrugged out of his coat and handed it back to him, then crossed my arms, waiting for him to chide me for going out or ask what I'd been thinking.

He surprised me. "Come on," he said, walking toward the kitchen. I followed.

Doyle reached onto the back of a shelf and came down with a half bottle of whiskey. "Bonnie's nearly a teetotaler herself," he said. "But she keeps this around for medicinal purposes." He found a glass and poured a healthy slug into it before handing it to me.

"I don't—"

"Drink it. You're still shaking," he said. "And it will soothe your throat."

I did as he said and choked down the liquor. It hurt to swallow, but the warmth pooled in my stomach, and I felt myself relax.

"Let me see your neck," he said, picking up the lamp.

I tilted my head back and to one side, looking up at him as he stepped closer. He looked at my throat for a long moment before he touched a gentle finger to a spot below my ear. I had a flash of a thought about how different two touches could be, and I barely managed to suppress a gasp as my insides went liquid.

Doyle pulled back at once. "Hurts?"

My face heated. "No . . . I just—A little."

"It's going to bruise, I'm afraid."

"So are Johnny and Seb," I said with a half smile. "You paid them for their work."

"Not half as well as I wanted to," he said.

He was still only inches from me, and after a long moment he seemed to remember it. He stepped back. "You've had a long day, and I'm sure you're worn out."

"You're right," I said. I took my own step back, turned, and left the kitchen. He followed.

I made my way to the stairs, my legs trembling only a little. I didn't let myself glance back, but I could feel him watching me go.

⸺

Alone in my room, I waited in the dark until there was no further sound from downstairs. In the aftermath of what had turned into an extremely long day, I was exhausted, but I didn't dare lie down. Even in my clothes and boots I was certain I would fall asleep and miss my chance. Fortunately, it was a clear night. I counted off an hour by the movement of the stars, then emptied my bag, took off my boots, and crept down the stairs, keeping to their edges in the hope they wouldn't creak beneath me.

In the kitchen, I took the lamp from beside the back door and carried it into the storage room before lighting it.

The flame flickered over the shelves and bundles, casting eerie, dancing shadows. I set the lamp atop the smaller trunk and opened the larger one, half expecting it to be empty, or at least for the magical items to be gone. But everything was where I had left it.

I hadn't actually touched the bowl earlier, and I hesitated before reaching for it with a tentative finger. It was there, an ugly remnant of magic, just like what I'd felt at the Jensens' homestead. It made my stomach cramp, and I used a fold of my skirt to lift the bowl and set it inside my bag, then turned to the books and papers and did the same with them. When it was all in my bag, I closed the trunk lid, blew out the lamp, and hauled everything up to my room.

Back behind my locked door, I upended my bag onto the bed. I hadn't felt anything magical on the paper I'd touched earlier, so I started with those. There were a few more propaganda posters like the one I'd already read and some newspaper clippings about the war.

I tossed them aside in disgust and turned to the books. I drew the *DE VOCATIONE* toward me with a mixture of dread and fascination.

Inside, it was page after page of closely written Latin, interspersed with drawings—mostly sigils, though there were a few pictures of creatures so warped and grotesque they could only be demons. I tried to ignore them and paged through until I found the symbol etched in the bottom of the quartz bowl. *Ligere* was printed beneath it. I set the book aside and turned to the bowl, studying the text carved around its interior.

Per verbo et per sacramento vique ligeris Per sanguine et per magiaque vique ligeris In hoc aeno ligeris Usque aenum

The last word or words were missing, though I could tell the last few letters were *t-u-m*. I had very little Latin—enough to guess at the meanings of some of the words. *"Sacramento"* and *"sanguine"* and *"mag-iaque"* were easy enough. That, combined with the greasy film of magic clinging to the quartz, made me certain the bowl had something to do with summoning demons. I set it aside, scrubbing my hands on my skirt as if I could wipe away the feel of it, and turned to the second book.

It was nothing but an almanac, largely unmarked except for the section that charted the phases of the moon by month. Starting in April, there were notations written in ink. *Failure. Pig*, read a note on the night of the full moon. Similar notes, with *goat* and *sheep* instead of *pig*, marked both the full and new moons in May. My chest went tight. These were early attempts at summoning demons. I paged forward, through several more failures, until July's entry made my skin go cold.

Written beside the date of the new moon were the words *Success. Man.*

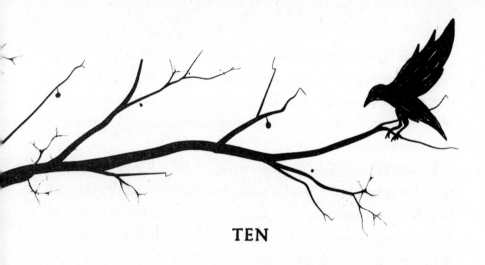

TEN

Based on the notes in the almanac, Broaderick had successfully summoned at least three demons—one each in July, August, and September. Each had involved a human sacrifice. There was nothing written beside the October new moon, but he wouldn't have had possession of the books or the bowl by then. I suspected their loss had not stopped him. He already had the knowledge he needed. And the men the night before had talked about bringing someone—presumably Broaderick—another piece of quartz, which meant he knew how to make a new summoning bowl.

The timing puzzled me. The summonings had happened at the new moon, but neither the Jensens nor the patrol had been killed on those dates. Had someone else summoned those demons? Or was there still more to this than I understood?

I slept badly, too disturbed by my discoveries to settle. When I did drift off, my dreams were full of men with rough hands and pools of blood on white stone.

Bonnie rapped gently on my door at daybreak, and I dressed, bleary-eyed. It hurt when I yawned, and I leaned over the little washstand to peer into the mirror above it. The bruising wasn't obvious, but when I tilted my head, I could see the faint marks from Johnny's fingers on the sides of my neck.

I stood still for a long moment, staring at them. Given everything that had happened afterward, I hadn't had time to dwell on the attack itself, but now, looking at the signs it had left behind, it struck me how narrow an escape I'd had. Both Seb and Johnny had come out of the encounter worse off than I had, thanks to Doyle, but it didn't change what had happened. A low, burning anger ignited in my gut, but I forced it down. It was done. There was no point in obsessing over it now.

I washed my face, then hurried downstairs to help with breakfast. I dished up plate after plate of pancakes and bacon until the first rush passed and I could sit and eat my own. I'd had two cups of black coffee by then, and I was jittery and nauseated from fatigue and too much caffeine. I picked at my plate until Samantha approached me.

"Good morning. Could I sit with you?"

I was not in the mood for company, but her face was so hopeful that I couldn't refuse. I gestured to the seat across from me and tried to smile.

"Where's your plate? Or have you already eaten?"

"I'm waiting to eat with my pa. He had to get up early to go to the barn and look after Patch. He doesn't like anyone else to do it."

"It's nice of you to wait for him."

"I do it whenever he's here."

"How often is he gone, usually?"

She shrugged. "It depends. If he has to go after someone, he stays gone for weeks. Lately he's been doing lots of short trips. I think it's because of what happened to the Jensens and the patrol."

"You know about that?"

Samantha sniffed. "I heard Pa telling Aunt Bonnie about it when they thought I was asleep. She told him not to tell me because it would be too frightening. But I'm not a child."

"She was trying to protect you." I hesitated. "Is she your father's sister?"

Samantha shook her head. "My mother's. She died when I was a baby, you know."

"I didn't," I said, parsing this new information. "I'm sorry." The girl's answer told me about Bonnie's relationship with Samantha, but not about her relationship with Doyle.

Abruptly, Samantha reached across the table and touched the binding on my wrist. Again, the touch of her nascent power plucked a harp string in my head, and I held my breath as a frown flickered over her face. She probably felt it as well, though she wouldn't know what it was or what it meant.

She drew a breath. "That's pretty. Was it a gift?"

It wasn't what I expected her to say, and I answered slowly. "You could say that."

"From a beau?"

"No," I said shortly.

"What's Boston like? I heard Pa say that's where you're from," she added.

She probably heard a lot, with those sharp ears. "It's different than here," I said. "Greener, for one thing. But let me ask you about something else. Have you heard anyone talking about a man named Marcus Broaderick?"

"Of course," Samantha said. "He used to come here to eat. I didn't like him."

Before I could formulate another question, her eyes focused on something behind me, and her face brightened.

"Mr. Northcutt!" Samantha said, sounding delighted.

I looked over my shoulder. The schoolteacher I'd seen leading the chanting boys the day before stood just inside the dining room. Samantha popped up from her seat and hurried to lead him to a table. "I'll go and get your breakfast right now," she said.

He smiled his thanks at her, then sat and opened the book he'd brought with him.

An idea occurred to me.

Leaving my now empty plate behind, I approached his table.

"Good morning," I said.

He looked up at me, seeming surprised. "Good morning, miss." Up close, he appeared to be in his fifties, with a ruddy, fleshy face framed by neatly trimmed whiskers. He wore a pale gray suit, fashionably cut, with a crisp white shirt and a cravat of bright blue silk. On one uncalloused hand he wore a heavy gold ring with a crest atop a red stone.

"You're Mr. Northcutt, the schoolteacher?"

"For my sins," he said in a jovial tone. "And whom do I have the pleasure of addressing?"

"My name is Joya Shaw," I said. "I don't mean to disturb you, but I wonder if I might join you for a moment."

"Having a lovely young lady join me at my breakfast could never be disturbing," he said, marking his place in his book and setting it aside. There was nothing even vaguely flirtatious in his manner, despite the flattering words. In fact, the impression I got from his overall manner and bearing was that women did not interest him in that way.

It didn't bother me, but I wondered at his reception in such a rough and rugged area of the country. Samantha certainly liked him, and his pupils seemed to as well, from what I'd seen the day before. But it was no matter at the moment, and I turned back to my immediate purpose.

"I'm working on some Latin translations," I began.

"Ah," he cried, nearly clapping his hands. "A fellow classicist!"

It was impossible not to smile at his enthusiasm. "Hardly. I'm afraid I have only a little Latin, and the work is beyond my skill level."

"I'm happy to help. If you'd like to show me—"

"No," I blurted.

Northcutt's eyebrows went up at my vehement response.

"I mean," I said, modulating my tone, "that I appreciate the offer, but I want to do the work myself. How else will I improve? I merely meant to ask if you could recommend a good Latin dictionary. I'll have to send away for it, but I don't even know what I need."

"A fair question," he said, nodding seriously. "There are several excellent options available. What are you translating? Sermons or poems? It makes a difference, you know."

"Poetry," I said after a moment. There was something of poetry to spell casting—cadence and intonation mattered.

This time he did clap his hands. "Wonderful! You must read the *Aeneid* in the original Latin—there's nothing like it."

His enthusiasm was infectious.

"I'm afraid that might be too far over my head at this point," I said, smiling. "But perhaps I'll work up to it."

"Oh, you must," he said, stabbing the table with a forefinger for emphasis. "For my money, the most beautiful poetry in the world is in the Latin. Some people say Homer, in the Greek, but I disagree. Virgil? Ovid? Sublime. None of this modern claptrap with its 'how do I love thees' and going a-roving and wandering lonely as a cloud." He made a derisive sound. "Pedestrian. A truly refined sensibility appreciates the Romans. The pinnacle of our culture."

"The dictionary," I prompted, barely managing to suppress a laugh.

"I know just the one," he said. "In fact, I'm happy to let you borrow my copy while you wait for yours."

"I couldn't do that," I began, but he cut me off.

"Nonsense—it will take weeks for you to get yours, and I don't want you having to wait. I don't have an immediate need for it. I board nearby. I'll run right back over after breakfast and bring it to you."

"If you're certain," I said.

"I insist."

Samantha arrived, carrying his breakfast, and set the plate down before him with a grin. "Here you go."

"Thank you, my dear," Northcutt said. "This looks delightful. Now, have you been practicing your lines?"

"I have," she said, beaming.

"Samantha is playing the Virgin Mary in the town Christmas pageant," Northcutt said to me. "She has a lovely soliloquy about birthing the Christ Child. Will you be in town for the holiday?"

"I don't know if we'll—"

"Oh, Joya, say you'll come back for Christmas," Samantha said. "There's the pageant, and then a party at the Broadwell House. Everyone will be there. And being out there on the farm won't be any fun at all! You should come and stay with us!"

"I'll have to see what Uncle Josiah says," I told her. "So I can't promise. But I'd love to come if I'm able."

A new wave of diners was arriving, so I excused myself to begin helping with them, wondering all the while if I'd be able to persuade Josiah to come back so soon. I needed time in town if I was going to track down Broaderick and whoever was helping him. Christmas was three weeks away. With Northcutt's dictionary, I should be able to make some progress on the *DE VOCATIONE* translations by then. And Samantha's enthusiastic invitation was touching. I liked the girl, and more time around her would give me a better sense of how close she was to coming into her power.

I was finished helping with breakfast by midmorning. When I emerged from the kitchen, Northcutt had been and gone again, leaving the promised dictionary on one of the tables with a note inside.

Dear Miss Shaw—
    This is the best-organized and most comprehensive Latin dictionary I have ever found for use by the intermediate translator.

Any of the shops should be able to send away for it for you. If you
are able to come for Christmas, your copy might even be here by
then. In any case, keep this one as long as you need, with my
compliments.

Yours,

B. Northcutt

Sapere Aude

I took the note and dictionary upstairs and stuffed them into my
bag—now overfull with the inclusion of the bowl, books, and my old boots.
I managed to force it closed, then hauled it to the front door, where both
Bonnie and Samantha were waiting to say goodbye. Samantha reiterated
her invitation to come for the holiday, this time with Bonnie's agreement.

"We'd be glad to have you," she said. "And hopefully I won't have to
put you to work."

"I'll try to come if I can, and I'm happy to be a worker or a guest, either
one," I said. I hesitated. Then, realizing I was hoping Doyle would appear,
I straightened my shoulders. "Give Ranger Doyle my best, please," I said
precisely, and departed.

I forced myself not to look for him as I walked. I didn't have a clear
picture of his domestic arrangements, but the last thing I needed was that
sort of complication. I stopped at Tuttle and Veach to place an order for the
dictionary and thank Mr. Veach for sending me to Bonnie's the night before.

It was going on toward noon when I reached the livery stable.

The wagon was out front, full of supplies, and the mules were already
hitched to it, stamping their feet and whisking flies off their flanks with
casual flicks of their tails.

"'Bout time you turned up," Josiah snapped as I approached.

"You didn't tell me to be here by a certain time," I said, taken aback
by his tone. "And you knew where I was staying. If we needed to leave
earlier, you could have sent Peter to get me."

"You're wasting more time standing there jawing," he said, scowling. "Get in the wagon, and let's get going. We're already going to have to hustle to make it back home afore dark."

My back stiff, I strode toward the back of the wagon. Badger tried to turn his head and bite me as I passed, but Peter had a hand on his bridle, so the mule flattened his ears and settled for an irritable snort. Thoroughly put out, I almost responded with one of my own.

Peter followed me to the wagon bed and reached for my valise. I hesitated for an instant before I handed it to him. It was silly. He couldn't know what was inside. He seemed not to notice the extra weight and swung it over the wagon's side into the bed, where it landed with a thump. I suppressed a wince, wishing I'd had more to wrap around the stone bowl than just my dirty shift.

The books and bowl fairly blazed at me from inside my bag, and I held my breath as we got underway, more than half expecting Josiah to turn to me in the wagon bed and demand to know what I was about, carrying things like that.

But he said nothing, and the longer he went without noticing, the less I feared he would.

I broached the subject of Samantha after we'd been underway for around an hour.

"How old is she?" he asked, after I told him what I'd sensed from her, using carefully oblique language out of deference to Peter's presence.

"Eleven." I'd confirmed her age while we peeled potatoes the night before.

"Then we've got a couple of years, most like," Josiah said, seeming unconcerned.

"Maybe," I said. "But I'm not so certain. She's showing signs." I let a beat pass. "They've invited me back for Christmas. It would give me another chance to gauge where she is. Or maybe if you met her, you could tell."

Another beat.

"We'll see," he replied without looking at me. His tone made it clear he was finished with the subject, and I sat back, having risen onto my knees as I spoke.

The wagon bed was more crowded now, but also more comfortable, with sacks of flour and beans to cushion the ride, and I lounged against them as we trundled over the grass, retracing the faint tracks we'd made the day before.

It was all I could do not to pull the books from my bag and start working on the translations. Instead, I mulled over everything that had happened during the past day.

I thought about Samantha, about her potential power, her brightness. I thought about Bonnie, ill but working so hard to keep herself. I thought of Doyle, then cut myself off.

I wasn't going to think about Doyle.

I thought about Inge, the prostitute I'd met at the post office, instead, and hoped the tea would work. I wondered how she'd come to her current situation. It couldn't be an easy life for her. A baby would be a disaster.

I thought about the miners I'd overheard and failed to follow. I thought about how I might try to find them again when I got back to town, and how I would know them if I did, since they'd been protected by some sort of enchantment.

I thought about Seb and Johnny and how their hands had felt on me, and the low anger simmered within me again. If I hadn't been able to make that spark, I wouldn't have gotten away.

But that might not be true. Doyle had come along only a moment later. He would have stopped them. I put a hand to my throat. Their bruises were worse than mine, and I was glad of it.

Doyle's response had been a surprise. Not that he was angry, but the cold, businesslike nature of it. Unlike at the Jensens', however, none of that anger had spilled over onto me. When he'd touched me—

I stopped, chagrined. There I was, again, thinking about Doyle. But there was nothing wrong with thinking about him, I decided after a moment. Thinking wasn't doing. It didn't hurt anyone if I admitted to myself that I found him interesting. That I desired him, even. The surge of heat I'd felt when he touched me had been unexpected but far from unpleasant.

I allowed myself to linger over the memory for a time, but in the end, even it wasn't enough to keep my mind off the contents of my bag. The urge to open the bag and at least page through the *DE VOCATIONE* was almost overwhelming, but I managed to suppress it. Then I stiffened, realizing what that meant.

I wasn't going to tell Josiah what I'd found.

I didn't even know I'd made the decision. It had happened without my ever consciously thinking about it.

Josiah had not summoned the demon that attacked the patrol. But there was a group of men involved. He could be a part of it.

The logic was shaky, at best. Josiah had shown no sympathy for the rebels, no signs of any demon magic—almost no sign of any magic at all, in fact—and the rules he'd imposed on me before he'd agreed to let me stay didn't seem like the sort of thing someone who embraced demon magic would set. But I'd known a fair number of people who were eager to impose rules on others they themselves didn't abide by, so Josiah's rules for me didn't necessarily mean anything.

At least, that was what I told myself.

The real heart of the matter was this: if I told him about the books, Josiah would take them away from me. Of that, I had no doubt. He'd forbidden me to have anything to do with magic without his permission. It seemed unlikely he would make an exception for studying demon texts, even though I wasn't fool enough to attempt any of the spells.

There was no way Broaderick was going to all this effort just to murder a relative handful of Unionists in a place with no direct connection to the war. No, the Colorado Territory was the testing ground. He had bigger plans.

There was a strange symmetry to it all. I'd exposed the rebels inside the Magisterium. I'd been bound and sent out here as a punishment, only to stumble over something much bigger.

I couldn't let Josiah keep me out of it.

I was so absorbed in all these thoughts that I didn't realize how late it had gotten until I began shivering and looked out over the horizon. The shadows had lengthened. I twisted to look past the mules' heads. The sun was low in the sky, hanging no more than a handspan over the mountains.

Even as I drew a breath to ask how much farther we had to go, Josiah nudged Peter, who slapped the team with the reins, urging them to pick up the pace. They broke into a jarring trot, making the wagon bed bounce and sway. We went on that way for a time, my teeth feeling as though they would rattle out of my head. I unfolded one of the buffalo robes and wrapped myself in it.

Finally, as the edge of the sun touched the top of the mountains, Josiah spoke. "It's no good. We're not going to make it."

Peter glanced at him, a question on his face, then sighed. He pulled the team to a stop and set the brake, then leaned into Josiah's side and pointed his arm straight ahead.

"I've got it," Josiah said. "Let's get the lamps lit before you go."

"Go?" I asked, confused.

Josiah ignored me. He reached into the compartment beneath the footboard and extracted a pair of lamps. He trimmed their wicks and lit them, hanging them from posts on either side of the wagon seat. That done, he reached for the reins and glanced at the sun.

It slipped behind the mountains.

"We'll see you in the morning," Josiah said.

Before I could ask what he was talking about, the air around Peter shivered. I gasped and came up onto my knees in the wagon bed as the big man shuddered and threw his head back. His face twisted in a grimace, and his body collapsed in on itself, his clothes wilting onto the seat beside Josiah. I would have screamed, but before I could gather breath enough to manage it, there was a muffled cawing noise. The pile of fabric moved, and a crow poked its head from the collar of Peter's shirt. It wriggled free, fluttering its wings. I inhaled again, nearly strangling myself on this second gasp of astonishment.

The crow—*Peter*—cocked his head and cawed at me. He flapped his wings and took to the sky.

ELEVEN

They're crows," I said in a voice gone thin with shock. My eyes followed the large black bird that had been Peter as he circled above us once, then set off in a straight line—*as the crow flies*, my brain supplied, with a sort of lunatic hilarity—in the direction he'd pointed out for Josiah.

Pointed out with his arm, which was a thing he'd had a moment before, but no longer did, because he was a *crow*.

When he was out of sight, I managed to drag my eyes down to look at Josiah. "Peter? And . . . Paul, too? They're . . . crows?" My voice scaled up at the end of every word, turning each one into its own question.

Josiah stared at me staring at him. My face must have been a sight to see, because the corner of his mouth twitched, and he let out a rusty, wheezing sound of disbelief. "Moon and stars, did you only just now figure that out?"

My face went hot, and I crossed my arms.

A grin split his face, the first I'd ever seen, and it added another layer to my disorientation.

"You did, didn't you?" The grin became a chuckle, which grew into full-blown, almost braying laughter that went on far too long for my liking. It turned into coughing, eventually, until I rose and thumped him on the back, possibly harder than necessary.

"Merlin's balls, girl," he said once he'd gotten himself under control and waved me away. "Are you trying to make me spit my lungs out?" He drew a handkerchief from his pocket and mopped his face.

"They're crows," I said again, and this time my tone was indignant. "How could you not tell me?"

He must have seen that I was contemplating violence, because he made an effort to suppress the grin threatening to break out again. "I thought you knew."

"How could I have known?" I said, feeling harassed. "I never saw them change, never heard you cast a spell."

The sun was fully set by then. The moon had yet to rise, and the circle of light cast by the lamps was tiny. From where I sat, I couldn't even see the mules' heads. I jerked my chin in their direction. "The mules are still up there, right? They haven't shrunk down and run off to hunt mice?" My tone was admittedly snide.

Still wearing that infuriating expression of suppressed amusement, Josiah turned to face forward. He moved the brake handle, lifted the reins, and clicked his tongue. He gave me a sideways glance as we lurched forward.

We made our way slowly through the dark while I worked through the implications of what I'd uncovered. Josiah had been genuinely surprised I hadn't already known about Peter and Paul. He'd expected me to feel the magic on them. Which meant he wasn't concerned about it. Which meant it wasn't demon magic.

Probably.

I suppressed a sigh. There was no way to be sure about anything, and I was worn out with trying to logic my way out of this tangle. Either he was one of the summoners or not. I would never find out for certain if I didn't start pushing. Before I could think better of it, I reached over the seat and pitched Peter's clothes into the wagon bed, then climbed into the place he'd vacated. "How did you do it?"

Josiah glanced at me.

"Even with this," I said, lifting my arm and shaking the bracelet on my wrist, "I should have felt a spell that powerful. Transfiguration of birds into men, linked to the sunrise and sunset? Held day after day? That is enormously complex magic."

His only response was a grunt.

This time I didn't bother to muffle the sigh. I was too far in to stop now. I wanted answers. "Forgive me for being so blunt," I said. "But I've been in your house for better than a month now, and I've never seen you do any major magic—you don't even do cleaning charms. I would have sworn you didn't have the strength for something like that."

"It ain't about strength," he said.

"What does that mean?" I asked, exasperated.

He looked sideways at me. "Do you really want to know?"

I tried not to squirm beneath his gaze. "Yes."

Josiah looked at me for a long moment. "All right. But not right now. I need to concentrate on getting us home. Not so easy to drive a team and loaded wagon in the dark."

I bit down on my impatience. He was right. There were barely any landmarks to follow in the daylight; the featureless blackness around us would have been terrifying if I'd had any room for such an emotion.

Fortunately, the mules seemed to know where they were going. We plodded onward for perhaps an hour before the ward snapped over my skin. I let out a startled gasp, not having realized we were so close to the farm.

Minutes later, Josiah pulled to a stop in the yard. "Hop down for me and open the barn door while I get them unhitched," he said. "The boys can unload the wagon in the morning."

I did as he said. "Where are they now? The . . . Peter and Paul?" I asked as he led Badger inside. I took hold of Fox's bridle and followed.

"Cold nights, they roost in the bunkhouse. Night like this, they're in a tree somewhere around the place." He began stripping the tack from Badger, who lashed out with a back hoof. The mule was tired, and the effort was half-hearted. Josiah idly sidestepped it and gave him a slap on the rump.

"How do you make them come back every morning?" I asked as I settled Fox in his stall. He lipped at my sleeve.

Josiah looked at me as if I were simple. "I don't. If they didn't want to be turned into men every day, they would fly away one night and I'd never see them again. But they're there waiting every morning. They like it."

I thought of Peter feeding the goats and Paul scooping Shadow into his arms. I thought of the alert way they watched everything and Peter's reaction to his reflection in the polished copper at the general store. It was true.

Josiah scooped oats into the feedbag and hooked them over the mules' heads. He picked up a brush and began drawing it over Badger's coat with long, deliberate strokes.

I drew a breath to speak, to prod him for the explanation he'd promised me, but I didn't get the chance.

"What is magic?" he asked abruptly.

The breath huffed out. "Josiah, I don't need—"

He cut me off. "You want to know how I do the spells I do with the power I have?"

I bit down on a sharp reply. "Yes."

"Then you'll let me explain it my way. Now answer the question. What is magic?"

"Elemental power, shaped by focus and bound by will." It was a rote response, one any child of the Magisterium could recite. There were multiple theories about exactly how magic worked, about where the power came from and why some people could use it and others could not. I'd never paid much attention to the debates. I found them tedious. I didn't need to know exactly how magic worked to use it.

"And how does that geegaw stop you from doing magic?" Josiah asked, jerking his chin at the binding. He stepped out of Badger's stall and into Fox's. The sound of the brushstrokes resumed.

"It restricts my access to the power," I said impatiently.

"But you aren't cut off completely," he said. "You've still got a little left."

I pulled a face. "Not enough to do anything."

"That's where you've gone wrong," Josiah said. "I'm thinking that before they put that thing on you, you could hold a fair bit of power, am I right?"

It wasn't bragging if it was the truth. "Yes."

"One thing I've noticed," he said. "Witches who can hold a lot of power don't put as much effort into focus and will. Power comes easy to them, so they lean on it. They run into a difficult spell, they sling more power at it. That sound familiar?"

"I've never thought about it," I said.

"I'm right," he said. "I'd bet a gold nugget on it. But power isn't the only thing that makes magic. Focus and will are just as important," he said, nodding. "If you have less power, you can make up for it by having better focus and a stronger will."

I barked a laugh. "That's all?"

"Ain't no 'all' about it," Josiah said, pinning me with a dour look. "I've been practicing for nigh on fifty years to be able to do what I do. It takes work, lots of it. But at the core of it, yes." He came out of Fox's stall and set the brush aside. "Now. My old bones want to be in bed." He reached over the wagon's side, and my heart jumped into my throat as he tried to lift my bag. I'd all but forgotten about it.

Josiah grunted. "What did you bring back from town, rocks?"

"Some books," I said, hurrying to take it from him. "And my old boots are in there, too."

He didn't appear to notice my sudden agitation. "Glad you got what you needed. Means we won't have to go again for a while."

I didn't say anything. It didn't seem like the right time to prod him about the Christmas invitation. I followed him to the cabin, thinking about what he'd said. Focus and will. It seemed too simple. There must be more to it. Maybe he was lying, and his power really did come from another source.

But if it was true . . . If it was true, then maybe I could have my magic back.

I waited until we were inside to ask. But with my hand on the ladder to the loft and my heart pounding in my ears, I turned to him. "Will you teach me?"

He looked at me for a long moment, then nodded once. "Get some sleep. We'll start tomorrow."

⚬━━⚬

"Power, focus, and will," Josiah said. For each word, he used the stick he held to tap one of the points of the triangle he'd drawn in the dirt of the yard.

It was after breakfast the following morning. I'd barely slept, too excited by the idea of getting my power back to quiet my mind even after an exhausting pair of days. I took a last bite of the corn cake I carried and tossed the rest in the direction of the chickens. Shadow lazed among them, his slitted eyes on the tip of Josiah's stick as it trailed along the ground.

Peter and Paul, men again now that the sun was back up, also watched us from beside the corral. I'd been unable to stop myself from staring at them since they'd emerged from the barn, now that I knew what they were. Everything seems obvious in retrospect, but I couldn't help feeling foolish for not seeing it before. They looked like men, but the way they moved, the way they observed things, their interest and their curiosity, all had a distinctly birdlike quality.

"You need all three to do magic," Josiah went on, waving the stick at me to reclaim my attention before drawing another triangle, this time with one wide angle atop two narrow ones. "But the proportions are flexible. You feed in enough power, you can get by without as much focus or will." He drew a third triangle. "You feed in less, you need more of the other two."

"It still seems like too simple an explanation," I said.

"Nothing simple about it," he said. "Learning how to refine your focus and shape your will are the hardest parts of doing magic."

My skepticism must have shown, because he sighed. "Why do we use potions for some spells?"

"Because they're too complex to cast otherwise."

"Because of the amount of power they need?" Josiah asked.

"No," I said. "Most potions don't need that much power to be invoked."

"That's right. And it's not because the ingredients themselves are magic. Otherwise, they would work even if a Mundane mixed them. It's because complex spells require you to focus on more things at once. So we use the ingredients to help us fix the focus—each ingredient represents some aspect of the spell."

"But that can't be—I've used potions before without giving any thought at all to what the ingredients represented, and they worked just fine. And lots of the ingredients we use in potions are also used in Mundane remedies."

He nodded as if conceding the point. "That's because on some level, magic is about collective belief."

"What does that mean?"

"How do you think of magic? Everyone sees it differently."

"Water," I said without hesitating. "I've always thought of it as water. As a river I can reach into and dip out what I need."

He made a considering noise. "I've always thought of it as wind, myself, breathing it in and such. But water works. Think of the power as water running across a sheet of rock," he said. "Without something to shape it, it will spread out in every direction. Your will holds it in place. Your focus tells it where to go. Eventually, like water running over rock, magic carves a channel, so you don't need to use as much control to get it to do what you want—you just pour the power into the channel you've chosen, and off it goes."

I frowned. It made a certain intuitive sense, put like that.

Josiah went on. "Belief that magic will work helps reinforce it. That's why new spells are so much harder to control than old ones—there's no channel carved yet, no collective belief to help harden your will. If you're the first one who's ever done a spell, whether it works or not comes down to whether you have enough focus and will to make it work. Course," he added, "if you don't, you can always sling more power at it and hope some of it ends up where you meant it to go, but that's a sloppy way of doing things."

I thought of some of the spells I'd created and the unintentional effects they'd had. Like the time I'd invented a new spell to boil water and wound up melting the pot it had been in. Or the time I built a spell to clean a marble floor and instead scoured away the top layer of the stone.

Looking at those incidents the way Josiah described them, as an uncontrolled release of power, as reckless rather than innovative, made something in my stomach go hollow.

I pushed the feeling aside to consider later and nodded. "All right. I don't have much power with the binding on, so I need more focus and will. How do I do it?"

"First thing, you need to find out exactly how much power you can draw without that thing burning you." He nodded toward the bangle on my wrist. "Pain makes it hard to focus—that's part of how it works to hobble you. I want you to reach out and touch the power. Think of yourself putting your hands on the surface of the water. Don't try to scoop anything up yet."

I closed my eyes and took a breath. As I'd done so many thousands of times before, I opened that extra sense inside myself and reached out to the reservoir of power all around me. I could feel it at the edge of my awareness. Carefully, so carefully, I laid myself against it. It ran beneath my hands, tempting.

"You feel anything from the binding?"

"No," I said, my eyes still closed. It was torture, feeling the power there and wanting to fall into it, knowing I couldn't.

"Now," Josiah said, "I want you to draw up the smallest bit of it you can manage."

I visualized a bead of dew standing on a leaf. Round. Perfect. Tiny. I pulled it into myself and gasped.

It was the first time I'd held power without pain since the Magistra put the binding on my wrist, and the sweetness of it brought tears to my eyes. The yearning for more was almost overwhelming, and my breath quickened.

"Now try a bit more. Not too much."

It took all my self-control, but I pictured a second dewdrop running across the surface of the leaf to join the first, and they merged together.

"Again," Josiah said. "Keep going, a little bit at a time, until you feel the binding warn you off."

Droplet by droplet, I added to the little pool of power I was collecting. Far too soon, the bangle heated around my wrist, and I stopped with a regretful sigh. Altogether, if power really were water, it might have been enough to half fill a thimble. "Now what?"

"Now let it go and draw exactly that much again, but more quickly."

"Why?"

"Because you've got to know where your limit is, instinctively, without having to stop and think about it. It doesn't matter how good your focus is, it won't be good enough to ignore the pain if you draw too much. Any spell you try will be over before it starts."

I did as he said, drawing and releasing the power half a dozen more times. It got easier each time to recognize when to stop.

"Now," Josiah said when he was satisfied I understood where the boundary was, "time for the next step." He broke the stick he'd been holding into kindling and piled it around a tuft of grass. "Set that on fire."

I made an exasperated noise. "How? What I can hold isn't enough to do it. It's not enough to actually do anything."

"You only think it's not enough because you're used to having power to waste. You've been spoiled. I'll bet when you made a fire before, everything around it heated up, too."

I thought of the pot again, and my face went hot. "So?"

"So, that means your focus was no good and you were wasting power, letting it spill over from your actual goal. You don't have that luxury anymore. Have you ever seen someone start a fire by catching the sun with a piece of mirror?"

"Yes."

"See yourself doing that, but with magic. Pick one spot, and put everything there. No waste."

I'd managed to make a few sparks when he'd told me to light the stove, and, of course, one notable one during my desperate struggle in the alley against Seb and Johnny. But each of them had come at the cost of a new burn mark on my wrist. This was different. I gathered the power and narrowed my focus to a single blade of dry grass the width of a bit of thread. I focused on it and willed it to burn. I concentrated until my eyes blurred and sweat stood out on my forehead. Finally, finally, it began to glow. I gasped, and the tiny ember grayed and died at once, sending up a thin wisp of smoke as it crumbled to ash. But I'd done it.

I turned to Josiah expectantly.

He grunted. "That wasn't fire. Do it again. And don't let go this time."

Josiah was a hard taskmaster, but his methods worked. After three days of practice, I could reliably make fire, and we moved on to other things. I mastered several cleaning charms, as well as a spell I could use to turn the windmill's blades and make drawing water from the well far easier. It was no coincidence that the spells were all things I could use in my chores—they were practical, and I got plenty of opportunities to practice them. It was beginner's magic, all of it, and though having it at my fingertips again was glorious, I chafed at the painful simplicity of it. It was far from what I'd been capable of doing before, and I pushed at every opportunity to go further.

"Show me the spell you use for Peter and Paul," I said one morning as they emerged from the barn.

Josiah grunted. "You're not ready for that one," he said. "Might not ever be, as long as that binding is on you."

"So focus and will only go so far—there are some spells you can't do without having the ability to draw up a certain degree of power?"

"Maybe," he said with a shrug. "I don't know. In theory, enough will and focus could compensate for anything but a total lack of magic. And the other way around, too. But in reality? Seems likely there's a limit."

I looked around at the farm. "If you won't show me how you turn Peter and Paul into men, then what about the ward? How did you do that? It's strong. And holding something that large should take both a lot of magic and a lot of focus. Even before I was bound, I don't think I could have kept something like that up all the time without the effort showing. But it doesn't seem like it taxes you."

Something changed in the set of his shoulders—he was not entirely impervious to praise, apparently—and his voice was less gruff when he spoke. "The ward is just a modified protection circle. Come on. I'll show you."

He walked me in a rough loop around the edge of the property, stopping every twenty feet or so to nudge aside a tuft of grass or lift a pine bough and reveal the protective symbol carved on a half-buried rock or gouged into the soft wood of a tree trunk. "Think of each one of these as its own amulet. They're linked to each other."

It made sense. An amulet holds a spell within an object. It was more durable and convenient than having to do a spell in the moment.

We walked on to the next symbol. There were long scratches on the trunk beside the carving. It looked as if Shadow had found this tree ideal for sharpening his claws. One of the scratches intersected the outer edge of the symbol.

Josiah grunted and withdrew a carving tool from a pouch in his pocket. "If that damned cat of yours takes down my ward, his hide will wind up stretched on the side of the barn." He scraped the old symbol away, then re-carved it, higher this time, before putting his hand on it and closing his eyes. Concentrating, I felt the tiny pulse of power he sent into it as he connected it to the other carvings.

"How do you know when someone passes through it?"

He fished inside his collar and hooked a finger under the leather thong around his neck. Strung on it were several wooden disks the size of dollar coins. He selected one and held it so I could see the same symbol carved on it. "With this. Anything bigger than a fox touches it, I feel it go warm."

"What are the other amulets for?"

"This and that," he said shortly, dropping them back into his shirt and turning toward the cabin.

I followed. "So you've set a permanent magic circle without drawing a physical one? I've never heard of anyone doing something like that."

"It's like anything else," he said, glancing at me. "The drawn circle is to help hold the focus for the magic. If you can hold the focus without it, you don't need it. Technically, if I had enough power and will, I wouldn't need the runes either. But I tried it without them and it was a lot harder. So I use them."

"Can I learn it?"

"Why do you think I showed you?"

<hr />

That night after dinner, Josiah drew the protection symbol on a sheet of newsprint, then pushed it toward me. "Copy that a few times. Get the feel for it." While I worked, he went into his sleeping alcove and returned with a handful of thin wooden disks like the ones I'd seen that morning. He put them on the table beside me, then added a small engraving tool. "Once you can draw it, try carving it."

I nodded without lifting my eyes from the paper. Amulets are more powerful when you put more effort into making them. I could make one out of pencil on newsprint and keep it in my pocket, but it would be weaker than the same spell carved into wood. Stone or engraved metal would be even better.

When I was sure I could draw the symbol from memory, I sketched it onto the first of the disks, then carved over the lines with the awl. It was awkward, and I ruined several disks before I got one done well enough to be worth trying to invoke.

Under Josiah's direction, I gathered the power and trickled it into the lines of the carving. I knew it was working even before I was done. I could almost see the power glowing in the thin channel of the carving before it sank away into the wood.

"Good," Josiah said when I'd finished and he'd run his thumb over the symbol and felt the magic.

"The symbol itself isn't magic, right?" I said. "Just like the words of a spell or the ingredients in a potion."

"That's right."

"So in theory, I could use a completely different symbol and get the same outcome."

"Maybe," he said. "I've never tried."

I took up the disk and hesitated for a moment before adding lines to the rune until it formed the outline of a mayflower. The tiny fragrant flowers were my favorite, and both the blossoms and leaves were used in potions and Mundane remedies. It spoke of home to me, of safety and familiarity. If magic was strengthened by association, I could think of no better substitute symbol.

Josiah watched with interest. I was certain the charm still worked, even before Josiah took up the medallion and confirmed it.

"So where does it end?" I said after a moment.

He raised an eyebrow.

"I mean," I said, trying to explain, "what is the limit? If the symbol on an amulet or the ingredients in a potion are all nothing but aids to focus, then couldn't a witch with strong enough focus do any spell at all without any of those things?"

"Maybe," he said. "But I don't know. I've been practicing for decades and I still use them. It's all a balance between the three—power, focus, and will. Might be that a witch strong enough with all three could do it. I've never met one. Not sure I'd like to—no one should have that kind of power. Everyone needs limits."

I went silent for a long moment before I spoke again. "What would the Magisterium say about you teaching me all this?"

He glanced at me, an eyebrow raised.

"They bound me as a punishment," I said. "They didn't want me doing magic. Aren't you defying them by helping me learn to do it anyway?"

"They bound you because they didn't want you doing magic the way you'd been doing it. They can't afford to have powerful witches out in the world who can't control themselves. Might not matter so much if you were a minor talent—it's why they don't much bother running off to punish hedge witches and the like. No one cares what they do because they can't do much. But someone with your potential can't be allowed to run wild."

I blinked. He'd called me powerful. Twice. His tone dampened it, but it was still the nearest thing to a compliment I'd heard from him since I'd arrived. I didn't know whether to feel pride or chagrin.

"It's fine if you don't like the rules," he went on. "But they exist for a reason. The point of binding you was to teach you a lesson. You bending your neck enough to learn the lesson is what will convince them to take it off you. If you can master the level of control needed to do magic despite the binding, you'll have gone a long way toward proving you can be trusted with the responsibility."

There was a rough logic to it, though I wasn't certain the Magisterium would agree. I took a breath to say so, but Josiah held up a hand to stop me.

"And make no mistake, magic is a responsibility. If I don't teach you anything else, I want you to learn that you are responsible for the effects of your magic. If you fly off the handle and hurt someone, it's on you. If you work a spell and it has effects you didn't intend, you bear that burden. This power we have is a gift. Misusing it, or allowing someone to be hurt because of it, is the worst thing you can do as a witch.

"As for the Magisterium, well, they shouldn't have put you under my authority if they didn't want me using it. I wouldn't have agreed to teach you if I didn't think you were ready to learn."

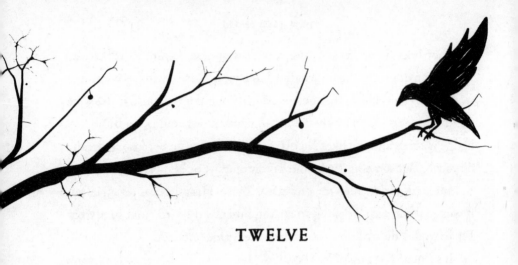

TWELVE

H is words echoed in my mind as I climbed the ladder to my loft. I waited until his snores began, then lit my little stub of candle and pulled the *DE VOCATIONE* from its hiding place beneath my mattress, just as I had done every night since getting back from town.

The guilt was especially stinging tonight, with Josiah's words about responsibility and his quiet approval still fresh in my mind.

I'd spent some part of nearly every night since returning from Denver City working my way through translating the book. It was slow going. I knew enough Latin to understand nuances mattered. There was a big difference between "it will kill" and "it will be killed."

The first thing I'd done was translate the words carved on the quartz bowl. To my shock and fascination, they turned out to be a binding spell. The bowl had been meant to capture and hold a demon.

I wrote the spell and its translation on the page beside the sigil.

Per verbo et per sacramento ligeris. By word and power be you bound;

Per sanguine et per magiaque ligeris. By blood and magic be you bound;

In hoc aeno ligeris. Be you bound within this vessel

Usque aenum. Until this vessel—

The missing final words must be something like "be breached" or "be broken." I made a list of possibilities beside the rest of the spell.

The discrepancy between the dates of the successful summonings—the nights of the new moon—and the attacks on the Jensen farm and the patrol made sense now. Broaderick had trapped the demons and held them until he could set them loose on their targets. The implications were terrifying. I imagined a demon set loose among the Union army. Or in downtown Boston. Or the lawn of the White House.

The slaughter would be breathtaking.

A few pages into the book, there was a mention of a ritual for making oneself invisible to a demon. There was a drawing of a sigil called the Broken Eye, though the facing page—presumably where the text of the spell itself had been located—was missing. I thought of my inability to recall the faces of the men at Bonnie's and wondered if they'd been wearing it. If it could make a man invisible to a demon, perhaps it also had the effect of making him, if not invisible, then unmemorable to people. It would be useful, if one were up to no good.

There were other tidbits, as well. There was both a summoning and a banishing ritual—I made a careful translation of the latter and committed it to memory. Apparently even a Mundane could perform either of those, but no human could do demon magic unless given the power by a demon in exchange for some promise or service. The book offered several warnings about such bargains.

I didn't spend much of my time on that section. I had no intention of bargaining with any demons.

Every night, I wrestled with the idea of telling Josiah what I'd done, and every night, I decided against it. It was a breach of his trust, and I knew it, and yet I persisted. I told myself I couldn't tell him now because I hadn't told him before. He would be angry with me for the deception.

He might refuse to keep helping me with my magic. Might even tell the Magisterium I was not, after all, learning the lesson they'd intended for me to learn. For a certainty, he would never allow me to continue studying the book or searching for Marcus Broaderick and his men. And I was too far involved now to let it go. I'd seen what happened to the Jensens. Doyle had known some of the men of the patrol, and I'd seen what their deaths had done to him. I couldn't let it keep happening.

⚬—•—⚬

I waited until the week before Christmas to remind Josiah about my invitation to spend the holiday in town.

"I'd like to go," I said. "I think it would be a good idea for me to have more time around Samantha. She's going to need instruction sooner than you think."

He shrugged. "Hay's in. Butchering's done. If you want to go, it's fine by me."

I hadn't expected him to agree so easily, and my next argument was already on my lips. It took me a moment to reorganize my thoughts.

"I thought I might stay a while," I said carefully. "Maybe two or three weeks?" If I was going hunting for demon summoners, I'd need time. A few days wouldn't be enough. *And it's more time with Doyle*, a little voice said in the back of my mind. I tried to ignore it. I'd spent more time than I cared to admit thinking about his fingers against my skin.

Again, Josiah surprised me. "How will I know when to send one of the boys to fetch you back?"

"No need. I'm sure I can get someone to bring me." *Doyle*, the little voice said, and again, I shushed it.

"All right."

"All right?" I repeated.

"You going deaf, girl?" Josiah asked irritably.

"No. I heard you."

He didn't reply, and I studied him from the corner of my eye. It was hard to tell, but I thought the lines around his mouth might be deeper than they'd been when I arrived. He looked . . . not older, exactly, but more worn. We'd been working hard over the past few weeks, and it occurred to me that he might have agreed to my going because he needed the rest.

The question was on the tip of my tongue, but before I could ask it, he spoke again.

"Mundanes give gifts at Christmas. If you're going, you can't go empty-handed."

Dismay flooded me. "Oh no. I hadn't even thought of that."

"You can use my account at Tuttle and Veach," he said. "But might be I can help you with the Ranger's gift, at least." Josiah hauled himself to his feet and went into his alcove. There was a creak as he lifted the lid of the trunk. He emerged a moment later holding one of the knives I'd seen while searching his things and handed it to me.

I drew the blade from its hard leather sheath. It was heavy but well-balanced, with a handle of antler and a fine steel blade the length of my hand.

"There's a charm worked into the metal," Josiah said. "Helps keep it sharp. And with a little bit of power fed into it, it can cut through most anything. That part will be wasted on the Ranger, him being a Mundane, but a good knife is always handy."

"You're sure you want to give it away? This must have been hard to make."

Josiah shrugged. "It's doing no one any good sitting in the trunk."

"It's an excellent gift. Thank you."

It was only later, as I lay in my bed in the loft, listening to his snores, that I realized he'd seen me watching him. He'd known what I was thinking. He'd changed the subject to stop me from asking a question he didn't mean to answer.

Peter took me into Denver City on Christmas Eve. We left at first light, wrapped in buffalo robes against the frigid air, our breath making clouds of mist as the mules plodded along under the brightening sky. We made far better time riding than if we'd brought the wagon and reached town by midday.

From the look of things, every rancher and miner in the territory had come into Denver City for the holiday. The streets were jammed, and as we turned onto Wazee Street I worried Bonnie might not have a room for me. There hadn't been any way to tell her I was coming, and with so many people in town, the temptation to rent out her spare room might have been too much to resist.

But she looked pleased to see me when I arrived, smiling from across the front room, her hands full of plates. She put the dishes in front of a pair of men at a corner table, then stopped for a moment to speak to a plain-faced young woman wiping up a spill from one of the long trestle tables before making her way over to me.

"Joya! You made it."

"I did. And I see you have some new help." I nodded toward the girl.

"I do," Bonnie said. "MaryAnne. She's a hard worker." She lowered her voice. "And she's not pretty, so maybe I'll get to keep her for a while."

"I wouldn't count on it," I said, watching as one of the miners leaned toward the girl and whispered something that made her giggle.

"Oh, I know it," she said with a wry smile. "But let me have my delusions, if you please."

"Then I'm sure I'm wrong and she'll stay a year," I said. "It looks like there's still plenty I could help with. Do you have a room for me, or is MaryAnne staying in it?"

"She's not, and of course I do," she said. "Do you think Samantha would have let me give it away? She's been counting on your being here. Lang and I tried to tell her you might not be able to come, but she wouldn't hear it."

"Oh good," I said, not bothering to disguise my relief. "When I saw how many people were in town, I was afraid I'd have to turn around and go right back to the farm."

"Not at all." Someone hailed her from one of the tables, and she flapped a hand at the man before turning back to me. "I need to get back to work. Go right ahead and take your things up if you like, then come have some lunch if you haven't yet."

I stepped outside to let Peter know I was settled. "Thank you for bringing me," I said as he handed down my bag from Badger's back. He gave me one of his gentle smiles, then turned and rode away, Fox now on a lead rope behind him.

I took my bag upstairs and unpacked, hanging my coat and the extra dress I'd brought on the hook on the wall, hoping the wrinkles would fall out of it overnight. I'd brought the *DE VOCATIONE* and dictionary with me so I could keep working on the translations, and I put them in the bureau. I tucked my bag beneath the bed, the only things left in it a pair of packages wrapped in newspaper and tied with string. One held Doyle's knife. The other was a pair of tortoiseshell combs Thomas had given me for my last birthday. I could never bear to wear them again. I didn't even know why I'd brought them with me, but now I was glad I had. They would look lovely in Samantha's hair, and this way they would go to someone who had no bad memories attached to them. That left only Bonnie to buy for.

There was a knock at the door.

"Joya!" Samantha exclaimed when I opened it. "You came. I knew you would!" Her face was alight.

"Of course I did," I said. "I didn't want to miss the pageant." I leaned down to give her a hug, and the protection charm I'd made swung away from my throat.

"That's pretty," the girl said, reaching for it and running a thumb over the carving. Her forehead wrinkled, and I held my breath, certain she was feeling the magic in it, even though she wouldn't know what it was. A half beat passed, and she pulled back. "It's a mayflower, right?"

"How do you know that?" I asked. "You can't have ever seen one before—they don't grow out here."

"Aunt Bonnie has a painting of them on the wall in her bedroom. They're her favorite—she says they remind her of home."

"They're my favorite, too," I said, wondering where Bonnie was from. "And speaking of Bonnie, I wondered if you might help me pick out a Christmas present for her?"

"And something for my pa?" She cocked an eyebrow at me.

"I already have his present. And yours, too."

Her face lit up. "Oooh, what did you bring me?"

"I'm not telling," I said, laughing at her naked acquisitiveness. "You'll have to wait until tomorrow. Now, I'm starving, so I'm going downstairs to have a quick lunch, and then, if Bonnie doesn't need my help, we can go, all right?"

By the time I'd eaten, the lunch rush was winding down, and Bonnie was happy to send Samantha out with me. "I know it's just the season and all the excitement," she said when I asked, "but she's been a trial—anxious about the pageant but snapping my head off every time I ask her about it."

However she'd been toward Bonnie, Samantha seemed pleasant enough as we departed for Tuttle and Veach's. There was a display of scented soaps near the front counter.

"Would Bonnie like these, do you think?" I asked, lifting each of them to my nose in turn. Roses, lavender, cloves. I lingered on one with a fresh lemony tang. There was mint in it, too, and I gave it another sniff before I put it back.

"She would, but Pa already got some of them for her," she said.

I grimaced. So much for the easy route. "Maybe I could make her some sachets? Which scents does she like? And what colors for the fabric?"

"Lavender for the scent, and she likes blue."

Mr. Veach showed us several bolts of blue calico, and I bought half a yard of the one Samantha chose, as well as a tiny sewing kit in a leather pouch.

"We still have the Braddon novel you were looking at last time you were here, miss," he said as he wrapped my purchases in brown paper. "Could I wrap that up for you as well?"

"Not this time, I'm afraid, but thank you," I said. "And merry Christmas."

On the way to the apothecary shop, Samantha chattered to me about the upcoming Christmas pageant. It would be held at the Broadwell Hotel, a choice of venue that had apparently caused some consternation among the town's churchmen.

"They all wanted to host it themselves," Samantha said. "And some of them are temperance, and the hotel serves spirits. They kept bothering Mr. Northcutt about it. He finally told them Jesus drank wine, so if they thought they knew better than the Son of God they were welcome to go around saying so and see how far it got them. Then he quoted some Latin at them—something about wine making glad hearts—and said he wasn't going to listen to any more of their nagging, the pageant would be held at the hotel, and no one would make them come if they didn't want to."

We'd reached the apothecary by then, and I pushed open the door, amused at the picture she'd painted of the genteel schoolteacher facing down a contingent of moralizers.

"The party afterward will be the best part," Samantha went on as I examined the glass jars of herbs lining one wall. "Pa and Aunt Bonnie said I can go this year. It's a dollar per person, and there will be all sorts of food. And music—last year the dancing went on all night."

I bought dried lavender, as well as cedar shavings and a trio of phials that held aromatic oils. I could make several different combinations, some Bonnie could use for her linens and some for the kitchen pantry. They would smell pleasant and help ward away bugs and mice. I could even put a bit of magic in them to make them work better.

I thought of Inge as I bought the supplies, hoping she was well.

My shopping done, we walked back to the house, where I nearly collided with Doyle as I walked through the door.

"Joya," he said, his face brightening. "Bonnie said you'd made it into town. We're glad to have you."

"I'm glad to be here," I said as warmth spread up my neck. Damn it. I tried to will myself to composure as I went on. "And ready to help Bonnie and MaryAnne with the rush tomorrow."

"Oh, no," Samantha said in an offhand tone. "She closes the restaurant on Christmas Day. She says it's a day for family."

Family. Which I was not. My face blazed hot.

Samantha seemed not to notice that she'd said anything awkward. "Pa," she went on, turning to Doyle, "will you come listen to me practice my lines for tomorrow?"

"I will. Why don't you go on upstairs," he said, shooting me a glance over her head. "I'll be along in a minute."

Both of us waited until she'd disappeared through the doorway, then spoke at the same time.

"I don't want to intru—" I began.

"Don't worry about—"

We both stopped.

"Let me go first," he said, raising a hand when I opened my mouth to start again. "We're all happy to have you here. Bonnie wouldn't have invited you if she hadn't meant it."

"I don't know," I said ruefully. "Samantha was really the one who invited me. Bonnie couldn't very well refuse to go along with it once it was out there. This is her home. I hate to feel like I'm intruding."

"You're not intruding. We all want you here," he said. He reached for my hand, and the sudden, unexpected warmth of it startled me into stillness. It seemed to shock him, too. We stood for a long instant like that, staring at one another. My pulse beat in my throat.

The squeak of the kitchen door broke the spell, and we pulled apart as Bonnie entered the room. She didn't say anything, but there was something in her face that made me think she'd seen him holding my hand.

"If you'll both excuse me," I said over the blood pounding in my ears. "I should put these away." I held up my shopping in front of me like a shield, then turned and fled up the stairs without looking back.

I spent the next few hours in my room, making an array of sachets and feeling guilty. I'd never been the type to go with other women's men, and I had nothing but disdain for women who did, women who were willing to be someone's dirty secret. I wasn't certain what Doyle and Bonnie's relationship entailed. But it hardly mattered. They were a family in every respect that mattered, and putting myself in the middle of it could only complicate everything.

By the time I finished Bonnie's gift, I'd resolved to myself that I would do nothing further to encourage Doyle. My attraction to him was irrelevant. It wasn't something I was helpless to resist. I was too unsettled to find the focus necessary to enchant the sachets, so they remained stubbornly un-magical, but the herbs alone should make them effective enough. Perhaps I could try again later in the evening.

I went down the stairs and stopped in the kitchen to get an apron. MaryAnne was there, filling pitchers with water and beer. Bonnie flashed me a brief smile but said nothing before turning back to the pots bubbling on the stove. The dining room was already beginning to fill as I came out of the kitchen, and I was glad for the distraction. I lost myself for the next few hours, carrying plates and wiping tables and casually flirting with miners and merchants alike.

As before, I tried to keep an ear on the conversations around me, but I didn't see or hear anything that might have to do with demons—unless you counted demon rum. I suspected the men at the corner table were the disgruntled churchmen, based on the filthy looks they were shooting at Mr. Northcutt, who sat three tables away, placidly spooning up the last of his dessert.

He waved when he saw me, and I made my way over to him and thanked him for the use of his dictionary.

"Think nothing of it," he said with a gallant gesture. "If you'll save me a dance at the party tomorrow night, I'll consider the debt repaid."

"Any one you like," I said with a smile as I took his empty plate. "Just come and find me when you're ready."

The dining room emptied, finally, and I wiped the last of the tables clean and went back into the kitchen. Bonnie was counting out coins for MaryAnne. There was a quarter of a pie in a tin beside her. "Tell your parents merry Christmas from me," Bonnie said, handing the girl the tin along with the money.

The girl bobbed her head at both of us and departed.

I murmured my own goodnight to Bonnie and turned to leave.

"Joya," she said from behind me.

I turned, dreading whatever she was about to say.

"There's pie left. Share it with me? It won't keep."

There was something in her tone I couldn't identify, but it didn't seem to be anger. I sat, and she lifted a cloth off a plate to reveal another wedge of pie. She split it in two and slid half onto another dish, then scraped up a big spoonful of whipped cream from a bowl and plopped it on top before she passed it to me.

It was apple and custard, spiced with cinnamon and nutmeg and nestled into a flaky crust. I closed my eyes in bliss after the first bite and opened them to find her regarding me. "It's delicious," I said, swallowing.

"I know it is," she replied. "I'm an excellent cook."

"One of the best I've known," I said truthfully.

"Lang likes you." Her voice was steady. "And you like him."

I straightened, the bite of pie suddenly sitting like a burning coal in my stomach. "Bonnie, I'm not—"

"It's all right," she said, and there was both amusement and sadness in her voice. "He likes you. And Samantha likes you. And that's a good thing. For both of them."

"I—" I pressed my lips together. "I wasn't sure whether you and Doyle were . . ." I cast a sideways glance at her to make sure she understood what I was asking.

"No," she said. "It's never been like that with us. He loved my sister. We both did." She went quiet for a moment, lost in thought, before going on. "Samantha wasn't even a year old when Caroline died. I'd been widowed for several years by then. I had room, and he needed help. We've all been here together ever since."

"Did the two of you ever think of marrying?" I asked. "You're raising Samantha together, and you obviously care for each other. Successful marriages have grown from less."

She half smiled. "We might have, if we'd been back east, just to stop tongues wagging over us living together. But out here? No one cares, so it's never come up.

"Besides," she went on, "he's already lost one wife. I'd never want him to have to go through that again."

It was the first time I'd heard her refer, even obliquely, to her illness and to the fact that she knew how it would likely end.

"I want him—I want *them* to be happy. I love them both," she said, the utter truth of it in every line of her body as she spoke.

"They love you," I said, certain it was true. She and Doyle might not be lovers—and, oh, how that little bit of knowledge brightened something in me—but he still lived in her house, still trusted her with the raising of his child. I felt sure he would never do that if he didn't have enormous affection and respect for her. "And you're Samantha's mother, in all but name."

"I know," she said. "And I know she loves me, despite the way she's acted these last few months. She's growing up. Pulling away. And you're younger, and new, and more fun to be around. She's relaxed around you."

"I'm not the one telling her to do her chores or eat her turnips," I said with a shrug. The conversation had turned in a less uncomfortable direction, and the pie looked interesting again. I took another bite. It was still heavenly, and I finished the rest of my wedge in a few bites while I thought about mothers and daughters.

"I think," I said as I put my fork down, "that mothers aren't really women to their daughters. Maybe to their sons, either—I don't know one way or the other about that. The woman who raised me wasn't my mother. But she was, all the same," I said, thinking of Marthe. "Just like you and Samantha. And I haven't always treated her well."

That was putting it mildly. I grimaced, remembering all the grief I'd caused her when I was younger. Not to mention everything that had happened since. It was a wonder she hadn't washed her hands of me. "I suppose all that is a roundabout way of saying that part of why I like Samantha is she reminds me of myself at that age. Perhaps that makes me something of an egotist." I gave her a sardonic smile.

"Or maybe it means you're the right person for her to be around right now," Bonnie said. "You might know what she needs better than I do."

There was no way she could know how true that statement was, and I fought to keep my face neutral.

Bonnie pushed her own plate aside with a sigh. "I'd hoped for children, but none ever came, and then my husband died. When Doyle turned up on my doorstep with Samantha all those years ago—just a tiny little thing, and needing a mother so badly—it was like I'd gotten a chance after all."

I hesitated, unsure how to convey what I wanted to tell her. It was ridiculous to talk about what might happen between Doyle and me. Nothing had. It might be nothing would. I fumbled around for another moment, then sighed and looked at her. "There isn't anything—or anyone—who can take away what you are to her. I'd never try."

Bonnie glanced down as I spoke, and when she raised her head again, her eyes were, if not teary, then suspiciously shiny. "Thank you for saying that." She coughed once and straightened, the movement somehow the turning of a page. "Now, you've had a long day, and I don't want to keep you. I'm going to finish up down here, but you should go on up to bed." She reached over to pat my hand, but I turned it over and grasped hers instead, holding on until she squeezed back, then let go and left the room.

When I got upstairs, I looked at the brown paper package holding the sachets I'd made for her. They were too paltry a gift now. Too devoid of meaning after what had just happened. I was a threat that could—maybe, eventually—disrupt her family. And Bonnie had given me her blessing. Willingly. Generously.

Some impulse made me pull the mayflower charm from my neck. There was a bit of my magic inside. Bonnie wouldn't know it, but it was a tiny piece of me, of my effort and my intention and my hope for the future. I untied the string around her present and laid the pendant inside before retying the bow. It was little enough, but it felt right.

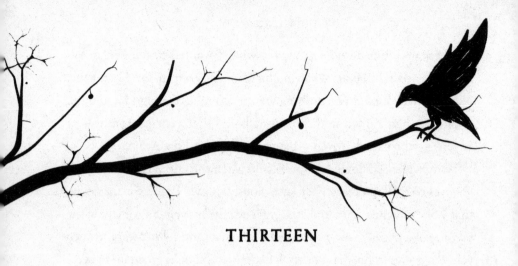

THIRTEEN

Christmas Day dawned bright and cold.

Samantha was up with the sun and all but quivering with excitement. "Can we do presents first? Please?" she asked as soon as we were downstairs. She had brought an armload of packages with her.

"It's up to your father," Bonnie said.

She turned a pleading gaze to him.

"Well now," Doyle said, attempting to sound serious, although anyone could see his amusement. "I'm pretty hungry. Maybe we should wait until after breakfast."

Samantha let out a groan and tugged on his arm. One of the presents started to slip from her grasp, and he leaned over to catch it before it hit the floor.

"All right, all right," he said, allowing his grin to spread across his face. "Can't have everything getting broken. Guess we'd better go ahead."

I went back to my room to fetch my gifts, and we gathered around the fireplace in the common room. Bonnie put on water for coffee while Samantha handed around the presents.

"Open yours first, Joya," she said, handing me two packages.

"How do I have presents?" I asked, eyeing them. "You didn't even know I was going to be here until yesterday."

I knew before I'd even gotten the smaller package open that it held the citrusy soap I'd smelled at Tuttle and Veach's the day before.

"Pa and I went back while you were upstairs," Samantha said, her eyes bright. "I could tell you liked that one best."

"Sneaky girl." I smiled at her, already suspecting what the second gift would be. Sure enough: the Braddon novel I'd been tempted to buy.

"Thank you very much," I said. "These are lovely gifts. Now mine for all of you."

Samantha went into raptures over the combs. "Oh, Joya, thank you! They're beautiful." She turned to Bonnie. "Can I wear them tonight?"

Bonnie smiled. "I'm not sure the Virgin Mary wore tortoiseshell combs. Mr. Northcutt probably wouldn't approve. But," she added when Samantha's face fell, "we can take them with us and you can wear them to the party afterward."

I gave Bonnie her present next, and her face softened when she saw the pendant. "Joya, this is lovely."

"She made it herself," Samantha said. "And the sachets, too. I helped her pick the smells for those."

Bonnie lifted them to her nose. "I love them. Thank you both."

Doyle's face went slack when he saw the knife. "This is a fine blade," he said, withdrawing it from its sheath. "The balance is perfect, too."

"It was Josiah's," I said. "There's no telling how long he's had it, but he said it had plenty more years left in it."

"I'll say it does," Doyle said. "Thank you."

Pleased with how my gifts had been received, I sat back and watched as they opened the rest. Samantha gave Bonnie the soaps, and Doyle gave her several yards of pretty, sprigged calico and a small sack of almonds in their shells. "Grown in California," he said.

For Doyle, there was a heavy sheepskin coat, well-made and warm, and two pairs of socks, which I could have guessed from the uneven stitches had been knitted by Samantha, even if she hadn't blurted the information out as soon as he opened them. Samantha got several books, a packet of hair ribbons, and a packet of maple candy "all the way from Vermont," her father told her.

After breakfast, Doyle headed over to the stables, and Samantha went with him, planning to call on her friend Ruthie Hawkins to show off her gifts. Bonnie declared that with no lunch crowd to serve, she meant to take a Christmas nap, and after reading a few chapters of my new book, I decided to follow her example. It was the sort of long, deliciously lazy day I hadn't had since leaving Boston, and I shamelessly wallowed in it.

As the shadows lengthened, I rose from my bed to get ready for the party. There were only my two drab, serviceable dresses to choose between, so once I'd washed my face, I brushed and re-pinned my hair and declared myself finished.

Samantha was downstairs, already in her costume. The blue of the robes made her eyes glow. Bonnie had curled her hair with heated tongs, and it flowed down her back in ripples like melted toffee.

She seemed unusually subdued.

"Are you nervous?" I asked.

"Not really," she said. "But Aunt Bonnie made me take a nap, and I think I slept funny—my neck is a little stiff."

The four of us walked to the Broadwell House together. The streets were full of people, not all of them headed to the pageant—Bonnie might have closed her restaurant, but it seemed every saloon in town was open, all pouring unlimited holiday cheer for anyone who had coin or gold dust to trade for it. For now, at least, the shouts and jostlings were good-natured, with none of the ugly edge that would likely come on as the hour grew later and the drinking grew heavier.

I got separated from the others when passing in front of one of the saloons, and while maneuvering through the throng, a gentle hand on my elbow stopped me. I turned. Inge stood beside me, with a man, already red-cheeked and bleary-eyed, waiting a few feet away on the sidewalk.

"Merry Christmas," she said, with a quick glance around us. "I don't want to keep you, but I saw you and wanted to say hello."

"Merry Christmas to you as well." I lowered my voice. "How are you feeling?"

"Just fine," she said, lowering hers to match. "Worked a treat—hardly anything to it."

"I'm glad to hear it." I squeezed her arm, then shifted my eyes to the man. "You're all right?"

"Better than all right," Inge said. "He's one of the good ones."

There was a gap in the scrum around us, and I caught a glimpse of Doyle on the sidewalk, his neck craned as he looked for me. Inge and her customer faded away through the crowd as I wove through the men on the sidewalk and made my way to Doyle, wondering if he would ask about her. He only gave me a small smile and offered his arm. I took it, and a minute later we reached the hotel.

The doors were thrown open, but the big interior lobby was full of people and had a roaring fire going in each of the huge hearths that bookended the space. The mantels above were decorated with sprays of holly leaves and fresh pine boughs. More evergreen garland swirled around the banister of the staircase, and a huge tree in one corner was draped with paper curls and cutouts of angels and bells. Long trestle tables were already set with plates and glassware, and the smell of cooking wafted from behind a swinging door every time someone opened it.

Doyle led me through the crush to the back room where the pageant was to be held. Bonnie had saved us seats, and we dropped into them as the children took their places on the makeshift stage.

Mr. Northcutt clapped his hands, and the room quieted. He raised his conductor's baton—*more appropriate for the venue than a buggy whip*, I thought with a suppressed smile—brought it down, and the chorus began to sing. It was beautiful. The children's high, sweet voices sang of silent nights, of midnights clear, and of the advent of the faithful, while behind them the players reenacted the Nativity. In between songs, one of the boys recited from the gospel of Luke. Samantha's pale little face with its pointed chin was poignantly beautiful as she cuddled a blanket-wrapped doll with real tenderness. The angels wore wings of paper and wire, but the lamplight hid their flimsiness and made the crushed quartz coating them glitter like tiny diamonds. It was possible to believe we were witnessing something holy.

There were more than a few teary eyes in the room by the time the Three Kings departed and the children took their bows, and even I, with my distant attachment to the Christian faith, found myself moved. I applauded til my hands were sore, along with everyone else there, then exited with the throng back into the main room of the hotel, blinking in the brighter light and louder atmosphere. I lost track of Bonnie and Doyle, and being surrounded by strangers was disorienting. I had a moment's apprehension at the idea that anyone in the room might be one of the demon summoners.

But they wouldn't come to a Christmas party, surely. They would be at a saloon somewhere or out on the prairie holding some sort of Black Mass. They weren't summoning a demon, at least—the new moon was more than two weeks away. Still, I tested myself, choosing strangers from among the crowd, studying their faces, then looking away and making sure I could still picture them. It was silly—it was not as though I could have done anything if I found one of them. I'd examined at least twenty people without finding anyone suspicious by the time Samantha found me.

"Joya! What did you think?" She was still in her robes, but now the combs I'd given her held her hair back from her face. She was flushed and breathless. One of the girls from the chorus stood behind her.

"You were wonderful," I told her, then widened my gaze to take in her friend as well. "Both of you."

"Thank you, miss," the girl said, her apple-cheeked face going pink.

Samantha reached for her hand and dragged her forward. "This is Ruthie."

"It's nice to meet you, Ruthie," I said, offering my hand.

Ruthie giggled as she took it, her touch fleeting and soft.

Samantha glanced to one side, where another pair of girls stood waiting.

"Go on, have fun with your friends," I said.

They scampered away, and the little group made a beeline for the tables, now half-bowed beneath the weight of food and drink.

I scanned the crowd again, this time looking for familiar faces. There were few enough of them, but I found Mr. Northcutt and made my way over to him.

"Bravo," I said when I reached him. "It was magnificent."

His smile was all delight. "Thank you. I thought it went rather well myself." He pulled a crisp handkerchief from his pocket and dabbed at his forehead, which was shiny in the warmth of the room. "They are a lovely group of children. I enjoyed working with them." He tucked the square of cloth away. "If you'll excuse me, I'm going to get something to eat. I've been so nervous I haven't had a thing today. And I haven't forgotten your promise—I'll be along to collect my dance later."

"I look forward to it," I said, smiling. His courtly flirtation was charming, and the fact that I was certain there was nothing in it made it easy to banter back.

Northcutt wasn't the only one who was over-warm. The room was full of bodies, and between the press of the crowd and the massive fires still burning away, I was parched. At the drinks table, there were half a dozen different ciders and punches. I couldn't hear the server's descriptions over the din of the crowd, so I pointed at something at random. It was fruity and refreshing, and I was so thirsty I drained the cup at once. The man behind the table grinned at me and refilled it. I drank half the second cup by the time I was three steps from the table.

Whatever it was, it was potent. I had never been a heavy drinker, and I'd had nothing alcoholic over the past few months and hadn't eaten in hours, to boot. Within a few minutes, my legs were tingling, and the room was all softened outlines and droning noise. It was undeniably pleasant, releasing a tension I hadn't known I'd been carrying around. I was tempted to down the rest of my cup but thought better of it, deciding I'd better eat something first.

There was a bounty spread out on the tables. Roasted chickens, sliced beef, heaps of roasted parsnips and potatoes. Fresh wheat bread, still steaming from the oven, with sweet butter and pots of jewel-bright jams. Salt-herring and pickled vegetables. Savory puddings and cheeses. Another table held nothing but desserts. Canned peaches with spiced whipped cream, fresh gingerbread, tarts filled with dried apples or mincemeat and glazed with honey.

I filled a plate, then found an empty chair along the wall between a plump, matronly-looking woman and a rangy-looking miner so sun- and weather-beaten he could have been forty or seventy. He gave me a gap-toothed grin as I sat, but it wasn't a leer, so I returned the smile and wished him a merry Christmas, then turned my attention back to the room.

Samantha was huddled with her girlfriends, their heads together, sharing a plate of sweets and giggling the way only girls can. Nearby, Ruthie's parents—the resemblance was unmistakable—stood watching them with tolerant smiles. Doyle stood talking with a group of men, his partner, Garvey, among them, though he kept a watchful eye on his daughter all the while. I didn't see Bonnie, but Mr. Veach gave me a nod when his eyes met mine, his round face shining with sweat.

Across the room, a quartet of musicians gathered and began to play. There was an accordion, a piper, and a pair of lively fiddlers. I tapped my foot beneath the hem of my dress and joined in the applause when they finished their first song. The lead fiddler called out a reel, and couples began lining up in the middle of the room. The miner beside me turned and held out a hand with a raised eyebrow. I hesitated for half an instant, then downed the last of my drink, set my plate aside, and put my hand in his. Whatever his age, he turned out to be a spry and enthusiastic dance partner. He whirled me down the line, spinning me away and back again until I was breathless and laughing.

At the end of the reel, Mr. Northcutt claimed his dance, and we galloped through a polka together. There weren't enough women present, of course, and I danced without stopping for the next two hours, with miners and farmers, with a tavern owner and a stage driver and once with Mr. Veach, who was surprisingly nimble for such an enormous man. Every one of them was a perfect gentleman. It was the most fun I'd had in months.

Finally, breathless and sweating, I begged off and made my way back to the drinks table. Feeling light and reckless, I downed another cup of punch, then spotted Bonnie, Samantha, and Doyle all standing together and made my way toward them. They turned to me as I approached.

"I'm going to take Samantha home," Bonnie was saying. "I think we've both had enough." Indeed, Samantha looked drawn and tired, with dark shadows beneath her eyes. Bonnie, too, appeared exhausted.

"I'll come, too, then," Doyle said, setting his empty plate aside.

"No, there's no reason for you to do that," she said. "We're just going to head home and go to bed."

"Are you sure?"

"Yes," she said firmly, glancing at me. "Both of you. Stay." It was a benediction, and my heart felt light as a cloud as she spoke it.

Doyle and I hugged Samantha and watched as the two of them made their way out the front of the hotel.

"Samantha is lucky to have her," I said.

"We both are," Doyle replied. "Are you having a good time?"

"A wonderful time," I said with a smile. "I love to dance."

"I could tell," he said with the sort of loose smile that owed something to the punch. "I wonder if I might have the next one, now that I've got you here?" He held out a hand, and I took it. My whole body went warm, and this time it had nothing to do with the temperature.

The current dance, another polka, ended, and the two violinists began to play a high, clear waltz.

Doyle led me back to the floor, lifting my right hand in his left. I looked up into his face, feeling the broad pressure of his other hand as it came to rest on my back, just beneath my shoulder blade. I couldn't suppress a shiver, and something darkened in his eyes as he felt it.

"I didn't know the Rangers taught their men to waltz," I said. My voice was breathless.

"I'm a man of many talents."

He swept me around the room as the strings shivered and sang. The dance went on and on, a moment suspended, out of time. Everything was a blur except his face, and I barely felt the floor beneath my feet, so conscious was I of his touch. His shoulder beneath my hand was hard with muscle and warm through the heavy cotton of his shirt. His eyes were on mine, and the desire in them was unmistakable. It was a goad to my own, and when the music ended, I pulled him by the hand—or he pulled me, I didn't know which—through the nearest doorway, not caring where it went, only seeking somewhere, anywhere, where I could have more of him.

We were in a dim hallway, then stumbled together through an unlocked door, and I caught a glimpse of a rolling chair and a desk strewn with ledgers, a manager's or bookkeeper's office, but it didn't matter because Doyle's mouth was hot on mine, and my hands were fisted in his hair. His hands roamed over my back and hips, and I cursed the cage of my corset, that I could feel their pressure but not their warm roughness.

Skin, I wanted his skin, and as his mouth left mine to blaze a fiery trail down my neck, I yanked the tail of his shirt from his trousers and ran my hands beneath it, over the smoothness of his stomach and back, and he groaned into my neck and pressed the hard length of his thigh between my legs. I leaned into it with a breathless little gasp as everything inside me went liquid with want.

I was a minute away from reaching for the buttons on his pants, two minutes away from lifting my skirts and having him right there in that office, so greedy for him I wouldn't have stopped myself even if I hadn't been out of my head with liquor.

When the voice came from the doorway, it was as shocking and unwelcome as a dash of cold water.

"Lang? Are you in he—Oh." Garvey, his voice now amused. "Ah, my apologies. I didn't know you were . . ."

We froze, and when Doyle spoke, his voice was rough. "What is it?"

I pulled away, with some difficulty, and my body cried out at the unfairness of it. If I'd had focus enough to attempt it, I might have struck Garvey down where he stood. I glanced over my shoulder at him, standing in the doorway, very intentionally looking away from us and utterly failing to hide his grin.

"I'm sorry to interrupt," he said. "But one of the miners who came in just told me he overheard someone saying he thinks he saw the Reynolds brothers out at the old Harris claim southwest of town. You know the bounty on them is up to a hundred dollars."

There was a long pause before Doyle spoke again. "All right. Give me a minute, will you?"

"Of course," Garvey said, still not looking at us. "I'll meet you at the stables. Say twenty minutes?"

"Make it thirty," Doyle said. "I'll need to walk Miss Shaw home and leave a note for Bonnie and Sam."

Garvey, who hadn't yet acknowledged me, perhaps because he was trying to do me the courtesy of pretending he hadn't just seen me in an intensely compromising position, gave me a sort of half-sideways nod, still not looking at me. "Miss," he said, then withdrew.

"Well," Doyle said when he was gone. "I, ah . . . I don't usually . . ." He flushed. "I'm—"

"Don't you dare say you're sorry," I said, then cast a quick look at him. "Unless you are, I suppose. Unless you don't want . . . this?"

"No, I do," he said quickly. "I very much do. But this isn't how I intended *this* to begin."

"I suppose," I said, "we could blame it on the punch and pretend not to remember it in the morning. We could be embarrassed and awkward around each other for a few weeks. But I'd rather not, if that's all right with you. Nothing happened here that I didn't want to happen. Except for maybe Garvey walking in." I shot him a grin. "Though that was probably for the best."

He exhaled, and the tension left his shoulders. "Probably. So when I get back, we'll start again. Without the punch."

"I look forward to it," I said, giving him a direct look.

He leaned down and kissed me again, and this time it was gentle, full of promise. Still, it was heady enough that when it ended, we both pulled away with real reluctance.

"Come on." I sighed and pulled him toward the door. "You have outlaws to catch."

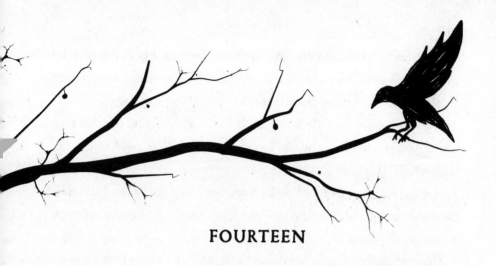

FOURTEEN

It took a long minute for my half-sleeping brain to register someone knocking—insistently—on the door to my bedroom. My head throbbed, and my mouth tasted foul. I forced my eyes open. They were gritty. The room was still dark. I couldn't have been asleep more than an hour.

"Joya, please." Bonnie's voice jolted me awake. It held a degree of barely restrained desperation. I hauled myself out of bed and stumbled to the door, shivering in the frigid air. Bonnie's house was even colder than Josiah's cabin.

Bonnie wore a heavy dressing gown over her shift, and her hair was still in its nighttime braid. Her eyes were shadowed, her forehead lined with worry.

"It's Samantha."

I didn't take the time to dress, merely yanked the heavy quilt from the bed and wrapped it around myself before following her back down the hallway to Samantha's room. Samantha lay on the bed, the coverlet and sheets fouled with vomit. She was flushed, her lips bloodless white and cracked. Her eyes were closed, and her breathing was ragged.

"I heard her cry out," Bonnie said. "I came in and found her this way. Could you stay with her while I get some water? We need to get her cleaned up."

"Of course." I perched on a clean spot on the edge of the bed while Bonnie was gone and reached for the girl's hand. "Samantha, can you hear me?"

Her eyes flickered open but didn't focus, and they drifted closed again after only a moment. I put a hand to her cheek. It was like touching the side of a stove.

"She's burning up," I said when Bonnie returned. "Have you sent for the doctor?"

"Just now," she said. "I ran next door and asked one of the neighbors to fetch him."

We peeled the soiled bedclothes back and slid Samantha's nightgown off her limp body. A red pinprick rash covered her chest and neck.

"Lang mentioned you've done some nursing," Bonnie said. "Have you seen a rash like this before? Do you know what it could be?"

I pressed it with a finger. The redness didn't fade beneath the pressure. "I don't know for certain," I said. "Lots of things cause rashes. It doesn't look anything like smallpox, at least," I said.

"Thank God for small favors."

We didn't speak as we cleaned the girl and changed her sheets. She mumbled and tried to pull away but didn't wake.

Two hours passed, and the sky outside began to lighten.

"Where in the blazes is Shaver?" Bonnie snapped, twin flags of color in her cheeks. "He should have been here by now—he lives above his clinic, and it's only two blocks over."

"Is there another doctor? I can dress and go for him."

"There's Dr. Foster, over in West Denver," Bonnie said. "But I've never trusted him. He drinks."

"What about the apothecary? He must have something for fever."

"Yes," she said, looking at the window. "It's got to be going on seven o'clock. He'll be open soon."

I rose and went to dress. I was fumbling with my buttons when there was a knock at the front door and Bonnie's hurried steps passed my room. A minute later, the sound of a man's voice on the stairs reached me, and I flung my bedroom door open as Dr. Shaver and Bonnie passed.

". . . third call I've had since midnight," he was saying. His face was tight and fatigued.

"Samantha's not the only one," Bonnie said in response to my questioning look. "Two of the other children from the pageant took sick overnight."

I followed them back to the girl's room, my gut tightening. There weren't many illnesses that could come on so fast and sicken so many. None of them were mild.

Shaver set his bag on the dresser and turned to Samantha. He placed a hand against her forehead, then felt beneath her jaw. He nudged aside the neck of her nightgown and frowned at the rash on her chest before pressing his fingers against it as I'd done earlier.

"Was she complaining of any symptoms last night? Headache? Tiredness? Anything like that?" he asked without looking at us.

"She seemed tired at the party," Bonnie said. "But I thought she'd just overexerted herself."

"She also said her neck hurt," I volunteered.

Shaver gave me a sharp glance. "When?"

"On the way to the pageant," I said. "I didn't think anything of it at the time."

The doctor pursed his lips. "The symptoms are similar in all the cases. I'm afraid it's brain fever."

I closed my eyes in horror. I'd seen cases of brain fever before. Some of them had recovered, but the ones who didn't had died gruesome deaths, their limbs turning purple and gangrenous before the poison overwhelmed their bodies. I glanced at Samantha's hands where they lay atop the blankets. So far they looked healthy, but that could change in a matter of hours.

"I'll send over some powders that might help the fever," Dr. Shaver said. "I've already given out the ones I had in my bag, so I'll need to have more made up. When they get here, give her one in a cup of water every six hours. You know how to wake her if she won't rouse?" He glanced at us, and I nodded.

"Rub the breastbone hard with the knuckles." My voice sounded hollow.

"Good." The doctor paused. "Is her father here?"

Bonnie shook her head. "He rode out after some fugitives last night. His note didn't say where."

"Southwest," I said, then frowned, trying to remember the name Garvey had mentioned. "Harris," I said after a moment. "They were heading toward the Harris claim."

"Send someone after him," Shaver said flatly, and a chill went down my spine.

Bonnie looked stricken, dropping into the chair beside Samantha's bed as if her legs would no longer support her. "It's as bad as that?" Her voice was barely a whisper.

Shaver put a hand on her arm as he lifted his bag to leave, but he didn't say anything to reassure her.

It would have been a lie.

Bonnie remained frozen for a long moment in the wake of his departure, then sprang to her feet with an air of furious resolve. "I'll go find someone to send after Lang. I'll—"

"You stay with her." I moved toward the door. "I'm already dressed. I'll go over to the Rangers' station and ask them to send someone." I wanted to stop at the apothecary as well. The doctor would send his powders, and we would give them to her, but there must be more I could do. Healing had never been my gift, but I had to try. Stars knew will and focus wouldn't be a problem. The little bit of magic I had reclaimed had to be enough.

An hour later, I was back. Bonnie had been back downstairs at some point—there was a sign on the door: CLOSED DUE TO ILLNESS. I went straight through the darkened dining room to the kitchen with my bundle.

I found a pot to make the potion and laid the herbs out on the worktable.

They hadn't been grown, harvested, dried, or stored the way I'd been taught they should. But, I reminded myself sternly, it didn't matter. All the strictures around the making of potions were ways of building belief, of reinforcing the notion that the spells involved would work. None of them, if Josiah was right, had anything to do with the magic itself. Focus, will, and power. Those were the only things that mattered.

If I allowed myself to doubt I could make a healing potion, it would undercut my will and focus, and I wouldn't be able to do it. To counteract any worries about the herbs, I'd tried to choose ingredients that had some medicinal purpose among the Mundanes. Vervain and chamomile, snakeroot and lemon balm. The apothecary, who had been hard at work mixing the powders Dr. Shaver had ordered, said they were mostly willow bark, or I would have included that as well. I also bought a vial of oil of peppermint. Mixed with cooking oil and rubbed on Samantha's feet and the back of her neck, it would help cool her fever without chilling her.

Bonnie came down while I was heating the water. "What are you doing?"

"Making a tonic," I said. "Dr. Shaver's powders are on their way, but hopefully this will do some good in the meantime. How is she?"

"The same." Bonnie wrapped her arms around herself. Her voice was tight as a bowstring. "What did they say at the Rangers' office?"

I grimaced. "They say the Harris place is close enough that if the fugitives were there, Doyle and Garvey will be back with them tonight, so there's no point sending anyone out after them." I glanced at her. "Hopefully they're right. If not, I'll go ask them again tomorrow morning."

Bonnie looked no happier with this answer than I had been when I heard it, but there was nothing we could do. She hovered as I chopped herbs for the potion. I needed her out of the way if I was going to add magic, so I hurriedly mixed the peppermint with some corn oil from the pantry and told her to rub Samantha's feet with it. "It should make her more comfortable," I said.

She left, seeming happy to have something to do, and I went back to work, steeping the herbs in hot water, stirring clockwise with a wooden spoon as I gathered my focus and called up my small store of magic. "Be healed," I chanted under my breath. "Be healed. Be healed." When I apprenticed with Giraud, I'd watched him use all sorts of complicated spells for healing various ailments, but they all meant the same thing. Like the rules around how the ingredients were grown, the words of the spell shouldn't matter as long as I believed they would work.

I forced my little bead of magic into the tincture, and for a moment there was a glowing swirl in the mixture. Two more circles with the spoon, and it faded as the power melded with the liquid. I hesitated, then, more from instinct than as part of any plan, pricked my finger with one of Bonnie's knives and added a drop of my own blood to the potion. It was my essence. My magic, poured out and given to another.

I let it cool, then strained it through a cloth into a jar and took it upstairs with me.

Samantha's room smelled heavily of peppermint. Bonnie was still beside her bed, but now she had her knitting on her lap. "I needed to keep my hands busy," she said at my glance, her tone defensive.

"I'm not criticizing. If I had something to distract me, I'd do it, too." I turned to Samantha. "I'm going to wake her to give her some of this." I held up the jar.

Bonnie nodded.

"Samantha," I said gently, "I need you to wake up." I shook her shoulder, hoping I wouldn't have to cause her pain to rouse her, but she didn't wake. With a resigned sigh, I put my fingers against her breastbone—stars, she was hot—and rubbed until she grimaced and her eyes fluttered open.

"Hurts." Her voice was a croak.

"What hurts, sweetheart?" Bonnie asked from behind my shoulder.

"Everything."

"You need to drink a little of this for me," I said. "It will help you feel better."

She was too weak to lift her head, so Bonnie had to help her as I held the jar to her lips. When she'd managed a couple of swallows, I traded the jar for a cup of plain water. "Now this."

After a few sips, she lay back, exhausted. "I want my pa."

"He's on his way," Bonnie said, trying to smile as she scraped Samantha's damp, tangled hair away from her cheek. "You rest until he gets here."

The girl's eyes drifted closed again, and Bonnie settled back into her chair. I couldn't be still and paced around the room, wondering how long it would be until I knew if the spell was working. Even Giraud's cures weren't immediate. I watched the clock for fifteen minutes, then, unable to make myself wait longer, went to the bed and put my hand to Samantha's forehead. She felt cooler, and hope leapt inside me like a startled hare.

My magic was working.

It was a temporary reprieve, however; an hour later her fever rose again. Shaver's powders arrived, and we dosed her with the first of them. It, also, worked for a time, and we alternated my remedy and his the rest of that day and throughout the night. Both of us sat up with her, bathing her with the peppermint mixture, urging her to drink. We slept, both of us, in short, anxious snatches that bore no resemblance to rest, starting guiltily awake and exchanging strained, rueful half smiles.

The doctor came again the next morning, wearing the same clothes he'd had on the day before and looking as though he hadn't stopped moving long enough to sleep in them.

"How bad is it?" I asked as I followed him up the stairs.

"Three more down overnight," he said.

"All children?"

"One parent," he replied. "So far. How are you and Bonnie faring?"

I shrugged. "We're tired, but no signs of illness."

We were nearing Samantha's room by then, and he lowered his voice and glanced back at me. "Keep an eye on Bonnie," he said. "Get her to rest if you can. The consumption makes her vulnerable. If she catches this, I don't like her chances." He didn't wait for me to reply, merely opened the door and strode through, already focused on his patient.

He examined the rash on Samantha's body, which had spread into large purple blotches, and felt her neck again. Bonnie and I waited anxiously throughout his appraisal. It was silly, really. There was nothing he could tell us we couldn't see for ourselves. Samantha was gravely ill. If she was not notably worse than the previous day, she was also no better.

Shaver tucked the coverlet around her with a gentleness at odds with his general demeanor. "Any word from her father?" he asked without looking at us.

"Not yet," I said. "I'll go to the office again today."

"I'll do it," he said. "It's on my way." His voice held no inflection, but I sagged anyway, knowing what he meant. The Rangers would be more likely to listen to him when he said they needed to fetch Doyle back here. I glanced at Bonnie. Tears stood in her eyes; she knew, too.

Our silence must have betrayed our understanding, because Shaver glanced over at us and made a visible effort to sound reassuring. "She's young and healthy. Keep bathing her and giving her the powders. The next day will decide." It was the best he could offer us.

I made another jar of healing potion. I don't know whether my increasing desperation interfered with the magic, or if Samantha's illness had simply advanced beyond my ability, but unlike the first batch, this one did nothing. I doggedly spooned it into her mouth anyway. Shaver's powders were similarly useless. She remained in a heavy, restless sleep all that day. By nightfall, her fever was so high I despaired. Bonnie and I sat, silent and frightened, beside the bed.

If I'd been alone, I would have tried another spell. But there was no way Bonnie was going to leave Samantha's side voluntarily. My chance came an hour later.

"I should get more water," Bonnie muttered, and rose. She wobbled and groped for the back of her chair as if to steady herself, but missed the handhold. She staggered and would have fallen if I hadn't made it to her in time to get a shoulder beneath her.

"Are you ill?" I tried to put my free hand to her forehead, but she brushed me away with an irritable gesture.

"I'm fine."

"You're not fine." I guided her toward the door. "You need to rest."

She tried to glare at me, but the effect was muted by the sheer exhaustion in her face and the fact that this close to her, I could hear the rasp in her chest when she breathed.

"You haven't really slept in two days," I went on. Neither of us had, and I didn't remember eating, either, but we must have. But I was younger than she was and didn't have consumption. "It doesn't do anyone any good if you get sick, too. I'm taking you to your room."

"I can't leave her," Bonnie said, trying to pull away.

I tightened my grip and hauled her along. Her room was next door to Samantha's. I nudged the door open with my toe. "I'll stay with her, I promise." I guided her to the bed.

She sat and looked up at me. "Promise me you'll come and get me if . . . if it looks as though she . . ."

"I will," I said.

"Swear it."

"On my own life."

Bonnie sagged. "All right. I'll rest. Just for a few minutes." She lay back on the bed and closed her eyes. I left her there, her breathing already deepening by the time I eased her door closed.

Back in Samantha's room, I pulled the chair so close to her bedside my knees brushed the mattress. I took her hot little hand in mine, meaning to close my eyes, slow my own breathing, and gather the focus I would need to attempt a spell. Instead, my breath hissed out as if a giant fist had crushed my lungs.

Samantha's fingertips were dark.

I lunged toward the foot of the bed, where I flung back the coverlet and tore her stockings from her feet. They were dusky and cold to the touch.

A low, keening sound filled the room, and it was a long moment before I realized I was the one making it. I went to my knees beside the bed, groping for her hand. I pressed it to my cheek and closed my eyes, my mind searching desperately for some hope to cling to.

But there was nothing. No matter how much I wanted to pretend otherwise, Samantha was dying.

I don't know how long I stayed there, furious, terrified tears leaking from my eyes, whispered words—prayers or spells, I don't know which, but they were useless either way—falling from my lips. I might have stayed there forever, except for the voice.

"Witch."

The timbre of the word was harsh and masculine, a rasp dragged along my spine.

I jerked upright.

Samantha's eyes were open. But it wasn't Samantha who was looking at me. The cast of her eyes had changed, and her expression was knowing. My breath caught in my throat as I stared at the thing looking out from her face in dawning horror.

I had been reading about demons.

And now I had met one.

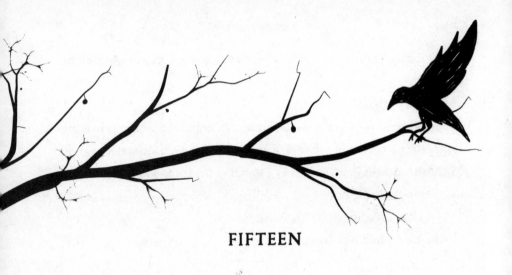

FIFTEEN

I scrambled away on legs I couldn't feel and pressed my back against the wall. My heart galloped like a stagecoach team beneath the whip, a relentless thundering that pounded against the wood behind me.

The demon drew Samantha's parched lips back in what might have been a smile. The skin of her lower lip cracked, and a bead of blood like a tiny ruby welled up. Her tongue, white-coated and dry, came out to lick it away. Her body shuddered in what looked like pleasure, but the slitted eyes never left mine.

"The child is dying."

I managed to shake my head, just an inch. It wasn't a denial of the statement but of the whole scene before me. It wasn't real. It couldn't be. It had to be a nightmare. I'd been reading the *DE VOCATIONE* every night for the last three weeks. I was exhausted. I'd fallen asleep sitting by Samantha's bedside again, and now I was dreaming. I dug my fingernails into my palms hard enough to leave little half-moon bruises, hoping to wake myself, but it was no good.

The voice coming from Samantha's body went on. "I can feel the life draining from her, even now." It paused. "When she's gone, I'll be free until sunrise."

I glanced reflexively at the window. Sunrise was hours away. The image of the Jensens' bodies strewn about their cabin flashed through my mind, and a wave of panic rolled through me. How many people were there in Denver City, and how many of them could the demon destroy before sunrise banished it? The first man who rode into town the following morning might find the sort of horror legends were made of.

I couldn't let it happen. There must be something I could do. My mind stuttered from thought to thought, a stone skipping over the surface of a pond. I had to bind it somehow. Once I'd done that, I could banish it back to its own realm. I knew the words.

It was possessing Samantha. Casting it out would be more akin to an exorcism, but surely it amounted to the same thing.

I had to get it into a circle. Everything else flowed from that.

Josiah had said it was possible to set a circle without physically drawing it. We hadn't gotten around to practicing it yet, and I didn't trust myself to be able to do it, not when the stakes were this high. But there was salt in the kitchen. I could use that, make a physical barrier and trap it that way.

My hand fumbled for the doorknob.

It saw the movement, and its voice was a whipcrack. "If you leave this room, I will tear my way free of the girl even as she lives. She will die in agony, split open like an overripe plum. And you will be next."

The threat was enough to freeze me in place.

"You cannot master me," it continued in a conversational tone. "Not as you are now." It dropped a contemptuous look at my wrist, then brought Samantha's eyes back up to meet mine.

There was a long beat as it looked at me. The expression on her face was expectant. The silence stretched.

Understanding came slowly. "If—" My throat was so dry the word emerged as a strangled croak. I coughed and tried again. "If I can't stop you, then why have you revealed yourself to me at all? What do you want?"

It smiled again, lazily this time. "You."

My heart tried to squeeze its way out of my mouth. I swallowed it back down. "What does that mean?"

"I like walking beneath the sunlight. Once this body is dead, I can take another from among the townspeople. And I will if I must. But I want yours."

"Why?" The word was more mouthed than spoken, but the demon understood.

Its eyes—Samantha's eyes, but somehow not—narrowed. "I took the child because I could feel the power waiting within her. But now I do not need to wait. I know what you are. I knew as soon as I saw you, as soon as I felt the binding that holds you. And I tasted your magic—your true magic—when you put it in the potion you fed the child."

My blood. A demon had tasted my blood. I couldn't suppress a shudder.

"I want it," the demon went on. "And I will have it. Allow me to possess you, fully and willingly."

"What difference does it make if I'm willing?"

It sighed. "Fighting you for control of your magic will be tedious."

It was like a hammer blow to my stomach. My power. Once it had me, it would break off the binding. With my full abilities at its disposal, there was no telling what sort of havoc it could wreak. Until the Magisterium caught up with me. It. Us.

I swallowed against the sudden choking feeling in my throat. "No."

It sighed. "I do not believe you understand the reality you face. You cannot stop me. I will take you either way. If you agree, however, there are things I can give you in return."

It didn't matter. I wasn't going to agree. But the longer I kept it talking, the closer we got to sunrise. "What things?"

"Most humans go mad eventually. If you agree, I can preserve your sanity while I possess you—allow you to keep the core of your personality. Someday, when I have tired of you, I might see fit to release you." It paused, as if gauging my interest. Seeing that its offer hadn't moved me, it threw out another lure. "And the child need not die. If you agree, I will heal her."

It felt as if every drop of blood in my veins froze in an instant. I could fight the demon. But there was confidence in its voice; it believed it could take me. If agreeing meant it would heal Samantha . . . I bit the inside of my cheek. It was a demon. It dealt in trickery and false hope. "Why should I believe you?"

"If we enter into a bargain, I must keep to it or be banished. As must you, else you forfeit your soul."

That was what the *DE VOCATIONE* said—that demons could not betray a bargain, once it was made. But they were slippery, alert to the details not spelled out, always looking for a way to uphold the letter of the agreement while getting what they wanted. I would have to make certain I didn't leave it any cracks to wriggle through.

I went cold to my core as I heard my own thought. Stars help me, I was truly considering it. I must be mad already. I thought of the stories, of the screams from behind locked doors and the witches who'd never been seen again. Of the Jensens and the Union patrol. What if it used me to do such things? It said it could preserve my sanity, but could anything save my mind from seeing things like that happen—not merely seeing them, but knowing it was my power being used to do it? Would I have to watch, like a fly trapped behind glass, as the demon—

My mind caught on the image, and I fought to keep my face from revealing the sudden glimmer of hope that appeared, like a faint star peeking through the clouds on an overcast night.

There might be a way. A way to save Samantha and banish the demon before it could harm anyone—even me. I needed to contain the demon. I knew a spell that could do it. I didn't have an engraved bowl, but maybe I didn't need one. Hadn't Josiah just spent a month telling me that all magical items were merely ideas made solid? Nothing more than aids to focus? I could be the vessel. I could trap the demon within me, then banish it.

It could work. It had to work. And even if it didn't, I had to try it. The alternatives were unthinkable.

It felt like a year since I had drawn a breath. I made myself inhale slowly. Once. Twice.

"Let us discuss the terms," I said, hardly able to believe what I was about to attempt. I cursed myself for not reading that section of the *DE VOCATIONE* more carefully.

A wheezing laugh came from Samantha's mouth. "I already gave you my terms. You let me take you, willingly. The child lives, and you keep your sanity."

"What about Samantha's sanity? Is she . . ." The question was too terrible to finish.

"I have made no real use of her thus far. Her mind remains unbroken."

"It's not enough," I said, trying not to let my voice waver. "I have other questions. I want answers to them before I agree."

It laughed, seeming genuinely amused. "Oh, how I do enjoy humans. You think to outwit me. Very well. Let us bargain."

"These are my terms," I said, trying not to let its confidence shake me. "You will heal the child before you leave her. You won't hurt her—or use me to hurt her. Ever. You will answer my questions fully and truthfully."

It narrowed Samantha's eyes, but her hands clutched at the blanket covering her and betrayed its excitement. "Do you think me a fool? You will not catch me out with such a simple trick. You will ask questions until the sun rises and I am trapped, and then you will put a circle around me and attempt to banish me."

"You would kill the child if I did that," I said, trying to sound reasonable. I clasped my hands together to stop them shaking.

"I would," it said. "But it would not be the first time I have seen a human make such a sacrifice." It tugged up a corner of her mouth in a knowing smirk. "Canny of you to try. Three questions, no more. And not until after you have agreed to the bargain."

I felt as if I were preparing to step over the edge of a waterfall. In fact, this was far more dangerous. A waterfall could only kill me. My heartbeat was so loud in my ears I could barely hear the words as I spoke them. "You heal the child. You fully and truthfully answer three questions. After you have done those things, I will not resist your attempt to possess me."

The smile on Samantha's face became a rictus. "Done. The bargain is sealed."

There was a vibration in the air around me, as if distant thunder boomed below the level of my hearing.

Samantha's eyes closed, and her lips began to move.

I stepped forward. "What are you doing?"

"Healing her," it said, without opening her eyes. "Be quiet, witch." The muttering resumed, the words too low for me to make out.

There was a drawing sensation in the air around me, a draft I felt not on my skin but beneath it. The power had that taint to it, the faintest tinge of rot, and I wrinkled my nose. But even as I did so, Samantha's breathing eased. Her face, which had been as pale as the pillowcase beneath the flush of fever, evened to a healthy pink. I took another step forward and put my hand to her forehead. Cool.

When the demon opened her eyes again, they were clear, no longer sunken. The dark half-moons beneath them faded with the next breath.

"She will sleep until morning," it said. "And she will be weak when she wakes. But the sickness is gone. Ask your questions."

It had done it. It had healed her. And now I would have to live up to my end of the agreement. I swallowed hard, fighting a nearly overwhelming urge to flee the room. But if I did that, I'd be forsworn. It would take me. I took another breath, steadying myself.

All right.

Three questions. I hadn't had time to think what they should be.

"Were you—" I stopped. I'd been about to ask the demon if it had been in the bowl I'd found in the storeroom. But that wasn't a useful question. I was certain it had been. Something else, then. I wanted to know how long it had been inside Samantha and how it had come to be there, but those were also wasteful questions. I could guess the answers. Samantha had somehow stumbled across the bowl. She dropped it, it cracked, the demon was released, and it had taken up residence in her body. Whether it had tricked her into agreeing or overpowered her, it hardly mattered. Even if my guesses weren't entirely correct, such details were irrelevant. I had to ask questions that could get me what I needed.

But first, I needed to find out if the hazy plan I was holding in reserve could work. If it couldn't, none of the other questions mattered.

I thought for a long moment.

"You will not wriggle free of the bargain by delaying," the demon said in a warning tone. "If the sun rises before our bargain is met, you are forsworn, and your body and soul belong to me."

"I'm not delaying," I snapped. "I'm thinking."

"Think more quickly. I grow impatient."

"I want to know how the possession works," I said after another moment.

"That is not a question," it replied.

I drew a breath, then forced myself to slow down before responding. If I said "Will you tell me how possession works?" it could answer "No," and there would be nothing I could do. I could not afford to be thoughtless.

I thought back to what I'd read in *DE VOCATIONE*.

I formed the question and thought through it several times, looking for traps. When I was satisfied, I spoke. "Once a demon has possessed a physical being or been bound inside an object," I began, "what happens to its corporeal form, and how does it interact with the outside world?"

"An excellent question," it said. "Asked as one who has studied the ways of my kind. You may be an even better choice of host than I thought, if you already have some useful knowledge."

"Now you're the one who is delaying. You must answer me, truthfully."

It raised Samantha's hand in a calming gesture.

"I will," it said. "And because I want our partnership to be a fruitful one, I will do so even though you have posed what are really several questions as one." It gave me a knowing look, like a teacher who wants a student to know their transgression has been noticed but will be allowed, this time.

I didn't let myself react.

"Demons do not have a defined corporeal self in your world. We can take any shape we please, or none at all. When we have possessed a living being, we take no shape, as a rule, but usually remain in what you might call our spirit form, though that is not quite a correct construction."

"But you threatened to tear Samantha's body open to leave it." I was careful to phrase it as a statement.

"Indeed. And I could adopt a form that would allow me to hurt a body I possessed in a thousand ways, if I chose." Its words were pointed; I suppressed a shiver. It wasn't talking about Samantha. It was a warning to me. "But damaging a host serves no purpose. Remaining in my spirit form is the best way to preserve the physical body. As for being bound to objects," it went on, "that is a different matter. There is no corporeal being in that case. A demon bound to an object is in a state of suspension. It has no interaction with the outside world."

I swallowed. It was useful knowledge, but also frightening. If I failed to trap the demon, it could hurt me. Would hurt me. But I couldn't worry about that. I would simply have to succeed.

I took a moment to steady myself and frame my next question.

"What is the name by which a human may summon and banish you?"

It hesitated, and hope jolted through me, hot and jagged as a lightning bolt. If it refused to answer, it was forsworn, and according to *DE VOCATIONE*, it would be drawn at once back to its own realm.

But it was not to be.

"My summoning name is Zalgammon." The words came like a too-full bucket drawn from a deep well, hauled out an inch at a time. The demon's gaze bored into me, in it a promise of pain. "One question remains to you. Ask it, and let us be done."

I had what I needed to trap and banish the demon. I could use the last question for something else.

"What are the names of the people in the Colorado Territory who are summoning demons?"

"I do not know," it said promptly.

I had no time to feel disappointed.

"That was the last of your questions," Zalgammon said almost gleefully. "It is time to complete our bargain."

Terror flooded my body. "How?" My voice was thready.

"I will leave the child's body now. If you attempt to move against me, you will be forsworn. I will—"

"Kill us both, I know," I said, my voice made sharp by fear.

"No," Zalgammon said. "I will kill the girl. You, I will leave alive. I will take you with me back to my realm and keep you as a plaything for the next thousand years. I do not think you would enjoy it. But I would." It studied me and seemed to decide I was adequately cowed by the threat.

Samantha's eyes closed, and her body exhaled. I felt that breeze waft over me again, fetid and sour. The girl's body lay perfectly still. She did not inhale, and my own breath froze in my lungs. She was dead. She was—

Her chest lifted. Once. Twice.

I sagged in relief.

"Joya."

Every hair on my body stood. The voice had come from behind me.

Full of dread, I turned, the way you turn in a nightmare, slowly, not wanting to move, terrified to behold whatever is waiting for you and yet having no choice.

My knees nearly gave out. Standing behind me was . . . me. It was like looking into a mirror, and the vertigo of it twisted my insides. Another thought struck me: if demons could so perfectly mimic a human form, then I could never again be certain I wasn't talking to one. I would go mad. Anyone could be—But no. Even as the horror of that idea washed over me, I realized it wasn't so. The wrongness, the ugly, sickening taint of the demon was palpable. It could look like a human, but it could not hide what it was, not fully.

I straightened. "What happens now?" I asked, proud my voice didn't waver. Much.

"There is a knife beneath the child's mattress."

I frowned, then stepped backward toward the bed and slid my hand gingerly between the mattress and the wooden platform. I found a rounded handle and pulled the knife free.

"This is one of Bonnie's kitchen knives," I said, chilled. "Why did you take it? What were you going to make her do?"

Zalgammon shrugged. "It is no matter now."

I swallowed against a surge of nauseated horror. It could have made Samantha hurt herself. It could have made her kill Bonnie or Doyle in their sleep. Its destruction would have been limited only by the strength of Samantha's body.

"I need your blood for the ritual. And it must be willingly given."

"Did Samantha give you hers when you possessed her?" I couldn't imagine it.

"I took the child unknowing." The demon curled its facsimile of my face into a smile. "Our bond will be all the greater, since you have acquiesced."

Again, my stomach threatened to revolt. "How much do you need?"

"Not much. A cut on your finger will do."

Before I could think better of it, I drew the edge of the blade across the pad of my left thumb. Bright blood welled.

Zalgammon inhaled, raising its head as if catching a tantalizing scent on the air. "Give it to me."

I reached out, and it caught my hand and guided it to its mouth. Its tongue swept across the cut, rough as a cat's, and its eyes—mine, but not mine—closed as an obscene look of languor spread over its face. My face.

I still held the knife in my other hand, and the urge to use it, to drive it into the gut of this foul thing wearing my face, was almost overwhelming. I knew what would happen if I did. I knew my body and soul would be forfeit. I knew Samantha would die, and still my right hand twitched with the need to try.

The demon began to chant.

It wasn't Latin. It wasn't any language I had ever heard. It scraped against the inside of my head like fingernails against a slate, sending a chill down my spine and thickening in my throat until I gagged on the wrongness of it.

It was happening. I closed my eyes and tried to shut out the words, the feel of its hand holding mine. I reached, carefully, so carefully, for my magic, and drew into me the tiny amount I was capable of holding. It was a drop of liquid gold, a bead of molten potential, one that could be forged into any shape I needed, if only I had will and focus enough.

The hand holding mine abruptly vanished, and I felt the demon enter my body. It was painful the way putting your hand into too-hot water is painful—icy cold for an instant before your nerves recognize the sensation of scalding.

Panic swelled, and I fought desperately to hold on to the magic as it tried to slip away. If I lost it, I would not get it back. I would fail, and I would belong to the demon for as long as it cared to have me. I had to cast the binding spell now, or it would be too late.

I squeezed the cut on my thumb. The blood welled again, and the pain focused me. I drew the rune from the bottom of the bowl on the palm of my uninjured hand, the strokes certain after so many nights of staring at it. My body was the vessel, my skin its edges. I sent the tiny drop of magic to trace my outline, visualizing myself as whole, uninterrupted. The split skin over my thumb knit itself back together as the magic rolled over it, and I suppressed a gasp.

Zalgammon's voice, when it came again, was its own, but came from inside my mind.

The words it spoke meant nothing to me, but the magic in them was undeniable. It crept along the crevices of my brain. It flowed out to the rest of my body along with my blood, building in force and intensity with every inch gained.

I could not speak the binding spell aloud. But I did not have to.

Per verbo et per sacramento ligeris, I thought. By word and power be you bound.

Zalgammon's voice spoke again, in eerie counterpoint to my own.

Per sanguine et per magiaque ligeris. By blood and magic be you bound.

In hoc aeno ligeris. Be you bound within this vessel.

Usque aenum . . . Until this vessel . . . I hesitated, stumbling over the last word, the one missing from the bowl. I pictured the list of possibilities I'd written. I had to choose one, but what if it was wrong? The demon's spell was peaking. I could feel it, settling into me. No time. I snatched at a word.

Destructum est, I breathed, and the spell snapped into being an instant before Zalgammon's spell did the same.

The demon screamed, and a billion stars exploded inside my head.

SIXTEEN

What did you do? Zalgammon's voice was a whiplash inside my head. "I bound you," I said aloud, my voice thick and shaking. I was on my hands and knees, though I didn't remember falling. The grain of the wood floor wavered in front of my eyes.

That is not possible, it snarled.

Claws raked the inside of my body, and I cried out and collapsed all the way onto the hard planks. Gasping, I rolled onto my side and looked down at my abdomen, expecting to see my entrails spilling from bloody rents in my clothing.

But there was nothing.

The demon shrieked, and there was fury and disbelief in the sound. I thought my head would split wide open, and I clapped my hands to my ears as if that would block out the noise. It raked at me again, but this time I knew it was only pain, not injury, and somehow that made it less. It couldn't actually hurt me.

You said you would not resist me. You are forsworn. Its voice was choked with rage.

"I am not forsworn," I said, hoping it was true. "I said I wouldn't resist your spell, and I didn't. I merely did my own spell at the same time."

You are forsworn, it said again, its voice shaking. *You are mine, body and soul, and for your insolence, I will make you suffer as no human has ever suffered before.* There was a twisting sensation, and the world doubled and faded for an instant before swimming back into existence.

No, Zalgammon said, as if in disbelief. The twist came again, more powerful this time, but again I came back to myself.

"I'm not forsworn, and you can't take me anywhere." Giddy relief washed through me. I had no idea what authority determined whether you'd broken your bargain with a demon, but apparently it had decided in my favor.

Something writhed in my head. The demon, rummaging, feeling the contours of the spell I'd wrought. *It was a binding spell*, Zalgammon said, sounding more shocked than angry. *You made yourself the vessel. How did you do that?*

A little worm of unease wriggled through my gut. Why could I still hear it talking? Wasn't it supposed to be asleep, the way it said it was while it was in the bowl?

"It doesn't matter," I said as I pushed myself carefully to my feet, not sure if I was answering its question or my own. "I bound you, and now I'm going to banish you."

No! The raking came again, along with the feeling of the demon throwing itself against the confines of my body. I grunted and staggered from side to side with the force of it. A bowl wasn't alive. It had no senses. Maybe that was why this was different.

"It won't work. You can't stop me." I picked up Bonnie's knife from where I had dropped it and made my way gingerly into the hallway and down the stairs.

Witch, I will destroy you. You will never be safe from me. The next time I am freed, I will find you, I swear it.

I did my best to ignore the threats. There were protective charms against demons. I would make one. I would make ten, if I had to, and wear them all every day of my life. I would jingle with charms like a fortune teller. Anything to never encounter a demon again.

In the kitchen, I lit the lamp with a trembling hand and found the salt cellar. I'd managed to trap the demon without a circle before, but there was no point in taking chances. I wanted a physical barrier before I tried to banish it. If it somehow got loose—the thought made my insides feel as though they were shriveling—it would be trapped inside the circle. It might kill me—*or worse*, I thought—but it wouldn't be able to hurt anyone else. Sunrise would see it gone.

I knelt and poured a ring of salt around me. Maybe, I thought as Zalgammon continued to rage within me, I'd start sleeping inside one of these. Just to be safe. I gasped out a laugh, imagining Josiah's face.

I was aware that I'd gone a little giddy, but my relief and elation were too great to contain. I'd outwitted a demon. I'd managed to trap it with less magic than I'd have used to warm my coffee cup three months before. It turned out there was no better teacher than desperation. Wait until I told Josiah. And Marthe. They would be . . .

On second thought, maybe I wouldn't tell them.

I knelt in the center of the circle and took several deep breaths, trying to calm myself. The next part should be simple. Demons did not belong in this realm. Their own always sought to draw them back.

Zalgammon knew what was coming. It stalked around inside my body like a tiger in a too-small cage.

All I had to do was say the ritual three times, then breach the vessel containing the demon. I took up the knife again. Another small cut on my finger would be enough.

"Zalgammon, I banish thee," I said. "I banish thee, Zalgammon, back to thine own realm. Zalgammon, walk no more upon this earth."

There was a tugging sensation inside me. I repeated the words, and the pulling grew stronger. By the time I neared the end of the third repetition, it was all I could do to take a full breath. "Walk no more upon this earth," I said from between clenched teeth. I ran the knife across the tip of my finger.

A tidal wave of pain slammed through me. Every muscle tried to tear itself from my bones as my bones tried to wrench themselves from my body as my marrow boiled within them. Every nerve and sinew felt limned with fire.

I cried out and pitched forward, dropping the knife, slamming my hands into the floor, and only barely managing not to fall across the salt circle and break it. I retched and writhed, groaning, curling in on myself, feeling Zalgammon doing the same inside me. Endless seconds crawled past as I waited to feel the demon drawn out of me, waited for it to be gone.

Finally, finally, the pain began to ebb.

Zalgammon was still there.

"It didn't work," I panted. I was covered in sweat, and my entire body felt like one enormous cramp. "It should have worked. I should be free."

But I wasn't.

"Why didn't it work?"

I do not know, said Zalgammon, sounding as wracked and exhausted as I felt.

I lay on the floor for several minutes, until I'd caught my breath, then hauled myself to my knees and reached for the knife, grimly readying myself to try again.

No, Zalgammon said.

It wasn't the word that stopped me. It was the faint note of pleading in it, along with the fact that I didn't especially want to go through that again, either. "I have to. You'll try to hurt me if I don't."

I felt its slight hesitation.

I offer a truce. Until the next sunset. I will make no attempt to hurt you as long as you do not do . . . that . . . again.

"No hurt to me or anyone else."

Agreed, it said quickly.

I slumped back to the floor, relieved. My finger was still bleeding. If I hadn't been so utterly drained, I might have tried calling up another bit of power and willing my skin whole as I had earlier—that was a useful bit of magic. As it was, I winced and reached for the shelf where Bonnie kept the rags for mopping up kitchen spills. I tore a strip from the most tattered of them and bound it around my finger, then sat inside the circle until I thought my legs would be able to hold me again.

I cleaned up the salt, then trudged up the stairs. Samantha was sleeping peacefully, her forehead still cool. Whatever else I had failed at that night, I had saved her, and that was worth being proud of. I thought of waking Bonnie, then decided against it. Let her sleep. There would be time enough to celebrate in the morning.

I went to my room and bathed the sweat from my body with the last bit of water in my pitcher, then climbed into my bed. Every inch of me ached.

"A truce for tonight," I said to the darkness. "But you cannot stay. I don't want you."

Want has nothing to do with it, witch. You are mine, and I will have what I bargained for.

There was no heat in the words, but no doubt, either.

I fell asleep, eventually, somehow.

⁌—⁍

When I woke, I didn't get even a moment to hope it had all been a dream. The demon spoke before I'd even opened my eyes.

Awake, finally. You mortals have so few hours, and you waste so many of them.

I stopped myself from replying. I wasn't going to converse with it. I was going to spend the day making a plan for being rid of it, and as soon as the sun went down and our truce ended, I would banish it. Successfully, this time.

I dressed and went to Samantha's room, expecting to find Bonnie with her, but the child was alone. Asleep. She woke when I touched her forehead.

"Joya." Her voice was weak, but her eyes were clear.

"Good morning," I said. "How are you feeling?"

"Better. Thirsty."

"I'll get you some water," I said. "And maybe something to eat?"

"Oatcakes? With jam?"

"I'll make them myself," I said with a wink.

Her mouth turned up at the corners. "Maybe just some toast, then."

I laughed and put a hand on her shoulder. "You have no idea how glad I am that you're better. I'll be back soon."

"Where's Aunt Bonnie?" she asked.

"Downstairs, probably," I said. "I'm sure she wanted to let you sleep. I'll send her up."

Leaving her, I hurried down to the kitchen. The room was dark and the stove cold. Something turned over in my stomach. Bonnie had been exhausted, but for her to still be in bed was unprecedented. She must be ill. I climbed the stairs again and rapped on her bedroom door. "Bonnie? Are you well?"

There was no answer. I hesitated, then twisted the knob. Unlocked, thank the stars.

The curtains were drawn, and the bed was deep in shadow. Bonnie lay on her back, her face gray and wasted. I couldn't see her chest moving, and I crossed to her bedside in one long, horrified bound.

Hardly breathing myself, I put a hand to her cheek, expecting to feel the chill of death, and almost screamed when she let out a ragged gasp and her eyes flickered open. She blinked at me, and her mouth moved, but no words emerged. One of her hands half lifted from the bed and fluttered for a moment before falling back to the sheet. Her movement was enough to shift the neck of her nightdress and expose the amulet I'd given her for Christmas lying below the hollow of her throat. The flower design I'd carved into it was almost illegible, the extra strokes barely noticeable beside the lines of the protection rune, which were now scorched and black.

<hr/>

"It's not the same thing the children have," Dr. Shaver said, standing in the hallway outside Bonnie's room. "Or if it is, it's showing up in a damned strange way, if you'll pardon my saying so. There's no fever, no swelling of the glands, no stiffness in the limbs or neck. It looks more like a case of exhaustion—perhaps from wearing herself out taking care of Samantha."

"So she'll recover?" I stood across from him with my arms wrapped around myself as if trying to hold my own body together.

The doctor sighed, then lowered his voice. "I don't know. She wasn't strong to begin with. And now it's as if something has drawn the life from her."

I pressed my lips together and didn't reply. That was exactly what had happened. I'd realized it while sitting beside Bonnie's bed and staring at the amulet as I waited for him to arrive. But it wasn't as though I could tell him so.

I followed him to Samantha's room, where he confirmed something else I'd already known: the girl was recovering.

"Keep her in bed for a few more days," he said as we left her room. "Make sure she gets plenty of water. Feed her things that are easy to digest. Now that she's on the other side of it, she should be fine."

"And Bonnie?"

Dr. Shaver's face sobered. "Help her eat and drink, if she can and wants to. Try to keep her comfortable and warm. I'll stop back by when I can, but there's nothing I can do for her, and I might be able to do some good for the others."

In my worry over Samantha and now Bonnie, I hadn't even thought to ask after the rest of the people who had fallen ill after the party. "How are your other patients?"

He shook his head. "I'm doing all I can," he said. "But I don't think they're all going to make it. Ruthie Hawkins is hanging on by a thread."

My chest tightened. Samantha's friend. I thought of them giggling, their heads pressed together. "Please give her family my best," I said.

"I will," he said. "And it will give them hope to hear Samantha is recovering. You and Bonnie deserve credit for your nursing."

The praise felt worse than a lashing would have, and it was all I could do to manage a tight smile as I bade him farewell.

When he'd gone, I dropped into a chair in the empty dining room and put my head in my hands, remembering the way the demon's power had felt as it brushed past me the previous night, the moment before it had healed Samantha.

"You stole the life from Bonnie to heal Samantha," I said.

Where else was I to get the power? Its tone was appallingly matter-of-fact.

My stomach curdled. "That's where demons' magic comes from? Stealing the life force from the people around them?" I expected it would refuse to answer, but it surprised me.

When we are in this realm, yes.

"If she hadn't happened to be wearing that charm I made her, would you have killed her last night?" I tried to keep my voice level, to act as if this were a casual conversation and not a matter of intense interest to me. It was answering questions—volunteering information, even—and anything I could glean might be useful.

Of course. I did not know at the time what stopped me. The charm was well-made, it went on. *I am pleased to know that even in your weakened state, your skills are well honed. You will be an even more useful host than I realized.*

The pleasure and confidence in its tone was chilling, and its casual admission that it would have killed her left me breathless.

"I'm not going to be your host," I said, barely able to choke the words out through my horror. "As soon as the sun goes down and our truce ends, I'm going to banish you. I don't care how painful it is."

Why?

"Why?" I repeated, incredulous. "What you did . . . It's grotesque."

The child will live when she would have died. I have watched the woman these past months. She loves the child. She is as a mother to her. She would willingly die to save her.

"Perhaps," I said. "Probably, even. But it doesn't matter. There is a difference between willingly giving one's life to save another and having it taken for the same purpose."

How is it different? If the end result would have been the same, why does it matter how it came about?

"I'm not going to debate moral philosophy with you," I snapped. "It matters." I glared at nothing for a long moment, then sat back in the chair as another thought struck me. "You would have taken the last of Bonnie's life force if you could have. But you healed Samantha with what you got. What would have happened to the rest?"

I would have kept it. Used it to fuel other spells. It spoke as if the answer were obvious, as if I were stupid for asking. There was a definite edge of complaint in its voice as it went on. *As it was, I used everything I took from her to heal the child.*

"You're powerless?"

I would not say that. It stretched within me, and I felt the sensation of claws resting against my flesh, as if readying themselves to split me open from the inside.

I tensed. "You swore not to cause me hurt."

And I have not, it said.

The "but I could" was implied, and I changed the subject hastily.

"Will Bonnie recover?"

I do not know, it said, in a tone that indicated it also did not much care. *I have never been stopped on the brink of taking a life before.*

I was trying to formulate a response when Doyle burst in through the front door, his saddlebags over his shoulder and his face frantic with worry and red from the cold.

"Joya," he said when he saw me. "There was a message for me at the Rangers' station. Samantha. Is she—"

"The fever broke last night," I said. "Dr. Shaver was just here. He says she'll make a full recovery."

He sagged in obvious relief, then straightened, his face going cautious as he noticed my own expression. "What?"

"It's Bonnie. She's . . . ill."

He grimaced and allowed his bags to slide to the floor. "It's bad?"

My throat tightened, and I nodded. Tears pricked at my eyes, and I turned away, embarrassed by them. I despised people who made a show of how deeply affected they were by tragedies that barely touched them. I didn't know Bonnie well enough to claim such grief. But exhaustion, fear, and guilt were all working on me, and my guard was weak.

Doyle didn't seem to find my display of emotion off-putting. He crossed the floor and wrapped his arms around me. He radiated cold, and he stank of horse, and sweat, and several days' travel, but the hard solidity of him felt wonderful, and I let myself lean into him as the tightness in my chest eased.

He held me for a long moment, and as the seconds ticked past, what had started as comfort began to turn into something else. The memory of his mouth on mine at the Christmas party intruded, and a jagged thrum of arousal streaked through me.

Mmm, now this is interesting, Zalgammon said, and I felt it shift restlessly within me.

I jerked away from Doyle, aghast.

"Joya?" he said.

"You should go upstairs," I choked out, my face lava-hot. "Samantha was asking for you. And you'll want to look in on Bonnie."

"You're right." He stepped back, and I fled to the safety of the kitchen as he mounted the stairs.

Behind the closed door, I put my hands on my cheeks. "You felt that," I said.

I did, Zalgammon replied. *You want him.*

"I—"

I have never been inside a human while they rutted before, it went on in a musing tone.

"Well, I'm not about to volunteer to change that for you," I hissed, careful even in my outrage not to raise my voice. All I needed was to be discovered talking to myself.

It sighed. *How prudish of you. If you had not bound me, I would have relieved you of such inhibitions. You would be writhing on the floor beneath him even now.*

A bucket of ice water could not have dampened my interest any more thoroughly. "Do not speak to me of such things," I said, disgusted. Deliberately, I made plates for Doyle and Samantha. The last of the bread, some cheese, and a pair of wizened apples from the storeroom. I filled cups with water, then added a third for Bonnie.

I carried it all upstairs.

Doyle sat beside Samantha's bed, holding her hand. She already looked stronger, sitting propped up in bed, her face alight.

"Joya, look who's here," she said.

"I know," I replied, keeping my attention on her. "I brought you both something to eat."

I left the tray with them and took the extra cup of water to Bonnie's room, pausing outside her door to settle myself before going in. She was asleep, her breathing harsh and irregular. Her eyes were dark-shadowed and sunken. She woke, a little, when I put a hand to her shoulder. "Bonnie, you need to drink." I put a hand beneath her head and helped her sit up—in truth, I lifted her from the pillow; she could not manage it on her own—and held the cup to her lips. She spilled as much as she drank, and the neck of her nightdress was soaked by the time I eased her back down. I hoped at least some of the water had made it into her.

Bonnie looked up at me. "Sa . . . man . . . tha?" Each syllable was less a whisper than a pant, the effort of shaping the word all at once too much.

"She's going to be fine," I said around a lump in my throat. "And Doyle's back. He's in with her now. He'll come see you soon."

She let out a sigh and closed her eyes, the corners of her mouth fluttering up into a faint smile before going slack again as she lapsed back into unconsciousness. Tears burned my eyelids again as I looked at her. Zalgammon was right that she would have been willing to give her life for Samantha's. The desperate way she'd forced out the question and the tiny flicker of a smile at my response would have convinced me, even if I hadn't already known it. But she hadn't made the choice. The demon had. And, even if it had been unwittingly, I had helped it.

⚬━⚬

I had to get away. I left the house with no real destination in mind. The sky was low and gray, the air frigid. I pulled my coat tighter around me. I'd been cloistered in the house for days, and the noise and activity in the streets was disorienting. It seemed wrong, somehow, that these people had been going about their normal routines while Samantha fought for her life and Bonnie nearly lost hers. I found myself vaguely angry with all of them.

I trudged along the freezing sidewalk, my head down, and passed the apothecary shop just as the door swung open. Mr. Hawkins emerged, a paper packet in his hand and a tight expression on his face. He checked when he saw me.

"Miss Shaw." He tried to smile, but it was a weak and watery effort. "I hear Samantha is better. I'm glad of it."

"We are too. How is Ruthie?"

The smile died. "As sick as I've ever seen anyone be," he said, then visibly rallied himself. "But the doctor says Samantha was sicker, and she recovered, so we have hope."

My heart clenched. "You're in my prayers," I managed.

"Thank you. I need to get home," he said, lifting the packet slightly. "More medicine."

More useless medicine. I stood on the sidewalk, watching as he hurried away, then pushed open the door to the apothecary shop. I could make more of the tonic I'd given Samantha. It might help.

It will not be enough, Zalgammon said.

I froze. How had it known what I intended? I fought down the desire to scream.

Zalgammon, I thought deliberately. *Can you hear me?*

Yes, it replied at once.

A wave of panic washed through me, strong enough to make my knees go weak. I reached out and gripped one of the shelves for support. The apothecary was at my side in an instant.

"Miss Shaw, are you ill?"

"No," I managed. "It was only a moment's dizziness. I'm fine," I said, forcing my lips to spread in an expression that had to be more rictus than smile.

"If you're certain," he said doubtfully.

"I am. I just stopped in for more ingredients for the tonic. I thought I'd make a batch for some of the others who are ill."

"Of course. I think I remember everything you bought before. Why don't you sit while I get it all together for you?"

I let him lead me to a chair and sat while he bustled around the shop.

Can you hear everything I think?

No, it said. *Only the thoughts you form clearly or direct to me.*

I almost sobbed in relief.

Human minds are too much of a jumble, it went on. *Trying to listen to them is like trying to pick one voice from a chorus. I get fleeting impressions and the occasional word, but usually not more than that.*

How did you know I intended to make more tonic for Ruthie?

It scoffed. *What else would you be doing?*

I had a moment's relief, quickly squashed as it went on. *But your magic is not strong enough to save her.*

You don't know that.

I do. I know what it took to heal Samantha. You do not have the power. A beat. *But you could.*

My chest was so tight it was a good thing I didn't have to speak.

At what price?

You already know.

No.

You will let the child die instead?

I am not letting her die, I replied. *I am doing what I can for her.*

But it is not everything you could do.

I will not let you make me a murderer.

I would let you choose who I take, it said.

I shuddered. *That doesn't make it better.*

"Miss Shaw?"

I started, having been so intent on the conversation that I hadn't noticed the apothecary's approach. He held a packet out to me. "This should be everything."

"Thank you." I stood and reached for the bundle. "I'm afraid I didn't bring any money with me. I can come back—"

"Don't give it a thought," he said. "I trust you for it."

I left with the packet under my arm and walked back to the house. My stomach was tight. With fear of seeing Doyle and the demon's reaction, of attempting to banish it again, with worry for Ruthie, with the poorly suppressed suspicion it was right, that I couldn't heal her.

Doyle was in the dining room when I returned, eating a plate of hot-cakes smothered in butter and berry syrup. They smelled divine.

"Samantha asked for them," he said when he saw me looking. "There are plenty more, if you want." He gestured to another plate, covered with a cloth.

I was about to say I wasn't hungry when my stomach betrayed me, letting out a growl so loud I clapped a hand over it, embarrassed.

Doyle grinned, and my stomach fluttered again, this time not with hunger.

Zalgammon noticed. *Are you certain you will not—*

Yes. I'm certain.

Pity, it said, then sighed. *It would be especially interesting to experience in the body of a young-bearer.*

I blinked. *A young-bearer? Does that mean you're a . . . male?* I'd had no sense of gender from the demon before now.

More or less. Demons do not fall so neatly into human categories, but there are those of us who bear young and those who do not. I do not.

I was trying to decide if I wanted to know more about demon repro-duction when Doyle interrupted. "Joya?"

I blinked. He was looking at me with a quizzical expression. "Sorry," I said. "Woolgathering. Hotcakes sound wonderful."

He passed me the covered plate. There were four perfect brown cakes on it.

"You don't want any more of these?" I asked.

"I'd be embarrassed for you to know how many I already ate," he said. "Go ahead."

I polished them off, then pushed the plate away with a sigh. "You cooked, so I suppose I should do the dishes."

"No," he said. "I make a mess when I cook, so I'll do them. Besides, I know you've been up day and night looking after Samantha and Bonnie while I was gone. You must be exhausted."

"If you're expecting me to insist," I said, "you're about to be disappointed."

"Not at all." His face was serious. "I can't thank you enough. I hate that I wasn't here. Dishes are the least I can do."

"Then I'm happy to let you do them." I lifted my packet from the apothecary. "If I won't be in your way, I'm going to make up some tonic for Ruthie while you're working."

"Of course," he said.

He finished before I did and went up to check on Bonnie and Samantha. As soon as he left, I called up my magic and stirred it—what there was of it—into the potion, knowing, even as I did, that Zalgammon was likely right. It was not going to be enough. I poured the finished tonic into a jar and capped it. I would take it to Ruthie's family in the morning. Tonight would be better, but there wasn't time. It was nearly sunset. The bargain I had struck with the demon would be ended, and it—he—would be free to act. I needed to be inside a circle before that happened. I found another jar and filled it with salt. With Doyle in the house, I'd have to do the banishing spell in my own room. I put the jar in my pocket, took a knife from the drawer, and hurried up the stairs as the evening shadows gathered.

An hour later, I lay sprawled on the floor of my room, the door locked, a thick circle of salt spread around me on the floor. I was covered in sweat and trying not to whimper from the pain as my muscles twitched and spasmed.

You cannot banish me, Zalgammon sounded as wracked as I felt.

He was right, and the knowledge made me frantic with terror. Our bargain was ended, and only the fact that he was inside a circle stopped him from reaching out and taking the life of anyone he pleased. And since I was in the circle with him, there was nothing at all to stop him from hurting me until I gave in and let him out.

I had to force him into a new bargain, and I could think of only one way to do it. Unless he was playacting for some reason I couldn't guess, trying to banish Zalgammon hurt him as much as it did me—maybe even more.

"I'm going to keep trying," I said aloud, forcing myself to my knees as if preparing to start the ritual again. I wanted to sob at the thought, but I made my voice hard and hoped he was too distracted by the threat to feel my reluctance. "As many times as it takes. I will be rid of you."

Why? It hurts you to try, just as it hurts me. And it does not work.

There was a hint of desperation in his voice.

"If I don't banish you, you'll kill people," I said. "I can't let you do that." I reached for the knife and drew a breath.

I offer a new bargain, Zalgammon said quickly.

Suppressing a throb of relief, I made a show of pulling my hand back. "What bargain?"

You will not attempt to banish me again.

"No," I said at once, proud that my voice was steady. "That could leave you within me for the rest of my life. I will not agree to that."

Then swear you will make no further attempt for a year and a day.

My heart pounded. Longer than I would like, but tolerable. And it might take that long for me to figure out how to be rid of him, anyway.

"And in exchange you will agree that for as long as you reside within me, you will cause no harm and take no lives."

He laughed, a harsh, abrasive sound that scraped against the inside of my head. *And if you cannot separate yourself from me, I am to remain powerless forever? No. To this I will agree, and no more: for a year and a day, I will cause no harm, nor take any life where your will forbids it.*

It was not exactly the bargain I'd offered, but it was good enough. "I agree."

Then it is done.

Sagging, I sat back on my heels, then reached out and broke the salt circle. I would sweep it up in the morning. Exhausted, I climbed into bed, unable to stop my relief from showing. It was no matter. Zalgammon had made the deal and would have to live with it. I knew he could feel my satisfaction, and I half expected him to be angry. Instead, as I sank toward sleep, I caught a faint, disquieting echo of his own feelings. It felt, I thought vaguely, strangely like triumph.

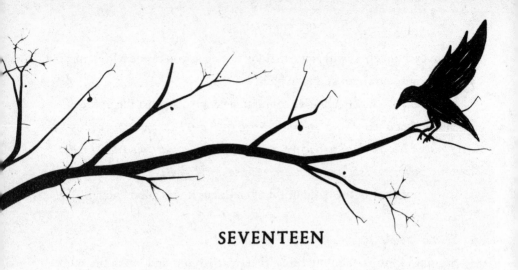

SEVENTEEN

I never got the chance to find out if the tonic would have done Ruthie any good. She died in the night.

We got word the following morning, and my guilt would have undone me, had there been any room in the house for such self-indulgence in the face of Samantha's grief. She sobbed so hard at the loss of her friend we feared she would make herself ill again. She begged to attend the funeral, and it would have taken a harder heart than Doyle's to deny her the opportunity to say goodbye.

And so it was that two days later, he carried her in his arms to the Church of St. John in the Wilderness, a tiny frame building with a sagging canvas ceiling on the corner of 14th and Arapaho Streets.

Ruthie's funeral would normally have been held at home, but the day before, her young brothers, both of them, had fallen ill.

They weighed heavy on my mind as I followed Doyle and Samantha into the church, wearing a black armband and holding my breath as I stepped across the threshold. It didn't look like a particularly sacred space, but even so, the idea of entering it with a demon inside me was enough to make my palms sweat.

Nothing happened. There was no dramatic crack of lightning. No ringing voice denying me entrance. I took my place in the pew, relief and vague disappointment now included in the chaotic swirl of emotions I'd been feeling ever since hearing Ruthie had died.

The little church was near full when we arrived, and it was only a few minutes before the minister, a thin, balding man wearing a worn cassock, stepped up to the pulpit.

"O God, whose beloved Son took children into his arms and blessed them: give us grace to entrust Ruth to your never-failing care and love," he began.

Zalgammon snorted. *What a tortured comparison.*

I gritted my teeth.

"And bring us all to your heavenly kingdom, through Jesus Christ our Lord, who lives and reigns with you and the Holy Spirit, now and forever. Amen."

Well, I suppose it is good she is dead so soon, then, since this life is such a burden and that is where you all want to go anyway. The contempt in the demon's voice was palpable.

The minister went on, speaking about a merciful God and a plan beyond mortal understanding. He read from the Bible, some verse about how the souls of the righteous were in the hands of God. There was a hymn, then more talk of the glorious eternal life Ruthie had been so blessed as to enter and how she slept now in the bosom of the Lord.

Zalgammon interspersed his acid commentary throughout, and at times it was hard to tell where his thoughts ended and my own began. There were witches who practiced versions of the Christian faith—Unitarians and Quakers, mostly—but I wasn't one of them. I didn't know what I believed happened after we died, whether we went to Heaven, or to the Summerland, or were reborn into new bodies, or merely rotted in the earth. But I didn't—couldn't—find any comfort in the notion that Ruthie's early, pointless death was somehow a beautiful gift.

When the rest of the congregation bowed their heads for a prayer, I glanced at Samantha, sitting between Doyle and me, tears streaming down her cheeks. Doyle held her hand so tightly I wondered that he did not crush it, and I knew he was thinking of how close he had come to sitting through a service like this for her.

I looked across the aisle at Ruthie's mother. She was pale and dry-eyed, wearing a hollow expression that made me think the doctor had dosed her with something to help her get through this excruciating day.

"Amen," the minister intoned as the prayer came to an end.

"Amen," the congregation repeated, raising their heads.

Four men rose and lifted the small wooden coffin from its plinth. They carried it down the aisle. Samantha let out a sob as it passed us, and the sound of it twisted something inside me.

I could have saved her, I thought.

You could have saved her, came Zalgammon's voice, hard on the heels of my own thought. He went on. *Sleeping in the bosom of the Lord? What pablum. She could have been sleeping in her own bed. Would have been, but for your stubbornness and timidity. Tell me there is no one in this town who deserves to live less than that child? You could have saved her, and this was the choice you made?*

The words were a goad and a torment. I could not argue with them, but neither could I bear to admit he was right.

Be silent, I all but snarled. *I swear, if you say another word, I'll find a way to hurt you.*

The demon must have heard the sincerity in my tone, because he fell quiet, though I could still feel his contempt.

We rose and trailed behind the coffin out of the church. Doyle decreed it was too cold for Samantha to attend the burial, and she was exhausted enough not to fight him. He took her home, and I followed the little procession to the graveyard on my own, my mind dull and twisted.

For all that Denver City was a young town, it had a well-populated graveyard. At least a hundred mounds dotted the acre of ground inside the plank fence, most of them covered in bent, brown grass. There were a few carved granite headstones, with names and dates and poetic sentiments. More were marked with chunks of rough stone, the resting places of those too poor or too poorly regarded to warrant the extravagance of identification. The three newest, all in a row, drew my eye. They were so small, no larger than the gaping hole beside them waiting for Ruthie.

The coffin bearers set their burden on the ground beside the open grave. I hadn't thought about it until that moment, but the fact of the yawning hole struck me with a tiny, discordant note of relief. The ground hadn't been too hard to dig. Ruthie's body wouldn't sit frozen in some storehouse until spring. The funeral wouldn't remain unfinished, a thing to be dreaded throughout the rest of the long, gray winter.

Once we were gathered, the minister began another reading. When Mrs. Hawkins began a low keening, he stuttered over a word, then pressed on, raising his voice. Mr. Hawkins hugged his wife harder into his side, but it was no good. The protective fog of whatever sedative she'd been given had burned off, and her grief broke through.

"My girl. My baby girl." She let out a low, ragged cry and fell to her knees beside the grave, covering her face with her hands. Her body heaved with sobs. Her husband tried to lift her to her feet, but she tore away from him and flung herself on the coffin with a scream. "Ruthie! No! Nooooo," she wailed. "Oh God, please take me too, I can't bear it."

My throat was tight with horror and sympathy.

The minister, somehow still talking, gestured to another man, who stepped forward to help Mr. Hawkins restrain his wife. Her nails scraped across the wooden lid as they pulled her away from Ruthie's coffin.

Together, they got her to her feet and held her back as the box was lowered into the earth.

"In the sure and certain hope of the resurrection to eternal life through our Lord Jesus Christ," the minister intoned, his voice raised to be heard over Mrs. Hawkins's sobs, "we commend to Almighty God our sister Ruth, and we commit her body to the ground. Earth to earth, ashes to ashes, dust to dust."

He nodded to Mr. Hawkins, who, still holding his wife, somehow managed to bend enough to scoop up a clump of dirt. He edged forward to toss it into the grave. The other mourners lined up to follow.

The hollow thumps as the clods hit the wood below were nauseating, audible even over Mrs. Hawkins's cries. I tried to shut it all out, tried to listen to the minister's words, to find some comfort in them, but there was nothing.

"The Lord bless her and keep her, the Lord make his face to shine upon her and be gracious to her, the Lord lift up his countenance upon her and give her peace. Amen."

Zalgammon did not speak again, but as I stepped forward to drop my own cold chunk of earth into the grave, it was not the minister's words that rang in my head, but the demon's.

You could have saved her. This was the choice you made.

⊶

Zalgammon was quiet the rest of the day. If I had been thinking clearly, I would have realized it was because the demon could feel the decision I was sliding toward and knew speaking might turn me from my course.

But I was not thinking clearly. I was hardly thinking at all. I lay on my bed in my darkened room, hearing, over and over, the sob Samantha let out as her friend's body was carried past her. Hearing Mrs. Hawkins's screams and the sound of her fingernails on Ruthie's coffin as she tried to cling to the last remnant of her daughter. Imagining her having to endure it all again when the boys died, as they would, today or tomorrow or the day after that.

Unless I saved them.

And I could save them. If I were willing to take a life to do it.

I had no right. I knew it, had learned it the way one learns a mathematical equation without ever bothering to examine the why of it. I knew, but I couldn't remember why it mattered, not with the sound of the mother's grief echoing in my head.

With the choice laid out before me now, it seemed obvious: some lives were more valuable than others. The ministers and philosophers might disagree, but their view rarely meant much in the raw, messy reality of the world. Generals sacrificed soldiers to hold ground. Captains decided who got seats in the lifeboats and who went down with the ship.

Most people never faced such choices. They didn't have the power, so they never had to decide.

But I did. I could choose who lived and who died. And because I could choose, I had to. Refusing to act was a choice with its own consequences. I'd gone down that path when I'd chosen not to save Ruthie, and now I would live with that failure forever.

Could I bear to do it again?

There were men in Denver City who were running from terrible acts committed back east. Men who would kill for the gold dust in someone's pockets, or out of drunken rage, or for the sheer thrill of it. They did not deserve to live more than those little boys did. No one could argue otherwise.

And so, sometime during the afternoon, without fully acknowledging I was doing it, I decided.

I waited until well after dark, until the house was quiet and the lamps doused, then put on my coat, crept down the stairs, and left by the back door. I had no precise destination in mind, no real plan, but I found myself turning down the rougher streets, the ones with more saloons and fewer houses. I'd decided I was willing to take a life to save a life, but some part of me knew it would be easier to actually do if I was defending myself. And so I walked the streets of Denver City, waiting for someone to attack me.

Perversely, no one did.

I walked until I was half-frozen and entirely frustrated, then turned and headed toward the largest concentration of saloons in town. I paused outside the Cibola Saloon, then pushed the door open and stepped inside, the relative warmth making me all the more aware of how cold I'd gotten.

It was too much to hope Seb and Johnny, the pair of men who'd attacked me on my previous visit to town, would be there, too much to hope the only two men I knew for certain were not worth the breath they drew would be sitting at the bar, already drunk and feeling vengeful.

I was right.

They were not at the bar, but at a table in the back. And they hadn't been there long enough to be drunk, though they had an unlabeled bottle of amber liquid and a pair of empty glasses sitting between them. Their bruises had healed, but Seb's arm was still splinted and bound. I suspected that wouldn't stop them from doing something foolish.

There were only a few other women in the place, all obviously prostitutes. My presence as a "respectable" woman was beginning to draw attention. Best to move things along.

I walked past Seb and Johnny's table, pretending not to notice when Seb half choked on his drink and nudged Johnny, his eyes wide. I lingered for a minute more, as if looking for someone, then made my way back to the door. I had to rebuff several offers on the way, and as I walked outside and tucked myself into the alleyway beside the building, I hoped none of the strangers would be the ones to follow me. I was in luck. The door opened not half a minute later, and Seb and Johnny appeared. A strange, cold pleasure washed through me as they squinted out into the dark, their faces alight with savage intent.

"Hello, gentlemen," I said.

Seb started, but recovered quickly, turning in the direction of my voice. "You caused us some trouble, you uppity little whore. Gonna take it out of your hide."

"You don't want to do that," I said. My voice, even to my own ears, was flat and cold.

"Don't want to do that," Seb repeated, mocking. "What I want, bitch, is you on your back, fucked bloody. And when we're both done with you, I'm going to give you a hurt to match every one that bastard of a Ranger gave us. Break your arm. Knock out a few teeth. See what else we can come up with." Confident, he was already fumbling at his belt as he strode toward me.

I let Johnny get a hand on my chest, let him push me back against the wall, before I spoke. "Take him."

Zalgammon's presence swelled in my head. *With pleasure.*

Nothing happened. I felt the demon's surprise, his frustration.

"What's happening?" I asked, startled into asking the question aloud.

"What's happening, bitch, is that I'm going to—" Johnny's hand slid up from my chest to close around my throat, and as his skin touched mine, Zalgammon's confusion became exultation.

The drawing sensation began, though this time, instead of whispering over my skin, it surged beneath it. It was thick and heady, overripe fruit with an edge of rot, sweetness and decay. I gagged as Johnny's eyes bulged and the energy flowed into me, and the demon groaned with something too like ecstasy.

Seb, seeing that something was wrong, tried to pull his friend away, and without ever forming a conscious intent to do it, I yanked off my glove, reached up a hand, and clamped it around his wrist. That was enough for the demon to take him, too.

I might have been able to stop it, but I didn't even try.

Eager, avid, Zalgammon drank them both in like mother's milk, stripping away their lives until their hearts stuttered and their breathing stopped. I felt it when the last of their life force guttered like the flame of a candle when the wax drowns it, narrowing and attenuating until there was nothing but a tiny filament left, then gone with barely a wisp of smoke to mark the passage.

They fell away from me and crumpled to the ground, empty shells.

I swallowed against a surge of nausea and averted my eyes from what the demon had done—from what I had done—but even if I could have, I would not have taken it back. They had not been good men. I would spend their lives better than they would have.

"Is it enough?" I said, hearing my own voice as if from a great distance. "Is this enough power to save all the children who are still sick?"

"Enough and more," Zalgammon said, sounding dazed and sated.

I left the bodies lying in the alley and didn't look back.

EIGHTEEN

It would be too strange for me to visit all those who were ill—I didn't even know most of them. Zalgammon assured me he could put the healing spell into my tonic, much as I had my own power.

I sent a message to Dr. Shaver at sunup and set about brewing a new batch, this time infused with demon magic. The process was not much different. A gathering of power, a few words to shape it, then an exercise of will to push it into the simmering liquid and set it there. It made me queasy for a moment, and a faint stench lingered in the air when I was finished, but it dissipated after a few minutes.

Will this help Bonnie, too, if I give some of it to her?

Zalgammon paused before replying, as if having to consider the question. *It will cure her consumption, but that is of little matter now. The spell will not restore her life force to her. That is not a sickness that can be healed.*

Why? I asked. *She is missing life force. The magic in the tonic is made of life force. Why can't it replace what she lost?*

That is not how it works, Zalgammon replied.

It wasn't much of an answer, but no matter how I pushed him, he would not—or could not—give me a better one. Regardless, curing Bonnie's consumption could only help her, so I poured off a dose of the tonic into a cup when it was finished.

Is this enough? I asked.

It is. For all the good it will do her, the demon added.

I ignored him, and as soon as it was cool enough to drink, I took it upstairs and gave it to her. She fell asleep again as soon as the cup was empty, and though I watched her sleep for a time, there was no sign of the sort of dramatic improvement I'd seen from Samantha. Dr. Shaver arrived midmorning. The strain of the last week had worn on him. He looked older than he had at the Christmas party, which felt like it had happened a lifetime before. I offered him a cup of coffee—Doyle had brewed it before he left, so it was palatable—and he accepted with pleasure.

"How many are still ill?" I asked as he drank.

"Six," he said with a sigh. "Three of those will recover, I think. They're not as sick as Ruthie was. Or Samantha."

Is there enough to cure them all? I asked Zalgammon.

Yes. For those not as ill, a partial dose will do.

"I've made more of the tonic I gave Samantha," I said aloud, indicating the four jars lined up on the table. "It seemed to help her. I made some for Ruthie, but she never got to take it. I thought it might help the others."

"I'm sure the families will be glad to have it," he said. "There's little enough I can offer them. And it very well could be whatever is in that tonic was the thing that made the difference for Samantha."

It was, but I could hardly tell him the secret ingredient was demon magic made of stolen life force. Instead, I forced a smile and told him to split one jar among the three he thought would recover anyway and give the rest to those who were sicker. I made him promise to go to the Hawkins family first, then sent him on his way.

When he was gone, I wandered aimlessly around the house, wiping a table here, straightening a chair there. There was nothing in particular I needed to do, and I felt strange: restless and jumpy. One emotion I would have expected, however, was not present. I had killed two men the night before. I should have felt guilt.

Instead, killing Seb and Johnny felt like the memory of a bad dream—unpleasant, but not the soul-wracking experience I would have expected. It came to mind, but I was not dwelling on it. I did not feel burdened. Two bad men had died; six innocent children would live. I knew the saying about good intentions and the road to Hell, but any way I looked at the choice I'd made, it felt justified. Surely, by some measure that made me a bad person. It had to. But then, what would it have made me if I'd let the children die, knowing I could have saved them? If I was damned either way, better damned for saving them than for not.

I made lunch for Samantha and Bonnie, who managed to sit up to eat a few bites. I carried the tray back to the kitchen, optimism blooming in my chest.

Zalgammon couldn't help himself. *It will not matter.*

His certainty was annoying. *You don't know that*, I said.

I know what my magic is and is not capable of doing.

Oh really? You couldn't take those men last night until they were touching me. You didn't expect that. And don't try to deny it. I felt how surprised you were.

That is true, he replied after a moment, his words stilted.

It was not much of a concession, but I still felt as though I'd won something.

"How much of them is left?" I set the lunch tray on the counter.

Zalgammon knew what I meant. *A fair amount.*

"Enough for more healing spells?" I thought of the other consumptives in town. Maybe I could help them as well.

Healing spells, he said. *Or others.*

I frowned. "What others?"

Thousands of others, Zalgammon replied. *Millions. Demon magic can do anything your magic can and more. We have been making and storing spells for eons. We have forgotten more magic than witches have ever known.*

The thought of such a store of magic touched off a powerful yearning in me. New spells. Knowledge no other witch had. And a way around the binding without taking it off.

It would be almost as if you did not have that thing on your wrist, Zalgammon said, and the fact that his words so closely echoed my own thoughts brought me up short.

"You want me to do demon magic."

You have already done demon magic, he said.

"You want me to do more. Why?"

Why not? he replied. *You have the power now. Why not use it?*

"No," I said. "You will not convince me that way. Why do you want me to do more spells?"

There was a long pause, and he sounded frustrated when he replied. *Before you were bound, did you like using your magic? Did you enjoy being a witch?*

"Yes," I said slowly. Having magic, having the ability to alter the world at my fingertips . . . it was glorious. I had not realized how glorious until it was gone.

And being bound? How does that feel?

"Like a death. Like part of me has been stolen," I said.

And the bit of magic you have been able to recapture. Is it enough?

"No," I said after a moment. It was true, and there was no point in pretending otherwise. Having any part of my magic back was an enormous relief, but it was not the same thing as being unbound. I missed the thoughtless ease of my magic before, though I accepted that Josiah was correct about my need for greater control.

It is no different for me, Zalgammon said. *We are both of us creatures of power. I refrained from using my power while I possessed the child—I dared not risk damaging her before she came into her magic. And now I am bound within you and cannot use it against your will.*

There was both resentment and wistfulness in his voice, and despite myself, I felt a pang of sympathy, followed by irritation. He was a demon, for stars' sake; he did not deserve sympathy.

There is much I could teach you. And you want to know more about the men who summoned me.

I straightened. "You said you didn't know who they were. Did you lie?"

I did not. You asked for their names, he said. *I do not know them. But that does not mean there is nothing more I can tell you.*

"And you will only tell me if I agree to do spells for you." It wasn't a question.

I have been generous with answers to questions up until now, he said, and there was a haughtiness to the response. *I see no reason to continue without payment.*

I thought for a long moment. There was something unnerving about the idea of agreeing to do more demon magic. But if he knew more about the men who'd summoned him, it might be worth it.

"I choose the spells. One per day," I said. "And you truthfully answer all my questions."

At least one new spell each day, he countered. *And there are some things—information about demons and our society—that I am forbidden to share. If your questions touch on that knowledge, I will not answer them.*

"But you will not lie to me or pretend information is forbidden when it is not," I said.

He didn't hesitate. *I agree.*

I paused. Negotiating with Zalgammon felt like playing the children's game where you race while carrying an egg in a spoon, but with far more terrifying consequences for a moment's inattention. "Our earlier agreement remains intact, as well," I said. "You cannot harm anyone or take a life against my will. None of the spells may do so, either. And when you run out of power, this part of our agreement is at an end. You cannot require me to kill anyone else to keep it going."

Done, he said. *What sort of spell would you like to learn first?*

"I have already learned a spell today," I said.

The healing spell was before our agreement. It does not count.

I hesitated. "What about a cleaning spell?" The kitchen wasn't filthy, by any means, but both Doyle and I had been using it, and though we tidied up behind ourselves, it was no longer the pristine room it had been when Bonnie was in charge.

Dull, Zalgammon said, *but very well. Attend.* He led me through the spell, and within moments, the kitchen gleamed as if freshly scrubbed. Again, using the power left me feeling faintly ill, but it passed quickly. It was not so different from using my own magic, aside from that. But there was one crucial difference: the binding on my wrist did not react to Zalgammon's magic, though I was the one using it. It was not so surprising. Its makers had no reason to include a block on the use of demon magic—if they'd even had any idea how to do such a thing, which was doubtful.

"Now, my questions," I said. "What do you remember of being summoned?"

There were two circles, he said. *An outer and an inner. I could hear men chanting, but I could not see them.*

"They wore the Broken Eye charm," I said.

The scowl was in his voice when he went on. *Be damned to whichever of my kin gave that to them.*

"Could you see anything?"

Their leader. He stood with the sacrifice in the space between the inner and outer circle.

"What did he look like?" I asked. It had to have been Broaderick, but best to confirm it.

A dirty, bearded human male, Zalgammon said, sounding impatient. *I did not concern myself with the details. He bargained with me, offering the sacrifice in exchange for a gift of power.*

"Who was the sacrifice?" I interrupted. I would rather not have known. All I could do was torture myself with the knowledge. But Broaderick had recorded the details of the sacrifices in his almanac, and they were seared into my memory. It would tell me exactly when Zalgammon had been summoned.

One of the native men, he said. *Young. Already injured. There was not much left of him.*

I shuddered. That meant Zalgammon had been the second demon Broaderick summoned. "And what did you give him in exchange?"

The ability to hide himself from the sight of other humans.

My jaw dropped. "You can do that? Give someone an ability? One they can use without your aid?"

It is not permanent. I gifted him a portion of the power I gained from the sacrifice, the demon said. *He will have it for as long as the magic lasts. How long that is will depend on how much he uses it.*

Perhaps that was how he'd escaped after Doyle and Garvey caught him. I frowned, wondering how they'd managed to do that, since he had magic at his disposal. But he'd been injured. Maybe that had prevented him from using it against them. They'd been lucky.

I bit my lip. "What happened next?"

We agreed to the bargain.

"What was it, exactly?"

That I would gift him the power and harm no one there except the sacrifice. I agreed. He and the men holding the inner circle stepped back, then dropped it.

I deliberately did not ask about the details of what I knew had happened next. "How did you wind up trapped in the bowl?"

The bowl was beside the sacrifice, full of its blood. After I drew the life force from the sacrifice, I reached for it. There was a hint of defensiveness in the demon's voice as he went on. *Blood is not my preferred sustenance, but there was no point in wasting it. The vessel was bespelled. I fought, but the enchantment was too strong. It pulled me in and trapped me.* Zalgammon's voice hardened. *If I see the man again who did it, I will make him pay for that trick.*

"Not without my permission, you won't," I said, and the demon's fury and indignation seared my insides. "But it seems we have a mutual enemy," I continued, as if I hadn't felt it. "His name is Marcus Broaderick. Perhaps there is something we can do about him."

You offer a bargain?

"Only the potential for one," I said. "But for now, I have another question. How long had you been inside Samantha when you revealed yourself to me?"

I was some three months inside the child, he said.

Zalgammon couldn't have been the demon who killed the Jensens. I'd thought it unlikely, but knowing it sent a faint rush of relief through me. It was nonsensical—I would be a fool to believe he was not capable of doing such a thing. But knowing I was not bound to the demon who was responsible for the carnage I'd seen was a comfort. Small as it was, I would take it.

⚬━⚬

Bonnie grew steadily stronger over the next few days, then plateaued. She could venture downstairs for short stretches, and she joined us for meals. But she tired easily, and there was no question of reopening the restaurant. "I have a little money put by," she said, determinedly cheerful. "There's no hurry."

I worried about what she would do over the longer term, if, as Zalgammon claimed, she was as well as she was going to get, but there was nothing I could do about it.

Samantha was almost fully recovered, though she was different than she had been before. Her grief over Ruthie's death was sincere and piercing, but that wasn't the only change. She seemed to have reverted to a younger, milder form of herself. She was clingier with her father, softer and more loving toward Bonnie. They both remarked on it, putting it down to the toll her illness had taken. For myself, I was inclined to think Zalgammon had influenced her more than he'd realized, and the absence of a demonic presence had let her naturally sweeter temperament show again.

A week passed, and the other children recovered, thankfully not instantly or all at the same rate. Demons, it seemed, like witches, had a hard-earned understanding of the importance of keeping themselves hidden. It was generally agreed that while my tonic might have done some good, it was no miracle cure. Prayer and Dr. Shaver were given most of the credit, and I was happy enough to let that judgment stand.

The threat of illness had kept the town's schools closed after the holidays. They opened again, and either Doyle or I saw Samantha off every morning, heavily bundled against the January wind.

The three weeks' stay I'd mentioned to Josiah was coming to an end. Every day, I thought about going back to the farm, and every day, I put the decision off. On my twenty-third day in town, I was in my bedroom just after sundown. Something rapped at the shutter of my window, and I nearly jumped out of my skin. Cautiously, I eased it open, then yelped when a glossy black blur swooped through the opening.

I reached for my power, misjudging the draw and singeing my wrist. Peter landed on the bed, cawing at me.

"Stars, you scared me," I said. I let go of the spell and gingerly rubbed the skin beneath the bangle.

He croaked in response, looking not at all regretful.

"What are you doing here?"

Peter flapped his wings, lifting himself a few inches from the bed before settling again and dipping his beak toward his leg. There was a small strip of paper tied there. I reached forward and carefully worked the knot free.

The note was characteristically brief.

Joya—Expected you back by now. Please send word with Peter. Will come to get you if need be. Josiah

What will you tell him? Zalgammon asked, sounding interested. *The truth*, I thought back, not wanting to speak in front of Peter. *Just not all of it.*

I penned my response on the other side of the paper.

Josiah—Sickness in town. I am well. Samantha recovering, Bonnie still ill. Staying a while longer to help. Don't come.

I considered for a moment, then erased the last line. Telling him not to come would bring him faster. *Will return soon*, I wrote instead. I added my name at the bottom, tied the message back to Peter's leg, and watched as he flew away.

I was only delaying the inevitable. The thought of it left a cramp in my gut. I'd had no idea Samantha had a demon inside her before Zalgammon had revealed himself to me, but the idea of trying to hide such a thing from a witch as canny as Josiah made me feel as though a hand were squeezing the breath from my lungs. But there must be a way. I couldn't avoid Josiah forever.

On the other hand, going back to the farm would let me avoid Doyle, which was becoming increasingly awkward. Once or twice over the preceding days he'd looked as though he were going to say something personal, and once, he got as far as saying my name in the tone of a man who is determined to make some sort of declaration. I had hurriedly exclaimed about a forgotten task and left the room before he could get out another word.

After a few such interactions, he subsided, apparently concluding I had changed my mind about our encounter at Christmas. I let him think so, though every time he was near me, my lower body tightened with the memory of his mouth on mine.

Zalgammon was certainly aware my feelings hadn't changed. He commented at such length and in such florid detail that I walked around much of the time with a face as red as a poppy—another physical reaction of mine he seemed to find entertaining.

At any rate, Doyle began staying out of the house as much as possible, which meant I only had to hide my use of demon magic from Bonnie, who napped most afternoons and went to bed early.

Despite Zalgammon's constant offers of ever more potent spells, I chose cautiously. I used demon magic to dry a load of damp wood. To remove weevils from a sack of flour. To mend a dress of Samantha's that ripped in the wash. Even doing only minor spells, however, I was growing more deft at using the demon's magic, and the taint of it bothered me less.

That isn't to say there were no effects. I fell asleep easily at night but dreamed strange dreams, intense and fragmented.

I stood on the prairie outside of town beneath a star-strewn sky and lobbed spells hot and jagged as lightning bolts. I called small animals to me, foxes and mice, and once a cat that wove a sinuous path from one of the town's outbuildings, and flayed them with a flick of the wrist, before burning the corpses. I crept into a strange bedroom and watched a man as he slept and whispered words I couldn't hear, words that made him cry out as his face clenched in pain. I wandered the darkened streets of Denver City, seeing them as through a heavy veil, and found a man alone, drunk and half-frozen against an alley wall. I drew the life from him with shuddering pleasure and left his body where it lay.

Each morning when I woke in my bed, I recalled the dreams with disgust but no great alarm. They were less disturbing than my old nightmare, on the whole, and they faded by the time the breakfast dishes were done. I regarded them as nothing more than flashes of Zalgammon's desires, his darker yearnings. The things he wished he could persuade me to do if only I would agree. Unpleasant, but of no great import.

I believed it, or wished to.

Until the night I woke in the kitchen with a bloody knife in my hand.

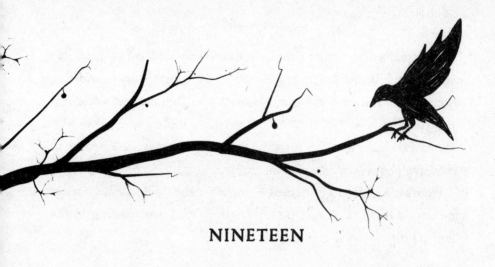

NINETEEN

F at drops of blood pattered onto the kitchen counter. My blood, from
a long, thin cut on my wrist. The knife was still wedged between my
skin and the Magisterium's binding, the charmed silver stretched taut
over the blade.

Disoriented, it took me a long moment to come fully awake, to understand what it meant. When I did, the knife clattered from my nerveless
fingers as Zalgammon raged inside my head.

"You were going to cut it off," I said, my voice hoarse with horror. I
groped for a rag to stanch the blood.

Zalgammon did not answer, but I could feel his fury and chagrin.

"You would have seen me killed."

We would have been strong, he said. *Once the binding was gone, you would
have had no choice but to embrace all our powers. Your pitiful council could not
have stood against us. I was clumsy. After you did not wake when—*

He cut himself off before finishing the thought, but I realized at once
what he'd been about to say.

The dreams. They weren't dreams. They'd been real. All of them. My legs wouldn't hold me, and I collapsed to the floor, the room whirling around me. "You are forsworn," I choked out. "You promised no harm to anyone."

No, Zalgammon said. *I promised no harm where your will forbade it. While you sleep, your will forbids me nothing.*

He was right, and I remained slumped on the floor, cursing myself for a fool. I had thought I was in control, but I was dancing to the demon's tune.

⚜

I crept back to my room after a time, then paced the floor the rest of the night, terrified that if I so much as sat, I'd fall asleep again and Zalgammon would finish what he'd started. He had no reason not to, now that I knew. Not even a salt circle could protect me, since he could use my sleepwalking body to break it.

I packed my bag and took it downstairs with me before first light.

There was no other option. I needed Josiah's help. I had to go back to the farm and tell him what I had done.

"You can't ride back alone," Doyle said when I announced I was leaving. "I'm going with you."

"It's not necessary," I said.

"I'm not offering to go," he replied, reaching for the coffeepot. "I'm telling you I'm going. Patch has a cracked hoof, but we can rent horses. I'll bring them both back to town."

I played my last card. "You can't leave Bonnie and Samantha alone."

"It's one day. They'll be all right." He was immovable, and I capitulated.

I bade Samantha and Bonnie farewell with a lump in my throat, not knowing when, or if, I would see them again. I didn't know what Josiah would do when I told him about Zalgammon. At the very least, I wouldn't be making any more solo visits to town.

He might kill you, Zalgammon said. He'd been trying all morning to convince me not to go back to the farm, which I took as evidence that going was absolutely the right decision.

He isn't going to kill me, I replied, as much to convince myself as to quiet the demon. It was the first time I'd spoken directly to him since the night before. I was angry and frightened. And, ridiculously, there was a tinge of hurt at the betrayal. It was stupid. Zalgammon was a demon. Of course he would do whatever he could get away with doing. I'd left him an opening, and he'd used it. The important thing was to make sure he couldn't do it again.

Shortly after dawn, we set off for the stables, where the bandy-legged proprietor looked surprised to see me accompanying Doyle.

"Morning, Lang. You're early today. Something wrong with Patch?"

"No, nothing wrong, Franks. He's healing fine. But we need to rent a couple of horses."

Franks frowned. "For how long? I don't have much stock available."

"I'm hoping to be back tonight," Doyle said. "But better say tomorrow noon to be safe."

"Well, I can put the lady on Dapple. But for you . . ." He gave Doyle an apologetic look.

Doyle grimaced. "Aw, hell. He's all you've got?"

"Sorry," Franks said with a shrug.

"I guess he'll have to do." Doyle's tone was as sour as I'd ever heard it.

Franks snagged one of his men. "Get Dapple and Buck kitted out for overnight."

Buck? I raised an eyebrow but kept my questions to myself.

Dapple turned out to be a compact gray mare, named for the stippling on her coat. She was soft-eyed and calm, and I stroked her velvet nose and murmured to her while the stable hand tossed the saddle over her back and tightened the cinch. He'd just finished when another hand exited the barn at a run, clinging to the bridle of a nervy-looking bay, who tossed his head and snorted with every step.

"That must be Buck," I said to Dapple, and she pricked her ears forward. "I'm just as glad to be riding you."

Buck had to be double tied to be tacked up. When that was done, Doyle shoved his rifle into the saddle scabbard and mounted.

"Stop that, you." He hauled on the reins to pull the horse's head down as Buck immediately twisted beneath him and tried to kick up his back legs. "Ought to be gelded," Doyle said. "Stallion's no good for a riding horse."

"He's pretty," I said, looking at the glossy coat and fine conformation.

"He's going to spend the day trying to yank my arms out of their sockets," Doyle said dourly.

"It's not too late to change your plans," I said. "I can find some other way out to the farm."

He gave me a look that spoke volumes and put his heels into Buck's sides. The horse leapt into a fast trot out of the paddock. I sighed and turned Dapple to follow.

We didn't speak as we made our way out of town, largely because it took all Doyle's attention to keep Buck under control. The young horse started and shied at every unusual noise, tried to bite other horses when they came too close, and generally made such a nuisance of himself that I understood within the first mile why Doyle hadn't wanted to ride him.

He calmed somewhat once we were out on the prairie, and we rode together in silence for a time.

We came upon the Indians when we stopped to water the horses. They were camped by the creek, a ragged little band of seven men, three of them too injured to even rise with our approach. The other four raised their weapons, and Doyle's hand went to his gun before I recognized High Walking's apprentice as one of them. He still wore the red-and-blue-beaded buckskin shirt, though now it was ripped and stiff with blood in places.

"Wait," I said. "We mean you no harm." Doyle glanced at me, but I focused on the apprentice. "Do you remember me?" I asked, having no idea if he understood me.

"I remember you," the young man said, to my relief. "You are the apprentice of Netse Ôhtseve'hâtse."

"That's right," I said. "What has happened? Where is your leader?"

He said something in his language, and though the others didn't fully lower their weapons, they relaxed enough to feel a fraction less threatening. He turned back to me. "He is gone," he said, weariness and grief in his face. "Two nights ago. We were camped. It was the Hestovatohkeo'o."

"What is that?" Doyle said.

The apprentice glanced at him. "I do not know the word in your language. It is a being from the spirit world. It comes with many faces."

Zalgammon stirred with interest. *One of my kin.*

I pressed my lips together as the apprentice went on.

"It appeared in the night and attacked us. Our warriors fought bravely, but it tore them to pieces before us. Our shaman ordered us to run. He stayed behind to face it. Because of that, this few of us still live."

"My condolences for your loss," I said with a heaviness in my chest. More of Broaderick's work. More death, more fear. "What will you do now?"

"We go to join our kin in the south," the young man said. "Tell Netse Ôhtseve'hâtse of my master's death."

"I will," I said. "I know he will be sorry to hear of it."

There was nothing more to say, and we left them there.

Doyle seemed troubled as we rode.

I knew why but could offer nothing, so I kept my thoughts to myself. The Indians had been attacked by a demon. Why? They weren't part of the war.

But they have magic, Zalgammon said. *Perhaps Broaderick wished to see if it was enough to defeat a demon.*

It made a terrible sort of sense. If Broaderick was trying to open another magical front in the war, he'd have to expect resistance. In fact, it explained why he was summoning demons so far away from the fighting. He could experiment here, in secret, where no one was paying attention, then fall like a hammer blow on the Union forces back east, where no one would be expecting anything.

<hr />

We were perhaps an hour's ride from the farm when the wind abruptly shifted into our faces. It brought with it a rank, musky smell. The horses reacted at once. Dapple snorted and danced in place. Buck's eyes showed white all the way around, and he whirled in a circle and began proving he'd earned his name. Doyle managed the first few jumps, but the stallion eventually caught him off balance, sending him flying over the horse's head.

Doyle managed to control the fall and rolled away from the lashing hooves. Freed of any restraint, the panicked horse bolted back the way we'd come, carrying Doyle's gear, including his rifle, away with him. Dapple would have liked to follow, but I was ready for the attempt and reined her in with a haul on her head that brought her under control, though she shuddered beneath me, blowing as if she'd galloped a mile.

"Are you all right?" I called down to Doyle as he climbed to his feet.

"Rang my bell, but I'll be fine," he said. He drew his revolver and turned in a slow circle, the barrel coming to rest pointing at a broad thicket of pine and tangled brush, the edge of which started some thirty feet ahead of us.

I drew a breath, but before I could speak, the tree branches shuddered, and an enormous, shaggy brown bear shouldered its way into the open.

Every bit of moisture in my mouth dried up.

What is that? Zalgammon asked, sounding impressed.

I was too frozen with terror to think a reply to him.

The bear's undercoat was the color of strong tea, with lighter, almost blond patches on its back and rump. From where I sat, it looked as large as Dapple, but stockier and more heavily muscled. It lifted its muzzle—bloody, I noticed with the detached calmness of terror—and sniffed at the air.

Doyle backed up, one slow step at a time, until his shoulders pressed against Dapple's flank. The horse trembled beneath me, and my hands were so tight on the reins my leather gloves felt as if they would split over my knuckles.

I swallowed. "I thought the bears were hibernating."

I kept my voice low, but even so, the bear reared onto its hind legs as I spoke, and Dapple snorted in fear.

Doyle's reply, when it came, was barely more than breath. "Some of them don't den until the heavy snow starts. That one's not more than half grown. Got a fresh kill nearby." He thumbed back the gun's hammer, the flat *click* loud in the still air.

"Can you kill it with that?"

He huffed out a half laugh. "I don't like my chances."

"Then what do we do?"

Let me have it, Zalgammon said eagerly.

How? I thought. *I'd have to be touching it.* I choked off a terrified laugh at the idea.

Doyle went on. "Back up, slowly. We show him we're not a threat, hopefully he'll leave us alone."

I squeezed my knees into Dapple's sides and tugged on the reins. One step. Two. Doyle moved with us.

It wasn't enough.

The bear let out a deep, coughing roar, dropped to all fours, and charged. Everything happened at once. Dapple whirled away with a terrified whinny, kicking up her back legs as she tried to flee. Doyle dove to one side, firing.

The bear was on us in a blink, raking at Dapple with claws like short, curved daggers. She squealed as they gouged shallow furrows into her rump.

Doyle fired again, and the bullet must have stung, because the bear turned and lunged at him. He got his left arm up, and the bear's jaws clamped down on it. The bear shook its head, and I swear I heard the snap as Doyle's arm broke. He screamed.

There had to be something I could do, some spell that would make the bear leave us alone. I tried to gather my magic, tried to draw up that measured drop of power. I moved too quickly, reached for too much. The bangle seared my wrist, and my focus disintegrated.

Let me do it, Zalgammon demanded.

No, I thought, more out of reflex than any deep consideration.

Fool witch. He will die. Zalgammon showed me an image as crisp and real as life. Shoved it into my brain as if it were in front of my eyes. Doyle, on the ground with his throat ripped out, blood fountaining into the air.

The image cleared, and I found somehow I was down off Dapple, still holding her reins in my hand. My throat rasped with every breath, and some part of me knew I was screaming, but I couldn't hear myself.

I didn't even have to think the words, let alone waste time speaking them. Zalgammon felt the direction of my will. The demon knew, and he was already moving within me. His power swelled. My arm came up, my finger pointed, and his eagerness and triumph rolled through me as his voice spilled from my lips, words I didn't know in a language I didn't speak.

The bear's neck snapped back until the top of its head met its spine, its roar becoming a strangled gurgle. It contorted so violently it flung itself half into the air. There was a sound of cracking bones and tearing flesh, and then the enormous animal simply . . . came apart. Blood and viscera slopped onto the dry grass as if dumped from a barrel. Its head and limbs thumped onto the ground, a heavy, macabre rain of fur and bone and meat.

I'd not done a demon spell of such magnitude before—not waking, at least. The utter foulness of the magic took my breath away. My legs went wobbly beneath me. My stomach twisted, and I struggled against a wave of nausea. An instant later the stench of the bear's spilled blood and torn bowels hit me, and I was lost. The world swam, and I clutched at Dapple's saddle for support as I heaved up the contents of my stomach onto the grass.

By the time the spasms stopped, I was covered in a film of sweat and shivering in the brisk air. Bleary-eyed, I groped for the canteen in my saddlebag.

"You . . . what did . . ."

I turned as Doyle spoke. He was on his back on the ground, his face bloodless and wide-eyed. He scrabbled for his gun with his good hand, then pointed it at me, the barrel dancing as his arm trembled.

I froze. My mind was an utter blank. I'd done magic in front of a Mundane. Explaining that it wasn't my own but that of the demon I carried wouldn't make it any better.

"You did it," he said. "Killed the Jensens. And the patrol."

"What? No," I said. "It wasn't—" I stopped, both my protests and my fear of the gun washed away by a wave of horror. There was blood spreading on the ground beneath him. A lot of it. I took an unthinking step toward him.

"Stay away from me." There was an edge of panicked terror in his voice.

"You have to let me—"

"I don't have to let you do anything!"

"Doyle, you're bleeding. Badly," I said, my voice shaking.

He blinked and looked down at the widening pool. Bleak horror spread over his face. "Sam," he said, his voice hollow. "What will happen to Sam without me?"

"Nothing is going to happen to Samantha, because you are going to be fine," I said, determined to make it true somehow. "I can help you, but you have to trust me."

He looked from me to the strewn remains of the bear, then made a strangled sound halfway between a laugh and a sob. He lowered the gun. "I suppose I don't have much choice."

"No," I said. "You don't."

I had to cut Doyle's coat off. His left arm was mangled, the flesh ripped and the jagged edges of bones visible halfway between his wrist and elbow. The bleeding was already slowing, but I tied a tourniquet above the break anyway and made a makeshift sling. Setting the break would have to wait until we had help.

Buck was nowhere to be seen, and I wasted a full minute scanning the horizon and whistling for him before giving it up as useless. The fool horse would either find his way back to town or not. There was nothing I could do about it.

I got my shoulder beneath Doyle's good arm, and we staggered to Dapple's side. Somehow, we managed to haul him onto her back, though the effort left him pale and sweating. I draped the remnants of his coat around him, then climbed up in front of him and clucked to her. Doyle held himself as far back from me as he could, though he must have been in agony.

After several minutes, I couldn't stand it any longer. "You need to lean into me and hold on."

He didn't move.

I blew out a breath through my nose. "If you pass out and fall off this horse," I said tightly, "there is no way I'll be able to get you on her again. We have to get to Josiah's. If I wanted to hurt you, I would have done it when I . . . before. You have to trust me."

Doyle didn't speak, but after a moment, his weight shifted against my back and his good arm came around my waist.

"Good," I said, and nudged Dapple onward again. I didn't know how long she would be able to carry us both, so I kept her to a steady walk.

Zalgammon was quiet, lazing like a cat in a sunbeam.

"How did you do that?" Doyle asked after a time. The words were slurred.

I hesitated. "Magic." There was no point in trying to say it had been anything else. He'd seen it. There was no other explanation that would satisfy him.

"What are you?"

I hesitated. I'd already broken stars only knew how many rules. I'd done magic—or the demon had done magic through me, and wouldn't that be a fine defense to use with the Magisterium, if they ever found out about it—in front of a Mundane, in a way that couldn't be denied or explained away. I was taking him to another witch, and I was going to do whatever it took to make that other witch help him, which would mean Josiah would be revealed as well. It was a profound violation of essentially all my oaths. But what did it matter at this point? "I'm a witch."

There was a pause, and then his breath huffed against my neck several times, warm in the cold air, and it took me a moment to realize he was laughing. It was the jagged, croaking laugh of a man who is half-drunk—or who has had a shock and lost a quantity of blood.

"So magic killed the Jensens?" he said, once the laughter tapered off. "And the soldiers? And the Indians?"

"Yes."

"But you didn't do it?"

"No, I didn't," I said, trying not to be annoyed. It wasn't an unreasonable question, given what he'd just seen me do. "I was on the stagecoach the day the Jensens died. And I was at the farm when the patrol was killed and in town when the Indians were attacked."

"You're taking me to Josiah. Is he . . . like you?"

In point of fact, Josiah was not like me, since he wasn't, as far as I knew, carrying an insufficiently bound demon inside his body. But I wasn't going to try explaining that to Doyle right then. It was too complicated, and he was already afraid of me. Telling him about the demons wouldn't help.

"He's a witch. He didn't kill anyone either," I added before he could ask. For months I'd been pretending to myself it was possible, but I was done with that farce.

"So who did?"

"I don't know exactly," I said. It was true as far as it went. I didn't know the name of the demons that had killed them. "I've been trying to find out."

He didn't say anything else, but after a few minutes he let himself relax further into my back. Despite everything, warmth flooded my lower belly.

Zalgammon stirred.

No, I thought at him. *I'm not talking about this with you.*

I saved him for you. You should be grateful.

I ignored him. Doyle didn't say anything for a long while, and if it hadn't been for his arm around my waist, I would have thought he'd gone unconscious. I started when he broke the silence.

"Joya?"

"Yes?"

"Did you use magic to save Sam?"

I hesitated. "Yes."

It was a long moment before he spoke again. "Thank you."

⚬━✦━⚬

My anxiety grew as we drew nearer. Josiah would be furious. About everything. I'd lied to him, even if only by omission. I'd betrayed his trust. I'd been unforgivably foolish. I'd broken my own oaths to the Magisterium and identified him as a witch to a Mundane.

And I desperately needed his help.

We reached the edge of his property. I took a deep breath to steady myself, then urged Dapple through the ward.

Lightning struck me. Everything flared bright, and an unseen force slammed into me, flinging me backward off Dapple, taking Doyle with me. I hit the ground flat on my back, knocking the wind out of me.

I lay on the dry grass with my eyes closed, gasping like a fish and with my head ringing as if I were standing inside a church bell being hammered by a man with a maul. My mouth tasted of blood. I must have bitten my tongue.

From my left came the sound of footsteps on dry grass. Josiah.

"Help," I managed to croak. "Help me."

The footsteps stopped beside my head, but he didn't bend down, didn't touch me or say anything.

After a long moment, I managed to turn my head and open my eyes.

I was staring into the barrel of Josiah's shotgun. Behind it, his face was terrible. "What are you?" His voice was a growl.

"It's me." My voice was barely more than a whisper.

"Do you take me for a fool? The ward rejected you. You show up here, wearing that girl's face, and expect me to believe your lies? Last chance." The shotgun barrel moved until it was pressed against my forehead, and his finger tightened on the trigger.

My hands clenched involuntarily at the grass. He was going to shoot me. Peter and Paul stood behind him, looking somberly down at me.

"Crows," I managed to rasp, looking at them. "They're crows. Sunrise and sundown."

Josiah's face went gray, and the gun sagged in his grip. "Joya? Moon and stars, girl, I almost killed you. What happened? What have you done?"

"Doyle," I said, remembering. "Where's Doyle?"

"The Ranger? He's over there," Josiah said, jerking his chin in the other direction. "Looks like he's pretty torn up."

"It was a bear. His arm is broken."

"That's a shame," he said in a flat tone. "What happened to you? Why did the ward reject you?"

I couldn't bring myself to look at him. "I—I made a mistake."

"Joya, tell me," he said. "I'm not bringing you onto my land until I know what you've done."

Shame and fear made me close my eyes.

"A demon," I said. "I made a bargain with it. It's in me, and I can't get rid of it."

There was silence.

I forced myself to look at him.

He looked devastated. Sickened.

"Please," I said, unable to keep the desperation from my voice. "I need your help."

"Damn me for a fool," he muttered after a long moment. "All right, let's get you both to the house."

Relief brought tears to my eyes. It was going to be all right.

Josiah made a gesture, and the air rippled as the ward dissolved. Peter and Paul came forward. Paul lifted me while Peter hefted an unconscious Doyle over his shoulders and laid him gently across Dapple's saddle.

In the cabin, minutes later, Josiah told Peter to put Doyle on the bed, then looked at me, still in Paul's arms. "You hurt or just shook up?"

I motioned for Paul to put me down, gingerly testing my limbs. I was sore, and my head still ached, but nothing was broken. "I'm fine."

Josiah nodded once. "Peter, you get two buckets of hot water, soap, and some clean rags, then bring them here," he said. "Paul, go see to the mare. Wash those scratches and put some of the salve we use on the mules on them. Joya, you come on back here with me."

I followed him. Doyle lay splayed on his back on Josiah's narrow bed. The wound on his arm was seeping blood despite the tourniquet, and he showed no sign of waking. Worrying the fall from Dapple's back might have injured him further, I probed gently at his head. There was a good-sized lump, but the bone was intact. Still, he could be bleeding inside his head.

"Doyle," I said, patting his face. "Wake up."

"Leave him be for now," Josiah said. "We need to clean out the wound and set his arm. Better if he's out for that."

Carefully, the old witch cut the shirt from Doyle's body, leaving the tourniquet in place. There were no other major wounds, but it was obvious he would be horribly bruised.

"Miracle it's not worse," Josiah commented.

"Doyle said the bear was young."

"Mixed blessing," he said. "If it had been full-grown, it would have killed him. But a grown bear might not have attacked. It's the young ones that are touchy. They haven't learned that not everything has to be a fight."

Peter returned with the supplies, and Josiah set me to washing the mangled flesh.

Doyle moaned and began to stir as I pressed the cloth against the wound, and Josiah put a hand to the Ranger's forehead and closed his own eyes. "Sleep," he said.

He is weak in the power.

Zalgammon had been quiet since we arrived at the farm, and his voice in my head was an unwelcome interruption. I tried to ignore him.

Doyle quieted, and Josiah left me to get on with it while he went in search of a splint.

The next hour was a horror, a gruesome ordeal I wished I could blot from my memory. Once the wound was as clean as I could get it, Josiah, Peter, and I managed to get the bones lined up and the splint tied in place with a trio of leather thongs.

That still left the terribly torn flesh to manage.

"Ought to be stitched closed," Josiah said. "You up to doing it?"

My stomach lurched, but I nodded. The feeling of sliding a needle in and out of human skin was not something I'd ever gotten used to while working for Giraud. While I found a needle and thread and began to close the wound, focusing on making the stitches as neat as I could as a means of quelling my nausea, Josiah made up a poultice. When I was done, he smeared the thick mixture over the stitches, then wrapped the arm in strips of clean cloth.

Zalgammon found the whole thing fascinating. *I could heal him, you know. Save all this bother with rags and sticks.*

I've already done my demon spell for the day, thank you very much, I thought back. I certainly wasn't going to so much as suggest using demon magic in front of Josiah.

With Doyle patched up, Josiah turned and walked into the main room and took a seat at the table. He gestured to the other chair, and I dropped obediently into it.

"Now, tell me. All of it."

I told him everything. The magical residue I'd felt at the Jensens. Suspecting him—or wanting to, at least. Discovering the bowl and books. Samantha. The spell I'd cast to trap the demon, and my failure to banish it. Zalgammon's attack on Bonnie. I hesitated over telling him about Seb and Johnny, but I couldn't keep it from him. There had been too many secrets, and they'd brought me here.

I risked a glance at him as I told him about giving them to the demon, and the expression on his face made something shrivel inside me, even as Zalgammon reveled in the memory. I swallowed hard and kept going, telling him about the new bargain I'd made, and what I'd learned in exchange for the spells I'd performed. I told him about waking in the kitchen with the knife in my hand, and how I'd realized I needed his help.

"So here I am," I said.

"You little fool," he said. His voice shook, and his face was a sickly gray.

"I know," I said in a small voice. "I'm sorry. For . . . for all of it. For suspecting you, for not telling you what I'd found."

"Sorry doesn't count for much," he said, pinching the bridge of his nose. He sighed. "But there's things I should have told you, too. I knew something was out there. I felt it test the wards, two nights before you turned up."

"The night the Jensens were killed."

"I didn't know that then, but yes. And then you showed up, with that hobble on your wrist and a belly full of resentment." He didn't look at me.

Realization dawned slowly. "You thought I'd done it?"

"Seemed a mighty big coincidence, you turning up right after something tried my ward," he said. "You wouldn't be the first bound witch to go looking for another source of power."

I flushed, not wanting him to know how near he was to having been right. "Once you knew I hadn't done it, why didn't you tell me then there was something out there?"

"You were bound," he said. "You didn't have the power to do anything about it. I wasn't going to let you get yourself killed trying."

I hesitated. "Why didn't you do something about it?"

He flushed. "I'm old, Joya. I've never had much power, and the little I do have is harder to use every year." He stopped, and I let him, too mired in misery to push him.

We sat quietly for a long moment. Finally, he heaved a sigh. "All right. We both have things we should have done differently. Let's see what we can do about not having more of them. Show me this book. And the bowl."

I fetched them both, the book—along with the dictionary I'd borrowed from Northcutt—from my bag and the bowl from the loft.

He ran a finger over the words engraved in the bowl. "Tell me exactly what you did when you tried to trap the demon."

I recounted it in as much detail as I could.

"And you used this spell? There's a word missing. How did you know what it was?"

I showed him the Latin dictionary and the list of possible words I'd made.

"And which of these did you use?"

"I . . . ah, I don't remember," I confessed. It had all happened so fast, and I had been under so much pressure.

Destructum, Zalgammon supplied helpfully.

My face went hot. "The demon says I used this one." I pointed.

Josiah gave me a sharp look, then pressed his lips together as if resolved not to comment. He thumbed through the dictionary. He ran a finger down the listings, then sighed.

"I'm no expert on demons, but here's what I think happened. I think the original word was something like *diremptum*, which has the sense of broken or disrupted. The one you used has the sense of destroyed or shattered."

"You told me the intent of spells matters more than the words themselves."

Josiah made an irritated noise. "That's true of our magic, but maybe it's not when you're talking about demon work. Might be that the exact words you use matter. It would make sense—that's why all the stories talk about how hard it is to successfully bargain with them. It might be that you've bound the demon until you're dead. Or maybe longer—if it's truly your body that's the vessel rather than your mind, it might not be free until your body rots away to nothing. Ashes to ashes and dust to dust."

The possibility struck me silent. Zalgammon, too—his horror mirrored my own.

Josiah sighed again at my look. "Or maybe it's not about the word you used. Maybe its spell and yours together did something new.

Maybe you made a new spell, and maybe that's just as dangerous to do with demon magic as it is with our own. There's no way to know. I don't know what possessed you to—"

A giggle spilled from my lips as the absurdity of his word choice struck me.

"A demon," I said with a gasp. "A demon possessed me." There was a thick vein of hysteria in my voice. The first laugh had pulled the cork from the bottle. I couldn't stop, laughing and sobbing. Tears of hilarity and terror and every other emotion I'd been bottling up for the last three weeks spilled out of me.

Josiah waited until I'd cried myself out, then handed me a handkerchief.

"Isn't there something we can do?" I asked, once I'd mopped my face.

"We can try banishing it again. I could smash your hand with a hammer this time. See if that makes a difference. I halfway want to do it on general principle," he added in a dry tone, then glanced at me and sighed. "But I don't think it will matter. I think for now you're stuck."

"Do you hate me?"

Josiah looked at me for a long moment before he spoke. "I don't. I would have made some different choices. Or maybe that's easy to tell myself from where I sit. Might be in your place I'd have wound up doing exactly what you did and be in the same spot you're in. Doesn't mean I'm not so angry I could wring your neck, though," he added.

"How do I keep it from taking me over at night? I don't want to make another bargain."

"No. Don't do that. We'll think of something."

"What about Doyle?"

"He saw you do magic."

"Yes."

He looked tired. "You know what the Magisterium would say."

I sobered. "They'd say we should let him die to keep the secret."

"They would," he said.

"I can't do that. He has a child. He got hurt because he was trying to keep me safe. And I—" My throat closed, and I shut my eyes against the tears threatening to well up all over again.

"It's like that, is it?" His voice was surprisingly gentle.

"I don't know," I said helplessly, swiping at my eyes with my sleeves. "I thought it might be, but it's out of the question now. But I can't let him die. We have to heal him."

"I don't have the power or the skill to fix an injury like that."

I do, Zalgammon reminded me.

Josiah must have seen my face change. "What?"

"Nothing," I said.

"No," Josiah said. "I can tell it wasn't nothing. Keeping secrets from me got you into this mess. We're not going down that road again. Tell me."

I sighed. "Zalgammon says he can heal Doyle."

Josiah scowled. "I'll just bet it does. And what would it like in exchange, I wonder?"

Noth—Zalgammon began.

"And don't tell me 'nothing,'" Josiah said, as if he could hear the demon's protestation. "There's always a cost. Every time you convince yourself it's all right to use demon magic, you get a little more comfortable with it. Makes it easier to use it the next time." He shook his head. "I know you have to keep the bargain you made. But promise me you won't do more than you have to."

"I promise," I said, meaning it. After discovering what Zalgammon had been doing while I slept, I wasn't eager to give him any greater foothold in my mind.

Josiah hauled himself to his feet and walked back into his sleeping alcove.

Zalgammon sulked as I stood and followed.

"I can't heal him," Josiah said, moving toward his workbench. "But that doesn't mean there's nothing I can do to help." He picked up a pair of the blank wooden disks I'd used to make my protection charm. With the tip of his athame, he carved something onto each one. He held one in each hand, closed his eyes, and spoke. His magic flickered and was gone so quickly I couldn't read the spells he'd cast. He put one of the disks on Doyle's chest.

I leaned over to look at it. "What is that? I don't recognize the symbol."

"It's a keeping spell," he said. "Useful for all sorts of things. There's different kinds. You can use them to make food stay good longer or slow the progress of an illness. In this case, it will help stop the wound from festering while it heals."

"What's the other?"

"Pain amulet," he said, showing me the sigil on it. He turned back to Doyle and put a hand on his forehead.

"Aren't you going to put the pain amulet on him before you wake him? He's going to be in agony," I said.

"I know." Josiah glanced over his shoulder at me and sighed at my expression. "I have to talk to him first. He's got to understand about what we are, and about magic."

"He already knows," I said. "He saw me kill the bear."

Josiah shook his head. "He saw, but he doesn't know," he said. "You'd be surprised the lengths Mundanes can go to in convincing themselves magic isn't real. He was afraid and hurt when he saw what you did. It's going to feel like something he dreamed. We've got to remind him it wasn't. He's got to be convinced to keep this on." He flicked the keeping amulet with his fingernail. "He'll convince himself it's all foolishness and superstition, and he'll take it off because it reminds him of something uncomfortable. If he does that, at best he'll lose the arm. At worst, he'll die."

He turned back to Doyle. "Wake."

A moment later, Doyle's eyes fluttered open. Pain and confusion colored his features as he tried to focus. His eyes wandered around the room before landing on me.

"Joya. Where—" He squinted at me in confusion.

I saw the moment he remembered.

It swept over his face like a summer storm. He instinctively tried to rise, then groaned and collapsed back onto the pillow.

"What are—What is—" The words came from between gritted teeth.

"Ranger," Josiah said.

Doyle's eyes flashed to him. "Josiah?"

"You're at my place. I can help you, but you need to listen to me. Do you remember what happened?"

"The bear. Joya killed it. She said she's—that both of you are . . . you're witches." The words were a whisper, but there was a question in them. Josiah was right. Doyle was white-faced with fear and pain. This was the time to convince him that he needed to accept our help.

"Yes," Josiah said. He held out the pain amulet. "Take this."

Doyle hesitated, then glanced at me. I nodded. With visible effort, he lifted his uninjured arm from the mattress and grasped the disk. His face went slack. "It helps. It doesn't hurt so much."

"It will keep helping as long as you keep that piece of wood against your skin."

"It's more magic?"

"Yes. And so is this one." He tapped the amulet already resting on Doyle's chest.

Doyle's eyes focused on it. "What does that one do?"

"Helps the wound not to fester. But you have to keep it on, touching your skin. Do you hear me? If you take it off, the wound will putrefy, and I all but guarantee you'll lose the arm, at a minimum."

Doyle swallowed hard, then nodded.

Josiah picked up the keeping spell, and panic flared in Doyle's eyes. "What are you doing with it?"

"Don't get your gizzard in a twist," Josiah said. He took a leather thong and strung the disk on it. When he gestured for the pain amulet, Doyle hesitated for a moment before handing it over. His face tightened as the pain in his arm returned.

With quick, efficient movements, Josiah strung both disks on the cord, knotted it so they wouldn't overlap, and looped it back over Doyle's head. The Ranger relaxed again.

"You can stay here a few days while your arm starts healing, and then we'll—"

"No," Doyle said, his voice surprisingly firm. "I have to get back to town tomorrow. Bonnie's still ill, and Samantha will worry if I'm not back when she expects."

"You can't ride," Josiah said. "Not with that arm."

"I'll be fine," Doyle said stubbornly.

"I'd tell you to get up and show me how fine you'll be," Josiah said, "but you've lost enough blood that you'll pass out before you take five steps. I don't think Joya wants to stitch you up again after you tear that wound open."

I repressed a shudder. I definitely did not want to do that. "What if we all go together tomorrow, in the wagon?"

Josiah gave me a look that could have curdled milk, but I ignored him.

"Stay tonight, let Josiah help you sleep. Tomorrow we'll go back to town together."

Doyle hesitated. "You promise?"

"I do," I said.

"All right, then."

As soon as Doyle was asleep again, Josiah turned to me with a scowl. "What in Sam Hell are you doing promising we'll all go to town?" He stomped out of the alcove, and I followed.

"We have to," I said, sitting at the table. "Broaderick and his group are summoning demons. Using them to kill." A thought struck me. In my worry over Doyle and my fear of Josiah's reaction to my confession, I'd forgotten to tell him about the Indians. I took a breath. "Josiah."

He turned at my tone.

"High Walking is dead." I told him what the apprentice had said, about how his master had fought a nightmare from myth so his people could escape.

The old man's eyes were suspiciously bright when I finished, and he cleared his throat before he spoke. "Like him, to do something like that. He was a good man."

"We can't let it go on," I said. "Broaderick and his men, they're murderers. And if the rebel witches back east start using demons, there's no telling what will happen. We can't do anything about it from out here."

"Might be you're right," he said.

I leaned back in my chair and closed my eyes, relieved. I was suddenly exhausted. Every inch of me still ached from running into the ward, and I was so tired I thought I might be able to fall asleep right there.

But I couldn't. Zalgammon would take advantage. I forced my eyes open and straightened.

Josiah was watching me, his expression inscrutable. "You hungry?" he said.

"I'm too worn out to be hungry." I massaged my temples and sighed.

"Have to see what we can do about that," he said, pulling the skillet from the shelf and setting it atop the stove. "But you need to eat anyway. I'll make you something."

The thought of food nauseated me, but I let him do it, knowing it was his way of showing concern and buying himself time to think. Soon, the smell of frying bacon filled the room, and there was a loud *mrraow* from outside the front door.

Josiah stepped away from the stove long enough to open it, and Shadow bounded inside, nose twitching. He saw me and stopped, blinking. I put out a hand, and he came forward to sniff it, then wormed his head beneath it until I chuckled and scratched him. He purred. Apparently, he either couldn't sense the demon or didn't care.

Zalgammon liked the feeling of the cat's fur beneath my fingers.

"Damned cat," Josiah muttered, but there was no heat in the words. He tore off a piece of bacon and tossed it to the cat, who pounced on it and swallowed it in a single gulp. Josiah set a plate in front of me, and I forced myself to start eating.

"First thing," he said as I chewed. "You need some sleep. I'm going to use the same sleep spell on you I used on Doyle."

"Will that be enough to keep the demon from wandering?"

"I don't know," he replied. "That's why once you're out, I'm going to set a ward around you like the one around the farm. You—and it—already both know what crossing it feels like. We'll both wake up if that thing tries to make you move."

Zalgammon said something in his language. Based on the tone, he was swearing.

A grin tugged at the corner of my mouth. "I think that will work."

"Good."

"What about Broaderick? How are we going to stop him?"

"I've got some ideas about that, but I need to think on them a little before I tell you."

"What—" I stopped as an enormous yawn rippled through me.

"Finish eating," Josiah said. "And then get some sleep. There will be time enough to talk it through tomorrow."

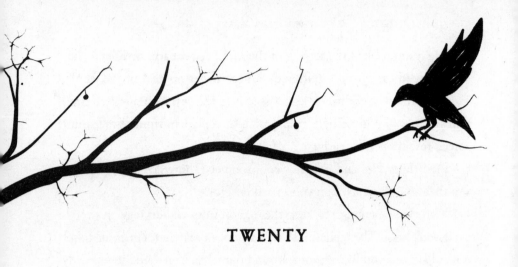

TWENTY

W e set out for Denver City at first light, under a low gray sky spit-
ting snow. Dapple was tied behind the wagon. Even with the pain
amulet and as much padding as I could find for him, Doyle lay white-
faced and sweating in the bed as we bounced over the rutted ground.

Josiah offered to put him to sleep again, but Doyle declined. "Talk to
me," he said. "Tell me more about magic."

I glanced at Josiah, who shrugged. *What did it matter now?* he seemed
to be saying. Doyle already knew enough forbidden things that holding
back the rest seemed silly, especially if we were going to need his help
to find Broaderick.

"What do you want to know?" I asked.

"Everything."

So I told him.

I told him about the Magisterium, its rules and structure, about the
way it had been riven by the war and my role in uncovering just how
deep that rift went.

"But if they took your magic away before they sent you here, how did you heal Samantha? And kill the bear?"

Stars, I didn't want to tell him about Zalgammon. "They didn't take all my magic," I said, uncomfortable. "Josiah taught me how to use what was left."

Josiah glanced at me, his face full of reproof. "If you're going to tell him, tell him all of it. He deserves to know."

My face went hot. He was right. I was still trying to run away from the choices I'd made. I took a deep breath and explained about Zalgammon.

Doyle, already pale, went white as flour. "Samantha had a demon in her? My God. How did I not know?"

"There was no way you could have," I said, meeting his eyes. "He didn't mean to be discovered."

I did not hurt the girl, Zalgammon said. *She is no different than she was before I possessed her. I would have made more use of her as she got older, had I stayed*, he added.

"He says he didn't hurt her, and I believe him." I left off his qualification about what he might have done later.

"It's talking to you, right now?"

I nodded.

"And you're doing spells for it? Using its power?"

"That was the bargain I made," I said. "I have to keep to it."

Doyle went quiet for a long moment, thinking. "It killed the bear. The Jensens and the patrol died the same way. And the Indians. But it couldn't have killed them if it was in Samantha. So there are other demons in the territory."

"There have been other demons summoned," I said. "I don't know if they're still here. I think they were freed to do the killing. Probably they were drawn back to their realm afterward, but I don't know for certain."

"And you think Broaderick is the leader?"

"We know he is," I said.

"Is he a witch?"

"A warlock," Josiah said, speaking for the first time in more than an hour. "Someone with the power of a witch but not the training. They're rare—usually they wind up dead or burned out."

"Burned out?" Doyle asked.

"Happens when you draw more power than you have the ability to hold. A little too much, you can't use magic until you recover. A lot too much, it's permanent. Or fatal. It's why the Magisterium keeps a close lookout for children coming into their power. If you don't find them quick, they don't learn to control it. A lot of 'em wind up killing people around them. An adult warlock is rare as hens' teeth. And they're usually crazy as bedbugs."

Which brought us to another difficult conversation.

"There's something else you need to know," I said reluctantly. "The demon chose Samantha because she has the potential for magic. It's going to bloom eventually, and she'll need training."

Doyle stiffened against the side of the wagon. "You're sure?"

I nodded.

"And if she doesn't get this training, she could die or . . . or go evil?"

"That's about the size of it," Josiah said, barely any inflection in his voice.

I shot him a look. This was a lot to ask Doyle to accept. The least he could do was sound sympathetic.

I turned back to Doyle, ready to reassure him Samantha would be all right, but he surprised me.

"Magic would explain how Broaderick got away after Garvey and I caught him." Doyle frowned. "But then why were we able to catch him in the first place?"

His apparent acceptance of Samantha's future power threw me, and a beat passed before I was able to reply. "He was hurt when you caught him. That probably dampened his magic. Also, there's no way of knowing how much magic he has of his own and how much he's gotten from bargaining with the demons he's summoned."

"That's how you healed Samantha? With power you got from the demon?"

"Yes," I said, leaving out the details about where the power came from, and this time I ignored Josiah's look. It didn't matter. It was done, and despite everything, if I could go back, I would still do it again.

"So now what we have to decide," I said, deliberately changing the subject, "is what we're going to do. We have to find them. They're somewhere in the mountains, but that doesn't narrow it down much."

"I've been thinking about that," Josiah said. "The Broken Eye hides them, but I bet it doesn't hide itself."

"Broken Eye?" Doyle asked.

I explained about the charm the summoners were wearing. "It's meant to protect them from the demons they're summoning. But it seems to work on humans, too. It doesn't make them invisible, but as long as they're not doing anything to attract a lot of attention, it makes them unmemorable, in an extreme kind of way. You could pass one of them in the street, or sell them a meal, or give them directions, and as long as they didn't do anything unusual, once they were out of your sight, you wouldn't be able to describe them."

"But Broaderick isn't wearing one," he said.

"No. He can't hide from the demons if he's going to summon and bargain with them," I said.

"Crazy as a bedbug," Josiah muttered, then went on in a louder voice. "But what I'm thinking is we need to be looking for the charm itself. Someone's going to have seen it or seen someone wearing it."

"I could ask the Rangers," Doyle said. "They'll help if it means tracking down the men who murdered the patrol."

"No," I said before Josiah could. "If word gets out we're looking, we'll be in danger. We have to be careful who we tell. Let's say we find someone wearing the charm," I went on, turning to Josiah. "What then?"

We argued through several possibilities. There were tracking charms. If we could manage to cast one on someone wearing the Broken Eye, we could follow them. But without more information about numbers, about locations, we would have no idea what we would be walking into when we found him. We could try to capture one of the summoners and force the information out of them. Zalgammon, in particular, liked that notion. But it had its own drawbacks, so we set it aside, agreeing to reconsider it if all else failed.

"Could you make a far-listening?" I asked Josiah after another round of rejected ideas.

"What's that?" Doyle asked.

"What it sounds like," Josiah said irritably, snappish and clearly out of patience with answering questions. "I've never made one, but I know how," he said to me. "But that doesn't solve the problem of finding the right person to listen to and getting it hidden where they won't find it."

"I've been thinking about that," I said. "I think I know someone who can help us."

⚬━╋━⚬

We made a pair of brief stops—one to drop off my message and the other to return Dapple to the stable. Franks was displeased to hear we'd lost Buck, but given the circumstances, he couldn't rightly claim it was our fault. As we left, he was telling one of the stable hands to get ready to ride out to search for the errant stallion.

We arrived back at Bonnie's shortly after midday. I went upstairs with Doyle, who looked half-dead from the trip, to check on Samantha and Bonnie. We found them together in Bonnie's room, Samantha knitting while Bonnie rested. They exclaimed over Doyle's injury, but he waved away their worry.

"Joya and Josiah fixed me right up and brought me back to town. I'll be good as new before you know it."

Hearing that Josiah was downstairs, Bonnie struggled to rise, but I made her stay down.

"Don't you even think about it," I said. "He knows you've been ill and won't want to be fussed over. You can tell him hello at dinner—which we'll put together," I added. "You rest."

"Can I come meet him?" Samantha asked.

"Better wait," I said. "He's tired and cranky after the trip. And speaking of tired," I said, looking at Doyle, "you should rest, too."

He agreed with ill grace, following me into the hallway. "Come get me when she gets here," he said before disappearing into his room.

While we waited, I watched Josiah construct the far-listening.

He looked over the items in Bonnie's kitchen, brightening when he found what remained of the almonds Doyle had given her for Christmas. "I thought we might have to go hunting for something over at Tuttle and Veach's," he said. "But this is exactly what we want." He chose several of the nuts, the ones with whole, unblemished shells, then brought them out to the dining room, where the light was better.

"You want something that's two parts of one whole," he said. "You can use two discs cut from the same piece of wood or the like, but it will work better if they are naturally of a piece. Even better if they're designed to split." He pulled his carving tools from his pocket and laid them out on the table.

With his knife, he carefully cracked each of the almonds, creating two oblong half shells about the size of the top joint of my thumb. The side of one nut splintered as he pulled it apart, and he brushed that one aside. He kept the split shells in their pairs.

Josiah selected the best two pairs and set them aside. "We'll practice on the others before we make the one we mean to use," he said, popping one of the nut meats into his mouth and crunching it. "Haven't had an almond since I lived in California," he said. "Always liked them."

I watched as he selected his smallest tool and carefully carved something into the inside of one half of the shell. It was fiddly work, and I wished for a magnifying glass.

"I can't tell what the symbols are," I said.

Josiah set the shells aside and drew two sigils on a sheet of newspaper. "These sigils draw in sound," he said. "So that's the 'listening' part of the spell. The 'far' part is why you need something paired. You convince the two parts that they're still one whole. So what one gathers, you hear from the other." He held the two halves together between his fingers. "Time to see if we did it right." He closed his eyes. "Born together. As to one, to the other. Apart, but whole. By will, so make it be." He grunted, then opened his hand and gave me the unmarked half of the shell. He stood with the other half and carried it to the far side of the room. He cupped his hand to his mouth.

"Joya. Can you hear me?" The voice came from the shell in my hand. It was raspy, and the words were difficult to make out.

"Not well," I said aloud.

Josiah came back with a shrug. "Thought that might be. I could feel the magic soak in, but the sigils were too rough. But good for a first try."

We made two more far-listenings before we got one that worked well enough that we were confident about using it. Josiah tied the carved shell into a handkerchief and put a keeping on it. "That will hold the spell. It won't start 'listening' until it's untied."

It was fortuitous timing; the knock came then, at the back door. I hurried to answer it.

"Inge," I said, ushering the prostitute into Bonnie's kitchen. "Thank you for coming. And I'm sorry I had to ask you to come to the back door."

"I understand," she said. "It wouldn't do for Mrs. Bonnie to have a woman like me be seen coming into her home."

"That's not why," I said, putting a hand on her arm. "It's because I need to ask you for a favor, but no one can know you're helping me."

"What sort of favor? I will help you if I can," she added. "I owe you a debt."

"Don't say yes until you hear what it is." I led her through to the dining room, where Josiah waited. Doyle was making his way slowly down the steps.

Inge's forward progress stuttered when she saw them, and her eyes widened when she took in Doyle's wrapped arm. He looked a little better after his rest, but his face remained drawn and pale.

"Ranger Doyle," she said.

"Hello, Miss Swensen," Doyle replied, and I realized I hadn't known her last name, or that Doyle knew exactly who she was.

"I heard your daughter was ill but has recovered?"

"Yes," Doyle said. "Thanks to Joya."

Inge nodded as if she understood. "Joya has good recipes." She turned to Josiah. "You I do not know."

Josiah introduced himself and took her hand without any sign of discomfort or judgment.

"Please take a seat," I said. "Could I get you coffee?"

"Thank you, no," she replied. "I cannot stay long. It will be dark soon, and the customers will be waiting. Mrs. Rose was unhappy when I told her I had to go out before I could start work."

"We'll be quick as we can, then," Josiah said. "We're looking for someone, and Joya thinks you may be able to help us find him."

"Who?" she asked.

"We don't know his name," I said. "We think he will have this symbol on himself somewhere, either on something he wears, probably around his neck, or maybe even on his skin—a tattoo." I showed her the drawing I'd made of the Broken Eye. "I thought maybe you or one of your friends might recognize it since—" I stopped, more out of deference to Doyle's sensibilities than out of any delicacy, but Inge took no notice.

"Since we see so many men's bodies," she finished, frowning at the drawing. "I have seen this." She looked up at me. "One of my men. A regular. He comes to me whenever he is in town. He wears it on a string around his neck and does not take it off."

"Do you know his name?" Josiah asked. "Can you tell us what he looks like?"

"Of course I can. His name is . . ." Inge trailed off, frowning. "This is odd. I know I have heard his name, but I cannot remember it. As to what he looks like, he is a miner. Rough hands. He does not trim his beard. I think it is blond?" There was a questioning tone in her voice, and her frown deepened.

"It's all right," I said. "We don't need to know his name yet. But we need to get something hidden. In his coat, ideally. Something he'll wear every day. Inside a seam or in a pocket. Somewhere he won't find it for a while."

I showed her the shell. "There's another like this inside this cloth," I said, handing her the handkerchief. "Don't unwrap it until you're ready to hide it. Will you do this?"

Inge picked up the unwrapped half of the shell and turned it over in her hand, squinting at the tiny carving on the inside. "This is a curse of some kind?" She grinned at our startled reactions. "My grandmother knew of such things," she said. "I never had the gift myself, but she could do things to those who crossed her—kill a man's pig or make his *kuk* unable to stand up." She demonstrated with her index finger.

Doyle shifted uncomfortably, but I had to smother a smile.

"I'll bet you'd like to know that one for some of your customers," I said.

"No," she said with a grin. "Then there would be no work for me."

"It's not a curse," Josiah said.

Inge shrugged. "It is no matter to me. There are always more men. I will not feel the loss of one. You helped me," she said to me. "I will do this for you."

"When?" Josiah asked. "How often does he come to you?"

The girl shrugged again. "Not so often. I think his claim is far. Maybe only once every two months. I last saw him before Christmas."

I tried not to let my disappointment at the idea of waiting so long show. There must be something we could do in the meantime. There would be another new moon before then, another chance for the summoners to raise a demon and set it on someone.

"Thank you," Josiah said, and I jolted, realizing he was doing what I should have.

"Yes," I added, rising to walk her out. "Truly, thank you," I said once we were in the kitchen. "You are helping lots of people by doing this."

"Then you are very welcome," she said with a smile. "Mostly I only get to help one at a time, so this will be a nice change."

I laughed as she gave me a naughty wink and slipped out the back door.

She ruts for a living? Zalgammon asked as I closed the door behind her.

"Yes," I said. "Perhaps you should have possessed her since you find that topic so interesting."

Perhaps, he said, as if seriously considering the notion. *But no. She sleeps in the daytime. It would have been harder to use her body without being seen. And besides, I would not get to have my revenge on Broaderick.*

"I'm so happy to know you don't regret your choice," I said sourly, then returned to the dining room, where Josiah and Doyle were deep in discussion.

"—think it's a good idea," Doyle was saying.

"I do," Josiah said.

They broke off as I approached. "I was wondering if there's another way to look for them while we're waiting," I said. "Inge said she thinks her man is a miner. And I remember thinking the same of the two I saw here that night. Don't mining claims have to be registered? Isn't there some sort of record of who has what?"

"In theory," Doyle said. "But it doesn't always work out that way. A lot of miners don't want to pay the fee to register a title—or tell anyone exactly where they're digging, which they'd have to do to register it. Especially since the war started, claims have been abandoned and then taken over by other groups, and almost no one bothers to file the papers. And there's no will to enforce it—not to mention the lack of manpower."

"So that won't work," I said, dejected.

"We're going to have to be patient," Josiah said. "There are hundreds of miners in the mountains, and they're most all tetchy about people poking into their business. We go asking who's digging where, word will go out faster than if we stood on the street and shouted. And anyway," he said to me, "we're not going to be here to be doing any asking. We're going back to the farm first thing in the morning. Both of us."

"But—" I began.

"No," Josiah said. "I don't want to hear it. We don't know how long it's going to be before we get anything from that charm. I'm not waiting around in town, and neither are you. I want you out at the farm where you can't get into any more trouble."

I was in no position to argue, so I only sighed and took myself up to my room.

⚬━┼━⚬

That evening, after dinner, there was a knock at my door. I opened it, expecting Josiah. Instead, Doyle stood in the hallway, a thoughtful look on his face.

"I've been thinking," he said. "I have some questions about . . . things." He shot a furtive glance down the hallway.

I sighed. "Do you want to come inside to ask them?"

He hesitated.

"I think we're past worrying about propriety," I said.

He stepped through the doorway with a rueful half grin.

I closed the door behind him and raised an eyebrow.

Doyle took a deep breath before he spoke, as if gathering himself. "Bonnie said she got sick the same night Samantha's fever broke. Between that and what you told me today, it got me to wondering. Did one of those have anything to do with the other?"

I closed my eyes for a moment before I answered, resigned to telling him the truth and hoping he wouldn't hate me for it. "Yes. The demon drew from Bonnie's life force to heal Samantha. I didn't know at the time that's what would happen."

He didn't look appalled, only sad. "That's what I was afraid of." He went silent for a long moment, then heaved a sigh. "I hate that. But if she'd been asked, Bonnie would have agreed."

I told you that, Zalgammon said.

I ignored him.

"I know," I said. "But I still wish it hadn't happened." I hesitated, but I was tired of hiding the truth. "The demon used everything it took from Bonnie to heal Samantha. To heal the rest of the children, it needed more."

He understood at once. "Who?"

I dropped my eyes as I told him about Johnny and Seb. There was silence when I finished speaking, and I waited a long moment before I looked up at him.

Doyle's lips were pressed together. "Someone would have knifed the pair of them sooner or later anyway," he said eventually. "At least this way something good came out of it."

"You don't think I'm some sort of monster?"

Doyle rubbed his good hand over his face. "Oh, hell, Joya, I don't know. I half feel like this is all some big confidence game you're pulling on me. Or else I'm going stark-staring mad."

"You're handling it well," I said.

He barked a laugh. "I'm scared half to death," he said. "But at the same time, a lot of things make more sense now. I've been feeling guilty for months, thinking I should have told people about the Jensens, that maybe it would have saved the patrol. But it wouldn't have, would it?"

"No."

We stood looking at one another for a long moment. "I had one other question," he said, his voice softer. "Was that—the demon—why you didn't seem like you wanted me around you after Christmas?"

I nodded, my cheeks warming. "It sees and hears what I do. And it feels what I feel."

He blinked as he grasped the implications. "Well. That's damned awkward."

"It is, isn't it?"

We looked at one another for a long moment.

Zalgammon stirred, and I spoke before the demon could interject.

"I expected you to ask about Samantha," I said. "The idea that she's going to develop magic, that she'll need training to keep her safe. Doesn't that worry you?"

"It terrifies me," he said. "But I'm trying to worry about what's next, not what's coming down the line. We should have some time, right? You said it mostly happens when they're older than Samantha."

"As a rule," I said. "It flares earlier, sometimes." But that wasn't likely. My own early flicker of power had been the result of a threat to my life. Watched over by her father and aunt, Samantha led a relatively sheltered existence. Doyle was probably right that we didn't need to worry about her magic yet.

"So we'll deal with it when it comes. And besides," he added, "you're here. You'll help her when it's time."

There was such faith in the way he said it. The idea that Doyle trusted me, even bound and demon-tainted, to keep his daughter safe brought a lump into my throat. I could barely speak around it. "I will."

How touching, Zalgammon said in a sour tone.

Oh, shut up, I thought.

I might have said more, but at that moment, the sound of Josiah stumping up the stairs reached me, and I quickly opened my bedroom door.

"Where'm I bunking, Ranger?" he said as he appeared in the doorway.

"With me, I suppose," Doyle said with a degree of resignation. "I'll go get my bedroll. You can have the bed."

Josiah didn't move. "I'm tired. And I'm going to bed," he said. "But before I do that, I'm going to put her to sleep"—he jerked his chin in my direction—"and put a ward around her. If you've got anything else to say, you'd best go ahead and say it now."

Doyle visibly suppressed a response, then turned and left.

I didn't bother to hide my own annoyance, which Josiah pointedly ignored. I didn't have to suffer it long, however. His spell was potent, and an instant after I put my head on the pillow, blackness overwhelmed me.

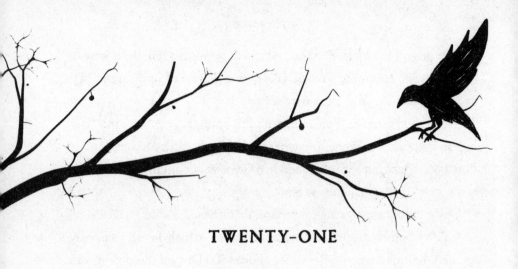

TWENTY-ONE

I went back to the farm with Josiah the next day, carrying my half of the far-listening in my pocket. I kept it with me every moment of the next few weeks—under my pillow as I slept at night and in my pocket as I went about my chores during the day. The protective circle Josiah put around me each night kept Zalgammon from leading me on further nighttime wanderings, though he complained bitterly.

The demon complained, but there were any number of ways he could have retaliated for having his nighttime excursions curtained. Yet he refrained.

Why? I asked him. *You could cause me pain to try to force Josiah to remove the warding. You could shout obscenities at me all day—or all night. You could keep me from sleeping at all, if you wanted. But you aren't, so there has to be a reason.*

I am sure I do not know what you mean, he replied.

Josiah sighed when I relayed the conversation to him. "Joya, it's immortal. It can afford to be patient. It's counting on getting what it wants eventually. No reason to drive you mad or make you its enemy if it can worm its way through you by grumbling and pretending you've bested it. You're learning spells. You're not trying to banish it."

He took himself off to the smokehouse, and I sat, feeling foolish.

Zalgammon didn't bother trying to deny it.

It was six weeks to the day after I'd given Inge the far-listening when it crackled to life in my pocket as I was doing the morning milking. Snores, deep, and ragged, echoed in the still air of the barn.

I jumped from my stool with a gasp, upsetting the bucket of milk and drawing a reproving look from the cow as I thrust my hand into my pocket. I ran out of the barn and burst through the cabin door, where Josiah was pulling breakfast off the stove.

"It's working," I said, thrusting the nutshell at him.

The snores had stopped, and now Inge's voice, hollow but recognizable, came from it. "—back into town?"

"Last night," an unfamiliar voice replied.

"So I am your first visit? I am flattered."

"You're my only visit, darlin'," the man said. "And now I got to get back." The clink of coins, followed by the sound of a door opening and closing, and a man's footsteps on a wooden floor.

Wherever the men were gathering, it wasn't far from the Golden Rose. Within ten minutes, another door creaked open, and another man's voice came from the shell.

"'Bout time you got back. He'll be here any minute, and we'd all pay hell if you'd been gone."

"Shouldn't have gone at all," a third voice said. "You know what he said."

"Aw, shut your gob," said the voice of Inge's customer. "I didn't go anywhere else, just there and back. And I didn't talk to anyone. What he don't know won't hurt him none. I only—"

The men fell silent as the door opened again, and even through the medium of the shell, I thought I could feel the sense of menace enter the faraway room. Broaderick had arrived.

"Mornin', boys," he said. "I hope you're all—" He stopped. There was the sound of shuffling feet. When he spoke again, his voice was deadly. "There's magic in this room. It wasn't here last night. Who's been here?"

"No one," said one of the men, fear evident in his tone. "I swear."

"Then one of you left and came back with something. Who was it?"

More shuffling. Beside me, Josiah tensed.

"McDonnell took a little trip over to the vaulting house this morning," one of the men said. "Thinks with his johnson."

Inge's customer—McDonnell—swore. "You son of a bitch. You—"

"Be silent." Broaderick's voice sliced through the chatter. "There's magic on you somewhere. Strip."

Broaderick's authority was such that the next sound was rustling cloth. When the voice came again, it was clearer. He was holding the far-listening. "Whoever you are," Broaderick said, and the hair on the back of my neck rose to attention, "this was unwise of you. The whore will pay for this. She'll tell me what I want to know. She'll beg to tell me. And I'll come for you next."

There was the sound of metal hinges, and our half of the far-listening, sitting on the table, blackened and burst into flames.

I yelped and grabbed for a cloth to bat it out, leaving a scorch mark on the table. The nutshell was nothing but a smear of ash.

When I looked at Josiah, his face was grave. I drew a breath to speak, but he moved before I could, heading toward the door.

"Where are you going?"

"Remember what I told you," he called over his shoulder as he stepped into the yard. "You are responsible for the outcome of your magic. I made the spell. Now that girl is in danger because of it. I have to protect her if I can."

I hurried after him, assuming he was headed to the barn. "You'll never get there in time. Whatever they're going to do, it will be over long before you can ride to town."

Josiah stopped in the middle of the yard and turned. "I'm not going to ride." He took a deep breath and dropped his chin to his chest. The air rippled around him, and his body collapsed in on itself, just as Peter's had that night on the way home from town. A moment later, a massive golden eagle stood in the yard, shaking itself free of Josiah's clothes. It fixed me with a fierce eye, and its sharp beak opened and let out a harsh cry.

I stood staring in shock as it—he, Josiah—spread wings wider than I was tall and flapped them as if stretching. He took off with a pair of hops across the yard and launched into the air. He was unsteady at first, circling the farmstead a few times as if practicing a long-unused skill. Then, with a few hard beats of his wings, he turned in the direction of Denver City, gaining speed until he was nothing but a dot in the distance.

My mind a blank, I bent to scoop up the clothes Josiah had left behind. Something fell to the dirt. The rawhide thong he wore around his neck, with a trio of wooden disks. Amulets. I picked them up. One was the link to the ward. The carvings on the other two were also familiar—they were the same two spells he'd cast for Doyle: a keeping spell, and a spell to relieve pain.

Dread clutched at my insides as I stared down at them in my hand. The coughing. His thinness. The way he rubbed at his hip and back without seeming to notice what he was doing. Josiah was ill. And he'd left behind the charms that were holding him together to try to make it to town in time to save Inge. I wheeled for the barn and shouted for Peter and Paul to saddle the mules.

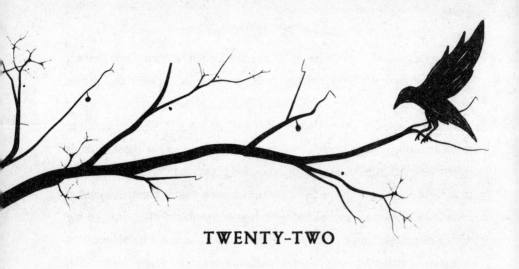

TWENTY-TWO

Peter and I were halfway to town when Doyle found us, riding Patch at a fast canter and leading Dapple behind him.

"It's bad," I said when I saw his face. A statement, not a question.

He nodded.

I could barely force the words out. "Is he alive?"

"He was when I left," he said. "But Doc said he can't last long."

"What about Inge?"

"She's fine," he said.

"All right," I said. I turned to Peter. "Take Fox back to the farm. Both of you should come after sundown."

Peter nodded, and the worry visible in his eyes made mine begin to sting.

"Tell me," I said to Doyle when I was mounted on Dapple and we'd gotten underway.

"I didn't see it. Only heard about it after. Four men came to the Golden Rose looking for Inge. They busted into her room. The man she was with took exception to being interrupted. It turned into a brawl that spilled out into the street. Someone called for the sheriff, and when he and his men got there, they tried to quiet things down.

"In all the hullaballoo, one of Broaderick's men put a knife to Inge's ribs and told her to keep quiet and come along. She says he took her down the alley to a pair of horses and was trying to get her onto one of them when a giant bird came falling out of the sky and went after the man who'd taken her. Cut him up pretty good. Near about took one of his eyes before the man started stabbing at it with the knife and beat it off him. Without that knife in her ribs, Inge managed to get away and start screaming for help, and two of the deputies came running.

"They arrested him for kidnapping, but they'd already let the rest of Broaderick's men get away—they hadn't known they were dealing with anything more than a brawl. Anyway, he's over at the jail."

Doyle paused. "Somone found Josiah a street over. Stab wounds in the arm and the gut. Naked." He glanced at me. "Been some talk about that. No one remembers him ever being a customer at the Rose before, but that's what they're assuming. I figure it's as good an explanation as any. They've got him over at the doc's, and I came after you as soon as I heard. Do you . . . Do you think you'll be able to help him?"

"Probably not," I said. "I've never been much good at healing, even before they bound me. I'll do what I can. But I think there's more than the stab wound wrong with him. I found these in his clothes after he left the farm."

I held up the amulets, and Doyle's face changed when he recognized the signs etched into them.

"He's sick. He didn't tell me," I said, my voice tight. "He should have."

We rode the horses hard and arrived in Denver City in the early afternoon. Doyle took me directly to the clinic, and I leapt off Dapple, tossing the reins at Doyle without a word.

Doctor Shaver was in the front room, talking to a miner with his hand thickly wrapped with gauze.

"Where is he?" I asked.

"Miss Shaw," the doctor said, surprised. "I didn't expect you to get here this quickly."

"Where is he?" I asked again, more insistently.

"I've got him in the back," the doctor said, turning to lead me down a narrow hallway. "I'm glad you made it. I've offered him laudanum, but he won't take enough to sleep. He insisted on waiting until after he'd spoken to you."

"How long does he have?"

The doctor didn't turn. "It's hard to say. The arm isn't so bad, but the blade nicked his intestine. There's nothing I can do to fix that, and it will be far better for him if he goes quickly. But we'll have to wait and see. He's a tough old bird."

I barked a laugh that came out sounding like a strangled sob. If only he knew.

The doctor glanced back over his shoulder, sympathy on his face. "You need to prepare yourself."

Inside the room, Josiah lay on a narrow cot made up with clean, dun-colored sheets. His face was gray and wasted, his eyes closed.

"Josiah, I'm here," I said, and his eyes fluttered open.

"There you are, girl," he said, his voice weak. "Wondered when you'd get here."

I fished in the sack as I stepped toward him and brought out the amulets. "I brought these," I said, fumbling with the cord.

He brushed away the keeping amulet with an irritable wave. "Stars, girl, not that one. You think I want to linger like this? I'll take the other one, though."

I helped him raise his head enough to slip the pain spell around his neck. He sighed in relief as he lay back, and some of the tension drained from his body, though he looked no less drawn.

"You're sure?" I said. "There might be something we could do."

"Not a damn thing you or I could do. We both know that. And I won't take anything from your passenger."

I dropped my eyes from his and pressed my lips together. *Could you heal him?*

Yes.

At what price?

The cost would be dear, Zalgammon said. *Apart from the injury, the rot is all the way through to his bones.*

What price? I asked again, impatient with the demon's word-mincing.

Another life, he said. *Perhaps the man who stabbed him? It is only fair, is it not? That death instead of this one?*

Josiah would be angry with me, but wouldn't it be worth it, to have him alive and whole? Wouldn't he forgive me, eventually?

You need only say the word.

I could feel Zalgammon's eagerness. It should have been off-putting, but I wanted it as much as the demon did.

Josiah interrupted my thoughts. "Joya, girl, whatever it's telling you, it doesn't matter."

I looked at him.

His face was resolute. "I won't do it. Whatever it wants to do, I won't have it on my conscience, or yours." He meant it, and the fragile resolve that had been holding me together collapsed.

"But you're going to die." My voice wobbled.

"We all die," he said. "That's the way of things. It's my time. Well past it, probably, if I'm being honest. I've had that keeping charm on for years." He sighed. "You're going to let me go, and you're not going to let that *thing* talk you into trying to save me. Promise me."

"I promise," I said, tears blurring my vision.

"And promise me you'll be careful," he said. "I'm not going to be here to help you get rid of the demon, and I'm sorry for that." A spasm of pain flickered over his face, and he took several careful breaths before he went on. "Every choice you make as long as you have it inside you has extra weight. It wants what it wants, for its own reasons, and it will try to use you to get it. You can't trust it. Not ever. You can't afford to make choices without thinking them through anymore. It was dangerous before, when you only had a witch's power. Now, it could be a catastrophe. Do you understand?"

I nodded. I did understand, truly. I opened my mouth to tell him so, but the doctor interrupted then, with more laudanum, and Josiah's talking had taxed him enough that he was willing to take it.

He slept until just after sunset, waking when Peter and Paul landed on the windowsill in a rustle of wings and anxious caws. Their bright, dark eyes were knowing.

"I should have taught you the spell," Josiah said, looking at them. "They'll miss being men." He sighed, his voice weakening as he went on. "If I had it to do over . . . But that's the way of it. Choices." The last word was little more than a mutter, and he lapsed into unconsciousness.

I sat beside him through the night, holding his hand. He died as the sun rose.

TWENTY-THREE

I was numb with grief and exhaustion as Doyle guided me back to Bonnie's. Stray thoughts floated through my head, every one of them adding to the leaden weight in my gut.

I'd have to decide where Josiah should be buried. He'd probably prefer the farm to the town cemetery.

What would happen to the farm? And the animals? Someone would have to go and tend to them in the next day or so, now that Peter and Paul couldn't do it. And—

Oh, stars, no. With Josiah's death, there was no one to set a ward over me at night. When I went to sleep, the demon would be free to overtake me again. Unless I made yet another bargain with him.

I almost went to my knees with the realization.

Much as I hated the idea, I was drawing nearer to the conclusion that with Josiah gone, I needed to involve the Magisterium. What was I going to tell them? It would have to be the truth—or at least most of it. This had all gone too far for anything else.

What would they do? Would they even believe me about the summoners? Maybe they would send someone to help, but it would take weeks at best, and there was no telling what might happen in the meantime.

And if someone did come, could I manage to hide my possession from them? And should I? I'd kept the secret from Josiah, and look what that had gotten me.

We reached Bonnie's house, and I waited as Doyle fumbled in his pocket for his key.

"How is your arm?" I asked, belatedly realizing I hadn't even asked him since meeting him on the trail. He still wore a splint and wrap, but had dispensed with the sling, and he'd been using it without obvious pain.

"Healing clean," he said. "Doc says the muscle damage is likely permanent, but the bone is set straight, and there's been no sign of festering."

As if to demonstrate how well he was doing, he shifted the key to his left hand and inserted it into the lock.

I stepped closer in anticipation, wanting nothing more than to fall into bed, to escape from this horrible heavy feeling for a few hours, then suppressed a sigh. I wasn't going to get that luxury. I'd have to make a pot of coffee and—

Doyle made a sound of surprise. The door was unlocked. He swung it open.

The front room was wrecked. Tables were askew, benches overturned, chairs tipped and splintered. Broken dishes were strewn across the floor. In the chaos, it took both of us a moment to realize the crumpled heap at the bottom of the stairs was Bonnie.

Doyle was across the room in an instant, falling to his knees beside her, his fingers seeking the pulse in her throat.

He looked up at me, his face hollow. He didn't have to say the words.

I shook my head, not disbelieving him, just unable to accept it. I bent to check for myself. Doyle didn't wait for me to get past my shock. He shot to his feet, taking the stairs three at a time. "Samantha!" It was a bellow, full of terror and rage.

Bonnie's face was drawn and white, her skin gone waxy. No breath. No pulse. She was dead. I dropped my head, trying to absorb this new loss on top of the one I already carried. I rolled her onto her back, straightening her limbs and smoothing her skirts, trying to give her some dignity. The broken ends of a worn leather thong trailed from her fist, which was clenched around something. Her fingers were already beginning to stiffen, and I had to work to pry them open.

Doyle appeared on the stairs.

"Samantha's gone," he said, panic in his voice. "She's—"

He stopped as he looked past me at what I'd uncovered.

We stared together at the Broken Eye amulet lying in Bonnie's lifeless palm.

⚬—✦—⚬

The sheriff wasted no time when we told him Bonnie was dead and Samantha taken. He ordered his men to fan out through the town, looking for anyone who might have seen Broaderick's band riding out with Samantha the day before. We left, too, then doubled back once there'd been time for the sheriff and his men to disperse, leaving a single young deputy to guard the prisoner they'd arrested the day before.

He was the key. He knew where they were taking her. All we had to do was make him tell us.

The deputy's face went wary as we came back through the door, his hands coming up in a defensive gesture. "I can't let you hurt him. The sheriff would have my hide." His voice wavered.

I didn't blame him. Doyle might have been made of stone, so rigid was his posture and expression. He had taken his grief over Bonnie and folded it away like a winter blanket once spring had come—a thing that had no purpose now but was carefully stored for the future. There would be time for mourning later. Once Samantha was safe. He'd shown no emotion since we left Bonnie's, and it was obvious he was holding back his terror and fury only by sheer will.

"They'll find something. You have to be patient," the deputy went on when Doyle didn't respond.

The sheriff might be doing his best, but I wasn't hopeful. People had remembered the brawl, yes. But it had attracted attention. A few men, riding out of town quietly, some hours later? No one would remember them, even if they'd had Samantha with them. All it would take was a gun in her ribs to keep her quiet and a Broken Eye charm around her neck, and no one would remember seeing a thing.

Doyle's hands clenched into fists, and he shifted his weight as though about to take a step forward. The deputy stepped back, swallowing.

"We only want to talk to him," I said.

The deputy flinched at my voice, apparently having forgotten I was there.

"I promise," I said. "Neither of us will so much as touch him." Doyle turned his basilisk stare on me, and I did my best to ignore it. If I handled this correctly, I wouldn't need to touch the prisoner to make him tell us what we needed to know.

The deputy looked uncomfortable. "I don't think—"

"Please." I put a hand on his arm and made my voice soft. "He killed my uncle. He knows where they've taken Samantha. What could it hurt to let us talk to him?"

The deputy heaved a sigh. "All right. If you're truly set on it, I'll let you talk to him from the hallway outside his cell." He looked at Doyle. "Unarmed. And you have to stay well back from the bars. I can't let you—"

"It's fine," Doyle said, the words coming like bullets. He removed his gun from its holster and placed it and his knife on one of the desks. "Let's go."

As we followed the deputy down the hallway, Doyle leaned down and put his lips to my ear. "What are you going to do?"

"I don't know yet," I whispered back. "But I'll get what we need. I swear it."

He pulled away, not satisfied, but apparently willing to go along for the moment.

My palms grew damp as we neared the cell. The spell I'd used on Thomas might work on this man, but even when I'd had access to my power, that had been a complex spell, and a potion to boot. I doubted I could make it work in my current state. I repressed a sigh. There was no help for it.

Zalgammon, I offer a bargain.

The demon stirred. *What terms?*

I need this man to tell us where they've taken Samantha. You can use any spell you like on him, but it can't leave a mark, and it can't be too . . . flashy, I finished.

I want what is left of him when we are finished.

No. It was a reflexive denial. I did not care about the prisoner's life. But I wasn't going to let Zalgammon kill whenever he wished.

Zalgammon sighed, annoyed. *Why? You wish to cause him pain. He killed your mentor.*

No, I thought again, the tone of it somehow sharper. I wasn't even certain why I was arguing. He was right. I did want to cause him pain, both to find Samantha and to punish him for Josiah's death. But he was unarmed, jailed, and no threat to me. I had to draw a line somewhere. *You don't need his life. You still have plenty of power left from the man you took while I was asleep.*

Then I decline the bargain, Zalgammon said. *You may use sweet reason with him and see how far that gets you.*

I ground my teeth. I had to make this work. I took a breath. *This man is the key to finding Broaderick,* I thought. *If you want to see him pay for trapping you, you must help me.* I let the bait hang there for a moment, then added to it. *When we find the men who took Samantha, we may have to fight them. You may have any of them who try to hurt us.*

I made that promise easily, without a qualm. Killing in self-defense was something I could live with.

Done.

The agreement eased one worry while creating a host of others, but I forced them aside. One thing at a time.

The man who'd killed Josiah sat on a narrow cot in an iron-barred cell at the end of the hallway. He was ragged and dirty, with a wide bandage wrapped around his head, covering his damaged eye. He sat forward and leered at me when I stepped into view.

"I ain't never been in a jail that delivered slit tail afore. Come on in here, darlin', and we'll have us a ride."

The deputy reddened and drew a breath, but I spoke before he could.

"Charming," I said. "I'm sure that invitation gets you no end of attention. But I'm afraid I must decline. We have other matters to speak of."

I turned to the deputy. "We'll be fine." My dismissal was clear in my tone, and he pressed his lips together and stepped back, but not far enough. At a glance from me, Doyle clapped the man on the shoulder and drew him farther away.

"Let's talk about how we're going to handle catching Broaderick and his boys once we have a lead on them," Doyle said. "We can't come at them straight on. Not when they've got my . . . a hostage with them."

As the deputy began talking, I turned back to the prisoner and lowered my voice.

"The man you stabbed is dead."

"Didn't stab no man," he said. "Stabbed a damn bird. 'Bout clawed my eye out."

"Yes. A bird clawed your eye. And you stabbed a bird, but no bird was found. It was a man. How do you suppose that happened?" As I spoke, I turned so my back was to Doyle and the deputy and moved my cupped hand in front of me. An effort of will, and fire bloomed in my palm.

The man's face went white.

"I know you've seen magic before," I said. "You're well acquainted with what it can do. Did you know, I wonder, that your Mr. Broaderick isn't the only one in the territory who can use it? Your Mr. Broaderick, who isn't here, while I am." I smiled, an unpleasant smile, then went on. "They left you behind, you know. Rode out of town yesterday. They killed a woman—an innocent woman—and took a young girl with them." I let the fire grow. "I want her back. And you're going to tell me where she is."

"I don't know," he said.

"I don't believe you."

"I don't care what you believe, bitch."

"You will," I said. "You're going to care." I paused, then echoed Broaderick's words when he'd discovered the far-listening. "You're going to beg to tell me."

Make him hurt, I told Zalgammon.

The demon spoke in his own language, and I felt his power flow through me.

The man groaned and clutched at his head.

I let it go on for a moment. *Enough*, I thought.

Zalgammon was displeased. *You said I could do as I wished.*

I said you could use the spells you wished, I replied. *Not that I would let you torture him for nothing. I need him answering questions, not writhing in pain for pain's sake. Now pull the spell back.*

The prisoner slumped forward, panting.

"Tell me about the leader of your band," I said. "Marcus Broaderick. What sort of magic can he manage? Beyond summoning demons?"

The man's eyes widened.

"Yes," I went on. "I already know a great deal about what you've been doing. You set a demon on a homestead. On a Union patrol. On an Indian war band. Probably others."

He didn't speak, and I sighed.

Another, I said to Zalgammon.

This one did something that made the cords in the prisoner's throat stand out. He looked as if he were screaming, but no sound emerged.

I stopped it after a moment, and Zalgammon sighed in disappointment.

"Tell me," I said to the prisoner.

He'd had enough. After a shuddering swallow, he began talking, to Zalgammon's palpable dismay. Broaderick had been in the territory for nearly a year. He'd come alone and began gathering followers from among the Southern miners. They'd been summoning larger and larger demons. He bargained with them for additional powers, promising them blood and lives. It served a dual purpose, making him more powerful and testing the binding bowls.

"Where is the camp?" I asked when he ran dry. It was the only thing he hadn't told me, and the only thing I needed to know.

"I can't," he said.

Zalgammon sent another spell at the man, and this time he curled in on himself, quivering in silent agony.

"Tell me," I said through gritted teeth. "Where is the camp?"

It went on for longer than I thought he would withstand. He was wet with sweat and shuddering as if with an ague by the time he gave me a look I interpreted as surrender.

"I'll tell you," he panted. "Just make it stop." He sucked in a breath. "West of town, in the mountains," he began, then stopped as abruptly as if a hand had gripped his throat, his good eye bulging.

"Go on," I said.

But he could not. His face reddened. Foam appeared at the corners of his lips.

"What's happening?" I asked, my heart racing.

There is a binding on him, Zalgammon replied. *It was invoked when he began to tell you where the camp is located.*

"Break it," I said. "He hasn't told us what we need yet."

I am trying. I cannot.

The prisoner's face was going purple, and a dark stain spread at his groin as his bladder gave way.

I spun to face Doyle and the deputy. "He's having some sort of fit," I shouted.

The men raced forward, and the deputy took one look inside the cell and swore, fumbling in his pocket for the key. He got the cell door open, and we all rushed inside, but it was already too late.

The prisoner was dead, taking with him our only link to Samantha.

⊙══╾═○

I'd never seen a man closer to the edge of despair than Doyle was as we left the sheriff's station.

Back at Bonnie's, the undertaker had come and gone. Her body had been removed, but the spot where it had lain still drew my eyes. The door was barely closed behind us before Doyle swung to face me and gripped my shoulders. "Please tell me he told you where she is. Please."

The raw pleading in his face made my throat ache. "There was a spell on him," I said. "It killed him when he started to confess. All I know is they're somewhere in the mountains to the west. I'm sorry."

I might have expected him to vow he'd find her, ride the whole of the mountain range if he had to. But he, better than anyone, knew how impossible it was—there were thousands of miles of wilderness in which they could be hiding. With no better direction than "west," he could search for the rest of his life without finding her. And Samantha didn't have that kind of time.

"Tell me you can find her," he begged. "Tell me there's something you can do."

I'd spent the walk back trying desperately to come up with just such a thing. A tracking spell, maybe, made from Samantha's hair. But I doubted I could make something that would work from so far away with my own power. I would have to use Zalgammon's.

"We're going to find her," I said. "I'll do whatever it takes."

He fell to his knees and broke then, weeping, wrapping his arms around my waist and burying his face in my stomach. It was grief, and terror, of the sort only a man faced with losing everything in the world that mattered to him can feel.

I stroked his hair, my hands numb with dread. I had no choice. I needed the demon's help, and I shuddered to think what he would take in exchange. But if I wouldn't pay, I would condemn Samantha.

Zalgammon, I began. *I need*—

Something crashed against the front window, and I let out a little yelp. Peter. He cawed and battered at the glass with wings and beak, holding something dark in his claws.

I unwound Doyle's arms from my waist and hurried to raise the window. Peter swooped inside, flying in circles around me twice before dropping his burden on the floor with a click and landing on the back of a chair, cawing madly.

I stared stupidly at the thing he'd dropped. It was one of the combs I'd given Samantha.

I looked at the sleek black bird, still perched on the chair. "Where—" It hit me then. "Was she wearing them when she was taken?"

He flapped his wings and cawed, and I knew it for a yes.

"You found them. The Broken Eye charms don't work on you. Is Paul tracking them? Can you show us where they are?"

Peter launched himself from the chair and out the window, then circled, cawing, waiting for us to follow.

TWENTY-FOUR

D oyle would have ridden out that instant, but I convinced him to give me an hour. He spent the time gathering supplies.

I used it to write a letter to Marthe.

We were about to do something unbearably dangerous. If we failed, the Magisterium needed to know about Broaderick and his plans. I outlined everything I'd learned and told her where to find the books and bowl if she needed help convincing the rest of the council. I explained about Samantha and asked her to make certain the girl was trained, if she somehow survived and her father and I did not.

I struggled with whether to confess to her about Zalgammon. If this letter was the last thing she ever heard from me, I hated to think of her left disappointed in me, yet again. In the end, I said nothing. If Josiah were right, and Zalgammon was bound to my flesh until it was no more, then even if I died in the mountains, he wouldn't be free to possess someone else. Marthe wouldn't have that particular bitterness attached to her memory of me.

I hesitated, then added one final paragraph.

I've learned a great deal over the past few months about what it means to make choices and how important it is to take responsibility for them. I wish you were here to advise me about this one, but however I look at it, I cannot fail to act. Broaderick must be stopped, and there is no one else here to do it, so I must try. I want you to know I regret every bit of pain and sadness I've ever caused you, and I wish I'd been able to make it right.

I signed my name at the bottom and added the date. Doyle hovered over me as I folded the letter into an envelope.

"We're all packed up," he said. "The horses are outside."

"I'm ready," I said, standing.

We stopped by the Golden Rose on the way out of town, and I left the letter with Inge, with instructions to mail it if I didn't return within a week.

Broaderick and his men had almost a full day's lead on us, and Doyle kicked Patch into a fast canter as soon as we were out of town. I dug my heels into Dapple's sides and followed, hoping she was as sturdy as she seemed. I knew a spell to wash away fatigue. Maybe I could try it on the animals once we stopped for the night.

Peter wheeled above us, leading us onward for several hours before Paul joined him. The pair of them circled, cawing to one another, before Peter broke off and flew like an arrow due west.

It was the first time I'd been west of the city, and the terrain was different than that only a few miles to the east, the grass-covered swells and rocky outcroppings more frequent and pronounced.

The day was cold, and I was grateful for the heavy buffalo robes Doyle had brought. Mine was long enough to cover my legs and Dapple's flanks, and it helped trap her warmth beneath me. It didn't help my face, however, and my cheeks were numb before we'd gone three miles.

There was no sign of Broaderick's band having passed this way, and I wondered if they'd taken a different route, or if some sort of magic had disguised their trail. The Broken Eye charm shouldn't be able to do such a thing, but there was nothing to say there wasn't another spell, one I didn't know about, that could.

I considered asking Zalgammon, then discarded the notion. The demon had been quiet since the prisoner's death. Brooding, I suspected, over his failure to sense the spell before it triggered. There was no point in stirring him up to satisfy my curiosity. We would have to trust Peter and Paul to lead us in the right direction.

We pushed onward, stopping only long enough to water the horses. We ate jerked meat and dry bread in the saddle. We didn't talk, Doyle because he was holding himself together by sheer force of will, and me because there was nothing to say. He drove the horses to the edge of their endurance, and I kept a careful eye on Dapple and Patch. If they collapsed, we were lost. But he knew it too, and each time I worried we were pushing them too hard, he slowed them to rest.

The mountains to the west gradually grew larger. The light began to dim.

"We have to find a place to stop for the night," I called ahead to Doyle. We couldn't travel through the night. It would be too dark, too cold, and the horses needed to rest.

"Not yet," he shouted back without turning.

I let another half hour pass. I was on the verge of insisting we stop when I realized Doyle had pulled us off course, bearing north of the line the crows had set.

We cantered over a ridge, and I drew up in surprise.

Tucked in behind a windbreak of pines, hidden in the shallow valley between two hills, was a tiny cabin and barn, hardly distinguishable from one another, with low roofs and no sign of habitation.

Doyle made straight for it. The barn was tight-chinked and snug, and we tied the horses inside. I untacked them and gave them their oats—whispering the refreshing spell as I did it—while he broke the ice over the stream and hauled in water for them. It was full dark by then, the only light that of the lamp he carried in his pack. We brushed the horses and flung a pair of the buffalo robes over their backs, and Doyle declared they would be warm enough.

Taking up the lamp and our bedrolls, he led me to the cabin door and pushed it open.

Inside, the single room was empty save for blown-in pine needles and dust. There was a fireplace, however, and split firewood was stacked four feet high all along one wall.

"What is this place?" I asked as I spread the bedrolls and he built a fire.

"Used to belong to a man named McGovey," Doyle said without turning. "He came out a couple of years ago. Thought he was going to set himself up to trade with miners. Put his outpost out here, where they wouldn't have to take the extra day to go all the way into town. It would leave them with more time to dig, and he could charge more. It wasn't a terrible idea, necessarily. But the miners don't just go into town for supplies. That's where the women and the whiskey are—McGovey didn't have either of those, though he'd have gotten them in time, I'd wager.

"He didn't reckon on the winter, though. It's too harsh this close to the mountains. Feet upon feet of snow. Winds so cold your skin freezes wherever it's exposed. Almost no one overwinters in the camps. McGovey thought he'd stay out here by himself."

"And?" I asked, knowing the story probably didn't end with the man giving up and going back east.

"The first miners on their way back out in the spring found him. Or what was left of him. Best anyone can tell, he'd gone out during a blizzard and had gotten turned around. Froze to death twenty feet from the cabin."

Doyle had gotten the fire going as he spoke, and he turned away from it with a sigh.

I handed him more bread and dried meat from the pack. He ate it as if he didn't much want to but knew he needed it.

"Get some sleep," he said. "We're starting out again before first light."

Zalgammon, I began, not sure what I was going to offer the demon in exchange for leaving me be as I slept. But he surprised me.

I will do nothing, he said.

Why? I demanded, instantly on my guard.

What is there to do? We ride toward what I want. If I hinder you, I hinder myself.

I'd sat up with Josiah all the night before, then ridden hard most of today, so despite my worry and heartsickness, I fell asleep at once. I woke sometime in the night. The fire was low, a mere glow in the hearth, but the cabin was better-built than it seemed, and the warmth hadn't leaked away. Doyle lay on his bedroll, but he wasn't asleep.

"They need Samantha alive," I said. "They won't hurt her."

"The new moon is tomorrow night," he replied. "You said that's when they conjure their demons. When they—" He cut himself off. "If we don't catch up to them before then, she's gone."

"We're going to catch them and get her back."

"You don't know that," he said. His voice was like a lash. "Ah, God, she's all I have. Those monsters have her, and they're going to—" He let out a strangled sob, then choked it back. "All this. It's too much. I wish I didn't know any of it, that none of it had ever happened. I wish you—" He managed to stop himself, but I knew what he'd been about to say.

"Do you think I don't know all this is my fault?" I said, sitting up. "Do you think I haven't been hating myself for bringing it into your life? Samantha would be asleep in her bed right now if I'd left you all alone. Josiah and Bonnie would still be alive if I hadn't been such a fool. They were sick, but they could have had more time if it weren't for me. I'd give anything to be able to take it all back, but I can't."

I was almost panting by the time I'd finished.

"No," he said after a long moment. "It's not your fault, much as I want someone to blame. Samantha had that demon in her before you came. Maybe it would have healed her if you hadn't been there, or maybe it would have let her die and killed most of Denver City just for the fun of it. And Broaderick was out there already, before you came, doing all this. He would have killed the Jensens and the patrol and the Indians and God only knows who else if you'd never come.

"Maybe you could have done some things differently," he said, fingering the amulet on his chest. He sighed, then dropped it and looked at me. "Or maybe we're all fooling ourselves. We think we're away from the war, but we're not. I fought the rebels at Glorieta Pass because I believe in the Union. If Broaderick's doing all this to help the rebs, then this is just another front. And there'd be no chance of winning without you."

Something loosened in my chest at his words. "You should get some sleep if you can," I said. "Tomorrow's going to be a long day. We're going to have to be smart about this fight, and we can't do that when we're exhausted."

⌖

We were underway again before dawn was more than a promise in the east. I had no idea if my spell had done anything, but both horses seemed fresh enough. They kept up their pace throughout the morning, cantering along beneath an ominous, smoke-colored sky. The air had the feel of snow in it, and at midday, when icy flecks began stinging my cheeks, I wanted to scream with fury and frustration. Real snow would slow us, perhaps fatally. I tried not to think about McGovey dying a few feet from safety.

But the weather held off, the snow only beginning to fall in earnest as we left the plains and entered the foothills. The terrain changed, growing steeper and rockier. Above us, the mountains loomed, white-capped and forbidding.

Peter and Paul had been leapfrogging ahead of us for a day and a half, but now they stayed close, flying from tree to tree and urging us on with their harsh calls. I took it for a sign that Broaderick and his party had reached their destination. A desperate hope filled me. They could not be so very far from us now. But every bit of this place looked like every other bit. It was all rock and scrub pine and snow. Samantha's life hung in the balance, and despite my trust in Peter and Paul, I worried.

Half a dozen times, I fished the comb Peter had brought me from my pocket and took a breath to try a finding spell. There were strands of Samantha's hair still in it. They would be enough. But each time, I let the words die unspoken and tucked the comb away again. Even if we were close enough to make it work, even if my magic were strong enough, it was too dangerous. Such spells put a rime of magic around the object being sought. If Broaderick felt it, he would know we were close. It was too great a risk when surprise was all we had on our side.

And Peter and Paul showed no hesitation as they led us on through what would without them have been a featureless maze of boulders and tumbled rock. I worried about sentries, but the crows were more likely to spot them than we were. So far, there had been nothing.

We found their camp just before sunset. It might have been set up to pass for a mining operation at first glance, but even a cursory second look was enough to reveal the charade. Tools were rusted, sluices off-kilter and leaking, and the pile of logs ostensibly meant to serve as tunnel bracing was slimy and rotted. There were half a dozen tiny, shed-like cabins, all empty, and a rough-hewn stable with a dozen horses tethered to a bar inside. They'd been fed and watered, but their coats were stiff with dried sweat. Wherever they'd taken Samantha from here, they'd left on foot and in a hurry.

Doyle and I led our mounts into the shelter and tied them. Before we could exit, Paul squawked a warning call from outside. An instant later, the sound of footsteps echoing over rock reached us, followed by voices.

". . . see why he won't let us stay for it," said the first one. It was young, male, with an overtone of complaint.

The second voice was older. "You don't want to stay. I saw plenty the last time. Believe me, brushing down the horses is the better job."

Doyle and I exchanged a glance. He drew his knife, his face cold, and I nodded, understanding. There was nowhere to hide, and we couldn't afford to let them give the alarm, couldn't afford to merely tie them up and leave them alive at our backs. They were a part of this, and there could be no mercy. I gathered myself and tugged the gloves from my hands.

The first one stepped through the door, the second on his heels. They saw us, and there was time for their faces to register little more than surprise before we were on them. I leapt forward to touch the face of the nearest one, and Zalgammon tore the life from him like a boy stripping the wings from a fly. He folded where he stood, crumpling to the packed dirt floor with a muffled thump that didn't even make the horses look up from their meals.

His energy flowed into me, and I doubled over with the force of it, full to bursting, a low groan that was half horror, half pleasure escaping from my lips. There was a whiff of sweet carrion stink, there and gone again so quickly I didn't have time to be sickened by it.

When I was able to raise my head, Doyle was watching me, warily, his face white and rigid. His knife was red, and the other man was also dead on the ground. Doyle had killed him so quickly and quietly I hadn't even realized it was happening.

I nodded that I was all right, and he bent to clean the blade on one of the dead men's shirts, then shoved it back into its scabbard without a word.

I stared at the bodies on the floor. The one I'd killed was little more than a boy. I studied his lifeless face with a mixture of sorrow and anger churning in my gut. It shouldn't have come to this. It was all the more bitter that I could feel Zalgammon glorying in the additional power.

How did you do that so quickly? I asked. *It felt . . . easy.*

It is easy when you are not fighting me.

I shuddered at the contentment in his voice.

Doyle bent to check the dead men for weapons.

"See if either of them is wearing a Broken Eye," I said, my voice rough.

They weren't. It was likely why they'd been sent outside.

We left the stable, cautiously. Peter and Paul took off from the roof and flew across the camp, both of them lighting on one of the stunted trees growing almost horizontally out of the jagged rock face.

In the shadow of its limbs was a dark, narrow opening in the stone.

"This is it?" I said to them, and they flapped their wings in affirmation.

I glanced back at Doyle. "I'm going first."

To his credit, he didn't argue.

Crouching to step into the passage itself felt like nothing so much as being swallowed by some ancient, long-necked beast. The absence of wind made it feel warmer than the outside, though the air remained chill and damp. The tunnel curved, cutting off the last rays of the sun and plunging us into blackness. I stopped, waiting for my eyes to adjust, but there wasn't enough light. I didn't want to use magic, not with Broaderick nearby.

Zalgammon spoke. *Use my eyes.*

I blinked, and the tunnel brightened, the divots and outcroppings growing sharper, the shadows separating. Somewhere behind me, Doyle stumbled and let out a muffled curse.

"Hold on to me," I whispered, half turning. "I can guide you."

Doyle's hands fumbled until they found my shoulders, and we shuffled along, my certain footsteps dogged by his hesitant ones, though they grew more confident as I guided him. The tunnel grew wider, taller. I was able to stand straight, and after another bend, so was he. I kept a sharp watch for light ahead, for guards, for any sign Broaderick and his men knew we'd followed them, but there was nothing.

It felt as though we'd been walking for hours, so far into the mountain I half expected to come out the other side. But there had been so many switchbacks I'd lost count; we couldn't have gone as far as it seemed. We had, however, been going deeper. I thought I could feel the tons of rock pressing down on me overhead, and thoughts of cave-ins, of winding up trapped as I did in my nightmares, made my chest grow ever tighter as we descended.

"Joya," Doyle murmured, his breath warm on the back of my neck. "I can see. It's getting lighter."

He was right. It was subtle, but there was light somewhere ahead of us. We slowed and kept going as the tunnel continued to lighten. Another turn, and the tunnel began to angle upward toward a doorway in the rock, too perfectly arched to be natural. The sound of low voices reverberated through it.

We were close.

I fought the urge to rush forward and pressed my back against the tunnel wall, easing toward the opening one slow, deliberate step at a time. I gripped Doyle's wrist, unsure whether I was urging him forward or holding him back.

At the edge of the doorway, I twisted my head far enough to peer around the lip. It opened onto a shelf of rock strangely reminiscent of a private box in an opera house—rounded, with a waist-high front wall I couldn't see over from where I stood. To the right, a set of rough-carved stairs led downward.

I went to my hands and knees and crawled out onto the shelf. Doyle couldn't do the same, what with one hand still hampered by the splint and wrap and the other holding his gun, but he dropped into a crouch and stayed low as he followed. We reached the front of the shelf, and I lifted my head just far enough to see over the edge. We were in an enormous cavern. The walls were shot through with veins of quartz, which shimmered in the flickering light of dozens of oil lamps tucked in niches around the space. The ceiling was barely visible, soaring some twenty feet overhead.

On the floor, an equal distance below, a pair of massive ritual circles had been carved into the stone, one nested inside the other. Seven men stood around the circumference of the outer circle. Five more stood on the inner circle, arranged as if at the points of a pentagram. In the space between the two stood a quartz-striped stone plinth holding a binding bowl like the one I'd found in the trunk. Beside it stood Samantha and Marcus Broaderick. One of Broaderick's hands was wrapped around Samantha's upper arm. The other held an enormous knife.

Beside me, Doyle tensed as if readying himself to leap down on them. I put a hand on his arm. "Wait," I breathed. "They haven't started yet. We have time."

On the heels of my words, Broaderick spoke, and the other men went silent.

"Brothers," he began. "The time of preparation has ended. Tonight, we strike the blow that will break the Union."

The men burst into excited mutterings, and he waited until they quieted before he went on. "All that we have done until now was meant to ready us for this moment. This vessel," he went on, pointing to the binding bowl with the knife, "will break, not here in the Colorado Territory, but on the battlefields of the east, and the being we summon this night will sweep our glorious cause to victory."

The men cheered and whistled, their jubilation echoing around the cavern until it sounded as though they were hundreds strong.

Broaderick cut them off with a gesture, then raised the hand holding the knife. "Begin," he said.

The men straightened and joined hands before beginning a low, rhythmic chant. Magic washed over me as the circles went up, and the sensation made every hair on my body prickle. I thought quickly. Broaderick did not seem to have sensed we were near—too focused on the ritual and perhaps too arrogant to believe we could have found him. Casting a spell would probably alert him, but if it were strong enough, it might be worth it.

Zalgammon, can we kill Broaderick from here?

No. He is inside an invoked circle. And even if he were not, he added, *he would have to be a very great fool not to have some sort of protection.*

Can you disable the men holding the outer circle? I asked.

I can see only the warlock and the child, he replied. *If there are others, they are hidden from me.*

I grimaced. They were wearing the Broken Eye charm.

Very well. At a minimum, we needed to break the outer circle. I was tempted to tell Doyle to shoot one of the men holding it. But there were more of them than us, and they were armed. Once they knew we were here, we would be wildly outnumbered. And they had a hostage.

We had to be cleverer than they were. They still didn't know we were here. The longer we could keep them from realizing it, the better.

Can you shield me from their notice if I approach? And hide me from Broaderick?

Zalgammon considered. *Perhaps. But you will not be able to use your power while hidden. It will reveal you.*

The chanting changed, and the air in the cavern went charged and heavy. My chest tightened. We were out of time.

"Can you shoot Broaderick from here?" I whispered to Doyle. We might have to kill him and risk having to fight the rest of them.

Doyle's mouth twisted. "No. The angle is wrong. He's too close to Samantha."

"All right," I said, deciding. "Give me your knife. I'm going down there. Zalgammon will hide me," I said, not mentioning the demon's reservations. "When I raise my hand, shoot one of the men in the outer circle. The outer circle," I repeated. "Not the inner. If they manage to summon the demon before I get to Samantha, we can't let it get free."

Doyle didn't argue, pulling the knife I'd given him for Christmas from the sheath at his belt and flipping it to hand me the hilt. I took it, remembering what Josiah had said—that with a bit of power fed into it, it could cut through anything. I hoped the power I could summon would be enough.

I eased myself up and toward the steps, slowly, my eyes on the men below.

I can shield you from their sight, but not their hearing, Zalgammon warned.

Fortunately, the chamber echoed, and the sound of the chanting bounced off the hard surfaces. It should cover whatever noise my shoes made on the rock. Still, I held my breath as I went. I was out in the open, and if Zalgammon's shield failed, I'd be spotted at once.

I reached the bottom of the stairs and began moving around the outside of the larger circle, making my way toward Broaderick. The floor was littered with jagged chunks of striped stone. Detritus left over from the making of the chamber, probably—I couldn't imagine it was wholly natural. I picked my way among the rocks, leery of tripping or drawing notice by crushing one of the smaller pieces with an errant step.

The cavern was even larger than it had appeared from our little balcony, and the amount of ground I needed to cross without being discovered made my palms grow damp. The lamps' flickering light cast long, dancing shadows and added a faint scent of smoke to the damp air. My eyes bobbed from the floor to the men and back again. The Broken Eye charms they wore kept me from focusing on their faces, so I couldn't tell if the two I'd overheard in Bonnie's restaurant that night were there.

One face stood out like a beacon, however. Even from this distance, Samantha looked terrified, her small face pinched and white. I wished there were some way I could reassure her.

I was looking at Samantha, not Broaderick, so I flinched when his voice rang out above the drone of the chant.

"Belmathok! Beneath the new moon I summon thee. Belmathok! With thy name I summon thee. Belmathok! With blood I summon thee," Broaderick said again. "Be free to cross the realms."

The air in the inner circle rippled. I was out of time. Noise be damned, I broke into a run, sprinting across the floor and skidding to a stop behind the man standing on the outer circle nearest to Broaderick, just as a snapping sound echoed through the cavern. An enormous billow of black, sulfurous smoke rippled into being inside the inner circle. The men holding it shifted nervously. There was a lull in their chanting—not a break, but a tiny stutter.

"Hold," Broaderick commanded. "The circle will contain it."

Gradually, the smoke cleared, revealing the demon now standing in their midst. Looking at it made my stomach twist. Some ten or twelve feet tall, and bulky, with sickly yellow, goat-slitted eyes the size of dinner plates below a pair of horns that spiraled into wicked points three feet above its head. A long, triangular snout with needle-shaped teeth the length of my thumbs. Three-fingered hands and feet, all tipped in curved obsidian claws. Over it all, a cracked, leathery hide, grayish-black and iridescent as an oil slick, its haunches covered in quill-like feathers.

Zalgammon recoiled within me, his horror as cold as falling through the ice over a lake.

What is it?

Broaderick has summoned a Greater Demon, he breathed, his voice filled with awe and terror. *We have to run. That circle will not contain her for long.*

She will break free?

Without a doubt, he said.

That changed things. The goal was no longer to keep the demon in the circle. Now it was a matter of breaking the circle when it was to my advantage.

Broaderick spoke. "Demon, I would bargain with you."

"What do you offer?" Belmathok sounded as if she were only half listening. She crouched, peering at the men holding the inner circle. They flinched away from her gaze. My breath caught in my throat. The Broken Eye wasn't working.

"These trinkets you wear may hide you from my lesser kin," she said. "But they will not protect you from me." She raised a taloned hand and flattened it against the air over the circle, as if against a pane of glass. But panes of glass did not usually flex, and I swallowed hard. Zalgammon was right about this demon's power. I had to hurry.

While all attention was on Belmathok, I edged forward, as close to the back of the man in front of me as I dared, my hand tightening around the hilt of the knife.

I raised my free hand to signal Doyle. A shot rang out, and the man directly across the circle from me staggered sideways and dropped. In the instant of confusion that followed, I plunged the knife into the back of the man I stood behind and put my other hand to the back of his neck. The contact was enough to overcome the Broken Eye. The wound I'd given him was likely mortal, but it didn't matter. Zalgammon took him, and he was dead before his body hit the floor. The power hit me, and I gagged, but there was no time to wait for the sensation to pass. I fought for control as the outer circle fell and the remaining men cried out in fear and confusion.

"Hold," Broaderick bellowed again, taking a half step toward the man who had been shot, perhaps still not realizing what had happened.

I lunged forward and snatched Samantha by the wrist, dragging her out of Broaderick's grip. He spun, and the shielding spell must have fallen, because furious recognition filled his face. "You."

He reached for me, and I slashed out with the knife as I danced backward, shoving Samantha behind me. Broaderick screamed as two of his fingers flew into the air, red droplets falling from their severed ends. He staggered back, clutching his mangled hand to his chest. His lips moved, and though I couldn't hear the words, I could tell he was muttering an incantation.

I kept an eye on the men as I pulled Samantha toward the stairs. The inner circle of men didn't dare move, too frightened by Belmathok to react to what was going on around them.

Those who had been holding the outer circle were in disarray. Two were dead. One was bent over one of his fallen comrades. Another was moving toward Broaderick. Two were staring in terror at the demon. One, however, had his eyes on us and was pulling his gun. Before he could aim it, there was another shot, and he went down, his head snapping back in a spray of dark blood.

Doyle met us at the bottom of the stairs, the barrel of his gun still trailing smoke.

"Take her back through the tunnel," I said, shoving Samantha at her father. "Take one of the lamps and go." I glanced behind me. With the second shot, more of the men had realized what was happening and were drawing their guns, shouting.

"What about you?" Doyle asked. He shot a third man.

We have to go, said Zalgammon. *You have the girl.*

I couldn't leave, not with a Greater Demon in a weak circle. She would get loose, and the destruction would be terrible. I had no idea what I was going to do, but there had to be a way to banish her, even if I wasn't the one who had called her. The men were afraid. Broaderick was weakened by his injury. It could be done. "I'll be right behind you. I—"

Broaderick's voice rang out, cutting through the noise. "Belmathok, I offer a bargain."

I snapped my head around. The demon was still in the smaller circle, though the men holding it looked as if they would break at any moment.

Broaderick stood outside the circle, facing the demon, who was regarding him with lazy interest.

"What bargain?"

"Leave me and those who wear my charm unharmed," he went on. He flung his hand out, and I had an instant in which to note that whatever magic he had used had sealed the bleeding stumps of his fingers before I realized he was pointing at me.

"In exchange, I will free you from the circle and give you the body and blood of a witch."

TWENTY-FIVE

E verything stopped.

The demon's eyes met mine, and her nostrils flared. She inhaled deeply, as if scenting the air. "A witch, indeed. Strong, but bound." Another breath. "And she carries one of my kin within her. Greetings, youngling."

Zalgammon moaned in fear, and any hope I had that one demon would hesitate to attack another died as Belmathok went on.

"Your power is hardly worth the taking, little one, but I have never been one to turn down a snack." Her tongue, long and thin and black, came out to swipe at her muzzle. "The witch, however . . ." She took another breath, and the expression of anticipation that spread over her face made me want to scream until my throat bled. "The witch is a delicacy worth savoring."

"Then you accept the bargain?" Broaderick asked.

The demon turned her attention back to him and smiled, and it was enough to make the air go cold. "I have no need of your bargain."

Casually, she shoved a hand through the circle, which fell with a crack like thunder. With another languid movement, Belmathok disemboweled one of the stunned men who had been holding the circle. His eyes went wide with shock and horror as he stared down at his entrails, now falling in bloody ropes to the stone floor.

Chaos erupted. Men screamed and ran, some firing their weapons at the demon with as much effect as boys shooting peas at a fence post. Bullets bounced off the cavern walls, striking sparks and sending chips of stone flying. Broaderick began bellowing spells, the words lost in the noise, but flashes of fire and the stench of burning flesh and singed hair began to fill the space.

"Go!" I shouted, giving Doyle and Samantha a shove.

An instant later, Doyle grunted and stumbled backward as a bullet punched into him. He fell.

I screamed something and went to my knees beside him. He blinked up at me, his shoulder blooming red.

Another bullet went past my head, near enough that I felt the hot wind of its passage. It was only a matter of time before we took another hit.

"Help me move him," I shouted to Samantha. "And stay down!"

She scurried to help, and we managed to drag him behind an outcropping of rock. That would stop further shots, at least.

"Pressure, put pressure on it," I said. I took Samantha's hands and put them on the wound, showing her where to press.

"I don't think it's so bad," Doyle gasped. "Probably just a ricochet. Doesn't even hurt much."

Idiot, Zalgammon said, and I agreed with him. Doyle wasn't hurting because he was still wearing the pain charm. And it didn't matter if it was a ricochet—he could bleed to death from an accidental wound as easily as an intentional one.

But it occurred to me with a horrible abruptness that bleeding to death might be a kindness. They couldn't get up the stairway now. There was no cover. Doyle would be slow from blood loss, if he could even manage to move under his own power. They'd be picked off by a bullet or an errant spell before they made it halfway. We were all trapped here with a Greater Demon. We were all going to die. Likely gruesomely.

For a moment, I wanted to cower there in relative safety and wait for it to be over. But that was foolishness. Better to die fighting.

I made myself move, calling up my tiny bead of magic and pouring it into the knife. I dragged the blade across the stone floor, inscribing a circle around them. Just as Josiah had promised, fed by power, the blade cut through the rock as if it were tallow. I nicked my finger and pressed the bloody tip to the circle and invoked it. It was a meager protection, but it was better than nothing.

"Stay here," I said. "Don't draw attention to yourselves. No shooting unless someone is coming right at you and you have no choice."

"Joya, what are you doing?" Doyle asked.

Samantha, her hands still pressed to his shoulder, was sobbing in terror.

"The demon is loose," I said. "I have to try to stop it."

You cannot, Zalgammon screamed inside my head. *You are not strong enough.*

Then you have to help me.

Me? he shrieked. *A hundred of me would not be enough to defeat her! Stupid witch—she is a Greater Demon.*

I am doing this, I thought. *Help me, or we both die.*

I stepped out from behind the outcrop. Almost at once, a reeling man stumbled into me, his face blank with terror. Zalgammon snatched his life away, and he fell. The power thundered into me, overwhelming, but I had no time to react. Bullets were still flying, and chunks of rock, and even a ball of fire, which streaked toward me from somewhere on the other side of the cavern. I dropped to the floor, and it passed through the space where I had been before exploding against the wall behind me.

I lifted my head far enough to look for the source and found Broaderick on the far side of the cavern, staring at me, his expression caught somewhere between terror and rage. Even as I watched, he gouged a chunk of rock from the wall of the cavern with his bare hand and flung it at me, its magic-assisted flight fast enough to blur. I twitched away, barely, and it smashed against the floor beside my shoulder. Another fireball bloomed in his hand. He hurled that at me as well, and I scrambled out of its path. I didn't know what he was doing, whether he thought he could regain control of the situation or whether he merely wanted to kill me for interfering, but I couldn't let him keep trying.

Zalgammon, hide me again, I thought.

I rolled hard to one side and scrambled to my feet as the spell settled over me. A third fireball slammed into the spot where I'd been lying. I darted a glance in Broaderick's direction and caught a flash of frustration on his face before the warlock disappeared as if blinking out of existence. I sucked in a startled breath.

He bargained with me for the power to hide himself, Zalgammon reminded me. *He has invoked it, just as you have done.*

Well. At least he wouldn't be hurling any more fireballs for the moment. I'd just have to hope I didn't blunder into him.

I turned toward Belmathok.

She had not moved from her position inside the second circle, but now she had a screaming man pinned to the floor beneath one of her massive claws. She was ripping pieces off of him in a slow, methodical way that seemed designed to leave him alive as long as possible. The area around her was littered with the remnants of at least one other man. The expression on her face was one of sublime pleasure, as if she were engaged in a favorite pastime and in no hurry to see it end.

Only four of Broaderick's original twelve men remained alive. All of them lay splayed on the cavern floor around the demon, staring at nothing and screaming as if in agony, though none had any visible injury.

She is a demon of the mind, Zalgammon said in answer to my unvoiced question. *She feeds not only on the life force but on the fear and pain of souled beings. She has overtaken them. Filled them with terror. They see their fears made real. She will do the same to you if you get too close. I am not powerful enough to hide you from her.*

As I watched, the man beneath her claws gave a final shriek and died. She tossed what was left of the corpse aside and plucked up another of the living men as if pulling a berry from a bush. His face changed, awareness coming back to him, and the tenor of his screams changed as she laid him almost gently on the ground and began to slice at him with her claws.

Pity and horror all but choked me.

Fool, Zalgammon said, feeling it. *These men are your enemy. They would have set you where they are now.*

I know. But no one deserves this.

She is distracted, Zalgammon said. *Take the man and the girl and get out. I can hide the three of you. You cannot hope to defeat her.*

I can't leave her free. She is too dangerous.

Then we will be destroyed, he said, despair in his voice.

Perhaps. I averted my eyes from the slow torture before me, and my gaze fell on the binding bowl sitting forgotten on the plinth. Both surfaces shimmered in the flickering light of the still-burning lamps, making it appear as if they were of a piece. A tiny tendril of an idea came to me. *Or perhaps not.*

I edged closer, thinking quickly. Yes. It could work. There would be no room for error, but if I could manage it . . . There it was again: hope.

Zalgammon, I thought. *Will you be able to tell when we're getting close enough for her to overtake us?*

Yes. What are you doing? I can tell you think you have thought of something clever, but I cannot see what it is.

Just warn me when we are within her range, I thought. *Then drop the cloaking spell when I tell you. I'll need my magic.*

Keeping well back, trying to ignore the slow-moving slaughter happening only feet away and shut out the screams filling the air, I made my way back around the remnants of the outer circle, toward the plinth, my heart hammering inside my chest.

I was still some feet away from my goal when Zalgammon spoke.

We are—

He didn't get a chance to finish. A spike of terror hammered through me, freezing me in place and tearing a groan from my lips.

Belmathok raised her head from the man she was savaging and looked in our direction. Her thin black tongue came out to lick at the blood dripping from her muzzle. "I know you are there, little witch." She drew her lips back from her teeth in a parody of a grin.

The terror redoubled. Zalgammon's, as well as mine. I could barely form the command. *Let it go.*

The cloaking spell fell away, and I scrabbled desperately to push the fear aside, to find enough focus to draw on my power. Somehow, I managed it. I drew the tiny sip of power into myself and held it.

Belmathok rose from her crouch and took a step toward me, reaching.

I let the bead of power roll into Josiah's knife and struck out with it. There was a sudden stench, and the demon yanked her hand back with a snarl. Thick black liquid dripped to the stone floor, sizzling where it landed and leaving little pockmarks in the stone.

Belmathok looked first shocked, then furious. "Little witch, you will pay for that."

The distraction loosened her hold on the men around her, and two of them began to move, trying to crawl away, sobbing. The other collapsed, apparently struck witless by whatever he had been forced to see.

Belmathok whirled and took two strides toward the fleeing men. She stepped on the witless man as she went, and his head burst beneath her foot like a rotten pumpkin.

I didn't wait to see what she did to the others. I lurched toward the plinth. I held my hand over the vessel and drew the tip of Josiah's knife over the fleshy spot beneath my thumb. My blood welled, and I squeezed until it covered the bottom of the bowl. Keeping my eyes down and trying to ignore the sounds of tearing flesh and breaking bone coming from a few feet away, I called up my power again.

My blood tempted this demon. I could bind her with it.

I closed my eyes and pulled on my power again. I sent it tracing my own outline, just as I'd done the night I bound Zalgammon, making the edges of my body into a circle of protection. The cut on my hand sealed as the magic passed over it.

I began the far-listening.

Born together, I thought. *Apart, but whole.*

I could bind this demon not in my body but in the vessel made for the purpose. With all the will and focus I could muster, I linked the blood in the bowl to the blood in my body, willing them together but twisting the intent of the spell into something different. If it worked, then I—and my power, the thing that had so excited two different demons—would exist in two places.

One hidden, inside my body, its allure muffled by the binding on my wrist and the protection of the circle.

The other visible and tempting, in the shallow bowl, proclaiming my true power and free for the taking. *Apart, but whole*, I thought again, and let the spell go.

I felt Belmathok's approach but didn't dare look up at her, too afraid it hadn't worked, too afraid I would see her reaching for me—the real me, not the false reflection in the bowl.

"It is time, witch," she said from far too nearby, and I couldn't suppress a tremor.

I almost screamed as her taloned hands reached past my face. They continued on, plunging into the bowl, and my heart leapt as they sank past the wrists, then past the elbows as the spell on its surface began to draw her into its depths.

Belmathok felt it take hold of her and shrieked, trying to pull away. She had strength enough to rip men apart, but the bowl stayed steady on its plinth as she set her feet and fought to free herself. Slowly, slowly, her arms began to emerge.

She is too strong, Zalgammon said, sounding frantic.

The spell carved into the bowl wasn't enough by itself. I had to reinforce it somehow or she would escape.

I dropped my circle, and Belmathok's eyes went wide with shock. "You, witch. You tricked me. I will make you suffer for this."

I drew a breath and gathered my power again for the incantation that would bind her to the bowl. I put a hand to its side and trickled my power into it as I spoke the words of the spell.

"*Per verbo et per sacramento vique ligeris*," I chanted. By word and power be you bound.

Belmathok shrieked in fury and snapped her head forward, trying to tear my throat out with her teeth. I ducked and struck with the knife again. It scored a deep cut across her muzzle, and the pitch of her scream changed.

"*Per sanquine et per magiaque vique ligeris.*" I spoke from between clenched teeth, one hand still on the bowl, still letting my power trickle into it. By blood and magic be you bound.

She did not try another physical strike, instead sending a heavier wave of power at me, and I broke off with a groan as pain bloomed in my head.

It disrupted my focus, and a fresh wave of terror welled within me as the demon's arms slipped another inch out of the bowl.

I was failing. I would fail. She would be free. She would take me. She would take me, and Doyle and Samantha would be helpless against her. They would—

"Witch," she hissed. "You are too late. They are already dead. *See.*"

Her voice scraped against the inside of my mind, an order, and my head swiveled.

Doyle and Samantha lay sprawled in front of the outcrop of rock where I'd hidden them, lying in a lake of their own blood, their throats opened so deeply the white of their spines showed. Their eyes were open, blank and accusing at the same time.

Shock and horror washed the power clear out of me. I let go of the bowl and the knife and the spell and fell to my knees, screaming. Broaderick. Broaderick must have done it, must have crept around the edge of the cavern and overpowered them while I played with my little bits of power and thought myself so clever. They were dead. I had failed them. My screams echoed off the walls, ringing in my head until I thought I would go mad with it, and the thought of madness was a comfort. It promised oblivion.

Someone else was screaming, too, not me, but in me.

Zalgammon.

Zalgammon was screaming, but it didn't matter. It would be over soon, for both of us. We would—His claws raked at my insides, and I screamed again, this time in physical pain.

It is illusion! Illusion! he shrieked. *You are seeing your fear! She found it in your mind and made it seem real. Wake up, you stupid witch, or she will have us both and then it* will *be real!*

I blinked and dragged in a choked, ragged breath. I was lying on my side, and Belmathok was nearly free of the bowl. I turned my head to look at where Doyle and Samantha's bodies had been lying.

There was nothing there.

Rage boiled up within me as I staggered to my feet.

I gathered the tattered remnants of my will and began the spell again. It was not enough. Belmathok was still pulling away, her wrists showing above the rim of the bowl.

Help me, I ordered Zalgammon, then suppressed a shudder as he poured his own power through me.

Belmathok screamed again as her progress stopped, but the bowl did not resume drawing her in. My focus had been disrupted, my will battered by her attacks. I drew harder on my power, pushing against the limits of the binding on my wrist. The silver grew hot, threatening my focus further.

We cannot last like this, Zalgammon cried.

Terror and fury and frustration all mixed together into some new, unnamed emotion, and on its heels, a realization.

He was right. We were at a stalemate, and stalemate meant the demon would triumph. I could not outlast her. I would tire. Will alone could not suffice. My focus would waver, my meager store of power would be exhausted, and she would win free.

If I did not end this, and now, I would fail.

The decision was no decision at all.

I crouched, swept up Josiah's knife from where it had fallen, and, with one swift slice, cut through the silver binding on my wrist.

Power—my full power, unbound—exploded through me.

The sheer pleasure of it tore a groan from my lips. I drank it in, pulled it into my body until it hurt, and sent it out again, straight into the bowl. The Latin of the binding spell rolled off my tongue, and Belmathok shrieked again as the bowl began to draw her in despite her struggles, first slowly, then faster and faster.

But binding her into the bowl was not enough. The bowl could be carried away, could be broken to loose her. The demon would be set free to visit destruction on whatever hapless souls were nearby.

It could not be allowed to happen.

Even as I continued to recite the binding spell, in a separate part of my mind, I began the far-listening again. The far-listening, now turned to a new purpose. The bowl was born of the mountain, carved from it. *Born together. Apart but whole.*

The power was still roaring through me, more than I'd ever dared draw before. More than was sane. Every nerve in my body sang with it, near flayed by the force. And with Josiah's teachings to guide me, I wasted none of it. My will harnessed it. My focus narrowed it until it bored into the spell like a beam of sunlight aimed with a mirror.

Belmathok's physical form began to disintegrate as the spells—both of them, twined together—took hold.

I shook with the strain of holding on to the magic. I couldn't last much longer.

"*In hoc aeno ligeris*," I said, my voice no more than a gasp. Be you bound within this vessel. "*Usque aenum destructum est.*" Until this vessel be destroyed.

With a final, faint shriek of protest, what remained of the demon fell into the bowl, then through it.

Bound.

Not into the bowl, cleaved from the mountain, but into the mountain itself. Bound into its shining, near-infinite veins, trapped so deeply that she could not be released unless the mountain itself were ground into dust.

TWENTY-SIX

I let go of the spell and collapsed in a heap on the cavern floor, numb, dizzy, and gulping for breath like a thing hauled from the depths of the sea.

How did you do that? Zalgammon sounded dazed.

I have no idea, I thought back, too wrung out to speak aloud. *But we're alive. We did it.*

I'd never attempted such a massive spell before, never held such power, and though it was gone now, its echo still rebounded through me, thrumming in my ears.

It covered the sound of Broaderick's approach.

He was beside the plinth when he dropped his cloaking spell, his face waxen.

I swallowed a gasp and made an instinctive attempt to rise, only to find my muscles too spent to obey. All I could manage was an ungainly lurch to one side. At the same time, I groped for my magic and found . . . nothing. The binding spell had taken everything I had.

I was burned out.

I had a moment's worry that it was permanent, that I might have condemned myself to life as a Mundane, before the threat of the here and now reasserted itself. The rest of my life might be measured in minutes. The realization sent a spike of fear through me, and I went still as a hare in the hunter's shadow.

Broaderick didn't seem to notice. "What have you done?" Shock colored his voice. He reached for the binding bowl, holding it in one hand, running his other over the carving inside. "Empty," he whispered. Rage swept over his face. "Useless! All my work come to nothing!" He smashed the bowl against the plinth. Both shattered. Broaderick turned to me, jagged shards of rock trickling through his fingers.

I read my death on his face.

Zalgammon, can you—

The demon interrupted me. *I used it all in binding Belmathok. I am as powerless as you are. I cannot save you.* There was a hint of something—was it regret? Sorrow, even?—in his voice.

Broaderick strode forward. I watched his hands, waiting for fire to spill from them, but they remained clenched into fists. He could have struck me with a killing spell, could have watched me burn. He could have stripped my life away with one ruthless gesture.

Instead, he kicked me in the ribs. Hard.

Pain lanced through my torso, and I felt the crack as at least one of my ribs broke. I might have tried to grab his booted foot, might have tried to get my hand on his skin so Zalgammon could kill him, but the pain was so shocking, so unexpected, that before I could so much as construct the thought, he'd already pulled his leg back and kicked me again.

I grunted and curled away from the blow, wrapping my arms around my head.

He gave me a third kick, this time in the lower back, and I couldn't suppress a ragged scream.

Broaderick bent and dragged me upright by the hair, then backhanded me across the face, the contact too brief for Zalgammon to take him. Pain exploded behind my cheekbone, and I tasted blood.

"Nothing left, is there, witch? The well's gone dry." His mouth split in an unpleasant grin. "I'm going to enjoy this."

Through the haze of tears brought on by the blow, I caught movement behind him.

Samantha.

She crept like a mouse from behind the lip of rock where I'd hidden her and Doyle, tiptoeing her way around the debris—both mineral and human—strewn across the cavern floor. Her hands, stained with her father's dried blood, were wrapped around the grip of his gun.

No, I begged silently. *Stay hidden. Stay safe.*

Broaderick hit me again. My lip split against my teeth. Blood trickled down my chin.

The gun was too big for Samantha, too heavy, and even with both hands she struggled to lift it. The barrel wobbled, dipping down as she reached to pull the hammer back.

The click was loud as a thunderclap in the echoing vastness of the cavern.

Time slowed to a crawl.

Broaderick dropped me and spun, fire already licking from between his fingers. I reached for him, but I couldn't make my body move quickly enough. The fireball was already on its way, already arcing through the air toward the girl, and I could do nothing to stop it.

I had an age to watch as Samantha's eyes widened. To watch as she dropped the gun. With a wordless cry of terror, she brought up an unthinking hand. It was a reflexive, warding gesture, as useless against the magic-bound flames as a shout against a windstorm.

Except it wasn't.

The fire was an inch from slamming into her upraised hand when I felt it, the lightning-quick burst of magic that came from her as her latent power asserted itself.

The fireball snapped back toward Broaderick and took him in the chest before he could so much as take a breath.

The flames rolled upward over his shoulders and face, setting him alight like a torch doused in lamp oil. He screamed, and kept screaming, until he fell to his knees beside me.

I reached out to clamp a hand to his wrist, and Zalgammon made an end to him.

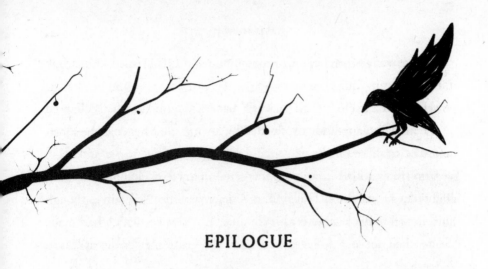

EPILOGUE

I raised my head from *DE VOCATIONE* when Paul's warning call
came from the yard. I was halfway through translating a spell I hoped
might help me turn the crows back into men, but I put down my pen and
stood, dislodging Shadow from my lap. He let out an irritable *mrraow*.

"I know," I said as I stretched the cramp from my back. "Your life is
very difficult." I lifted my coat from its hook. By the time Patch trotted
through the tree line and into the yard, I was waiting in the doorway of
the barn.

Doyle swung down from the horse's back, wincing only a little as the
motion pulled at his arm and shoulder, and strode toward me through
the calf-deep snow, leading the horse behind him.

"Did it come?" I called.

In answer, he dipped a hand into his pocket and withdrew an envelope.

My heart, already thudding against my ribs, threatened to explode
from my chest.

It had been six weeks since Zalgammon and I had sealed Belmathok into the mountain.

After sending the fireball back at Broaderick, Samantha had collapsed in a dead faint, her body overloaded by having used her magic—albeit unintentionally—for the first time. I managed to crawl to her and make certain she was breathing, then staggered to my feet, clutching my ribs, and went to check on Doyle. The Ranger was also still alive, though unconscious. The wound on his shoulder had clotted, which had made Samantha's decision to leave him when she heard me scream at least a bit easier.

I rested for a time, but there was no food or water in the cave, so eventually I slapped them both awake, and the three of us dragged ourselves out of the cavern. We spent several days in the summoners' camp, both Doyle and I too injured to start the journey back to Denver City. Doyle, still wearing the amulets Josiah had made for him, declined any additional aid from Zalgammon. I accepted a tiny healing spell—just enough so it didn't hurt every time I breathed.

Fortunately, there were supplies in the best-built of the cabins.

Broaderick's, obviously, but none of us complained.

We didn't talk much, though I explained about magic and witchcraft to a stunned Samantha, who asked fewer questions than I would have expected and spent most of her time cuddled up beside Doyle, asleep. Her powers didn't manifest again, which was normal, I assured her. They would come back in their own time, and when they did, I'd be there to help her learn to use them safely.

For a time, I wasn't sure how I was going to keep that promise. I'd used more magic in binding Belmathok than I ever imagined I could hold, and I was well and truly burned out. When it began to trickle back, I cried with relief. Even now, using my power still felt like stretching an injured limb, tender and hopeful at once, and I was being careful about the spells I tried.

A snowstorm further delayed our departure from the summoners' camp, and all told we were there ten days. When we got a break in the weather, we decided to make a bid to leave rather than risk being trapped in the mountains by the next storm. We loaded food and medicine onto the summoners' horses, tied them in a line, and departed. We lost three horses on the way down. By the time we got back down to the plains, another storm was brewing.

We made a beeline for McGovey's cabin, which we reached just ahead of the storm. We were there another week before striking out for town. Burdened by the extra horses and our own injuries, our pace was torturously slow.

The whole time, I was keenly aware of the letter I'd left with Inge.

I'd asked the young woman to wait a week before sending it to Marthe. Inge, apparently an optimist by nature, waited two. That was still fully ten days before Doyle, Samantha, and I reappeared in Denver City, bearing a carefully constructed story about a fatal confrontation with Broaderick and his group of outlaws.

By my reckoning, the letter telling Marthe of my death should have reached her at about the same time as the telegram I sent the day after we returned. It read: ALIVE DID FIRST LETTER ARRIVE SECOND FORTHCOMING ALL MY LOVE JOYA

I could only imagine what Marthe must be feeling, and that made the second letter even more difficult to write.

Technically, I wrote two new letters—one I intended for her to share with the Magisterium and one I hoped she would not. In the first, I described what happened after Doyle and I set out after Samantha. I explained about Belmathok and the spells I'd woven together to stop her. And I admitted I'd removed the binding.

I can make no apology for my actions, I wrote. *I could not have prevailed against the demon Belmathok without full access to my power. I hope the Magisterium will agree I had no choice and decline to sanction me further, given the circumstances.*

I tried to strike the correct tone. I wasn't going to run, and I wasn't going to cower. I'd made my choice and would live with the outcome. Still, I hoped the Magisterium would see reason.

In the second letter, the one meant for Marthe's eyes alone, I confessed to her about Zalgammon.

What are you doing? he asked, aghast when he read the words coming from my pen.

Trusting someone who loves me, I replied. *Josiah didn't turn against me. Marthe won't either.*

I sent them both in the same envelope, then went back to the farm.

Zalgammon wanted to stay in town, but since Josiah was no longer alive to ward me at night, I decided it was safer to be somewhere with less temptation. I still owed him one spell per day, based on the terms of our agreement. And there were plenty of farm chores I could do with magic—with my own now unbound, we'd worked together on several very effective new spells. Something had changed since we'd melded our magics in the cavern. He could hear my thoughts more easily, and I now sometimes caught a glimmer of his, which he found unnerving. Turnabout being fair play, I rather enjoyed it. Whole days went by when I spoke aloud only to the animals.

They belonged to me now. Josiah hadn't had a will. But he'd publicly accepted me as kin, and no one seemed interested in disputing my right to inherit the farm.

It was a safe place to spend the winter. A safe, private place for both Zalgammon and me to practice our magic and wait for the Magisterium's response.

Which Doyle had just brought me.

He handed me the letter and led Patch into the relative warmth of the barn. I held the door open long enough for Peter and Paul to swoop inside and perch on the door of Fox's stall. Even though I hadn't been able to recreate the spell that made them men yet, they remained on the farm, dark sentinels who spent their days flying lazy circles over the property, begging for food and harassing Shadow whenever he appeared in the yard.

The letter was sealed with Marthe's personal sigil, rather than the Magisterium's, and when I touched it, it was so familiar it gave me a wave of homesick longing.

I sent my own magic into the seal, taking a simple pleasure in an act I'd been unable to manage for so long.

The seal recognized me and snapped in half.

I unfolded the single page and began reading.

Joya,

I want to shake you until your teeth rattle from your head. And I want to hold you to me and weep with relief. Your first letter arrived a day before your telegram, and it was the worst day of my life.

I gave your account of the battle with the demon to the council. As I'm sure you've imagined, it created quite the uproar. Your description of Broaderick's plot accorded with some of the information we've uncovered from other sources. Even in a warded letter, I dare not be more explicit. Suffice it to say that matters here are sufficiently unsettled that I suspect it will be some time before anyone has the wherewithal to come looking to punish you, if indeed that is the decision of the council. I am doing everything I can to steer the outcome in another direction.

As to your other, private news, I can only say nothing has ever frightened me more. If I could, I would be on my way to you at once. As it is, I can only implore you to be careful. The fact that you told me, when you might well have decided not to, reassures me somewhat. I am proud of you. Keep yourself safe. I will write again soon.

With all my love,

Marthe

I looked up from the page.

"Well?" Doyle said.

I handed him the letter and watched his face as he read.

"She doesn't say much," he said when he'd finished. "I would have expected more."

"So would I," I said. "But it's enough for now. No one is coming for me, at least not officially. And she hasn't told them about Zalgammon."

"How are you doing with him?" Doyle asked.

"He gained enough power from killing Broaderick that I can keep our bargain without hurting anyone else," I said. "We're managing."

Killing him was a mercy as much as a meal, Zalgammon said, and I had to agree. The demon had been less difficult since we'd mingled our power to fight Belmathok. I couldn't tell whether something about that experience had satisfied an unknown need, or if he was merely biding his time before making some new demand of me. Whichever it was, I appreciated the relative peace.

"I can't stay long," Doyle said. "I don't want to leave Samantha overnight."

"How is she? Any more signs?"

"Nothing yet," he said.

We stood looking at one another for a long moment. Finally, as if he could bear it no longer, Doyle reached for me. I met him halfway, and the kiss—the first we'd exchanged since Christmas—left me lightheaded.

Zalgammon could not suppress his enjoyment of the moment, and though I managed to ignore it for a time, it eventually made me pull away. Much as I wanted Doyle, I could not bear the thought of a watcher in my bed.

"I—"

Doyle brushed his thumb over my lips. "I know. But I'm in no hurry. We have time." He kissed me again, softly, and I sighed against his mouth.

Time. A year and a day. Less, now. I was sworn to tolerate Zalgammon for that long. But once that time had passed . . .

There had to be a spell. If there wasn't, I would make one. A way to separate us, to send him back where he came from and give me my freedom.

The next thought to drift through my mind was Zalgammon's. It was faint, barely more than the echo of a whisper.

If you still want it.

ACKNOWLEDGMENTS

The Witch's Secret, even more than either of my previous books, was a team effort.

I am always profoundly grateful to the members of the Arlington Writers Group for their support, but this time they went above and beyond.

On a Tuesday in May 2023, I mentioned to someone that I felt really good about how the draft was coming along. On Wednesday I realized I'd written all the parts where I knew what happened and had absolutely no idea where to go next. I sent a panicked email, and by Saturday night, Michael Klein, Sarah Blumenthal, Colleen Moore, David Gould, and Jen Blanck had read forty thousand words of sloppy draft and synopsis and showed up at my house ready to plot.

They spent three hours helping me hammer out the rest of the book. By the time they left, I had ten pages of notes and a solid plan. Truly, it felt like I lit the Bat Signal and five batmen (or two batmen and three batwomen) showed up. I cannot thank them enough.

Klein, Sarah, Colleen, and David also beta read the draft once it was done, along with fellow AWG members Lori Sullivan and Dale Waters. I was so sick of looking at it by that point that the ending was very hand-wavy and the epilogue was a list of bullet points. Their insights and gentle nudges were invaluable.

Thanks also to my agent, Jill Marr, who took it in stride when I emailed her in late 2022 to admit I'd spent most of a year avoiding writing the book I told her I was working on but had a new idea I wanted to run by her.

The team at Pegasus remains the best. My editor, Victoria Wenzel, loved Joya from the beginning. Copy editor Laura Gilliam un-italicized nine thousand individual commas and fixed all the places where I incorrectly capitalized the cardinal directions. I still don't understand the rules on that one and will get it all wrong again next time. Sorry about that. Elisha Zepeda designed a cover so lovely it made me gasp, and Maria Fernandez's chapter headings made me want a new tattoo.

My thanks to Latin teacher Cheri Miller for the Latin translations, and to Gary Holtzman for making the connection. Any errors or misuses are most definitely my own, and let's say they're intentional.

Finally, and most of all, thank you to my friends and family, who love me even when I'm on deadline.